Dancer for the Goddess

by
Diana Rivers

Printed in the United States of America
ISBN: 978-0-9969617-3-8

Published by

 **Goddess Ink**
opening hearts and minds

Goddess Ink
WWW.GODDESS-INK.COM

Interior and cover designed by
Rebekkah Dreskin
www.blameitonrebekkah.com

Front cover art "Dancer for the Goddess" by
Cedar Kindy

Prologue

With all the dangers and uncertainties that filled their lives, these women needed something to entertain them during the long nights around the fire, something to give them a sense of normality. I was one of the new ones there. I thought Dance would be my contribution, but on my third night with them Altra said: "Tell us about your life, Zaia. We know you've been a Dancer on the road for five years. You must have many stories."

I shook my head. It was still much too painful to look back. She kept insisting, saying: "You owe it to us, Zaia. The rest of us have all told our stories, some more than once. If all goes according to plan, we have at least twenty more days in these cursed stony hills before we meet with the others and start moving back down into the valleys. That should give you time enough to tell us a great deal, one story of your choice for each evening. You could even Dance some parts of it. Start at the beginning and speak slowly so Jenoa can write down some of it. Later we will need our stories and she is a Temple-trained scribe."

I stared at Jenoa in surprise. With her rough scarred face and her ragged clothing, covered in places with scraps of filthy leather armor, she hardly looked to be Temple-trained. Then I blushed suddenly at my rudeness. I might as well be staring at my own future. Thesali came to sit next to me and took my hand in hers. The rest of them called out encouragement. I took a deep breath and gave Jenoa a nod. "I'll start with the first thing that really matters to me," I told them. And so I began my story ...

Picture, if you can, the city of Urshameel, great center of trade and culture, a jewel of beauty, the finest city in the region—or at least so we thought, those of us who lived there. And then picture in the middle of the city, like a jewel within a jewel, the vast complex of the Temple of Kernoss, famous as a Dance Temple and training center for all the sacred arts, the spiritual heart and core of the city.

CHAPTER 1
The Temple of Kernoss

B y walking past the Temple at that exact moment on that particular morning, my life was changed forever and set irrevocably on its new course. I had been sent out on some errand or other. Later I couldn't even remember what it was because I never reached my intended destination. I was very young at the time, ten perhaps, certainly no more than eleven, just barely old enough to be out in the streets alone. My older cousin, Renairi, the one who should have gone instead of me, was ill. I had been allowed to go in her place with the strict understanding that I was to come straight home afterward.

Of course I'd been on that street many times before with my family, but we'd never lingered in front of the Temple of Kernoss. My mother was so contemptuous of the Goddess and all things holy that we always passed by quickly, often with my mother making disparaging remarks. I knew my father had once been head gardener at the Temple, but that was long ago, even before my parents married. Sometimes he still spoke of it with longing and affection. My mother had no such feelings—and in our family, my mother held the power.

Those other times, the outer courtyard had been a bustle of activity, crowded with celebrants there for the holy days, or merchants who had business with the Temple. Throngs of people passed in or out of the gates, some from the city and some from the farmlands beyond. The Temple of Kernoss was immense, almost like a town within the city of Urshameel, with many to be fed and clothed and much sacred business being conducted there everyday. This time, however, it was early morning. For once, the front courtyard of the Temple was empty.

Feeling very daring and a little frightened, I stepped through the open gates to take a quick look into this forbidden place. I had only meant to stay for a moment or two, but I found myself lingering there, tempted by the beauty of the flowerbeds overflowing with spring blooms. I was also tempted by this unexpected freedom. After glancing around to make sure no one was watching me, I craned my neck to find the source of the waterfall that started from some high place in the polished black stones of the Temple wall. From there I followed with my eyes as the water fell, flashing and sparkling, into a shallow pool where gold, red and bronze fish swam in lazy circles. Past the pond the water flowed on into little streams that meandered about and watered the gardens. Of course, I had to stop for a little while and watch the fish. Then, humming to myself, I had to dip my fingers in the water and run my wet fingertips lightly over the flowers.

Drawn by curiosity, fears forgotten and responsibilities as well, I began walking further and deeper into the courtyard. At a bend in a low, curving, brick wall, I came upon an enormous stone statue of Great Mother, The-Mother-of-all-Things. She was surrounded by a multitude of tiny animals and humans made of painted clay. I sucked in my breath with delight. Wonderfully round and full of power, Her features were almost worn away from the touch of many hands. Awed, I stopped before Her and bowed. Then, feeling very daring but unable to resist, I scrambled up on a bench. With tentative fingers I stroked Her face. I wanted to pluck a flower and set it on the altar in front of Her with all the other offerings, but Temple ways were unfamiliar to me. I was afraid I might do something forbidden.

The courtyard was paved in dark stone with an inset of lighter stones in the shape of a spiral. Stepping with care, I followed this spiral pathway to its center where a small, round pool reflected the sky like an unblinking blue eye. From that center, I looked up in wonder at the pointed archway of black polished stones leading into the inner courtyard and the Temple itself. My eyes were instantly captured by the symbols carved around it, each one painted in a different bright color.

Errand long forgotten, I began moving toward the archway as if in a trance. I was reaching out my hand, intent upon touching one of those mysterious symbols, when a sudden movement caught my attention. A young woman, far back inside the archway, was bending over to fasten her sandal. Fascinated, I stopped to watch. Just then she stood up and swung her long dark hair back from her face with one sweep of her arm. Sighing deeply, she took an unconsciously graceful pose and stood looking past me into the outer courtyard as if lost in thought.

A ray of early morning light fell on her in the darkness of the archway. It flashed on the gold links of her necklace and lit the richness of her Dancer costume, red and purple with a blue vest and several multi-colored sashes. In one hand she held a glass tube or wand in which brilliant colors swirled and shimmered in constantly changing patterns. With the fingers of her other hand she absently twirled some strands of her dark hair. I stood gaping at her with my mouth open. Her beauty took my breath away—the Goddess Herself in earthly form. Flooded with admiration, in that instant I fell in love with my whole heart as only someone very young can fall in love. At the same moment the Dancer glanced down and noticed this little girl, staring at her so openly. She turned her full attention on me.

"Have you never seen a Dancer, Child?"

I blushed and stammered, "Yes, often, at festival times but always Dancing, never just standing still like a real person."

The Dancer threw back her head and laughed. "Oh, I'm real enough. Watch..." She did some quick intricate Dance steps ending with a slight bow in front of me. "You see, I'm very real," she said again, reaching out and touching me on the wrist. "I'm a Dancer for the Goddess and I'm training right here in this Temple."

I trembled at her touch and went on staring up at her, my eyes wide and unblinking. Words came tumbling thoughtlessly out of my mouth: "What's your name? Mine is Zaia. How old were you when you started Dancing? Can someone my age do those steps? Are they very hard to learn?" Then I glanced away, going suddenly shy and silent.

I think the longing and intensity in my questions must have touched her heart. It was certainly not my manners. "My name is Kendrin," she said with a smile. "I started when I was nine. Come, I'll show you where the girls your age practice. Melanthia is the Dance Mistress and she's very strict so we have to be quiet and not let anyone see us there." Kendrin slipped her wand into her sash. Then she reached out her hand and I took it without thought or question.

Together, hand in hand, we made our way through the Temple. To my young eyes it was a place of wonders, a vast jumble of vivid impressions. I could see now that the Temple was not just one massive black-stone building, as it appeared to be from the street but many interconnected buildings of different shapes and sizes. Kendrin led me through courtyards, gardens, archways, halls. I could hear bells and chimes in the distance and, from another place, the swell of music. Peacocks and other brightly colored birds strolled about like walking jewels. There was a constant flow of people moving purposefully, as if to some important task. They nodded to Kendrin and looked curiously at me, but no one blocked our way or stopped us to question my presence.

Off to the side I saw a long processional walkway. It was made of colorfully patterned tiles and lined on both sides by a row of carved columns. Beyond that loomed a huge ceremonial chamber hung with bright tapestries. Soon we turned from the main way and entered a series of twisting narrow passageways. "This is a way that few outsiders ever see," Kendrin told me. We passed shops where weavers, carvers or potters were bent over their work. From around a corner came a loud rush of sound, much clanging and bustling and the clamor of raised voices. In passing I caught a glimpse through a wide doorway of a huge, steamy kitchen.

Soon we were out again, hurrying past terraced kitchen gardens. Chickens and geese were running loose. There were pens of sheep and pigs.

What I remember best were the flowering fruit trees growing flat against red brick walls in the shape of giant harps. Next we came to an especially beautiful flower garden. Because of my father I knew much about gardens. I was tempted to linger at this one, but Kendrin urged me on, saying: "They've already started. You'll miss it all if you wait. The young ones are going to do *The Dance for First Harvest* here in the Temple Dance Court. It's for this they practice. You must get your parents to bring you at mid-summer."

I nodded, but even as I did a shiver went through me. My parents in the Temple? Not much hope of that! I pictured my mother's face contorted in anger and saw my father cringing at her bitter words. Then, with a will, I shut out all thoughts of my parents, shut out everything but what was happening right at that moment. I knew there might be trouble later but I told myself that no matter what happened after, this would be worth it.

At some point the way grew narrow and Kendrin stepped in front of me. It was then I noticed the woven knot of thick silken cord she wore in her hair. Intricately shaped and bright red in color, it was nestled at the back of her head in a cluster of small tight braids. I was just going to ask her about it when her hand went up to touch it. As if she had read my mind, she turned back and answered my unasked question: "That is my Dancer's Knot. We wear it any time we're not sleeping. It is one sure way to recognize a Dancer no matter what else she may be wearing. We earn it when we graduate from Novice to Apprentice."

With an odd little tremor, I touched the back of my own head as if I felt a weight there. My mother had always kept my hair cut short. She said it was too unruly and she didn't want the bother of untangling it. Looking at Kendrin's fall of long shiny black hair, I vowed to let mine grow. Of course it would not be quite the same since mine had red mixed in with the dark. Besides, it was wild and curly instead of straight.

Finally we came to a large Dance Court, a circle of short, well-tended, bright green grass. The Dance Court itself was sunken, with a few tiers of seats rising around it. At the very center it was open to the sky and surrounded by two sets of wooden pillars that supported the curved roof, each pillar carved with a representation of the Goddess. Three musicians were seated on a low stone bench at the edge of the court. Twenty or more girls of near my age were Dancing, while a stern-looking Dance Mistress put them through an intricate set of steps, using a wand like Kendrin's for emphasis.

"It's so big," I whispered to Kendrin, gazing in awe at the court.

"This is just the practice court. The formal one is much larger," she answered. Then she released my hand and whispered in my ear: "We can only go a little closer, just by that pillar there. Then we must stand very still."

I did as I was told and watched in silence as the other girls moved through their steps under Melanthia's direction. She was indeed an imposing-looking figure, tall and spare with a lean, well-muscled body. Her silver hair, pulled back tight, was in stark contrast to her dark skin. I found myself listening so intently to her words that my ears ached with them. Soon I could feel the music moving in my body. Though I was standing still, the Dance began flowing through me like an irresistible force, pulling and pulling at my core. I could do those steps; I knew I could. It was as if I already knew them, as if I had Danced them in my sleep.

Suddenly, with no thought and no intention on my part, I found myself walking or rather floating down to the Dance Court. I suppose Kendrin had been absorbed watching the Dance. Too late she must have realized that her charge had slipped away. To call me back or try to grab me would only have caused more disruption. I slipped in to join the others. Moving like someone in a dream, I began doing the steps as if my body had suddenly been freed to be itself. Some of the others girls saw me and hesitated with a look of shock on their faces.

"Please continue," Melanthia said sternly. "This class is not yet finished." Then she walked over until she was standing directly in front of me. I was concentrating so intently on following the steps of the other girls that I was hardly aware of her presence until she tapped me sharply with her Dancewand and asked in a loud voice: "Who are you, Child, and what made you think to intrude this way? Has no one taught you any manners?" The voice was severe, but there was an appraising look on her face. Most of the other girls moved away quickly, all except one whose name I later learned was Thesali. This Thesali looked to be a year or so older than I was. She stepped up right next to me as if to offer protection.

Startled, I looked up at Melanthia then quickly glanced away again, blushing deeply. At that moment I was aware of everyone's eyes on me. My tongue glued itself to the roof of my mouth and my stomach curled into a knot. I was frozen in place, unable to move or speak.

"Answer me!" Melanthia snapped. "I am not used to my students keeping me waiting in this way."

"Zaia, of the House of Anzor," I mumbled, glancing down at the floor. Then I took a deep breath and with a burst of courage looked up into that stern visage. "I didn't mean to cause trouble, but I couldn't help myself. Something came over me. The music called me."

At the mention of my name a strange expression passed over Melanthia's face and she muttered, as if to herself, "The House of Anzor? Goddess, how is that possible?" Then to me she said in a gentler tone: "The Dance called you, Zaia, that is what drew you here. Never forget that."

Kendrin had come forward and was looking back and forth between us, flushed and confused, twisting her hands in distress. "It was all my fault. She asked if girls her age could Dance. She seemed so eager I thought to show her. I imagined we could stand quietly behind a pillar and not be noticed. I had no idea she would..."

Melanthia put a hand on the girl's arm. "It's alright, Kendrin. You did well to bring her here. The Goddess moves Her will through us in mysterious ways. This was meant to happen—but don't think to ever do it again." After that Melanthia signaled, by a nod of her head, that I was to continue Dancing with the other girls. I shivered with excitement, very conscious of her shrewd, appraising eyes watching my every step.

Fortunately for me it was my father who came to look for me—or, more likely, he was the one who was sent. If my mother had come she would probably have made a dreadful scene. Likely she would have thought there was some intentional insult there, that her daughter had been lured on purpose by the Temple. Even my father sounded unusually gruff. "What are you thinking of, Zaia? The whole house is in an uproar. You were supposed to come right home. Everyone is out looking for you. If a little boy playing ball by the garden wall hadn't seen you go through the gates I would never have known you were here." He looked distraught and his hands were shaking. "Melanthia, my apologies," he said with a quick bow. "What a strange way for us to meet again."

"Do not be too harsh with her, Tomaire. I think she is drawn to movement the same way you are drawn to making things grow and with the same passion. She's a born Dancer. You must send her to the Temple soon for training. I see the hand of the Goddess in this, that Zaia came to us here in spite of all the..." Then she stopped in confusion and they both looked at each other strangely, almost as if they each wanted to reach out and touch, though neither moved to do so.

"Please Father, please. You must let me come." I reached up and tugged on his arm.

"Later," he said almost harshly. "We will speak of this later, Zaia. Now we must go home quickly. Everyone is worried about you." Turning to the Dance Mistress he made a slight bow again. "Melanthia, please forgive this intrusion. I'm sure the child meant no harm. She's young and impulsive. It was a mistake to let her out on her own this way."

Melanthia shook her head. "It was no mistake Tomaire, it was meant to happen. Remember what I said. Bring her here for training. Such a talent should not be wasted. There are not that many natural Dancers in the world."

Impulsively, I reached out and touched the older girl's hand. "Thank you, Kendrin. I'm sorry for the trouble I caused you. I didn't mean you any harm."

Then, gathering my courage, I said to Melanthia: "I'd like to come back to the Temple and Dance. I'd like that more than anything in the world."

She shook her head again. "Be very sure. Don't think it will be easy, Child. It will be very hard, I promise you. It will take everything you have, mind and body and soul. Look deep into your heart before you make that choice. Goddess bless you. Now go home quickly. You have frightened your people."

"Yes, quickly, the whole house is in turmoil," my father said urgently as he took my hand and hurried me out of the circle. I gazed back filled with longing, stumbled and would have fallen if my father had not grabbed my arm. "Look where you're going, Zaia," he said gruffly. "You've already caused more than enough trouble." But as soon as we were out in the gardens his whole manner softened. "So, Melanthia thinks you have a natural talent for the Dance. She's not known for being generous with her praise, in fact quite the opposite."

"Can I do it, Father? Can I come here to Dance?"

"Not now. We'll talk later." As he said that, he seemed more shaken than angry. Then he turned to look at the gardens and his manner changed again, a smile spreading across his face, a smile that had some sadness in it. "Did you ever see such beautiful flowers? It's a joy just to stand here among them."

"Father, did you plant these gardens?"

"I designed most of them. I even planted some with my own hands. I'm glad to see them still thriving. These trees were no more than little dry twigs and look at them now, spreading out over our heads and giving shade." There was such a tone of longing in his voice it made my heart ache.

"Did you plant this garden?" I asked, eagerly drawing him over to my favorite part of the gardens that Kendrin had just rushed me through, a place with several fountains and many little stone-paved paths that wound through the shrubs and flowers.

"Everything. From the very beginning. I still have the drawings for it rolled up somewhere."

And so, instead of rushing home, we wandered through the gardens on our way out of the Temple, with me asking endless questions about everything that grew there and my father answering patiently. At that moment I was trying not to think about home and what waited for me there. *It was well worth it*, I told myself again, *No matter what happens, it was well worth it.*

Finally, we reached the street. On sudden impulse I grabbed my father's arm, wanting to stop him. "Do I have to go back? Why can't I just stay here and learn to Dance? They want me. You heard Melanthia. I want to be just like Kendrin. I don't want to go into the family business. I have no head for it. It bores me. Please Father. I'll never ask you for anything again."

He looked away and shook his head. "You can't always do what you want in this world, Zaia. There are other people involved. You mother would never allow it. You know how she feels about the Temple."

"Please, Father!"

"No more! Not another word! Come with me right now, Daughter! Right now! We have tarried here long enough. You have worried everyone with your thoughtlessness. Now we must hurry." With that he took hold of my arm and rushed me down the street. Before we went around the corner I turned back for one last glance at the Temple gates. Kendrin was standing there watching us. She raised her hand in a farewell gesture and then disappeared inside.

Once home it was even worse than I had imagined. My mother's relief at seeing me safe quickly turned to anger and then rage when she realized the extent of my betrayal. "The Temple of all places!" she shouted. "You know how I feel about the Temple! You see what comes of all your stories about the Temple gardens, Tomaire? Or have you been secretly influencing her behind my back?" She was pacing up and down, spewing out furious words and then stopping suddenly to glare at my father or me, first one and then the other.

"All our neighbors have been out looking for you, you little monster! And there you were lolling around the Temple, making fools of us all. You have no heart and care for no one but yourself." Quickly, she resumed her pacing, as if all that anger could not be contained in a still body. Then she whirled on my father again, shouting, "Do those witches have nothing better to do than lure our children in off the street? I'll bet Melanthia was behind all this. She can't have you so she wants my child, my eldest daughter at that, the one who is destined to take my place in the family business."

With the courage of desperation I burst out, "But Mother, I'm no good at it. I have no head for numbers. Let Yanin take my place. I yield it to her willingly. She can be the eldest daughter. All I want is to go to the Temple and Dance. Melanthia says I'm a born Dancer."

That, of course, was the wrong thing to say. My mother whirled on me with her hand raised. She was so angry she would have struck me if my father had not stepped between us. "Thea, think what you're doing. She's only a child."

My mother lowered her hand and said with barely suppressed fury, "Never! I will never give my consent. Put such ideas out of your head right now, Zaia! You will take your place in this family as you are supposed to. Melanthia cannot have you. I won't allow it. Now go to your room and shut the door. You can spend the day there thinking on all the trouble you've caused with your selfishness. As for you, Tomaire, you have undermined me in this family and made a fool of me in the Temple world. You know I won't forget it—and I will never forgive you."

I crossed the garden court with a heavy heart, tears filling my eyes so that all the flowers ran together in a blur of colors. As I was about to close the door to my room I heard my father say, "Thea, I want you to know there was no intention to hurt you in this. She's only a child. The sight of a young Dancer standing in the archway caught her fancy, nothing more. Pay it no mind. She'll forget this notion soon enough."

But he was wrong. I didn't forget. I could think of nothing else. And now, of course, I was not sent on any more errands. In truth I was seldom allowed out, even with the family. And, if I did go with them, it was never by way of the Temple. My mother barely spoke to me and then only in the coldest tones; my father seemed awkward and embarrassed around me; and my little sister, Yanin, mocked me with sly looks and cruel words. I was a virtual prisoner in my own home, expected to study diligently to make up for my betrayal. But I had a hard time studying. Where before the work had bored me, now I loathed it. It seemed like part of the punishment.

All I could think of was the Temple: the beauty of the courtyards, Kendrin standing in the archway caught by that ray of sunlight, the Dance Court, the other girls my age being allowed to Dance, and Melanthia saying that I, Zaia, was a born Dancer. Even when I tried, the numbers swam before my eyes and sometimes in my tears. Then I would lay my head down on the table and let the visions come and of course there would be more trouble. My only comfort and my only confidant at that time was my cousin Renairi, the only person I could talk to. Though my mother had warned her to keep away from me, she managed to find ways to sneak into my room. Or we would meet in secret in the far corner of the garden under a tree whose drooping branches hid us from sight. There I would pour out my heart—all my grief and longing and my anger at the unfairness of things.

Whenever my father came to encourage me in my work, I would beg him to intercede for me. Then he would shake his head and look sad. "You know your mother will never agree. She has already told you so. Now you must accept that in your heart and make the best of it. There is a long-standing feud between your mother's family and the Temple. Thea is a proud woman. If nothing else, her pride would not allow it."

All that trouble with the Temple had happened so long ago it seemed like a myth to me. It was well before I was born, when my mother was a very young woman or perhaps still a girl. Her parents, who were also merchants, had had some dealings with the Temple. They felt they had been treated unfairly—cheated actually. When they went to the Temple for redress of their grievances, they found themselves met with arrogance and contempt, or at least that was how they perceived it. Anyhow, in their eyes, the matter was never made right. That was the story I was told, the source of all that anger. Now, these many years later, those involved were likely all dead, my grandparents as well as the High Priestess and others at the Temple, but because of what had happened back in that misty past, I was not allowed to go there and Dance. I raged against the injustice of it and often cried myself to sleep.

Finally, in tears, I begged, "Please, Father, ask her again for me." I knew my father loved me, but he was under my mother's power. He had come into the marriage as a poor man and he was never allowed to forget it.

"Are you very sure, Zaia? Your mother is a strong-willed woman. She does not forgive those who go against her. You may make an irreparable separation with this insistence."

"I'm very sure. It's all I want in my life."

"But you're so young. You can't know all the consequences. How do you really know if...?"

I grabbed his hand. "Please do this for me. I know what will happen if I stay here much longer. I'll die!"

He must have gathered his courage to ask because an hour or so later my mother stormed into my room. "So now you have taken to threatening your father with your own death. What kind of heartlessness is that? You know the man loves you and you abuse his love that way. Unnatural child! Understand, Zaia, I will never give my consent. Never! Get that into your head!" Then she left, slamming the door behind her so hard things fell off the shelves and crashed to the floor. I was in despair. Later my cousin Renairi found me asleep at the desk in a puddle of tears. She shook me awake. When I finally raised my face it was all crisscrossed with a design of wet ink marks. She showed me in the mirror before gently washing them away.

I had not planned it as an act of resistance or a last resort. It was simply what happened. I lost my appetite and stopped eating. I stopped studying. I no longer cared what was happening around me. My father's pleading and my mother's threats could not reach me. My cousin's worry had no effect. My aunt tried to scold me back to life and got no response. Nothing seemed to touch me. I had disappeared inside myself into a semi-dream state where I wandered freely in the Temple gardens, which seemed far more real to me than the rooms of my family home. Night and day began to blend together. I was sunk so deep into my stupor that I was hardly aware of anything until a loud shouting argument broke out. My aunt, alerted by my cousin, had come to confront my mother. "You will let your daughter die in your house just to satisfy your cursed pride, and then what will people say? Where will your pride be then, Thea? Have you thought of that? Let her go! She's not yours to hold. She has her own life. Let her go quickly before it's too late."

My mother shouted back, "You always thought you could tell me what to do, Veraine, but this is my family and none of your business."

"She is my business! She's my niece and my Goddess-child, the one I'm honor bound to guide and watch over and keep safe. I have no choice but to intervene. You're killing her with your stubbornness."

"No! She's killing herself with her own stubbornness."

"What does it matter, Thea? It will all come to the same thing very soon and then it will be too late!"

I felt myself slipping into a sort of dark pool and didn't hear any more until suddenly my mother and aunt and father all burst into my room. "Get up, Girl and get yourself dressed," my aunt Veraine said urgently. "You're going to the Temple to learn the Dance. Anyone who wants something so much they are willing to die for it should have it."

I saw the look of implacable hatred on my mother's face. "You will go to the Temple to live there like one of the country girls. I won't have you in my house anymore. The Temple can have you and good riddance. I won't pay them a single coin for your keep there. You are not my daughter anymore. Your sister Yanin will take your place in this house." I could see my sister and cousin crowding in the doorway, their eyes big and round. My father reached out his hands for me. "It has been decided, Zaia. Come, it is time to go." My heart was pounding wildly in my chest. I took his hands, struggled to my feet and instantly fainted dead away into total darkness.

I remembered nothing of my trip to the Temple. When I came to myself again I was lying on a bed. I was in a little white room I had never seen before, with colorful hangings on the wall and a blue vase of bright flowers at the window. Kendrin was sitting next to the bed, leaning over me. In back of her I saw Thesali, the girl who had stepped up next to me in the Dance Court. Her eyes were wide and she was looking anxiously over Kendrin's shoulder. Kendrin was smiling down at me. "If you are going to Dance, Zaia, first you must eat," she said firmly. Then she held out a bowl of food to me. And that is how I came to the Temple of Kernoss to be a Dancer.

CHAPTER 2
Novice, Apprentice and Lover

I recovered and I Danced. I Danced like one possessed. Dancing was when I felt truly alive, when I was most myself—and yet more than myself. That was how the Goddess first came to me, though I still did not recognize Her presence. She came to me then as energy and a flow of power, not yet words. For a while, Dancing was all that mattered in my life. Scarcely aware of my surroundings, I went about in a trance. But I learned fast, quickly reaching the level of the other girls my age and then surpassing them. Though Melanthia's praise and attention didn't make me loved among my classmates, I hardly noticed. At first I made no efforts toward friendship with the other girls and they, no doubt motivated by clannishness and envy, returned the compliment in kind. The only one of my age-mates who befriended me was Thesali. She had helped Kendrin with my care while I was recovering and had even chosen to share her room with "the newcomer."

It was Thesali who taught me the Dancer's prayer, the one especially used by young Dancers when they are about to Dance in public space for the first time. *Oh Great Goddess Who Dances all life into existence, please bless these feet, these hands and this body, that I may honor You by Dancing my part in the Great Dance of Life.* I learned the words of the prayer because Thesali wanted me to, because it was important to her to teach me, but it wasn't until much later that I really came to value them. At first I thought that the Dance just came from within myself, that I was the source of it all. I didn't understand that it was a gift and that some humility was required.

Thesali was also lonely there, another outsider, a country girl among the city-born. Gradually her kindness melted my reserve. We even formed a sort of alliance between ourselves, whispering together in the night long after the candles were blown out: gossiping about the other girls and the Dance Mistresses; sharing our concerns about family and future; sometimes even sharing a bed if our little room was too cold and damp for comfort. We were a strange pair. Thesali was good at all the book learning and lessons we were obliged to do as part of our training, while I barely had patience for anything but Dancing. I, on the other hand, quickly became the best Dancer among the novices while Thesali was just barely able to keep up, trying desperately to do better because she didn't want to be sent back to the family farm.

"I'm afraid as I get older that I'll fall further behind. I can't bear to go back to that life," she finally confessed to me in despair. "I'm not like you, Zaia. I know I'll never be a great Dancer. But if I could just stay and make my life here at the Temple that would be enough."

I shook my head. "They won't send you back, I promise." Then, seeing the pained look on her face, I asked gently, "Would it be so very bad?"

"It would be the end of my life," she said in a flat dead voice.

This seemed overly dramatic until I thought that I may have given the same answer for myself if I had been asked the same question. "Why? What is so bad there?"

She shook her head and kept shaking it. When she finally answered, it was an effort for her to speak. "I was by far the best Dancer in my village. They sent me here with pride, gave a feast and party for me when I left. How could I go back there in shame and disgrace? How could I face them all? Besides, my parents would not welcome me back. I was the last of too many children, one more than they had food for. They were only too glad to have the Temple take me off their hands. I would rather be dead than go back there."

"They won't send you back," I promised again. "I won't let them!" After that I began secretly coaching Thesali whenever we could find the Dance Court empty and deserted. In exchange she helped me with the book lessons that I struggled so hard over, groaning and complaining.

With all the new things I had to learn and adjust to, our little room soon became a haven for me in the vastness of the Temple. When I first came there it was quite bare, but every time my aunt or my cousin came to visit, they brought some bright gift from the market to cheer me up and make me feel more at home. They made sure to bring something for Thesali as well so no ill will should fall between us. Soon our little white room was bright and cheery with color: intricately embroidered cushions, soft woven covers for the beds, pictures for the walls, pretty objects for the window sills.

Just as Thesali looked up to me, filled with gratitude and admiration for helping her with the Dance, so I followed Kendrin about aflame with passion and devotion. Kendrin, for her part, did nothing whatsoever to encourage this. Though her friends must surely have teased her about "the puppy at her heels," still she could not bring herself to be unkind. It was not her way. Indeed, she became a sort of mentor for me, explaining the ways of the Temple and the mysteries of the Dance. One afternoon, after I had mastered a particularly hard step, I joyously threw my arms around her. Suddenly, filled with intense desires I couldn't understand, I clung tight and would not let her go.

Firmly, Kendrin unwound my arms, held me away and said gently, "I love you like a little sister, Zaia—but not more. My bond is with a young woman named Ushain who is a sculptor, an apprentice to the Master carvers of the Temple. You are too young for such feelings and I am much too old to be the object of them."

I blushed deep red with embarrassment. Then, with a cry, I tore myself loose and ran down the hall, not stopping until I reached my room. There I threw myself down on my bed, sobbing and beating the pillow.

That was how Thesali found me. At first I was too embarrassed to speak. Then, after much urging from her, I told the story, between sobs, while she patted my back. "It's nothing to be so ashamed of. Most of us have crushes on one or another of the older girls. It's normal. We're just not so forward about it."

I sat up, roughly scrubbed away my tears with my sleeve and said angrily, "Well, I'll never speak to Kendrin again. We'll see how she likes *that*." Thesali looked troubled and shook her head. She even tried to argue with me, but I had already set my formidable will.

For a while I was true to my word. I would pass Kendrin without a word or look, though sometimes I could not resist a quick sideways glance to see what effect I was having. Kendrin always appeared sad and puzzled. Then I would feel a strange mixture of hurt and satisfaction.

Finally it was Melanthia herself who put a finish to this little game, firmly taking my arm at the end of class one day and drawing me aside. "I usually don't interfere between my students, but Kendrin came to me because she was very troubled. She was afraid she had hurt you deeply. I have been watching. Instead of deep hurt I see a young girl who thinks she can just set her will and make others jump to it. But you need to pay attention, Zaia. Others have their own ways and needs that may sometimes conflict with yours. Kendrin has been very kind to you. She was one of those who nursed you back to health and she has helped you find your place here in the Temple. Now you're repaying her with anger and meanness because she can't be as you want her to be. Think on it carefully." Then Melanthia released me and turned away, striding off without a backward glance.

Later, when I could collect myself sufficiently, I went off to find Kendrin and apologize. I dreaded the encounter, but Kendrin was kind and gentle, as was her way, not mocking and cruel as some of the other girls might have been. "I was puzzled and confused. I've never knowingly done you an unkindness, Zaia. Instead, I loved you like the little sister I never had. I'd be only too glad for this to be over."

"Oh, Kendrin, I'm so sorry. Some spirit of meanness possessed me." I threw myself into her arms and hugged her hard, but this time I made sure to step back first. After that we became more like friends and equals in spite of the difference in age between us.

14

At first I had been too busy to miss my family as much as I might have otherwise. There was so much that was new to me, so much to learn and try to understand. There was the whole Temple complex to map out in my mind and all the Temple ways that had certainly not been taught in my home: the holy days, the prayers, the chants, the rituals, the processions, the many names of the Goddess. As a novice, one of my favorite jobs was helping to dress the older girls for their Dances. Each time, it thrilled me to be part of that miraculous transformation, to see some rather ordinary young woman magically altered by clothes and paint and jewelry, turned into a Dancer, that sacred being so full of mystery and power. When it fell my lot to be one of Kendrin's dressers it was a special pleasure to be the one to braid her hair or apply the blue-green shadow over her eyes, or choose the prettiest vest for her to wear. But, after Melanthia's scolding, I was always very careful not to intrude into her life.

For me, the hardest things to learn there were those that had nothing to do with Dance. The Temple was like a giant hive with endless needs for service and so, though there were cooks and servers and carvers and garden-ers, still all the young people who apprenticed there had daily tasks assigned by lot. I had grown up in a house with servants and so had no experience with such work. When I complained to Kendrin, saying, "All I want to do is Dance. Surely someone else can be paid to cut up vegetables," Melanthia overheard and descended on me like a hawk on a rabbit. "Do you think yourself better than the rest of us? We all do our service. That's how the Temple has survived for all these years. Service in the kitchen is as much of an homage to the Goddess as service in the Dance Court and never forget it. If you're too good to wash vegetables or cut them up or serve them, then per-haps you're too good to eat our food, or Dance at a ritual. If we are to pay for all that work where's the money to come from? Not your family surely. They haven't sent one coin in this direction for your support."

I was in an agony of embarrassment, face flushed, eyes darting about, looking for some escape. Fortunately, one of the other Dance teachers had heard it all. Raising her hands, Dhonir stepped between us. "Melanthia, do you always have to be so harsh with the students you love the best? Her crime is really not so big." Without waiting for an answer she made a little bow and disappeared.

Melanthia laughed suddenly and shooed me away. "Go, go, I suppose you're no worse than the rest of them. They all have to be taught."

After that I tried to do my tasks promptly and willingly. I even found myself doing them with a different attitude.

Because I was the new Dancer there, I drove myself harder than the others. There were nights when I fell asleep exhausted, with every muscle crying out in pain and the words of my Dance teachers ringing in my ears. Sometimes I was sure I heard the voices of Melanthia and Dhonir and Nekali and the others still talking to me in my sleep. And yet, as the year wore on to a close and there was still no word from my mother, there were some nights when I cried myself to sleep. Though I knew there was little hope that anything would change, still I longed for her approval. I wanted her to be proud of me. But, in truth, it was my father's desertion that cut even more deeply. The few times he came to see me it was a quick, guilty visit. He seemed evasive and distracted, too preoccupied to listen, not at all like the father I remembered. And I could never get him to walk in the gardens with me again no matter how much I begged. Mostly, except for Thesali who knew everything about me, I kept my grief to myself. I didn't share it with any of the other students, not even with Kendrin and certainly not with Melanthia. It was a matter of pride not to talk badly of my family at the Temple.

After a while I began to think of the Temple, or rather the Dance School, as my real home, since that was where I actually lived. Though it was at the center of Temple life, the Dance School was also quite separate, under somewhat different rules, like a village within a town. As a Dancer my life was much freer, not so closely bound up and supervised as that of a Priestess, especially a young one. The novice and apprentice Priestesses had a strict daily routine to follow, starting with the dawn bells at gray morning light and continuing through the day with an endless round of chants and prayers and worship in honor of the Goddess, nothing I wanted to do. For me, the Goddess was a very distant concept, much like the clouds and with as little connection to my life. At that time Dancing was my Goddess. Dancing was all that mattered to me. I cared little for anything else. But, as long as I practiced the Dance and completed my chores, I could do as I pleased the rest of the time.

Much as I felt at home there, sometimes the Dance School seemed too constricted to me, as if I were living in a closed little world of women. Though there were men in the rest of the Temple—Priests as well as Priestesses—and men among the workers and craftspeople, there were no male Dancers since the Dancer was intended to be a representation of the Goddess in bodily form. Curious, wanting to see a wider world, I took to exploring the Temple in my free moments, wandering about through the kitchens and gardens and workshops, talking and asking questions and making friends more easily than I had among the other Dancers. I hung about the potters so long they would either shoo me away or pinch off a little piece of clay and invite me to sit and work with my hands. I heard the chants and the sacred music, saw grand processions that wound through the Temple and sometimes poured out into the streets of the city. I envied the Dancers who went with the processions to Dance in the great Dance Court of the city and dreamt that, someday soon, I would be able to join them.

At that time I even met up with Old Selvi who was sometimes called Auntie. She was an old Dancer who had stayed out on the road far past her time and come back with Dancer madness, "fire-touched" as people said. Her hands shook so that she could hardly feed herself. She had a strange, unblinking stare and would sit for hours in a trance or talk on and on of her adventures with the Goddess to anyone who would listen. The other girls warned me about her and sometimes made fun of her, giggling and whispering to each other, but I liked listening to her stories and cared little whether they were truth or imagination or madness. There was something wild and strange about her that appealed to me. I knew that people mocked or pitied her, but Melanthia said she was a child of the Goddess now and we should see that she was fed and clothed and let her go her own way, that perhaps she saw deeper or further than all the rest of us. There were a few others like her who lurked around the Temple but none as interesting to me as Selvi.

In my explorations of the Temple I even poked about down seldom-used stairs and into back halls and alleyways. This is how I found the grotto of the Mother Toad. At the end of a narrow staircase, I noticed a rusted metal gate opening into a dimly lit grotto of natural stone. Full of wonder, I pushed open the gate and looked around. The floor was carpeted with moss and ferns. From one corner a little spring bubbled up to fill a tiny pool and then disappeared underground. The only light came from a small round window almost covered with vines. It gave the whole chamber a strange green glow. Intrigued, I sat down on the low, carved stone bench that was the only sitting place there. Listening to the music of the water and watching the ferns bobbing about, I found myself almost dozing off into a trance when, suddenly, a strangely dressed old man came bursting in. Startled, I jumped to my feet.

"Who gave you permission to enter the sanctuary of the Mother Toad? What are you doing here?" He was about to grab my arm and haul me away when he noticed my Dancer clothes. Then he made a slight bow. "Ah, little Dancer, did Melanthia send you here to inquire the future from Mother Toad?"

"I came here on my own, wandering about, but I beg you not to send me away again. Please show me the Mother Toad. I know nothing about Her."

He glared at me for a moment as if wanting to punish me for my impertinence. Then, his face softened and he nodded. "It's few enough that come this way anymore. I think this shrine is almost forgotten. Maybe you are meant to be here. Maybe you were led. Sit back down, shut your eyes, make a cup of your hands and stay very still. Don't be afraid."

I did as I was told and suddenly felt a soft, cool weight in my palms. When I opened my eyes the biggest toad I had ever seen was cupped in my palms. The creature was reddish brown with gold-flecked eyes. It looked ancient and enduring, like a rock or a mountain and was covered with a thick, lumpy hide. I leaned forward to peer at this wonder. "How does she foretell the future?"

"That's not for us to know, is it? The Priestesses of the Temple know how to make that magic. I'm only the guard of the shrine. Now, give her back and be on your way and don't intrude here again." Though his words sounded almost threatening, there was a secret little smile that showed at the corner of his eyes. Reluctantly, I gave back the toad, secretly vowing to myself that sometime I would show Thesali this strange, enchanted place.

In spite of his words, I went back many times. I had set my will on this thing. After a while, the old man no longer tried to interfere. If he was sweeping the floor or clearing away debris, he merely nodded to me and slipped out, leaving me in peace there. It became my favorite place in the Temple and I wanted so much to show it to Thesali but when she heard my description, she didn't share my enthusiasm at all. Each time I mentioned the grotto, Thesali would shake her head and make some excuse, promising to come with me the next day. Finally, I lost patience and said fiercely, "Come now or I'll never share a secret with you again."

I suppose Thesali saw the flash of anger in my eyes and the hard set of my jaw. The time had come. Not wanting to risk losing my friendship, she followed me down dark winding halls and narrow back stairs. When I pushed open the gate and swung my arms wide saying, "Isn't this a wonderful secret place?" she even followed me in across the damp rocks that were green with moss, but she couldn't suppress a shudder.

Looking around, she shivered again and shook her head. "It reminds me of the springhouse back home. I hated being sent there for water. The ceiling was covered with spiders. Sometimes they dropped on my back." Nothing I said could persuade her to sit down on the stone bench and hold the Sacred Toad in her hands. She wasn't able to breathe normally again until we were back up in a sunny courtyard. Then she turned and said defiantly, "Zaia, I will follow you anywhere else but not back down to that slimy grotto, so don't ask me again." It was the first time she had ever stood up against my will. Though I was deeply disappointed, somehow I looked on Thesali with new respect after that.

As the year was drawing to a close and there was still no word from home, I began to grieve all over again. For a while I had been too busy to care. There had been too much to learn and too many new things to absorb. But all that time, at the back of my mind, I suppose I had been hoping that a year would be enough punishment or enough time for a change of heart.

Meanwhile, my life went on and I said nothing, not even to Thesali. It would only have added to the hurt to speak my feelings aloud. Sometimes, on my free days, my cousin Renairi would come for me and we would walk around the Temple courtyards together or stroll out into the city streets. Sometimes my aunt Veraine would come to visit me at the Temple, though she never seemed very comfortable there. More likely I would go to my aunt's house on my free days or for an evening meal. Mostly I talked of the Temple and Melanthia and the Dance and the other girls, especially Kendrin and Thesali, but one day I poured out all my grief about my mother.

"Well, you made your choice, didn't you? And now you have to deal with the consequences. Not always easy in this life." The words sounded harsh, yet looking at Veraine's face I saw they were kindly meant. I suppose she was trying to strengthen me so I could deal with the realities of my life.

"But why did I have to choose between my family and the Dance? Other girls have both."

"You aren't other girls. Other girls don't have your talent, Zaia. Besides, you could have made a different choice."

"I would have died."

"Well, there you have it. You made the choice you had to make and have done it bravely and well. It's not a choice any child should have to make, but it's what was in your cards. We all get dealt a hand of cards by the Goddess. Our lives are how we play out that hand. No matter what hand we're given we all have some choices, more than we think we have, but never as many as we would like. That's what makes us human and mortal. If we had all the choices in the world, then we would be the Goddess Herself. You have done well with what you were given, very well. But great talent is not always a free card. In your case it was balanced out by a mother who wanted you in the family business and who doesn't forgive having her will crossed."

"But I never would have been good at it, even if I couldn't Dance a step."

"How do you know? You might have tried harder if you didn't have a different gift. But, the truth of it is, you weren't destined to be good at business. I knew that from the moment of your birth. The stars were all wrong. I told your mother, but she's stubborn enough to think she can alter even the stars."

My aunt was a great card player and loved games of chance, which she almost always won, so she saw life itself as a card game. "I never thought of Dance," she went on. "I imagined that perhaps it would be music that would pour out of you, or paintings. But, of course, it's all the same thing isn't it, those gifts of the Goddess? I knew it wouldn't be numbers—no gift there.

"You know your mother grieves for you also, Zaia. She feels the loss, but she's too proud to say so. If my daughter needed me I would never let pride stand in the way, no matter what had passed between us. That's not because

I'm such a good, kind person but because I have your mother for a teacher. I wouldn't do as she has done. I see the pain of that pride, what it has cost her and others in her life. She's also one of the cards in my hand, just as you are."

"I wish I had you for a mother," I blurted out.

"Well you don't, but you have me for an aunt and that's almost as good, though of course one always wants what one can't have. I doubt my own daughter thinks me such a piece of luck."

"Oh, but she does! She loves you very much. I've often heard her say how lucky she is."

"Well, look who she has to compare me to. And, the truth of it is, your mother loves you, too. I know she's also suffering. Maybe you should try one more time to patch things up. Go and tell her how much you love her and miss her. What harm could there be in that?"

"Oh no, I couldn't. When I left she told me to never come back, that I wasn't her daughter anymore."

"But that was almost a whole year ago. People change."

"Maybe I could try again, but I wouldn't think of going alone." Some little flame of hope was being rekindled in my heart. I tried to keep it under control.

Veraine grinned at me, a funny lopsided grin. "What if I went with you? I don't know if taking me along will make things better or worse, but I'll go if you want me to."

We debated for a while whether it would be better to surprise Thea or give her warning. Both plans had obvious merits and disadvantages. Finally we decided to send her a polite, respectful and rather formal letter that Veraine helped me write. We accompanied the letter with some flowers, a custom in Urshameel when one is trying to mend a rift. They were chosen with care, bright red, my mother's favorite color. At the same time, with Renairi acting as the messenger, I slipped my father a far more personal little note full of love and the deep grief of missing him.

It had been more than a year since I had crossed the threshold of my family home. Everything looked just the same—the heavy, deeply-carved blackwood door, the scarlet ivy growing up the stone walls next to it, the formal arrangement of shrubs and flowers. All familiar, yet all strange to me now. It seemed as if nothing had changed here. Hard to believe, when so much had happened in my life. Even the bell made the same sound, sending shivers up my back. After we rang, there was a long silence as if nobody were home. My legs were shaking. I was almost ready to turn and leave when a servant I had never seen before opened the door. She gave me a hard-eyed look as if I were the stranger there. Then, without a word, she escorted us into the big, front room. This was the formal gathering place of the house, the place where my mother conducted business meetings or entertained guests of importance. As children we had not been welcome there.

Thea was sitting with regal straightness in a big high-backed chair at the far end of the room. My sister, Yanin, was standing next to her, but one step back, and my father was standing several steps behind them. The furniture had all been pushed back so the room seemed almost empty. Everything had been arranged to present a picture of distance, austerity, formality and power, all centering around Thea. Holding my letter in one hand and the flowers in the other, she regarded us in silence as I made a bow.

"Mother, I..." I blurted out nervously.

"I will speak first," Thea interrupted coldly. "Since you had the chance to speak in this letter it is my turn now to reply. When you left I told you not to come back. Did you think I would forget so soon? That was only a year ago. I have a better memory than that. You knew the price when you chose to leave my house. The only way you could ever come back is if you gave up Dancing and came back to train for the family business. Even then I'm not sure I would ever trust you again. Besides, Yanin has been elevated to the place of oldest daughter. I could not take that away from her. The only letter from you that I'm interested in reading is the one that says you have left the Temple for good and severed all your ties there. Then I might consider seeing you again. As long as you Dance for the Temple I have nothing to say to you. I wish to hear nothing from you or even about you. Your father and sister feel the same way. There is no need for secret little communications with them."

Those last words were like a stab in the heart. My father had betrayed me. The child in me wanted to run to my mother and ask for forgiveness, to see Thea reach out her hand and smile. Even more, I wanted to throw myself into my father's arms, begging, *Please Papa, please come walk in the gardens with me again. Papa, come watch me Dance. Please, Papa. You'd be so proud of me. I've missed you so much.* But I knew it was no use. I could see the seething rage in my mother's face. I felt it like a blow. And it was the mute pain in my father's eyes that hurt me even more. Well, he had made his choice and I had made mine.

It was not the child of the house that spoke next. It was the trained Dancer of the Temple. I made a slight bow, then straightened my back, lifted my head and said, quite formally, the words I had memorized and even rehearsed in front of Thesali in case I should be rebuffed, "I had hoped we could find some way to mend this rift between us, Mother. I see now that it's not possible. I'm very sorry for all the hurt I've caused you, but I made the only choice I could. I would have died otherwise. I had hoped you could forgive me in time." Then I ended as I began, with a slight bow.

There was a long moment of total silence as if the whole world had sucked in its breath and was holding it. Then Thea suddenly shouted, "Out!" With the force of her anger she flung the flowers across the room in my direction. They spread across the floor like a long smear of blood. Next, she ripped up the letter and tossed the pieces into the air, white petals of anger that scattered all over that orderly space like ash. After that she turned her fury on my aunt. "You set her up to this, didn't you, Veraine? You needed to taunt me one more time, get a little last pleasure out of this."

Shaking her head, Veraine leaned forward and gathered up some of the flowers. "I didn't think of it as setting anything up. Zaia was in pain from missing her family. I knew you were in pain, too, so I suggested to her that she try one more time, hoping that it would be different. She was afraid to come alone so I said I would go with her. And now I see she was right to be afraid. You only have two daughters, Thea. Are you so sure you want to throw one of them away?"

"I only have one daughter now and she is standing right beside me. The other one is dead and has been dead for more than a year. I told her that when she left my house and chose the Temple. Let her live with it now." The expression on Thea's face was one of implacable hatred. When I glanced at my father I saw that he had taken a step back into the shadows and was staring at the ground. He would not meet my eyes, but Yanin was looking straight at me, not with malice or mockery this time but with some admiration and perhaps even a little envy. I acknowledged her by the slightest nod. We had both changed and grown much in that past year of separation.

Now we were all frozen in place again like the tableau at the end of a Temple performance. Finally, very slowly, Thea raised her hand to point at me and then Veraine. "I said out! Do I have to call the servants to have you removed or will you leave on your own?"

"We can manage, thank you, Sister. I remember where the door is," Veraine said dryly as she turned to go.

In a somewhat different tone Thea said, "You are still my sister, Veraine, and I have only one sister, but if you ever try to bring her back here again then you will be equally unwelcome in my house."

I looked one last time at my father before I also turned to leave. He did not return my glance. I followed Veraine out, our steps echoing strangely in that long, almost empty room.

When we were on the street again Veraine took my arm as if I were another adult. "Well, that's that. We tried our best, but we certainly lost at that hand of cards. I'm so sorry I talked you into this."

"Don't be. I'm glad. Now I don't have to cry for them anymore or carry around that little ember of hope. Now I know. My father wouldn't even look at me. He never said a word, not one single word the whole time." Angrily, I brushed away the tears that were forming at the edge of my eyes and vowed to myself that I would never ask my father for anything again.

"You acquitted yourself very well, Zaia. I was proud of you. It must have been hard."

"Dancer training stood me in good stead. I really wanted to throw myself down on the ground crying, but what good would it have done? I guess you're my only family now, you and Renairi."

"You could do worse, Girl, a lot worse."

"Why was she nice to you at the end? To hurt me more?"

"No, it's because I'm her sometimes business partner, especially when the big trading caravans come through in the summer and she needs some ready cash. She can't afford to throw me out the same way though, no doubt, today she would have liked to. Now she's probably in her room sobbing her eyes out over how much you hurt her. Such foolishness, all this pride and pretenses. Let's go back to my house, put these poor flowers in water and play a few real hands of cards."

Renairi was waiting eagerly to find out what had happened. As Veraine told her the story, I dramatized it with my skill at mimicry, acting out everyone's part, especially my mother's, giving just the right amount of exaggeration to her gestures and her tone of voice. Soon Renairi was choking with laughter and asking us to tell it all again. After a second retelling, it seemed more distant and had less power to hurt, like some miming in the street or a drama on a stage.

When I was back in our safe little room that evening, I told Thesali everything that had happened. Anger came rushing up as I paced back and forth, spouting off all the clever and cutting things I wished I had been able to say at the time—right into my mother's face. Truth was, I was still afraid of her. It had taken all my courage to go and face her, even with Veraine's support. Now I felt very brave as I stormed about but it had been a fierce act of will to walk into that room and face her without having my legs give way under me. Thesali was full of kindness and sympathy, even outrage on my behalf. Though it took some time, the anger eventually eased. Then the fear and the hurt began to dissipate.

After less than two years at the Temple, at Melanthia's insistence and over Dhonir's objections, I was moved up from novice to apprentice class. I had grown restless as a novice and was eager to move on. "She has learned everything she can learn as a novice," I heard Melanthia say. "She needs more of a challenge. It's time she earned her Dancewand."

Later I was to remember little of the formal part of the initiation that took me from novice to apprentice, little of the words and rituals. But I would always remember my own Dance and the feelings it released in me. I had been told to fast for the day, drink only kouri juice and meditate in some holy place. The Temple, of course, was full of holy places, but I chose the grotto.

I was the youngest initiate in a hundred years. Not since the famous Anuru had anyone been initiated so young. That morning I was full of nervous excitement, afraid it would make me restless and fidgety. Instead, I sat in the grotto for most of the day in a sort of kouri-induced trance, listening to the music of the water. It was Thesali who finally came to find me. "Time to dress, I've been looking for you everywhere," she said urgently. She had been willing to come look for me, though she made it clear she would not cross the threshold into that damp green chamber again.

When Melanthia had told me that Thesali couldn't be allowed at the initiation, that only those of apprentice level or above could be there, my eyes started to fill with tears. "But she is my only real friend at the Temple. How could something so important happen without her?" I objected. Then I began to set my jaw in that stubborn way I had.

Shaking her head Melanthia quickly held up her hands. "Wait, Zaia, spare me. Before we make a contest of wills out of your initiation, let me go ask the Temple Mother if we can make an exception this one time. You are, after all, an exception yourself, the youngest initiate we have had in our lifetimes." And so Thesali had been sworn to secrecy on what she was about to see. She was even helping Kendrin dress me and make me ready for this momentous event in my life. Thesali was almost more excited than I was. No doubt the kouri juice was helping me keep my calm.

The initiation was held at night and one of the things I was to remember later was the circle of candles surrounding the Dance Court. As I glanced around, the face of each woman was lit by the quivering candle-flame she held in a glass cupped in her hands, faces that were all familiar, yet strange and wondrous in that dancing light. All the Dancers of apprentice class and older were there, all dressed in Dance costume. Even the old Temple Mother herself was there, sitting next to Melanthia. "If you think so much of her, Melanthia, then I myself have to see this child Dance," she said, speaking loudly enough for us all to hear. Dhonir was there to add her support and Kendrin, sitting next to her, gave me a nod of encouragement.

The evening began with solemn ritual words and responses, then there was music, followed by more words. When the music began again, that was my signal. Now it was up to me to Dance. Melanthia called out the steps I was to do. She told me when to start and when to stop. I did my very best to send back to her everything she had ever taught me, wanting to make her proud, wanting to show all that I had learned there at the Temple. When she finally stopped me with a raised hand, she had a broad smile on her face. "You did well," she said with a little nod. Just three short words, but they meant the world to me. I must have passed the test, such as it was. *Now*, I thought, *Now I can finally become an apprentice. Now I will get to hold my own Dancewand in my hands.*

Melanthia stepped away and gave Kendrin a nod. Kendrin came forward and in her hands she held an intricate knot made of red cord and fastened to a comb, just such a knot as she herself wore in her hair. "Congratulations, Zaia. Today you have earned your Dancer's Knot." She fastened it carefully in my hair and then kissed me on each cheek. I flushed with pride and pleasure. Though it weighed almost nothing I felt a great weight there at the back of my neck. Quite solemnly we bowed to each other. Then she stepped back and Melanthia came to stand before me again.

In Melanthia's hands she held a black cloth edged with gold trim. Something was wrapped in it. As she laid back the cloth I saw she held a Dancewand. "Hold out your hands, Zaia. This is for you."

A shiver of excitement went through me. I did as she said, then had a moment of disappointment as I stared down at the wand. It looked gray and murky, almost lifeless, not at all like the others I had seen that were full of moving colors. I said nothing and only stared at it. Soon my hands began to tingle. Then, as I watched, pale colors came into the wand that slowly shifted and changed.

Gradually they took on life, first pearly iridescent hues swirling in its depths and finally stronger colors that deepened into brightness. There was a long moment of silence. When she finally spoke, Melanthia sounded very serious. "For as long as you Dance, this Dancewand will be your guide, your companion, the reflection of your moods, your connection to the Dance and to the Goddess. It will become a part of you and you will become a part of it. Respect it and keep it safe. Follow where it leads and trust its guidance. Let it help you move through the Dance and through your life." By now the Dancewand was surging with bright colors. I could almost feel it humming with energy in my hands.

"Thank you, Melanthia," I whispered. "Am I done now? Is it over?" I was exhausted. This day had been a long one. My excitement had awakened me well before dawn. I was ready to go and sit down. Actually, I was ready to go and eat a huge meal since I had eaten nothing all day. As I took a step to leave the circle Melanthia shook her head and held up her hand. "Not yet. You have shown us all what you have *learned*. Now show us what you can *do*. Dance your *own* Dance so we can see what you're capable of.

Whatever flows from your own spirit, or comes up from the belly of the night, or down from the stars, however you feel the Goddess speaking through your body, Dance it now."

That was all the direction I had. I was shocked. No one had warned me of this, not even Kendrin. *Not fair!* "Why didn't you tell me, Melanthia? I could have prepared something." Where moments before I had been filled with love for this woman, now I was angry at her and felt betrayed.

Melanthia shook her head again. "Because you're not supposed to know. We want to see what's inside you, how you Dance when you're not prepared."

"Not fair!" I hissed under my breath, my eyes flashing with anger. I had a quick instant of wanting to walk away. Then, just as quickly, I saw that I had no choice and that my anger would not serve me there. Instead, I nodded in acknowledgment. Then I stood still for a very long moment with my arms outstretched, drawing in deep breaths of the cool night air. My heart was pounding loudly in my chest. My head was empty. I had no ideas. It wasn't right. If only I'd known about this part I would have worked hard preparing something, something very grand, something that would be remembered. Every step would have been perfect.

In a sudden flash I understood. That was exactly why they hadn't told me, why they hadn't wanted Thesali there to watch and know more than she should know. Now it was just me and the Dance, no practiced steps. I had nothing that I'd learned to lean on. I shook my head to clear it. "Please help me, Goddess," I whispered as I knew other Dancers sometimes did, though in truth I gave the Goddess little credence at that time. In those early years at the Temple my passion was all for the Dance. For me the Goddess was no more than an insubstantial ghost or a series of painted carvings. In spite of that, somehow those words came to my lips on their own. With one more deep breath I gave a nod to the musicians.

As the music gathered and rose in volume I stepped forward into the Dance itself. It was time. At first, with thought and effort, I struggled to find my way. Then, abruptly, there was no more effort. I held my new Dancewand out before me and my body followed, moving to the passion in the music. The Dance was Dancing me. Where before my Dance had been about skill and practice, now it was about spirit. It was power and mystery, all rushing in and filling me. I had called on the Goddess, hardly believing in such an entity. Now the Goddess was inside me, Dancing. And She was outside too, watching and smiling. At some moment, as I moved through steps of my own making, I thought, *I'm making Her happy. She's Dancing with me. She's laughing.* I didn't know if it was the Goddess inside or the One outside who was laughing and I didn't care. I was in a trance of ecstasy that was like nothing I had ever experienced before. If my body could have held me up I might

26

have Danced forever, or perhaps grown wings and flown. I only stopped when Kendrin and Melanthia rushed forward to stop me before I fell. It took a few moments for the Dance Court and everything around it to stop spinning and come back into place. When my vision steadied I saw a circle of amazed faces, staring back at me. Then I remembered where I was and what I was doing.

It was a Dance that would be talked about for a long while to come. Though it was supposed to be secret, word instantly spread all through the Temple and even in the city. Soon there were people who made little bows to me in the street or asked me to bless their house or shrine or garden. They thought I had powers that I myself did not feel. It was as if Anuru had suddenly come back among them. Feeling unworthy and confused, I wanted to hide away from all that attention but Melanthia told me to be kind and gracious and that it would soon pass.

Dhonir was frightened for me, afraid I had been pushed too hard. I overheard her talking angrily to Melanthia. "I told you she was too young. Now look what's happened. How is a child that young to carry so much weight? They follow her around. It will age her too quickly, or worse, it will go to her head."

"I'll make sure that it doesn't." Melanthia had answered sharply. "Besides, how could we hold her back anymore? This way at least her talents will be challenged." Good to her word, Melanthia watched over her charge with all the fierceness of a mother eagle, quick to scold me for any infraction or carelessness. And, in spite of their worries, I felt blessed and even took Melanthia's rough watchfulness as affection.

Those next few years were happy ones for me. At first the older girls were no friendlier than my age-mates had been, but with the Dancing, Melanthia's praise and Thesali and Kendrin's friendship, my life was full enough. I put all of myself into Dancing until I became the best Dancer, even among the older girls. I even did my tasks willingly and with ease now that I had accepted the necessity for them. After a while, Kendrin's friends became my friends, accepting me in a way the younger girls never had. The Temple, or rather the Dance School, had now become my whole life. I felt loved and valued there in a way I never had in my mother's house. My grief about my family had finally faded into the background. By fourteen my body had begun to change, to blossom and fill out. New intense sensations coursed through me, sometimes waking me in the night. I took it all into my Dance, fuel for my power.

Since I had moved from novice to apprentice, I began to Dance in the main Dance Court of the Temple for rituals, ceremonies and celebrations. Soon after that I started Dancing in the great Dance Court of the city, quite an honor for someone so young. Though it was what I had longed for, the first few times I was a little nervous. I had been safe and sheltered, shut up in the Temple all this time. It felt very odd to be watched by a crowd of strangers that way but I soon grew accustomed to it and lost my fear. The first few times I was afraid my mother would suddenly appear and cripple me with a curse on my skill. Also, I secretly hoped my father was there watching and feeling proud of me. Neither happened, or at least if my father was there I never saw him. My aunt, however, came each time and often brought my cousin to watch. I could feel the glow of Veraine's love and support. It helped me gain confidence. But while my Dancing blossomed, Thesali, as she had feared, fell still further behind.

One afternoon, coming back from practice, I found Thesali desolately sobbing on her bed. I put my arms around her and rocked her, murmuring soothingly. Finally she was able to choke out a few words. Between sobs she said, "This time she's really going to send me back...I know she is...She was so angry..."

I shook her gently. "Who's going to send you back? Where? What are you talking about? Tell me! You have to tell me!"

Thesali finally sat up and the sobs stilled. "Melanthia. She hates me. She thinks I'm stupid and clumsy. I missed the last few steps of the Dance and she had me do them over and over. I was so nervous. I was trying so hard that it only got worse and worse. Finally she threw down her Dancewand and told me to forget it, that I wasn't worth my board here. She's really going to send me back this time, I know she is."

"No!" I shouted angrily, jumping up and starting to pace around the tiny space. "I won't let her! If she makes you leave I'll go too. I'll tell her that. I'll never Dance another step for her. I swear it."

Thesali looked terrified. "No Zaia, you mustn't talk that way! What if someone heard you?"

"I don't care. It's the truth. I'd say it to Melanthia herself."

There was no sound of steps, but the slight shadow movement made us both look up suddenly. With a little cry of despair Thesali covered her face with her hands. I gave a gasp of surprise and sank down on the bed beside her. Melanthia had come down the hall on silent Dancer feet and was now standing in the doorway of our room with an unreadable expression on her face. "And what is it you would like to tell me, Zaia?" she asked in a hard mocking voice as she took a few steps into the room.

I opened my mouth and I shut it again. No sound came out. I desperately wanted to know how long Melanthia had been standing there, what she had heard.

Melanthia nodded and said more gently to Thesali, "I thought I was too harsh with you today and so came to see how you were doing, but I see you already have your protector here with you." Then she turned her stare on me. "Have you nothing to say to me, Girl? No brave words now that I'm standing here before you?"

I blushed deep red, feeling chilled and fevered at the same time. "I...I..."

"Well, I will save you the trouble. I heard what you said. Not because I meant to listen but because you shouted loud enough so the whole hall could hear. Now tell me, would you really risk sacrificing your whole Dance future for the sake of your little friend here?"

I looked away, twisting my hands in my lap. I felt the knife blade turning slowly in my belly. Whatever I said now condemned me irrevocably with one or the other of them. I knew that Thesali and Melanthia were both staring at me, waiting.

"Well?" Melanthia asked impatiently.

Finally I looked up, caught Melanthia's eyes and stared back, holding my ground. I couldn't speak, but I nodded several times so there could be no mistaking my meaning.

It was Melanthia who grew uncomfortable first and finally looked away. "Very noble, Zaia, but not necessary. I wasn't really planning to send her off, though it might make my life easier if I did. Sometimes I think the Goddess didn't give me enough patience for this work. If you care so much, you yourself can teach her that last set of steps for the Spring Equinox Dance. And make sure she does them right. I don't have the time or, as I said, the patience."

Much relieved, I nodded again and bowed deeply. "Thank you for the chance, Dance Mistress. I will do my best."

"See that you do. You'll be held accountable." Though the words were harsh there was a hint of fond amusement in her eyes as she looked at me. Then, in two long graceful strides, Melanthia was at the doorway again. I let out a sigh of relief, but Melanthia turned suddenly in the entrance with a very different expression on her face. "And don't ever think to threaten me again with your Dancing. You've had your one chance with that little trick. Next time I'll send you home quick enough to your mother and you can see how she deals with you. After all, you're not the only Dancer in this Temple." This time she spun around and was truly gone. I slipped quickly to the doorway and watched Melanthia's back disappearing rapidly down the hall. Then I shut the door, latched it and threw myself down on Thesali's bed.

Thesali was trembling and there were tears in her eyes. "How could she be so mean to you? Sometimes I just hate her, don't you?"

"Hate Melanthia?" I asked amazed. "How could I hate Melanthia? She brought me here, made all this possible. She's the Dance to me. She is more a mother to me than my own mother ever was. Sometimes she may seem stern but underneath that her heart is kind."

"Kind? Is that what you call kindness? Well, she's not kind to me, I can tell you that. Did you see the way she looked at me, as if I were a bug in the soup? She wants to send me back. Maybe I should just go now before I get you into more trouble."

"Have no fear, she's not going to send either of us back. I won't let her. I'm going to be her best Dancer and she knows it." Suddenly recovered, I jumped to my feet and began striding about, doing my best imitation of Melanthia. "Now, no more of your tricks and threats, young woman, or next time I'll send you right home to your mother." Then I whirled about and shook my finger at the bed. "I heard every word you said, Girl, just remember that."

"Don't," Thesali said nervously. "She might hear you." Then, almost against her will, she began to laugh. I jumped on the bed with her and suddenly we were rolling around together, laughing helplessly. Then, just as suddenly, Thesali was crying again, and I was holding her and stroking her back. Then we were laughing again, even more wildly then before, rolling over each other like puppies. In the midst of this play I suddenly found my hand cupped around Thesali's firm new breast. A shock went up through my arm. I tried to draw away, but we were pressed together too tightly and Thesali's leg was shoved up between my own. The sensation there was too pleasurable to try pulling away. Instead, my body of its own accord was already tightening against that exciting pressure and I found my hand moving in a slow, hard caress over the breast I had accidentally taken captive. Thesali was moaning and twisting but making no real effort to escape. Instead, she shifted so she could cover my mouth with her own.

It was on that day that we discovered together what wondrous things, besides Dancing, bodies were made for. We tried to explore all the places where those strange and intense new sensations were hiding. As the afternoon turned toward dusk we used our hands and mouths and bodies to take each other places I had never even imagined before, the kind of ecstasy I had only found in the Dance. It felt as if I grew up that day. After that, I watched others much more closely and noticed all the little touches and looks and signs that passed between them. And I paid attention when the older girls teased and gossiped and made those little secret signs that had seemed so mysterious to me before. I even began asking questions, especially of Kendrin, not minding at all that I made my older friend blush. But I did not ask Melanthia anything. Somehow I sensed that she would not approve, would tell me sternly to keep my mind on my Dancing. Thesali, for her part, was delighted with this new discovery that bound us even more closely, lovers now, as well as friends.

*Every hundred years a Great Procession was held in Urshameel to cele-
brate the founding of the city and to re-dedicate the city and the Temple to the
Goddess. In our long history we had record of at least eight such Processions.*

CHAPTER 3
The Hundred-Year Procession

The Hundred-Year Procession was going to take place at the height of summer. I was fifteen that spring and full of my own power. Later, looking back, I was to think of that as one of the best years of my life. My young body had gained its full womanly shape and moved with an ease and power totally at my command. At fifteen, with the arrogance of youth, I thought it honest to say that I Danced better than any of the young women who were four or five years my senior, even as well as most of the Temple Dancers. Clearly, modesty was not one of my greatest virtues at that time. Even my stern, harsh Dance Mistress praised me in spite of herself. Somehow I had become the Temple pet, and the other girls were actually proud of me now. Instead of resenting me, they cheered me on. And, in addition to all that, I had a lover who adored me and all the pleasures of exploring together the secrets of our young bodies.

The only shadow that hung over me at that time was my fear that Kendrin would take her five-year pledge and go on the road as a Dancer for the Goddess, Dancing in towns and villages that had no Temple and no trained Dancers. She had spoken of it often enough. Like me, she had been born in Urshameel and had never been outside the city. Now she had an insistent longing to see more of the world. Thesali, when she heard about it, was appalled at the idea. "Why would anyone want to trade the comfort and beauty of the Temple for the dangers and hardships of the road? Sleeping on the cold damp ground? Eating rough food? Walking all day? I can't see the sense in it. Whatever can Kendrin be thinking of?" I shrugged and shook my head, wondering if this sounded, to Thesali, too much like going back to the hardships of her village after the relative ease of the Temple. Some part of me thought it sounded like a tempting adventure, but I wisely kept silent on my thoughts.

Ushain, Kendrin's lover, had her own opinions on the matter. "If we could go together it might not be such a bad idea. There's no future for me here. I'm sick of being an apprentice carver, being assigned to do toes or fingers or ears when I'm certainly skilled enough to carve a whole figure, but until the old ones die off there's no room for someone like me. Out there I could find real work, but the Temple demands a pledge of celibacy from their Dancers when they make their five-year pledge and that I'm not willing to do. I can't travel with Kendrin for five years as if we're just sisters. That's not my way."

In spite of anything we said, Kendrin insisted that she was going. To me, the Temple would have seemed very strange and empty without her. It was hard to imagine it. She had always been there, from the very beginning. Then, at the last minute, she changed her mind. "My grandfather is a sick old man. He's afraid if I go he'll never see me again and I'm afraid he'll die in my absence. Since my parents got taken by the fever I'm the only one he has left. Maybe...later..." So Kendrin was still in my life, though very busy with her duties as a Temple Dancer as well as with the care of her grandfather.

The Great Procession was something most people could only see once in a lifetime and then only if they were very lucky, but one old woman of a hundred and ten would be watching her second one and she was also going to be honored at it. The Procession occupied everyone's thoughts at the Temple, as well as in the city. All that spring and even the year before, things had been in a flurry of excitement and preparation. Walls were rebuilt or repaired and buildings were repainted in bright colors, some that hadn't seen a coat of paint in fifty years. Alleys were cobbled, streets were paved and widened, new gardens were made and older ones restored.

In the Temple itself old tattered banners were taken down and ceremonially burned, while new ones were woven and sewn by many eager hands. Altars were cleared and covered with bright new cloths. All the statues of the Goddess were removed to be cleaned, or to be painted, gilded and bejeweled again. Then they were returned to their places with all the appropriate rituals. A huge new figure of the Great Mother was being made in the Temple workshop. She had taken an entire year to complete and was the work of many hands. Just before the Procession She was to be placed in the central courtyard of the Temple in a grand ceremony. Meanwhile, no one but the carvers were allowed to see her.

Just as in the city, the gardens of the Temple were being beautified, enlarged, refurbished and replanted. Flowering trees and shrubs were being added everywhere. Fountains were being repaired and new ones installed. And, of course, it was my father who was called on to supervise all the work on the gardens by order of the Temple. Though this might appear to be a great honor and it was, in truth I suppose he had little choice. When the Temple Mother requested something it was more like a command. Few would have thought to refuse. It probably made his life at home even harder than usual, though he never once complained. Actually, he seemed delighted for this excuse to be back in his beloved gardens. And it meant we could visit together without fear. I was overjoyed. Now, instead of my task being assigned by lot as it usually was, I was assigned to help my father. In fact I was to be his assistant. Melanthia had seen to that.

I put in far more time than I would ordinarily have done on any task. Heads bent together over bright flowers, we talked of everything but Thea. I asked about her only once, but after Tomaire said, "Your mother is well, but I fear her anger toward you is unchanged," I never asked again. We carefully steered away from that topic. Instead, my father talked freely of his early life at the Temple, telling me many stories I had never heard before. He even mentioned Melanthia, wistfully, a few times in a way that suggested more. I knew better than to ask, but I watched how they spoke to each other, saw Melanthia's face soften with a look I had never seen before, heard the tenderness in my father's voice, and my heart ached for them both.

In turn I talked to him about my life there: about the Dance, the Dance school, the Temple, the other girls who were now my friends, and my love for Thesali. He listened to it all with delight. I told him about the Grotto of Mother Toad and he said he already knew it, knew it well in fact. "It was my favorite place to go when I was in the middle of a difficult task and needed some peace and solitude." I even shared with him the magic of my initiation Dance and knew from his expression that he understood. Eyes shining with pride, he often came now to watch me Dance and I was finally able to introduce him to my friends.

Among the young Dancers, the question on all our minds that spring— the thing we spoke of constantly—was who would be chosen to lead the first part of the Great Procession. It could not be one of the older Temple Dancers or one of the Dance Mistresses, nor could it be one of the young novices. The Dancer could only be chosen from among the apprentices or the new graduates. I was sure Kendrin would be picked for that honor and I desperately wanted to be one of her dressers. I was even ready to bribe or beg or bully to have a place there if it didn't fall to me by lot. In the end, I didn't need to resort to such strategies.

When Melanthia found me I was working diligently with two other Dancers, Noni and Essan, clearing away an accumulation of old leaves and debris from a flower bed. Actually, at that moment, we were being a little less than diligent. Screaming with laughter, Essan and I were trying to bury Noni in a mountain of leaves while she giggled and struggled, thrashing about wildly. At Melanthia's sudden appearance we all jumped up, quickly brushing ourselves off.

"Well, so this is how you do your work. Perhaps we should postpone the Procession until next year so you have time to make ready. Zaia, come with me and change your clothes to something more appropriate. You are summoned to appear before the Temple Mother."

I was totally flustered and said quickly, "We meant no harm here. It can quickly be repaired. Surely it is not so serious as all that."

Melanthia stared at me for a moment in surprise. Then her stern visage broke up into sudden laughter. "No, Zaia, the Temple Mother is much too busy to bother herself with a few leaves. This is another matter altogether. There is something of importance you must hear. Come quickly, we mustn't keep her waiting. Now, you two, get all this rubbish cleared away and make this garden ready for planting before the dinner gong." As Melanthia led me away the other two were hustling about, setting to work in earnest on the long flower bed. Though my hands were shaking, I dressed quickly in my best clothes. Full of anxiety, I tried to question Melanthia on our way to the audience chamber. She would say nothing except that we must hurry.

By the next morning the news that I had been chosen as lead Dancer had spread all through the Temple like floodwater and by afternoon it was all through the city. I, myself, had been dumbfounded. Being so young I had not even thought of myself as a contender for such an honor. "But I thought you would choose Kendrin," I had stammered out in confusion when the Temple Mother told me. She leaned forward and said solemnly, "You are the one the Goddess has chosen. We do not question her choices."

Though I knew perfectly well that it was the Dance Mistresses along with the Temple Dancers and the Temple Mother herself who had done the choosing, I blushed for my unintended rudeness, bowed and said humbly, "I am deeply honored and will try my best to deserve this honor."

"See that you do," Melanthia said sharply. "See that you don't disgrace the Temple of Kernoss or your old Dance Mistress before the town and the Goddess."

Stung by her words I turned suddenly and looked straight at her. "No need to worry, Melanthia. I will make you very proud of me." Melanthia stared back at me in silence for a long moment before she nodded. Then the Temple Mother made a dismissing gesture with her hand to both of us. I bowed again and we left together.

When we reached the hall my knees were suddenly shaking and my legs would hardly hold me. Now my bold words seemed flat and hollow. "I can't believe what just happened. What if I can't do it? What if I'm not good enough after all? Please Melanthia, will you help me with this?"

"Never fear, Zaia, you are good enough. That's why you were chosen in spite of your age. You're the best we have. And no, I can't help you now. I would be altogether the wrong person for that job. I have too much at stake here. I would drive you too hard. That's not what you need at this moment.

What you need is to find your deepest self in the Dance. I've already done you what good or harm I'm capable of doing. Nekali and Dhonir will be your teachers now."

"Oh Melanthia, how can I ever thank you for all you've done for me?"

"By doing your best." Suddenly, to my amazement, I found myself wrapped in Melanthia's arms, being hugged. It was the first time that had ever happened. Then, just as quickly she stiffened, straightened and drew back. "You've been almost like a daughter to me, the child I never had. Thank me in your Dance, Zaia. Watching you Dance is all the thanks I need." Though her words were gruff I saw a glint of tears in her eyes.

After that it felt as though time was rushing at me like clouds before the wind. I had little chance to see my father anymore. Melanthia had turned me over to Dhonir and Nekali. They were to get me ready for the Procession. I found them so different from Melanthia, both in appearance and in their ways, that at first it was hard to adjust. They were also quite different from each other. Though very agile, Dhonir was short and solid and seemed planted in the ground until she shifted and was suddenly somewhere else. She had reddish-brown skin so shiny it almost looked polished, a round, good-natured face and a gentle manner, with none of Melanthia's sternness and impatience, but I soon found that there was just as much firmness under that kindly surface. Nekali was almost ghost-like with light hair and pale skin. I think she must have come from somewhere far away, though she would never speak of it. Most of the time she spoke softly, but when she was displeased her voice could be heard across the Dance Court. I worked with them every day but not as I had expected, not at improving my stamina and technique or in learning new steps. No, it was something else altogether. Later, I was always to remember the strangeness and enchantment of that first lesson, but at the beginning, when they had tried to explain it to me, all I had felt was anger.

"Why didn't Melanthia teach me any of this?"

"It's not her job," Dhonir answered, firm but patient. "Melanthia's job was to work with your body, to teach you skill, agility, coordination, endurance, the pattern of the steps."

Nodding, Nekali took up the speech as if they had rehearsed it all beforehand or had already repeated it many times before. "But there are other things you need to learn and now perhaps you are ready for them. In truth, because you Dance in the Great Procession so soon, you have no choice but to be ready, isn't that so?"

"Besides, would you have listened back then?" Dhonir went on. "You wanted to use your body to Dance. That's all you wanted to do. You almost died from setting your will to it." Then she winked and gave me a sly little smile. "If I remember right, you didn't even want to do your share of the tasks here. You thought it a waste of your time even though that's what makes the Dance and all else possible at the Temple. Yes, those humble, ordinary little tasks are the core of all that happens here. Would you have listened then if someone had tried to tell you that the core of the Dance is stillness just as the core of music is silence?"

"This learning is about spirit," Nekali continued. "Finding your way to spirit through your Dance. That's really what the Dance is about. It's not just about learning steps, though that's clearly part of it. The real question is *'What is Dancing for?'* It's certainly not about raising sweat or training muscles. It's about *making spirit visible.* When you Dance, at that moment, you are the Goddess in earthly form to the people you Dance for. You bring Her radiance and Her blessings into their lives, an awesome responsibility. You cannot Dance just from skill. You must Dance from something deeper, find that part of the Goddess that lives in you."

I shivered, not at all sure I wanted to carry such a heavy burden. All I wanted to do was Dance. With no reply from me Nekali went on, "There's a center, a core to all the fast, skilled motion we call Dance. That core is stillness and at the core of stillness is spirit and at the core of spirit is the Goddess."

"You don't need to learn any more steps right now, Zaia, or any more skills," Dhonir added firmly. "What you need to learn has to do with spirit—spirit and breath. The Dance you did for your initiation was all wild energy and raw, untrained power. Now we will show you how to use and control and not let yourself be controlled by that power. And at the very heart of that power is surrender."

My head was aching from all this. It felt as if it might crack and I put up my hands to hold it together. I wanted to scream with frustration. "Why are you talking in riddles? Instead of teaching me to Dance you're telling me contradictions. Is this some sort of game? Are you making fun of my ignorance? I have only a little time to create a whole new Dance and you're talking to me of stillness and surrender?"

"And we have only this little time to teach you what you need to know. An older novice or a graduate would already know all this in her bones, at the core of her being."

"But you were the one chosen, so you are who we work with."

Turning from one to the other of them in confusion I burst out, "But how...? Why didn't Melanthia...?"

"Zaia, be still and listen. We said it starts with surrender. Do you trust Melanthia?" I nodded, mystified. "Well, she turned you over to us so we must be good for something. If you're going to learn from us, then you must trust us, too. This is learning on a different level, listening from a different place. For now you must set aside everything you think you know."

Dhonir shrugged and winked. "I told you she was going to be a hard one. The best ones always are. They think they already know everything. Well, Zaia, are you ready to learn something new? We're not like Melanthia. We won't threaten and shake our Dancewands at you. We'll wait until you're willing."

I looked down at the ground and mumbled somewhat sullenly, "I surrender to your will," thinking that now we could get on with the lesson. Full of resentment and confusion, I understood nothing that was being said to me. It felt as if, on some subtle level, I was being teased or mocked.

Nekali shook her head. "No, no, not to our will, Zaia. We have no wish to challenge your will. It has done you very well so far, but right now it is blocking the way. Surrender to the teaching itself or to the Goddess inside you if you wish, if you can understand that better."

"Look in your Dancewand and see what answers you find there," Dhonir added.

Somewhat resentfully I stared into my Dancewand. Dark turbulent colors were swirling about in it, murky and angry like an approaching storm, a very accurate reflection of my mood. I took a deep breath, trying to still myself inside. As I continued to stare at the wand in my hands, the colors slowly began to change to blues and greens. Now they were moving more gently in the pattern of slow breathing. *Help me Mother,* I said in the silence of my head.

As I went on staring and breathing, something shifted inside. Like a door opening, understanding bloomed. I looked up, staring past them both and put my hands over my heart. "I surrender to the teaching," I said softly, almost in a whisper. Then, I felt everything go soft within me. It was almost like surrendering to a lover's touch.

Dhonir and Nekali nodded to each other. "Lower your hands and try to follow the thread of my words," Dhonir said. Then she began intoning in a slow, steady, hypnotic way, "Stand balanced, centered on both feet. Breathe, breathe deeply, breathe into the core of your being, breathe into your center and feel the stillness there, feel the waiting. That is the still center from which the Dance grows, from which everything grows. Try to still your mind of thoughts. Bring it down to a tiny point of light.

"Now feel the darkness all around, feel it filling your body, spreading outward. Now bring the tiny point of light that is your mind down into your body, into your center, into the place that you Dance from. Put all of your power into that point of light. Feel it waiting, waiting, very still in the darkness.

"Now begin to feel it grow, slowly, ever so slowly, feel light growing and expanding in that darkness. Feel it grow until the light begins to fill your center and move out, lines of light moving out through your arms, your legs, shooting up through your head. Let those lines of light pulse out from your center.

"Now move on those lines and you will be Dancing."

Dhonir continued talking while I began to move. Following her words I Danced like one in a trance with Nekali guiding me, dancing at my side but never actually touching my body, using only the lines of light to keep her connection to me. I felt as if I were Dancing in a dream, my body moving freely and fluidly, almost without effort, light and power pouring from my center out through my hands and feet. *I could Dance this way forever without tiring,* I thought. Almost in the next instant Nekali nodded, Dhonir stopped speaking and gave a slight clap of her hands, the lines of light vanished and I was standing still, shaking my head to clear it and feeling a terrible sense of loss.

"Why did we stop so soon? Did I do something wrong?"

"No, you were beautiful," Nekali quickly reassured me. "But trust us, that's as far as you should go the first time. You went very deep." Then she winked at Dhonir. "See, I told you she could do it."

"There's no wrong to this part except in refusing to surrender, but you were probably Dancing for much longer than you realized," Dhonir added.

When the Procession was only one month away, I did nothing but Dance and eat and sleep. I worked with Nekali and Dhonir at their exercises, learning more and going deeper each time. I also worked hard on my own steps, trying to create the perfect Dance for the Procession. My teachers indulged me in this but did not seem to give it much importance. As the gardens had been completed I seldom saw my father anymore, but my aunt and cousin often came to give me their support and encouragement. Once or twice they even managed to bring my sister with them. They must have sworn her to secrecy. Yanin was wide-eyed with excitement at being able to watch her sister Dance and awed by the beauty of the Temple.

As the time of the Procession drew near, the silence from my mother hurt all over again, with a force it hadn't had for years. When Kendrin first talked of going on the road it had sounded exciting to me. Now I thought of it again more seriously. It would get me away from the endless tangle with my family. I would see new places, be on my own, test myself. I could feel the freedom of it tugging at me. When I mentioned it to Thesali I was met with total opposition. "How do you know you'll even come back? Anything might happen to you out there. Or you could turn out like Old Auntie Selvi, think of that."

I knew well enough who Old Selvi was, but it didn't frighten me. "You could come with me, Thesali," I told her eagerly. "We could do this together.

It would be a glorious adventure. We could see other cities, other Dance Temples. We could Dance for people who almost never see a Dancer."

Thesali was shaking her head vehemently. "I left the country. I have no wish to go back to that kind of life. Tramping about on muddy roads, carrying all our clothes, never knowing where we're going to sleep or if we're going to eat. No Zaia, I can't do that, not even for you. Why can't you just be content to stay here with me at the Temple? You have a glorious future here. You could be the best Dancer since the famous Anuru, maybe even better. Besides, Dancers on the road have to promise to live celibate. How could we do that? Is that really what you want? Oh Zaia! Forget this idea of taking the pledge. Please don't speak of it anymore. It breaks my heart."

But I couldn't keep silent. The idea pulled and pulled at me. What sounded to Thesali like hardship sounded to me like freedom. Even in the midst of my preparations, I longed for it. But each time I tried to talk to her it ended in a fight and so, for the first time, we found ourselves arguing constantly. As my training for the Dance deepened, it felt as if Thesali and I were drawing further and further apart.

At last, I went to talk to Melanthia. The Dance Mistress looked at me for a long time in silence. Finally, with some sadness in her voice, she said, "Child, I shall miss you more than I can say. I'll be very sorry not to have you here to Dance for the Temple. But, if this is where your heart leads you, then you must follow it as you have before. It was your heart that brought you here and it may well be your heart that takes you away again. I would not be the one to tell you no." But when I talked about leaving the Temple early, perhaps in the next year or so, since I had become an apprentice so young, Melanthia was adamant. "No Zaia, eighteen is soon enough. Before that you would be too young to go on the road alone. Put it out of your mind and do not set your famous will there. You will get opposition from your other Dance teachers and from the Temple Mother as well as from your family, but most of all you will get opposition from me. And, believe me, my will has been tested far longer than yours. But rest assured, when the time comes I'll help you on your way if that's still what you want. Now set all that aside, stop arguing with Thesali and put your mind on getting ready to lead the Procession."

After that, I said no more to anyone about taking the pledge. Instead I concentrated on my Dance and all the preparations for it. I needed a new costume which had to be cut and fitted, the fabric chosen, the vest embroidered. My aunt gave me a pair of long beaded earrings that shimmered in the light, my cousin gave me bells for my ankles and my father gave me a long, flowered sash for luck.

A week before the Procession was to happen the statue of the Great Mother was finally finished. She was shrouded in a dark cloth and carried on an ornate red and gold flower-covered oxcart to the central courtyard of the Temple with a large escort of Priests and Priestesses chanting and ringing bells and swinging incense. At dawn the next morning there was a very special ritual, attended only by the Temple Mother herself and a few of the oldest Priestesses and Priests. None of us were allowed to be there, but Melanthia told us it was for calling on the Goddess to bless this likeness of herself and to imbue it with power and presence. Later, the dark cloth was lifted so we could all see Her face.

Afterward the Temple was rededicated to the Goddess in a three-day ceremony. Most of the people of Urshameel came through the Temple gates in those three days, leaving offerings and paying their respects. The new Goddess was the center of all this. Made of dark polished stone, She was very grand and impressive. Even I, just beginning to find my way to the Goddess, felt chills and shivers when I looked up at Her. And, though I knew she was made by human hands, I was actually filled with a sense of awe when I laid my small offering at Her feet.

When the great day actually came I was in a dither of excitement and anxiety. I had to constantly keep reminding myself to breathe deeply and to reach for the inner stillness Dhonir and Nekali had trained in me. Dhonir came and did my face paint as this was to be much more formal than any Dance I had done before. With a steady, practiced hand, she painted dark lines around my eyes. Then she rubbed blue-green nithra-paste on my eyelids. Next she put her finger in a pot of red paste and made a focusing dot in the center of my forehead as well as ritual markings on my cheeks. When she was done she turned my face this way and that to look at it. Then she nodded her satisfaction and left me to Kendrin and Thesali who were to be my dressers.

Far from being jealous, Kendrin was very pleased for me and delighted that it had not been her. "You're not angry at me?" I asked her anxiously for the third time. "I thought it would be you and I had hoped I could be your dresser."

"No, I'm not angry at you, Zaia. I'm very grateful. I had no wish to carry that burden, but you will do it wonderfully well. I have secretly been watching you Dance whenever I could slip away. They couldn't have made a better choice."

"But, it's an honor, Kendrin, and surely you deserved it."

"If the finger had pointed at me, I would have had to choose between refusing that honor—which would not have gone well—or fainting from nervousness at the head of the Great Procession—which would have gone even worse. Thank you for saving me from such a fate. Now sit still so we can do your braids."

Then Thesali hugged me again and said for the hundredth time, "Oh Zaia, I'm so proud of you."

They sat on either side of me to make the Dancer braids and pin them up, leaving some of my hair to fly loose with the Dance. Then came the bright green Dance shirt with loose sleeves, a low bodice and a bare midriff. It was stitched all over with tiny mirrors that would flash in the sunlight. Over that went a long, blue vest of gauzy, almost transparent material that would float in the wind, and then the skirt of forest green that hooked on my hips and rode below the smooth roundness of my belly. Next came a snake bracelet for each arm, my aunt's earrings, my father's sash and the bells for my ankles. At the very end of all this, Kendrin fastened the Dancer's Knot into the mass of braids at the back of my head and pronounced me ready. "Look," she said, holding up the mirror for me as Thesali breathed, "Like the Goddess herself."

It was startling to see myself that way. I was indeed transformed, a stranger, both less than myself and more—touched with a sort of sacred power that thrilled and frightened me, and a sexual power that was bold and new, that spoke through the face paint and the clothing. I looked older by four years than when I had first sat down in that chair. Some part of me wanted to cry out, *No! Too young! Too soon!* In the next instant the trained Dancer took over, remembering what an honor this was and how glad I was to have been chosen. With a little nod, I leaned forward and mouthed to my reflection, *Luck be with you, Zaia.*

Kendrin went quickly to fetch Dhonir. She came at once. Her eyes went wide with pleasure and surprise at my appearance. With deft hands she laid a dark cloak over my shoulders and raised the hood, covering all my bright finery and my hair. It was a good disguise. On the street, at a quick glance, I could be anyone. After that, she and Melanthia led me out to where the Procession was already assembling in front of the Temple.

I blinked in the bright light. The sight of it all took my breath away. There were brilliantly dressed musicians with their drums and flutes, the other Dancers in their finest Dance costumes, the Priestesses and Priests of the Temple in their formal robes of purple and gold, the Head Mother being carried on a grand chair by four bearers. Right behind her was the old woman who at a hundred and ten was watching her second Procession. She was also being carried on a grand chair. Lined up in back of them were the dignitaries of the city, the seat-holders of the Council, several members of the wealthy merchant families and the heads of the craft guilds and the art alliances. After them came a mass of people who would shift back and forth from marching with the Procession to watching it. Sooner or later everyone would join in, if only for a short while.

The watchers were everywhere. Dressed in their best clothes, they were lining the sides of the streets, peering out windows, sitting on each other's shoulders, standing on the rooftops and on the tops of walls. Some had even climbed into trees for a better view. The streets were festive with color. Huge bunches of bright flowers hung from all the poles. A multitude of flags and banners were waving in the breeze, most of them adorned with brightly painted images of the Goddess. In fact the Goddess was in evidence everywhere. Many carried their house or hearth Goddesses in their arms or on raised platforms to receive the blessings of this occasion. Several of the Temple Goddesses were being carried in the Procession, all brightly polished and newly adorned with sparkling jewels.

This time the Dancers were to go in front of the musicians, and I was to go at the very front of the Dancers. We were to take a winding route through the city streets to end in the huge square at the center of Urshameel. There the rituals would take place and the speeches would be made. I was so glad I only had to Dance and did not have to speak. That would have frightened me far more than leading the Procession. Melanthia had already walked the route with me several times, but it was so well marked by banners and flowers I would have no problem following it. Now I stared around at the crowd with a moment of fear. "Am I late?" I whispered to Melanthia. "Have they all been waiting for me?" The excitement of the moment was so intense I thought I might be sick from it in spite of all my training.

"Yes, they have all been waiting for you. And no, you are not late. You are here at just the right time."

Then Dhonir on the other side said, "Remember, you don't have to lead the whole way. I'll signal you when it's time to change and other Dancers will come in your place. If you tire before that, signal to us and we'll get you out." With Melanthia, she walked me to the very front of the line of march. When we stopped, Dhonir whispered in my ear, "Now breathe deeply and find your calm center. Keep breathing deeply right to your core. You know everything you need to know. You have everything within you to do this."

I did as she said, breathing deeply and nodding to show I understood. She kissed me on the forehead and then Melanthia signaled to the musicians who began to play. Dhonir said, "Ready?" as she whipped off my cloak. There were gasps of delighted surprise and a hum of appreciation for my sudden appearance. It was as if I had dropped from the sky right in front of them.

I nodded to Dhonir. What else could I do? But, in truth, I was far from ready. I was in a frozen panic, unable to breathe, unable to move, unable to remember the Dance I had so carefully planned and rehearsed. I even tried saying the Dancer's prayer, but the words would hardly come to mind. I was so cold it felt as if all the blood had drained out of my body at that moment.

There seemed to be a cold winter wind blowing across my bare skin. What if I really wasn't worthy of this honor? What if I couldn't remember the way? Or remember the steps? Or ...

Then a voice in my head, like Melanthia's but much more forceful said, *Enough questions! It is time to Dance! That's what you were made for. That's what you were born to do. That's why you're here. Dance and all your questions will be answered. Dance and you won't need to ask any questions. Just breathe deeply and follow your Dancewand.*

There was no disobeying *that* voice. I took a deep breath and for a moment there was total silence in my mind. All the sounds of the city were shut out and I was alone in that core of stillness, alone but not alone, for it was filled with a vibrant sense of presence. Then the moment passed, I held my Dancewand out in front of me and all the sounds and colors of the city rushed in again, gloriously alive. This was the Great Procession and I had been chosen to lead it and now was the moment! The colors in the Dancewand swirled with red, orange, yellow. Power hummed in my hands and warmth rushed up through my body as I stepped forward into the music and into the Dance.

Dhonir and Nekali had prepared me well. I didn't have to think of the first step or the next. It just came, drawn before me in the air in lines of light. I only had to hold up my Dancewand and follow where the lines led, my body moving as I had already seen it moving in my mind. I don't know if I did any of the steps I had so carefully planned and rehearsed—and I no longer cared. The Dance was Dancing me. I had surrendered to the Dance. I had no will. And yet I was all will, all will burning like a bright clear flame. I felt powerless, a leaf on the wind, being carried along. At the same time, I was filled with power, power that hummed in my fingertips and under the soles of my feet. Some little part of my brain said, *Now I understand the contradictions* and then it fell silent. I was past words, deep into the Dance, yet everything entered my awareness, the music, the sound of the breeze in the leaves, voices chanting, the warmth of the sun, the earth under my feet, the hum of the crowd, a bird flying by, the smell of horses.

Then, quite suddenly, I slipped out of time and it was the Procession of a hundred years ago that I was leading. And perhaps I was Anuru or perhaps I was Dancing with her. Then there were other Processions in this city or perhaps other cities, perhaps even cities in other countries. I might have been going forward in time as well as back. *I am seeing through the eyes of the Goddess,* the little voice in my head said and then it was gone again. I was filled with the great sweep of all those Processions, all that human time, all the sounds of the music, the chants, the noise of the crowds, present and past. I was part of everything and everything was part of me and the motion of the Dance was the thread that held it together. I felt the Dance weaving through like a long, brightly colored sash and I felt myself at the heart of it all, weaving the tapestry and being carried along by it and Dancing as I never had before, as I could not even have imagined Dancing.

Suddenly, a venom-filled voice nearby hissed, "Only a beggar or a tramp would go dressed like that in the city streets. No woman from a decent family would show herself that way." It was my mother, so close I could have reached out and touched her if Thea had not been hidden by the crowd. Startled out of my trance, I stumbled and almost fell. It was fierce will that kept me on my feet, but I was not sure I could continue Dancing, certainly not the way I had been. The long, multicolored sash I had been floating on had been abruptly cut. Mercifully, just at that moment, there was a tap on my arm and then gentle hands on my shoulders turning me, Dhonir's signal that it was time to cede my place to other Dancers. I staggered a few steps, then Thesali's arms folded about me and Veraine came on the other side to give support. In another moment Kendrin and Melanthia were there too. I was gasping for breath, shaking and sobbing, "My mother, she came right next to me and said..."

"We heard her," Veraine interrupted quickly. "Once said is enough. No need to repeat such ugliness. We all heard her. Oh, why couldn't my sister have stayed home instead of coming out to try and spoil this triumph for you? I've forgiven her many things, but I don't think I can ever forgive her for this. That's why Dhonir pulled you out of the Dance."

"Not so," Dhonir said, shaking her head forcefully. "It was time to stop Zaia before she Danced herself into exhaustion, into oblivion. There's only so much a human body can endure. You Danced far beyond anyone's expectations. That was a Dance that will be talked about for years to come." The others joined in with a chorus of praise, especially Kendrin.

I knew they were right. It had been an extraordinary Dance. I also knew that they were trying to soften the blow. My mother had set out to spoil everything. It was at that moment I decided I was leaving the city of Urshameel. Even as I watched the Procession weaving its way past, some part of my mind was already looking ahead. After my eighteenth birthday nothing could hold me here and no one could change my mind. I would not live any longer than I had to in the same city as Thea. But I would heed what Melanthia had told me. Until then, I would bide my time and learn as much as I could. Standing between Thesali and Veraine I was able to catch my breath and watch the rest of the Hundred-Year Procession. Many came to bow to me or called out praises or tossed flowers at my feet, but none of that could change what had happened. Though I smiled and waved back and bowed in return, I watched it all at a distance as if there were a pane of thick, dark glass between me and the joyful, noisy, colorful crowd. For me, the day had been robbed of its charm.

CHAPTER 4
Departure and First Dance

W e no longer feared that Thesali was going to be expelled from the Temple and sent back to her village. She had grown much too valuable for that. Though she seldom Danced now unless a large troupe was needed and had given up any idea of moving from novice to apprentice, Melanthia had set her to doing work that was much more suited to her. Thesali had taken over teaching the young Dancers their numbers and letters, a task the Dance Mistresses disliked and for which they had little skill. Thesali was very good at it, "a born teacher," as Dhonir said. She had even crafted a course on the history of the city and the surrounding region, so our girls should not be altogether ignorant of the larger world in which they lived. Meanwhile, she was also learning how to weave. I could never have managed to sit still so long, but Thesali had the patience for it. Besides that, she had skilled hands and a good eye for color. It became her meditation after the noisy classroom. For my part, I was Dancing more and more often at the city Dance Court, the very thing I had most longed for.

With all that good fortune we should have been well content—in fact we should have been very happy together. Instead, we argued constantly. Two years had passed since the Great Procession and I was still just as determined as ever to leave right after my eighteenth birthday. Thesali, now deeply rooted in the Temple, was equally determined I should stay. Though Thesali had been my friend from the start, from that first moment in the Dance Court when she stepped up to defend me from Melanthia's anger, it was more that she had chosen me rather than the other way around.

Now she felt I was deserting her—and perhaps I was. Thea had unintentionally set me on this course and then Kendrin's absence had added to my restlessness. Kendrin had finally left a short time after her father's death, free at last to go on the road. I could feel her out there somewhere, beckoning to me, though of course I said nothing of that to Thesali. I found myself yearning for something larger than the Temple that had seemed so vast when I first came there. Even the city felt confining. There was a whole world to explore beyond its gates. With the increasing strain between us, Thesali and I found ourselves pulling apart, growing in different directions. Sometimes she almost seemed like a stranger to me—and not a very pleasant one at that.

Sometimes she even seemed like an enemy. I suppose I must have seemed the same to her.

My spirit felt tattered by the endless wrangling between us. I was finding it hard to concentrate on my Dancing. One morning, when Thesali and I were standing in the courtyard after our morning meal and I could hear us starting again on the same old argument with almost exactly the same words, I had an inspiration. "Perhaps this has nothing to do with us at all. Perhaps it's the will of the Goddess and She is the one we're really arguing with. Let me go ask the Oracle, The Mother Toad in the grotto and see what she tells us the future is to be."

Thesali grabbed my arm in a tight grip. "No, I hate that place. I don't want my life or anything about me to be decided by that creature."

"But she doesn't decide anything," I insisted. "She only lets us know what's already been decided."

"I don't care. I don't want to go there with you and I don't want you to go there alone."

With a sigh I unfastened Thesali's hand from my arm. I was beginning to feel that all too familiar anger and frustration rising from my belly and tightening in my chest. "We have to do something different. It's no use consulting with others. They simply side with one or the other of us but offer no new wisdom. This is tearing us apart anyway. Right now there's more anger than love between us."

Thesali turned away, saying bitterly, "Go then and ask what you will. I already feel you leaving and this is just another step in it. Ask your question. I'm sure you'll get whatever answer you want there."

"I will get what answer there is," I told her sharply. "I have enough honor not to twist a sacred thing to suit my own purposes and you know that. It makes me even angrier that you would suggest such a thing." But I was talking to empty air. Thesali had already left, vanishing down the corridor with swift, silent Dancer's steps.

I shrugged with a sense of futility. Now I was committed on a course of action that moments before had been only a chance suggestion. I didn't even know how to go about this thing and I was not about to inquire of anyone, least of all Melanthia who would want to know why I was asking. Quickly, I went to find some fruit for an offering. Then, with the pockets of my tunic bulging, I slipped through the Temple by little-used corridors and backstairs, hoping to avoid notice. I didn't want to answer any questions and I certainly didn't want any more advice. Nor did I want to see the looks of annoyance or superiority on the faces of others. I would discover the answers on my own, though I still wasn't sure how.

When I found the little secret stairs, I lit a torch and peered down. I had not been that way for a long while. Evidently, no one else had either. The path was blocked with spider webs and there were pools of moisture on some of the steps. It looked very uninviting. I wondered if it was no longer maintained. I almost turned back, amazed that I had found the courage to venture there that first year. Well, I had been in need of something then, and now I was in need again. I knew that, even if the stairs were forbidding, I would find comfort in the grotto. I wondered what had happened to the old man who used to tend this place. Perhaps he had died or gone away. "If it is decided that I have to stay then I'll take over that job. I'll come here at least once a week, leave offerings and keep the way fresh and clean," I promised myself aloud. Or perhaps I was promising the Goddess.

When I got to the grotto itself, after struggling through a mass of spider webs, it seemed somehow smaller than I remembered but other-wise unchanged. I had been so busy. It had been almost two years, perhaps more since I had come that way. I looked about hopefully for Mother Toad. Perhaps she was in hiding and I would not find her. Worse yet, perhaps she was dead from neglect. I felt a stab of grief and guilt. Then I saw Her sitting on a high damp shelf of rock next to a tiny waterfall, half hidden by some miniature ferns that were nodding in the drops of water. She was regarding me with Her unblinking gold-flecked stare.

After I set my offerings on the altar and spoke some ritual words, I made a slight bow and said directly to Her, "Mother, I mean no disrespect here, but I don't know how to do this thing so I have to ask in my own way." Then I stood on tip-toes and very gently lifted Her down. She made no resistance. I went with Her to the stone bench and sat with my back leaning against the ancient rocks of the wall, cupping the toad in my lap. Mother Toad settled her soft, cool, round belly in my palms as if we were still friends in spite of my long absence, as if I had been there only a few days before. I shut my eyes and leaned back as the coolness of Her belly turned to warmth in my hands. "What is it to be? What do you see? Am I to stay here or to go on the road?"

I sat very still, almost holding my breath. For a long while there was nothing but darkness in my mind. I was almost ready to give up, thinking I would have to go ask for advice after all on how to do this, when suddenly my mind was flooded with images, brighter than reality, images of myself on the road with a pack on my back, and others of myself Dancing in strange places, and more frightening ones of ruins and forgotten Dance grounds and ancient, long-abandoned Temples. Only when I opened my eyes with effort and deliberately broke the connection did the images stop. If I shut my eyes they instantly began again as if they had only been waiting there in the darkness for me. If I tried to see myself staying at the Temple after the end of that year everything turned gray and murky, and I felt a roiling sickness in my belly. "What about Thesali? Will she come with me in the end?" I asked aloud. Again, that same roiling sickness and nothing but gray murk. When I asked about Thesali staying at the Temple, my mind was filled with scenes of festivals and holy days as well as scenes of the daily life at Kernoss.

My answer had come through clearly enough and now I wasn't sure if I was glad or sorry. It was one thing to argue fiercely with Thesali for my right to go. It was quite another thing to see I really had no choice in the matter. In no hurry to go find her and tell her what I knew, I sat a while, seeking comfort from the warmth and softness that filled my hands. Finally I thought to ask a last question that had bothered me much of late. "What is my far future to be? Will I come back to the Temple or will I settle elsewhere?" This time there was no grayness and no bright scenes. A sudden dark veil settled over everything and with it a deep, pervading chill.

I shivered and opened my eyes. The chill was still there. What did this mean? My death? The death of others? What terrible thing was hidden in that darkness? Very much afraid, but needing to know, I shut my eyes and asked my question again. This time I saw the same darkness and with it I felt a terrible sense of dread. Quickly I opened my eyes. I would not ask again. It was clear that this was all the answer I was going to get. I sat for a long time, staring at the falling water and the little ferns bobbing in it, afraid now to shut my eyes for fear of more visions and, at the same time, not wanting to leave, because then I would have to put words to what I had just seen and speak those words aloud to others, especially Thesali.

That was how Thesali finally found me, nodding and dozing with my eyes half open and Mother Toad still in my lap. After waiting for what must have seemed to her like a year, Thesali had gathered her courage and come to look for me. Now she knelt by me and shook my arm until I finally came back to consciousness. "What did she show you? Did you see anything?"

"I'm so glad you came. You need to see it for yourself. Some of it is frightening and I have no idea what it means."

"No, I don't want to hold her! I don't even want to be here! I only came because I grew afraid when you didn't come back and I couldn't wait any longer." Scrambling to her feet as she spoke, she backed away quickly and held her hands up as if for protection.

I grabbed her wrist. "Wait, Thesali. She can't hurt you. She just feels warm and soft in your hands. And I want you to see for yourself so you'll understand, so you won't go away thinking I twisted the truth. You don't trust me anymore. I want you to ask her your own questions. I didn't come back yet because I couldn't bring myself to come and tell you, so this is much better. Here, sit beside me. I'll put her in your lap."

"What makes you think you can give me orders that way?" Thesali asked angrily. Then with a sigh she sat down. "Alright. Let's do this and get it over with. I can see that otherwise you'll just grind me down with that famous will of yours."

"Put your hands in your lap and make a bowl of them," I instructed. With another sigh Thesali did as I said. She shuddered as I gently set the toad in her hands but she didn't pull away. "Now shut your eyes and ask in your head or out loud whatever you want to know."

Thesali shut her eyes and was silent a long time. A frown deepened on her forehead. Twice she muttered, "Oh no!" When she finally opened her eyes again they were full of tears that spilled quickly down her face. "So you really are going and I'm staying here. I thought we'd be together all our lives. At the end I asked if you were coming back here when your pledge time was up and got nothing but a strange angry darkness. What can that mean?"

"I wish I knew. I saw the same thing. That's what frightened me so. I suppose we need to tell Melanthia, though I must say I'm not looking forward to it. But whatever's behind that dark veil it's at least six or seven years away. Now that it's clear to us both that I'm leaving and you're staying, let's be kind and gentle with each other for the time we have left. It's more than a year away." Hoping for some closeness I put my arm around Thesali. She stiffened angrily when I tried to draw her to me.

"More like nine months," she said bitterly. She was shivering with cold and damp and dread, but when I tried again to draw her close she pulled away. Finally, with another sigh, she let go and allowed herself to snuggle into the warmth of my embrace. This time, when she sighed again, it was with contentment. I held her that way for a long time in the stillness of that place, with neither of us saying a word. Mother Toad, comfortably forgotten, seemed quite content to sit in the warmth of her cupped hands.

Later I went and stood in the Temple archway, staring out into the courtyard, thinking about my many years at the Temple and all that I would soon be leaving behind. I'd never even been outside of the city and, in a few months, I'd be gone from there, wandering down roads that I'd never seen before to places that were only little dots on a map. Scenes from my time at the Temple kept playing themselves out in my head and I felt a sort of wistful sadness. Then scenes with my family intruded—my mother's anger and my father's pain. That, at least, I had no regret leaving. I stayed for a while in a daze of remembering until a sound brought me back to the present. A grubby little girl was standing just outside the archway, staring up at me with a look of wonder and admiration. "Are you a Temple Dancer?" she asked with awe in her voice. "Can I see your wand?"

I nodded and held up my wand. Pulled out of my dark mood, I beckoned to the child, feeling as if a page in my life had just turned over. Then I reached out my hand and after a moment's hesitation she took it. "Would you like to see where little girls like you learn to Dance?"

After that, Thesali and I no longer fought. We had made our peace that afternoon. There was a sort of sad sweetness between us as if one of us were going to die. The passion and intensity had gone out of our lovemaking. I suppose we were saying a long goodbye. It grieved me, though was far better than continued quarreling.

As the time to leave grew near, the eight of us who were to go on the road were put through some intensive training, working with Dancers who themselves had just come back. They were to teach us what to expect in our travels. Most of us were city girls and had no real experience of anything beyond the gates of Urshameel. Though we knew we would be fed and sheltered by the people we Danced for, we had to learn how to deal with life on the road—how to make a fire and how to cook simple meals and how to make or find shelter and even how to protect ourselves from wild animals. Some of the others found this alarming. I thought it exciting and challenging. I even discovered I had a natural skill for such things, something more for my mother to be shocked by, thinking of her daughter preparing herself to sleep by the side of the road with no proper roof over her and no proper bed to sleep in.

And it wasn't just our time on the road that would be strange and challenging, it was also the many new and different sorts of people we would meet along the way. Bhazrin, the tall wiry woman who was our main instructor, told us sternly, "You have to remember at all times that you represent the Temple of Kernoss and the city of Urshameel and, above all, that you represent the Goddess Herself to the people you Dance for. Do not in any way act superior. Do not be arrogant or give offense. Always be respectful of the customs of others, though they may be very different from our own. Be kind, be courteous and answer all questions politely." After that Bhazrin was showered with questions about her own adventures in the world out there, until she herself grew quite impatient with us and was not at all courteous and kind.

A few days before I was to leave I went to the early morning market on The-Street-Of-Many-Bells and bought a sleep mat, a light blanket and a basket pack, everything purchased with a chit from the Temple. Then I laid out all my things on my bed. Zindra, the woman who had made many of my Dance costumes, had also made me two sets of travel clothes: loose comfortable pants, gathered at the ankles and short loose tunics that slipped easily over my head. One set of these I would be wearing. I added to that the new blanket, two Dance costumes, several bright sashes, some underthings, a vest for the cold and extra sandals as well as a small cook pot with a cup and a bowl, a knife and a fork tucked away inside, also a spark-stone for starting fires. My feather-stuffed sleep-sack I rolled up tight and fastened to the bottom of my pack.

When I looked at it all it seemed like a pitiful little pile to last me five years. Then, when I tried to get it all in the pack, it turned into a mountain of resistance. I had to repack three times before I could make it all fit properly. Finally I hefted it onto my shoulder and groaned aloud. I thought I would fall over. Clearly, this would take some practice.

After I had everything settled to my liking, I tried walking up and down the garden paths for a while to get used to the weight. There was no need to practice sleeping outside. Thesali and I had done that often enough on hot summer nights, finding ourselves a secluded place in the garden. But I knew it would be very different out on the road, away from the shelter of the Temple and far from any city. Some of the other girls were doing a whole round of farewell parties with friends and family. I might have envied them, but all I wanted was to be quickly gone. The pressure of living in the same city with my mother's anger and my father's grief was becoming unbearable.

I was full of excitement when the time came to leave the Temple of Kernoss and set off on my own, the first day of my five-year pledge. After all the preparations it was finally happening. There were only six of us taking the pledge that morning. The other two had changed their minds during the training, having found the prospect too daunting. We were to start off together and then we would go our separate ways. Each of us would have our own Dance map that showed the towns and villages on our route, as well as the larger cities with Dance Temples of their own. We were free to choose our own way. The map was only our guide to what lay before us.

Pledging at the Temple was one of the high times of the year, as important in its own way as the Great Festivals. Everyone had come to the ceremony, friends and family from the city, the other students, the teachers, the Temple Dancers, some of the Priestesses, even the old Temple Mother herself.

At first I had been nervous before all those people. After all, I was used to Dancing, not speaking, but I had rehearsed the words several times and remembered them well enough. When I found myself saying my words and doing my part with the ease of practice, my nervousness vanished.

It was the Temple Mother who took my pledge, but it was Melanthia who blessed my Dancewand. She held it in both hands and stared into it for a long while. Then she touched it to her lips and handed it back to me, solemnly intoning the traditional words, "I bless this wand in Her name. Zaia, you are now a Traveling Dancer for the Goddess. May you always follow in Her path. May She always accompany you on your way. May you be blessed enough to Dance Her Dance all through your life. May She bring you safely home again." Afterward, she kissed me on the forehead. Then she leaned forward and whispered in my ear, "Blessings on you, Child. You are the best Dancer to pass through my hands in many years, perhaps ever. The sight of you setting out fills my heart with pride, though also with grief for I shall miss you sorely."

That was nearly my undoing. Tears sprung up in my eyes, making it hard for me to see where to put my feet. Just before I turned away she took my hand, set something in it and then closed my fingers. "It belonged to my sister who is no longer with us. My fingers are too big for it. All these years I have worn it on a chain around my neck. I think it will fit your hand. Wear it and sometimes think of me. Rub it when you need to call on my help." I slipped the ring on my finger and felt my own tears on the back of my hand. Who knew if we would meet again. Five years was not such a long time, but Melanthia was no longer young.

After the pledging ritual was over, my father kissed me on both cheeks and gave me a beautiful pendant in silver and gold that he told me had been his mother's treasure. It was the image of the Goddess as a Dancer, with Her arms raised over Her head and one foot lifted, ready to step into the Dance. With tears in his eyes, he slipped the chain over my head and said, "May it be well with you, my daughter, wherever you choose to go. May the Lady guard and protect you and bring you back to us when your time is up." His hands were shaking against my neck.

It had been hard enough to say goodbye to my father, but more painful still had been my mother's obvious absence at the pledging. Even my sister Yanin had been there teasing me good-naturedly. *Ah well, what had I expected after all?* My mother had been opposed to my being a Dancer from the very beginning. At least my aunt Veraine was there and so was my cousin Renairi. Veraine gave me a beautiful soft cape, dark as a raven's wing. She slipped it around my shoulders, saying, "This is to keep you warm on the road and also so you can hide yourself away when you don't want your bright Dancer finery to show. It even has a dark hood to hide your hair. I'll miss you so very much, Zaia. Play your cards well and have a good life. Don't look back until it's time to come home."

My cousin gave me a little travel drum for the road and kissed me on both cheeks. "This is to keep you company and to remember me by. You've been like my little sister all these years but even better because we never fought. Take good care of yourself. I almost envy you, but I would never have the courage of such a choice. You always were the daring one."

The other Dancers who had been my classmates accompanied me to the edge of the city with laughter and singing and best wishes. Thesali came with me to the top of the first rise where the hills that surrounded the city began their climb. There she tearfully gave me a beautiful djira-cloth made by her own hands. In it she had wrapped a tiny likeness of the Goddess, a lustrous shell from the faraway sea that had been her treasure, a small polished green stone in the shape of an egg and a candle. "With that you can make your own little altar wherever you go and perhaps you will think of me in those distant places."

That parting had been the most painful of all. When we were finally able to tear ourselves away, we looked back many times as we went our opposite ways; Thesali back to the familiarity and discipline of the Temple and myself to the fortunes of the road. I had been too excited to dwell on it long that day, but sleeping alone that first night there had been more than enough time to think on the emptiness of my bed. Years of such empti-ness lay ahead of me, since that pledge of celibacy was part of my five-year pledge to the Goddess.

My first night out I was exhausted, unaccustomed as I was to so much walking and the weight of the pack. I was very proud of being able to make my first fire on the road, but then much too weary to cook on it. Afterward, when I lay down to try and sleep, the grass suddenly seemed full of odd rus-tlings and the distant woods full of strange ominous noises. I felt very much alone there with no human sounds to be heard anywhere. Luckily, weariness overtook me before fear could get too much of a hold on my spirit.

The next morning, waking to find myself still alive and well, I felt a rush of joy and excitement that I was actually doing this thing. I jumped up and did a little Dance of my own on the very spot where I had slept. Then I consulted my Dance map. I hadn't left the city by any of the great trade roads but by a little-used farm road where there would be no cities and no Dance Temples. This meant more people would have a need for an itinerant Dancer. Even so, it was my third day on the road before I came to my first Dance opportunity, a village with a young girl celebrating her first-bloods. A new Dancer coming down the road seemed to them like a gift from the Goddess and an answer to their prayers. I suppose they were also an answer to mine. They rushed out to greet me and make me welcome.

The girl, whose name was Roshlan, was lovely and shy and as awed by me as I had first been by Kendrin. Her family claimed me for their house before the Headwoman could. They gave me their best room and fussed over me with offers of sweet juices and special foods and a hot bath, all very welcome after my time on the road. It was probably quite an ordinary little village, but since I had never been out of the city before, everything had the charm and enchant-ment of newness for me: the little winding paths that suddenly disappeared out of sight around the corner and beckoned me to follow, the reed-thatched, mud-brick houses with their brightly colored plaster, their curving walls and their delightfully fanciful shapes. Roshlan followed me around, making herself my guide and companion, until her family finally called her away to help make things ready for the next day's events.

The ritual and Dance were to be held the following evening. After a wonderfully comfortable night on a soft bed instead of the hard ground, I took all that day to prepare myself. I ate nothing and went down to the river so I could listen to the water for a while and find some inner calm. After all, this would be my first Dance on my own, away from the certainties of the Temple. I wanted to do my best for these people who were so kind and seemed so full of hope and expectancy.

While I was seeking solitude, Roshlan was spending her time in seclusion with the women of her family. They were having a small private ceremony for her before the larger public one. As I passed her house on my way to the river I heard the sound of chanting coming from it, followed by a loud burst of female laughter. At that moment tears stung my eyes and I felt a painful rush of envy, wishing I had been able to celebrate my time of coming to womanhood with my family. Later, as Roshlan's two older sisters helped me dress and make ready, I still felt a little touch of sadness as they went on and on, chattering about the events of the day.

I had put on everything red that I had with me: red blouse, red vest, red skirt and even a long, red sash. Over that I wore the dark cape my aunt had given me, wanting to remain invisible until it was time. The Dance Court was improvised, just a very level part of the cow pasture that had been surrounded by poles and rocks to make a rough circle. The grass had been clipped short and carefully raked so that not a pebble remained to hurt my bare feet. I think every person in the village was there to watch, from babes in arms to ancient grandmothers, all forming a larger circle around that circle. There were only three musicians: two drummers and a flute player, Roshlan's uncles and her older brother, but what they lacked in numbers they more than made up for in enthusiasm and energy.

Roshlan was sitting cross-legged at the center of the circle, all dressed in white with a white blanket beneath her. She kept her head down, not looking at anyone until Mallin, the Headwoman, stepped up in front of her with a large pitcher in her hands. Mallin signaled the musicians for silence. Then she raised the pitcher high and intoned, "Mother of us all, I beg of You, please be with us here for Your daughter Roshlan on this very important day in her life." Then, looking right at Roshlan, she said solemnly, "Roshlan, with the flowing of this blood you enter into the realm of womanhood." At those words she poured the bright red contents of the pitcher over Roshlan's head. Though I was expecting it and knew it was only berry juice mixed with a little of Roshlan's own blood, the sight was still a shock as the liquid instantly stained the girl's white dress and the blanket under her with the color of blood. Roshlan didn't flinch. She sat very still, but now she was looking right at Mallin and there was a little smile on her face. Mallin went on, "You are now sister to all these women. May they treat you as such. And may all the men of your people treat you with the love and respect accorded to women here. May this blood be a portent of future fertility. May you only bear children in your own time, if you are willing and able and never against your will. I ask the blessings of the Great Mother on your future life and on whatever children you choose to give birth to, for we are all in Her hands." Then, she bowed to me where I stood waiting at the edge of the circle in my dark cape. "Now this young woman from the Temple of Kernoss will Dance the Goddess into visible form for us as a way to further bless this special occasion."

All of this was so different from anything I had ever experienced at the Temple that I was almost in shock. I had to keep reminding myself that this was where I had chosen to be. At the Temple there would have been several Dancers for a first-bloods ceremony. Here, I was all there was. These people were looking to me to embody the Goddess and make Her blessings visible in their midst. I suddenly felt very much alone, not at all sure I could do this. *Help me Mother,* I found myself whispering under my breath. *Please, help me. I am here at Your bidding to do Your will.* After a moment of utter stillness it felt as if someone had put a warm hand over my heart. I then took a deep breath to find my center, nodded to the musicians, slipped out of my cape and stepped into the Dance Court.

As if from somewhere deep inside, power and energy rushed up through my body and with it joy. Many shades of red were swirling through my Dancewand when I held it out in front of me for a guide. After only a few steps the Dance began to Dance with me. Some of it was what I already knew from my years of training at the Temple. And some of it was new, creating itself moment by moment for this time and this place. Even as I leapt and swooped and turned, I always came back to bow to Roshlan as part of the Dance, remembering to honor her on her day. Each time I was rewarded with a huge smile and a look of delight. After my fourth or fifth turn about the circle, people began clapping and then stamping, not as applause but as a rhythmic accompaniment, something that would not have been allowed at the Temple but that here just seemed right. The sound lifted me up and carried me along so that, with my red sash flying in the wind, I felt as if I were Dancing on air rather than earth.

As the Dance finally began winding down I went to the edge of the Dance Court and drew Roshlan's mother and father into the Dance. Then I signaled to her sisters and brothers and aunts and uncles to join us and circle around her. At last I reached out and pulled Roshlan herself into the Dance so that at the end we were all laughing and breathless. Roshlan was flushed with excitement and pleasure. Before it was over, all the people who had been watching got to their feet and began to circle around us.

Afterward I was a guest at the Headwoman's house, enjoying the feast since I had fasted all that day. It was mostly the older folk. I wondered why Roshlan and her young friends were absent. After praising my Dancing and thanking me many times, the talk soon turned to crops and the weather. I was just nodding off from the exertions of the Dance combined with the heavy food and the long walk, when Roshlan burst in with some of her friends. "It's our turn now to claim her. You've had her long enough." She had changed into a bright red dress, and she seemed imperious and full of her own power, not at all like the shy young girl of the day before. Giving me no chance to say yes or no she grabbed my hand to rush off with me, while her elders made good-natured, but ritualized, objections and pretended to block the way.

Roshlan led me back to the Dance Court where I was quickly surrounded. Only a few of these young people had even seen a Temple Dancer and none had ever talked to one before. At first they were a little shy with me but that soon passed. They began asking me endless questions about my life and the city and the Temple. I remembered to answer politely and patiently as Bhazrin had instructed. After a while they each wanted to touch me as if I had magical properties I could pass on. I was glad when Roshlan interrupted this. "Stop pestering Zaia. Now it is time for us to Dance. We should invite her to join us."

And so I spent the night of my first Dance on the road singing, Dancing and drumming around a huge bonfire with a wild group of other young people, feeling a kind of freedom I had never known in all my years at the Temple. Roshlan and I were the center of the festivities. Every time I thought to sit down in some quiet spot, she had me on my feet again. We finally all went off to our beds by the gray light of dawn, those who didn't sleep right there on the ground. I didn't rise again until well past mid-day. When I finally left to get on with my journey I was showered with food and thanks. Roshlan made me a crown of ever-blooming flowers for my hair and kissed me on both cheeks. Not a bad start for my new life on the road.

I had been on the road a little more than three weeks and had Danced at least six times in as many places. Some of the excitement had already worn off. In fact, if there had been anyone to complain to I would have been complaining—and loudly. At that moment a five-year pledge seemed like an act of madness or at least utter ignorance. I even began wondering if I could really keep my pledge and what would happen to my life if I couldn't.

CHAPTER 5
Encounter on the Road

My back ached painfully. My pack was heavy with food as well as with my Dancer costumes and all else I needed on the road. The straps of the pack cut into my shoulders. In the last day or so I had lengthened and shortened them several times, seeking some relief from that relentless weight. After a mile or so the discomfort would set in again, each time seeming worse than before.

It was late in the afternoon. My last Dance had been two days before and I was headed for the town of Jakarth. I wished myself already there. Melanthia had warned me that the third week of walking would be the worst, but she hadn't warned me nearly enough. I felt some anger at her and at nearly everyone in the Temple for allowing me to do this. Why had they let me go? Why had no one told me how hard it would be?

That morning, to keep my spirits up, I'd started out humming gay little tunes I remembered from my apprentice days at the Temple, or from my childhood in Urshameel. I even accompanied myself on my little travel drum. After a while I fell silent. Now all I could manage was to put one foot before the other, keeping myself moving by a sheer act of will. It was still too early to make camp for the night. Besides, I had hoped to reach shelter in the town of Jakarth before darkness fell. That was the first town on my map with a Dance Temple, the first place on my journey where I could do a real Temple Dance. Besides that, I planned to soak in a hot tub until all the aches in my body were gone and even to sleep in a real bed which, at that moment, seemed like an unimaginable luxury.

For a while now the road had been deserted. Earlier I'd passed through orchards and planted fields. There had been many farming settlements and more than enough people and animals and dust along the way. Now that I wanted to ask directions, there was no one to be seen. The open land had turned to forest, and trees were rapidly closing in around me. I was afraid I'd taken a wrong turn at the last crossroads, though I'd stood there for several minutes, consulting my map. I had no desire to spend the night deep in the woods. After all, I was a child of the city, having been raised where all the streets were cobbled and well lit and clearly marked. Camping in fields or by the edge of the road was challenge enough. I found the woods more than a little frightening, especially with the coming darkness. My last two nights had been spent in a village where I'd Danced for the people in the Central Circle and been amply rewarded with food and shelter and gratitude. Now I found myself longing for more of the same without the hard effort of walking my body there.

The woods around me were strangely still and silent, almost as if waiting for something. In some places the branches crossed overhead, nearly closing out the sun. I felt the weight of it over and around me and sorely wished for the sound of voices, or at least the sound of birds. Before I'd left the Temple Melanthia had taken my face in both hands, looked into my eyes and said, "When the way gets hard, think of me. I will be there with you, offering strength and protection." Now, remembering those words, I tried hard to think of my teacher's strong, old face that could be so stern and so full of compassion at the same time, but I couldn't summon her up. With my thumb I even rubbed the ring she had given me. Nothing came but a sense of emptiness and with it fear, a very different fear from any I had ever known in the city or in the Temple either.

Wanting to hear the sound of my own voice, I said aloud, "I am all alone here." Instantly, I shivered. How often in the life of the Temple I had longed for more time alone and for some silence. The meditation time never seemed long enough. Now, at this moment, I would have given half the food in my pack for the sound of my classmates' careless chatter. As I went on my fear grew stronger with each step, though I had no choice but to keep walking forward. I certainly wasn't going to stop there for the night and it was far too late to retrace my steps. I could only hope that I would soon be through the woods and that the town of Jakarth lay close on the other side.

I didn't see him until he was standing on the road right in front of me, blocking the way. I had been watching the ground, making my way over a rough, stony place when he stepped out suddenly from behind a tree. Seeing his boots in front of me I looked up with a gasp of surprise. For just a moment I felt a sense of relief. Here was another person, someone to tell me the way. Then I saw the look on his face. All the vague fears I had been feeling solidified instantly around this stranger.

In the city of Urshameel there had never been any reason to fear men. For all the years I'd been in training as a Dancer for the Goddess, I'd been under Her protection. Besides, men in the city were respectful of women, that was the way in Urshameel. But I had been warned that there were occasionally "wild men" on the road who did not keep to the ways of the Goddess. One of the Dancers who had trained us for departure had even mentioned this, but at the time I had paid little heed to her words. This man must have been from some far place, the north perhaps. He had the strange appearance

I associated with northerners—sand-colored hair, pale skin and pale eyes. At least the few I had seen in Urshameel had looked like this. I remember when I was young, my aunt tugging on my arm and pulling me down the street. "Don't stare that way, Zaia. It's rude."

"But he looks ..."

"I know how he looks, like a peeled potato, but he can't help it. He was born that way." Actually the man in front of me looked as pale as if he had lived all his life underground with patches of angry red where the sun had bitten him. My own people, of course, are different warm shades of brown like the earth itself, with dark eyes and darker hair. The man who blocked the road had blue eyes so pale I could almost see his thoughts in them. It was clear from his expression that he was full of anger. Surely even such a man would be held back by a Dancewand. Almost without thought, I pulled the wand from my sash and found myself holding it out before me as if for protection.

The stranger cursed under his breath and took a step back. I saw his eyes widen. "So, you're one of those Goddess girls," he said contemptuously as he spit in front of me. "Curse the luck and devil take it! But don't think that little bit of glass will keep a strong man off your back for long."

In spite of his bold words, there was a look of uncertainty in his eyes. With a grunt he drew himself up straight and in one practiced gesture pulled a long knife from his belt. Quickly he thrust it out before him, holding it much the way I held my Dancewand. "Do you want to match weapons, girl, or will you give me what I want without getting yourself all sliced up? I've been watching you walking along without a care in the world and thinking how nice it would be to have you." His voice was full of menace as he thrust one hand suggestively between his legs.

I stared at him for a long moment, uncomprehending. Then his meaning hit me and I flushed with anger. Yes, I had heard of such men and even heard that there were some of them now wandering the countryside, but until that moment such stories hadn't seemed real to me. Who could imagine a man who would think to force the wants of his body on another? It went against everything I had ever known of the ways of men and women. Yet here stood just such a man before me. His meaning was clear enough and he was watching me closely, watching no doubt for any fear or uncertainty on my part, the weakness that would signal him to move.

Somehow I was less afraid now that the threat was real instead of the phantom menace of the forest. I was very glad for the defensive Dancing Melanthia had taught us, though I had certainly never imagined using it. Feeling my fear and containing it, I called on all my Dancer training, that training where fear and anger both can be channeled into movement.

Keeping my calm, I stared back at him from the core of stillness that lies at the heart of Dance.

"So you want to play, do you?" he asked angrily. "Women in this part of the world think themselves better than men but all that will change soon. Where I come from women know who has the power. No woman would think to be traveling alone and unprotected."

"Then it must be a sad, rude place to live." The words sprang from my mouth before I had time to think. I might better have kept my silence. Clearly my answer played right into his anger. He took a step forward with the knife held before him.

I could see my Dancewand filling with dark colors that swirled restlessly against the restraint of the glass. Beyond that I could see the flash of his blade. Keeping my eye on his knife, I called out in the silence of my head, *Goddess help me now. I am in Your hands, Mother.* At that moment it was Melanthia who came into my head. I heard her stern, strong voice saying, *Remember the Dance, girl. He has his knife, but you have the Dance. It is much faster than any knife. If he comes any closer, remember your training. Move and keep moving. Never take your eyes off that blade. You can be like a whirlwind around him.*

In spite of the fear clawing at my back I kept my calm and said forcefully, "Move aside and let me pass, Man. I am expected in the town of Jakarth tonight."

"After I get what I want!" he snarled back at me. "Then you can go any-where you please, for all I care." At least he hadn't laughed and told me I was going in the wrong direction. He took another step forward, watching the wand as if it might strike out at him at any moment. There was fear in his face but it was all mixed with greed and lust and anger. Clearly he would not let me pass, though he was also very wary of moving against me.

Never taking my eyes from his knife I shrugged out of my pack and leaned it against a tree. *Dance for your life,* the voice in my head said. I nodded, then muttered angrily, "Since there seems to be no other way, let the Dance begin." I was not going to abandon my pack there. It had in it every-thing I needed for surviving on my journey. And even without it, I certainly had no intention of trying to outrun him on the road or through the darken-ing woods. I had no wish to feel that sharp knife in my back. Taking a deep breath for calm, I looked him full in the face and called out loudly, "What you want from me you cannot have, I promise you that. But, if you think to get it anyway then you must come for it."

His eyes darted away from mine. I saw him hesitate, crouching, ready to lunge. It was growing late. It would soon be dark. I needed this to be over with. For that, I needed him to make his move soon. Raising myself up on the toes of one foot and bending my other leg high at the knee, I lifted my arms, ready to move into the first step of the Dance-of-Power. "Unless, of course, you're afraid of my Dancewand or maybe of my Dance," I added mockingly.

"Witch!" he snarled. The struggle in his face was almost comical as he shifted from foot to foot. Then, with a sudden cry, he lunged at me, knife flashing, more in anger now than lust.

I waited in my stillness until the very last moment.

As his blade flashed out at me, I spun about and was somewhere else, waiting for his next move. With a yell of surprise, he whirled to face me. When he struck next I was gone again. He struck a third time and the same thing happened. I was not where he had seen me last. I had vanished miraculously before him and had reappeared off to the side, safe and untouched while his knife slashed through empty air. Howling with rage and frustration, he began striking recklessly in all directions while I kept moving, always just out of reach, always keeping my eye on the blade.

In spite of the danger to my life the Dance began moving through me, my body responding from all my years of training. As if lines of light were drawn in the air in front of me, I could see just where he would move next and when he would strike. Each time, the Dancewand would pull me in the opposite direction, seeming to have a will of its own. Once we had started, we went on and on in this lethal "Dance," with me moving each time just before the stranger struck. It was almost as if we had rehearsed it all many times before, as if we were bound to each other by these strangely familiar steps.

Time seemed suspended. Shift and strike, shift and strike, over and over, almost like the Dance of Opposites that was used to train beginning Dancers at the Temple. There they had worked us in pairs. One of us would strike out with a stick while the other ducked and dodged and whirled and leapt away. When we were sufficiently trained, it was the Dance Mistress herself who flashed out with her Dancewand, and none of us escaped without a few bruises. But we all learned to move with speed and agility. This angry stranger was far slower than Melanthia and less of a challenge to my skill, but the blade he held was deadly. A misjudgment here could cost me far more than a tap with a Dancewand. It could cost me a limb or even my life.

We went on and on and on in our strange Dance. Turning and lunging and turning again, the man seemed to have incredible energy, fueled no doubt by his anger. His shouts of rage battered at the stillness until, at last, his hoarse ragged breathing signaled to me that he was tiring. *Maybe I can Dance him into exhaustion or into a stupor,* I thought with relief. *Then I'll be free to go.*

Almost as I thought this, I stumbled on some rocks and nearly fell. This was not the neat grassy turf of the Dance Court that we moved upon. With a roar of triumph the stranger rushed at me, sure of himself now. Instantly

I regained my footing and whirled away from him. "Enough of this!" I shouted at him, "Enough!" Stopping well out of reach, I turned to face him with my hands raised. He stopped too, standing in a half crouch, staring at me, sweating, gasping for breath, his sides heaving, a wild raging look in his eyes. I was panting too but not nearly as hard. My Dancer training was standing me in good stead, though never in all my years in the Temple had I Danced so hard or with such speed or violence. I reached inside myself for the core of deep calm at the center of the Dance, reached for it and held it. When I could catch my breath, I called out to him, "Man, it's growing dark. I need to be on the road again. Let's part now with no harm done. You go your way and I'll go mine."

At this he growled with rage and let out a string of harsh guttural words that I assumed to be curses, in a language I didn't understand. I could feel him readying himself to charge me again, no doubt thinking he saw a weakness there. Gathering up all my force, I called out louder, "Man, I have never injured anyone and have no wish to do so now. Stop this madness and go unharmed to your night's lodging before there is any blood spilled between us."

He seemed to grow even angrier at these words. Between gasps he snarled back, "It's not just your body I want now, it's your life as well. And I plan to have them both. No woman has ever treated me this way and lived to brag on it."

"What do you mean treated?" I shouted indignantly, suddenly losing my calm and shaking my fist at him. "It was you who attacked me on the road, or have you forgotten that already?" In spite of his threatening words I could see that he was exhausted. He was panting hard and holding his side as if in pain. Suddenly heartsick at all this ugliness, I dropped my hands and gave a deep sigh. Shaking my head, I said more softly, almost as if to myself, "I have no wish to brag. There is nothing here to brag on. I am dirty, dusty, weary and still have some distance to go this day. I have work to do. There are people in Jakarth for whom I am pledged to Dance. All I want to do is continue on my way in peace."

"Peace!" he spit out the word like an oath. "I'll give you some peace to chew on. I'll give you all the peace you could ever want on the end of my blade. Then I can have your body to use at my leisure." With that he seemed to rally some of his strength.

I felt a terrible deep weariness in me, not of the body but of the spirit. With a shrug, I turned to look for my pack in the gloom. Let him make his move then and be done with it. Thinking my guard down, he flung himself at me. I waited unmoving until he was almost on top of me. This time, when his knife flashed, I kicked high and hard. His hand flew open. He gave a shout of pain and surprise. The knife arched high in the air. Whirling, I kicked him again, catching him in the mid-section. I heard a sharp crack as he doubled up with a loud groan and went down like a sack of grain.

His wrist was flapping at a strange angle. I stood staring down at him while he lay rolling in pain on the ground in front of me. Feeling an echo of that pain in my own body, I wanted to scream or cry or vomit, or perhaps even fling another hard kick at him and be rid of this violent encounter. I did none of those things. Instead I carefully brought my breath back under control. When I could speak again, I said with pain and disgust, "Why did you make me do that? Why did you force me to hurt you?"

Clutching his wrist with his other hand, he looked up at me, terror mixed with the loathing in his face. He was taking great gulps of air that were almost like sobs. "You have me at your mercy, whore," he hissed through teeth that were clenched against the pain, "Kill me then and be done with it."

I shook my head again, "I have no wish to kill you. I don't have the stomach for it, though it might well be the best thing to do. May the Goddess have mercy on you if She can find it in Her heart."

Without looking back at him I went to pick up my pack. I shrugged into the straps, glad for the feel of its familiar weight on my back, even glad for the familiar bite of pain where the straps cut into my shoulders. Behind me I could still hear the man alternately groaning and shouting curses. I turned and was about to continue down the road when I saw a flash of light a little way off the road. The knife! Some last ray of sun breaking through the leaves was reflecting from it.

Pushing my way through the underbrush I went to stare down at his knife. Finally, I squatted by it. Reaching out very slowly, I picked it up with care by the handle. I held it in one hand, thoughtfully and cautiously touching the cold sharpness of the blade with the fingers of my other hand. That blade had been intended for my blood, my flesh, even my death. Balancing the weight of it in my hands, I wondered what it would take to make myself as familiar with the use of this knife as I was with my Dancewand. Slowly, I laid it in the open palm of my hand and held it there while I looked backward and forward in my life, back to all my training and forward to my pledged time on the road, weighing, judging, trying to understand what this all meant. I could easily finish off this wild man with his own knife. With one quick gesture I could slip it in under his ribs or draw it across his throat. And who would blame me? Then I could wipe the blade on his shirt and slip it into my sash or my pack for use against other such men in the future, if there were indeed going to be more of them. What was the path? What lay ahead in the future? Holding the knife balanced on my palm, I shut my eyes and said in a whisper, "Goddess, Great Mother, what do I do now? Give me some guidance, I pray of You, Lady."

As I waited, stiff and chilled, I could hear the night birds starting to sing. I could hear the breeze in the leaves. I could still hear the harsh animal sounds of the man from somewhere in back of me. Gradually, in the fading light, I became aware of the tears running down my cheeks and of the terrible deep ache all through my body. Suddenly there was a preternatural silence as if everything had been suspended within it. The sounds of birds, breeze and man were gone. With no will of my own the knife slipped from my hands and landed tip down in the earth. Staring down at it standing upright there in the leaves and dirt I heard the words as if the answer had been spoken in my head. *It is not the time yet for knives.*

"Thank you, Mother," I said softly. Quickly, pulling away the leaves, I began scrabbling in the dark soil with my hands, making the knife a burial place there in the woods. Now neither of us would have it. It could rust harmlessly back into the earth.

When I stood up my heart felt clear and light. I wiped my hands on my pants and almost absently brushed the tears from my face, probably leaving long streaks of dirt. Stepping back onto the road, I could just barely make out the man's huddled form. Off in the distance the owls began to hoot. With a shiver I wondered if he would survive the night, out there all alone. For just an instant I felt a tug of concern, as if I should sit watch with him till morning. Then I shrugged. After all I hadn't asked for any of this. He had made his own fate, insisted on it even. "In Your hands, Mother," I said aloud. Then, hitching my pack higher, no longer afraid of the forest, I turned and headed away from him, walking through the deepening gloom toward Jakarth and my new life.

CHAPTER 6
Dance of Healing

By following the road through the gloom until I was guided in by the lights of the town, I found my way to Jakarth that night and Danced for the people there the next day. But my heart wasn't in it and neither was my spirit. Only my body remembered the way to the Dance. I don't know if those good, kind people noticed or if they even would have cared. Pleased to have a Dancer from the famed Temple of Kernoss Dance at their small Temple, they were very grateful for my efforts and full of praise. They fed and sheltered me and would have been glad to have me stay longer, but I wanted to be alone with my thoughts. I knew I was in need of some healing, though I could not imagine what it might be. If I were back at the Temple I would have gone to soak in one of the mineral hot tubs and asked for a purification ritual. Here, among these strangers, I could not even bring myself to speak of what had happened back on the road. I felt dirty and confused and my heart was deeply troubled. It was as if everything I knew about life had slipped sideways, and a deep crack had suddenly appeared in the world.

Leaving the next morning, I was not sure which way to go. In fact, I was not sure of anything, not even sure if I should continue on the road at all or perhaps break my pledge and go back. My map showed that not far from Jakarth I would come to a Y in the road. In one direction lay the town of Versa, and the other road led to the city of Nhagail by a long, winding route. There was also a much shorter road to Nhagail, but it had an X marked across it.

The kind people of Jakarth all had advice to give me. I was told that the road to Nhagail led through a long, fertile valley of prosperous farms with several villages along the way. The road to Versa was higher, leading through some woods and then through a stretch of orchards for the growing of nuts and fruit, the famous orchards of Mazlin, they told me with some pride. Each had a favorite road that they urged me to take, but when I asked about the road with the X they all shook their heads in unison. Jarain, the woman who had been my dresser for the Dance, said vehemently, "Not a good road! Bad land! Very harsh, arid and steep. No water. It is even said to be haunted. Take heed Dancer, that X is there for good reason."

As I made my departure I put my Dancewand in my belt instead of my pack, thinking it might be some protection on the road. I had listened carefully to everyone's advice but still did not know which way I was going. Instead of trying to make a decision I left it to the Goddess—or in the hands of fate. When I came to the first Y, I found myself, with hardly any thought on my part, heading toward Nhagail. Perhaps I did not want to go through any more forest at that moment. When I came to the next Y, I found myself, again with hardly any thought, taking the road marked with an X in spite of all the warnings. I suppose I had no desire to walk through a green valley full of happy, prosperous people. It certainly did not suit my mood at that moment.

While I walked along, my mind kept churning round and round with troubling and contradictory thoughts. One moment I would be horrified that somewhere behind me a man's body lay by the side of the road, robbed of life by the skill of my well-trained hands and feet. It didn't matter what my head said, that he had given me no choice though I had begged him to stop, that in fact he might not even be dead. I carried the weight of it on my back like a second pack, heavier than the first. The next moment I would think of what he had wanted to do to me and I would feel sick all over—dirty and vile, though he had never even touched me. Rage would sweep through me in that instant. Then I would wish him dead twice over and painfully at that. I would even be sorry I had not stayed to make sure he was really gone. How could there be such men in the world? How could he want to do such things to another person? It was beyond my comprehension and totally outside of my experience.

At first the road had seemed no different from the one I had just left. Soon I became so absorbed in my own confusing thoughts I hardly noticed where I went. When the way began to rise and I found myself thirsty and out of breath, I finally looked around. It was indeed as they had told me, dry and harsh and barren. The fertile valley was far away below me and I was fast climbing into dry hills.

I stopped to drink, sharply aware that I would have to be very careful with my water, that I might, in fact, not have enough to see me through. I knew then that I should have given more thought to my departure. Most of that day I spent climbing a series of rises that seemed to go always higher until, by evening, I stood at the top looking down at a wide, brown plain. Weary and with no strength to go on, I found a sheltered place to sleep under a little overhang. It was part of the stone outcrop capping the hill. I had seen no other person that day and was glad of it. For safety, I slept with my back pressed against the wall of the overhang.

The next day I came down much faster than I had gone up, reaching the valley floor by mid-morning. The people of Jakarth had warned me that I would be passing through wild, desolate land. It was certainly true and, in some odd way, it suited me. The valley I'd entered was like nothing I'd ever seen before, sparse, harsh and dry, completely different from the lush green country I'd left behind. It was as if the hills themselves had stolen the rain and blocked all moisture from this place.

I knew from my map that I would have to cross that valley and climb another long hill before I could rejoin the road to Nhagail. The prospect before me was somewhat daunting. I wasn't accustomed to such dryness and the heat was fierce, beating down on me relentlessly with little shade from the few sparse trees that were able to survive there. The road had grown more narrow. It was rough and rocky underfoot and seemed to worsen as I went along. Now I began to wonder if perhaps I had made a serious mistake. I would soon be running out of water and was quite certain I wouldn't be finding another source ahead of me. For a while I even went back to agonizing over the man on the road. Then I wearied of this quarrel with myself and thought to turn it over to the Goddess. Let her decide if I did a wrong. Let her condemn me if she saw fit. I no longer cared. I had more pressing and immediate concerns.

After a few hours of struggling along—hot, sweaty and very uncomfortable under the weight of my pack—I saw ahead of me, at some distance, a cloud of dust rising. Finally, out of that dust, a wagon began to materialize, brightly colored against that drab landscape. It seemed unreal, a thing of dreams, quivering and shimmering in the heat. As I watched it approach and grow steadily larger, I felt a rush of fear. Before the attack, a stranger was only someone I didn't know, someone I hadn't met. Now I knew that strangers were dangerous. I would have stepped off to the side and hidden while the wagon passed, but of course there was no place to hide. Besides, I told myself, trying to hold on to what little courage I had left, they might have some water to share with me. I'd been carefully rationing my water and by now I had a monstrous thirst. When they got closer they hailed me, two rough looking individuals in clothing as gray and harsh as the landscape. My fear increased and I stepped back off the road to let them pass, but when they drew level with me, they stopped. I tensed, ready to defend myself. I even drew my Dancewand from my belt and held it up in front of me as if for protection. Then, much to my relief, I realized that they were both women.

The taller of the two said boldly, "Well, Dancer, what are you doing out here? Didn't anyone warn you? Only a fool would go through this land on foot. It's much too dangerous. We know it well, but even we are cautious here."

"I...I..." I found I could not talk. My tongue had dried and turned thick in my mouth. There was dust crunching between my teeth.

The other one leaned forward and said in a kinder tone, "You look tired and thirsty. We're headed for the spring to water our horses, fill our jugs and rest for a while in the shade. It's too hot to be traveling in the middle of the day this way. Would you like to come with us?"

"Spring? Shade?" I asked stupidly, regaining a little of my voice as I gazed around in puzzlement at that harsh shadeless land in which nothing green was visible.

"Don't argue. Get in," the first one said, reaching out her hand to help me up. "You won't survive long out here in this sun. My name is Karsha. I'm the rude, ugly one and this pretty thing is my sister, Sheeri. We know where all the springs are in this desert. We have a trade route and sometimes this is a better way for us to go."

Not having much strength of my own left, I took her hand and let myself be hauled into the wagon. Sheeri handed me a cup of water, saying, "Drink as much as you want. We will soon have plenty more." I could not imagine how, but I said nothing. My hand shook a little as I took the cup and I drank so eagerly I spilled part of it down my shirt. She quickly filled it again. I drank that too and then sank back in the seat with a groan.

In a state of weary befuddlement, I found myself being carried back the way I had just come. Not for long though. Soon we turned off on a little track even less traveled and much less visible than the road we had been on, a track I had not seen at all the first time I passed. The horses, who had been shuffling along in a dispirited fashion, suddenly lifted their heads and began to trot forward eagerly. I saw that Karsha was keeping a tight hold on the reins to stop them from breaking into a gallop. At that pace we quickly came to the top of a small rise and there, spread below us in the valley, I saw an island of green in the midst of that vast expanse of drab browns and grays.

"Elsion Spring," Sheeri said joyfully. "The best spring in this whole stretch of desert." We drew closer and I watched with amazement as the green island turned into a grove of trees, grass, ferns and moss, all flourishing in this dry land. I could feel a cool breeze coming from it. I could even hear birds singing and the lively sounds of running water.

The moment we stopped, the two women unharnessed the horses with skilled hands, took them to drink, and then staked them out to graze, doing everything together with some nods and just a few words, moving with the grace and ease of a much-practiced Dance.

Once done with caring for the horses, they slipped out of their gray travel cloaks and dropped them on the ground. Underneath, I was surprised to see they wore bright colorful clothes. In fact they looked quite different to me, no longer menacing, actually rather pretty young women. "Our disguise is for safety on the road," Sheeri said with a shrug. Then she spread out a cloth on the grass while Karsha went for the food basket. Once they had laid out a little feast they invited me to sit and eat with them. I sank down with a sigh of relief and for the next few minutes we ate in blissful silence, the only sounds being the burbling of the spring and the grazing of the horses.

I was just beginning to doze off when Karsha asked abruptly, "Well Dancer, what is your story? What happened to you? What are you so afraid of? I saw how you flinched away from us. I think you would have hidden if you could."

"Karsha!" Sheeri said reproachfully, "It is rude to question our guest so bluntly. Whatever it was, she may not want to talk about it."

"Well, I already said I was the rude one, didn't I? So, do you want to tell us or not?"

I nodded. Startled to find tears in my eyes, I began to talk. It was a relief to share what had happened with someone else. Here, in this place, with these two women, it seemed fitting, whereas in Jakarth it would have felt as if I was bringing some dreadful ugliness into the lives of the people I had just Danced for. When I finished, Karsha said loudly, "Well, I for one, hope the man is dead. One less such vermin on the roads to endanger the rest of us." Then she sprang to her feet and drew a long, curved knife from a scabbard I had not noticed in the folds of her skirt. Jumping into a fighting pose she swung it about several times in a menacing way. There was a sharp swish through the air. I drew back, alarmed, and she gave a harsh laugh. "No need to fear me, Dancer. This is not for you. But, any man who thinks to make use of our bodies that way or to rob us of our goods will quickly desist or he will soon regret it."

I glanced at Sheeri and saw she had drawn out a similar knife that was shining in her lap. "You, also?" I asked in surprise. She seemed so gentle and soft-spoken it was hard to imagine her wielding a knife and drawing blood.

"Oh yes, I have no choice. Lately there have been more and more such men on the road."

Karsha laughed again, a sound that sent shivers up my back. "Don't let her meek appearance fool you. She is much the better hand at it, almost as agile as a Dancer. We both learned from the woman who made these knives. We would not travel without them. It's a wonder to me that you walk these roads unarmed."

"She's not unarmed. You heard her story. She has the Dance," Sheeri said quickly.

"Still, it might be well..."

I shook my head, remembering the knife I had buried back there in the woods. At that moment Sheeri interrupted, "Enough of that kind of talk. Time for a swim to get rid of this itchy plague of road dust."

There were three pools, each one bigger than the last. Sheeri told me the small one right under the spring was sacred, used only for getting drinking water, never for washing. There was a lower one where they had watered the horses and a much larger one below that where we now went to swim, after all the food had been quickly and efficiently packed away.

Our clothes, thrown down along the bank, looked like huge, bright flowers against the dark green moss. I felt a moment of shyness about being naked before strangers, but the other two had no such hesitation. They were in the water in an instant, while I stood irresolute, wet to my thighs, gasping at the biting cold. In spite of the heat of the day, it took me a while to get my whole body immersed. Karsha splashed me teasingly and Sheeri told her to stop and splashed her back. Soon they were engaged in noisy water play with each other, screaming and shouting, while I was left in peace to tiptoe into the water, inch by inch. When I was wet all over I took handfuls of sand and scrubbed my whole body until my skin burned and I finally felt clean. Afterward, as we lay drying on the bank, my body tingled all over with a wonderful freshness. It felt as if some of that ugliness had been washed away in those sacred waters, a cleansing ritual of sorts after all.

When the day began to cool we went to the upper pool. There they filled all their water jugs while I filled my two gourds to the top. Then we climbed back into the wagon and returned to the larger road. As we parted, I thanked them several times and said I was ready to be on my way. "Are you very sure?" Sheeri asked with concern. "This is a harsh place, especially for someone on foot. You could go back to the crossroads with us and take the other road."

I shook my head vigorously. I had no wish to go back. Food and cool water and good company had revived me. I was ready to go on and see what lay ahead. "Thank you again, but I think this really is my road." I watched them leave, waving several times. Then I set out in the coolness of the late afternoon, walking with renewed energy. Looking around, I saw that there was a certain stark beauty to the land, now that I had grown more accustomed to it. Layers of rock in shades of brown, red and orange had been carved into fantastical forms by the wind, as if by a sculptor's hand. They contrasted sharply with the yellow sand and the stunted, twisted blue-green shrubs that dotted the ground, the only living things in sight except for the hawk that circled slowly overhead.

As the sun fell lower in the sky, I noticed a huge mound off to the side, rising out of the flatness of the plain like a small hill. In spite of the distance and the lateness of the day I left the road and turned my steps toward it. I was curious and there was no other point of interest in view. In truth, I felt strongly pulled in that direction as if by an invisible hand.

The mound was higher than I had first imagined and seemed to get larger, rather than closer, as I walked toward it. Finally after what seemed like an hour of trudging along and several times being tempted to turn back, I drew near enough to see enormous standing stones at the top. Now I speeded my steps, going forward with mounting excitement and a sense of discovery. At last I came to some stone steps that seemed to lead to the top. Almost covered with sand they were very long but quite shallow, hardly the width of my foot, and so steep that after a while I had to use my hands as well as my feet to struggle upward. They were also deeply worn in the middle from the passing of many feet over many, many years of time. These steps seemed to go on forever. I began to feel as if I might never reach the top. The one time I was foolish enough to look back, I grew dizzy and was afraid the weight of my pack would topple me over.

Out of breath and a little shaky, I finally reached the top and pulled myself over the edge. When I was able to stand, I gave a gasp of surprise and sucked in my breath, awed at the sight. Before me lay an ancient Dance Court built into a giant bowl of human design. The huge stone columns were even larger than they had appeared from down below. I could not imagine who had brought them there or how they had managed it. Eight in all and an equal distance apart, they were representations of The Great Mother.

Crude and very old, with only the suggestion of faces, breasts, belly and vulva, each was covered with an interlocking design of lines, circles, spirals and triangles. One of the faces had a bird-like aspect and others seemed to be some combination of creature and human. All were worn by sand and wind. All spoke of great antiquity, a shadow-time that lay well before anything I had ever learned about at the Temple.

If this was indeed a Dance Court, it had been long abandoned. There was no grass of course, only sand scattered with pebbles, brush and windblown debris. A shiver went up my back. How long had it been since human feet had Danced in this place? Years past comprehension. I hesitated, afraid to enter and break that ageless stillness with my presence. Without even thinking I touched my ring and then heard Melanthia's voice in my head, *You are a Dancer for the Goddess. Who better to enter the circle?*

As I stepped across that threshold I felt a sort of wordless welcome, a rush of warmth in my body. Wanting to honor the space, I broke off some branches from a low-growing shrub to use as a broom and a spicy smell filled the dry dusty air. Under some strange compulsion I set about sweeping the Dance floor clean, while the sweat poured out of me and ran off in little rivulets, mixing with dust.

When I was done I took out the djira cloth Thesali had woven for me. It was the first time I had used it on the road. With it I made a little altar of my treasures in front of the bird-headed Goddess. She was the one who spoke most clearly to me so I also lit my candle stub for Her. At that moment I felt Thesali there with me, felt her warmth and her love and had a sharp pang of missing her, though I think she would not have had much liking for this place.

Afterward I went about collecting little stones, ones that were shot through with brilliant colors and picking more branches of spicy leaves, some with bright red berries. With this stash of treasures I set to making more miniature altars, little offerings to the other Ancient Mothers until there was a small humble gift at the base of each column. Finally I looked about, pleased with the result of my efforts. I felt again that sense of welcome from the place itself, only more strongly this time, almost as I were being thanked for my work.

Tired from all this, I went to sit down in the shade of a column and almost immediately fell asleep, leaning against my pack for comfort. When I woke the air had cooled considerably and the light of the sunset was slanting in, casting long purple shadows across the sand. Somehow in that light the Ancients took on a different aspect, appearing to be more alive, more present. Some of their faces were cast in shadow and others in bright light. The bird-headed Goddess appeared almost golden in the setting sun and her round eyes seemed to be watching me.

I got up to stretch and my shadow stretched with me, reaching to the edge of the circle. The wind was rising, making a strange sound that was almost like music, a set of deep horns or pipes or perhaps a harp. I could feel Dance moving through me, not a particular Dance, but Dance itself, rising up through my body in coils of power. Then I heard a voice say, *Take off your clothes. Dance for us now. We are forgotten here. Dance and remember us. We are forgotten here.* It was not the clear voice that sometimes spoke in my head, it was more as if the wind was talking, had been talking for some time, and I was just now beginning to hear it. I almost looked around for the source of those words, but of course I knew there was no one else there, only me and the Ancient Mothers, silent for eternity. Perhaps it was the spirit of the place that spoke to me.

After a few moments of hesitation and uncertainty I did as I was told, leaving a small dusty pile of travel clothes by my pack and going to stand at the center of the circle. I shivered with the cool breeze on my bare skin. Down below, the harsh dry valley looked transformed, filled with slanting golden light. Floating mauve and violet shadows shifted about, turning it into a place of magic and mystery, a place of beauty. My own long purple shadow stretched out before me. Thin, angular and full of power, this shadow seemed to have some secret life of its own. "What should I Dance?" I asked the wind-voice, not really expecting an answer. *Let your shadow lead you,* it answered with the clarity of spoken words.

I took a deep breath and said aloud, not knowing where the words had come from but feeling the sharp pain of them, "My shadow has hands and feet that kill." This time when the answer came back it was in Melanthia's firm voice, *No one has the right to use your body against your will. Only you can decide who to share it with, no one else. If that man is dead he willed it on himself.* Then her voice fell silent and again I heard words in the music of the wind, *Dance for us. Let your shadow lead you. Follow your shadow.*

Not needing to be told again, I began to move very slowly, watching my shadow as I did so, almost as if it were a separate being with its own life. Each movement of mine was echoed and mirrored by a movement of *hers* but in a strangely altered way. I raised an arm and *she* raised an arm in response, reaching far away. I lifted a leg and moved a foot. *Her* leg and foot, attached to mine, stepped out into the distance. Very slowly I began to Dance, a Dance that was even slower and more attenuated than the Dance of the Fishing Cranes. Gradually I moved around the circle going in turn from one to the other of the Ancient Mothers, doing a Dance in front of each one with the moaning wind for music and my shadow for a partner.

Finally, after I had made my way around the circle twice, I ended in front of the bird-headed Goddess again. She seemed to regard me with a slight smile. I bowed before her and said aloud, quite formally, "Mother, I have done my best here. I hope my Dancing has been pleasing to You." Then I bowed to each of the others in turn. As soon as I stopped Dancing I felt deeply chilled. The sweat cooling on my bare skin sent shivers up and down my naked body. And yet I had no desire to dress again, not in my dusty road clothes, not even in the clean clothes the kind people of Jakarth had so thoughtfully washed for me. Somehow nakedness seemed more fitting in that place where everything was so spare and stripped away.

Instead, by the last remaining light, I quickly gathered some of the twigs and brush and litter I had already cleared away and made a little pile of them in the center of the circle. Then, with my flint, I lit the pile and watched with pleasure as it burst into flames. Light was going fast and with it any warmth from the day. Using my clothes for a cushion I sat down with my back to the fire and felt the warmth begin to move through my chilled body. I was facing the bird-headed Goddess, looking up at her so high above me. Now, with the firelight flickering on her face, I was sure she was smiling at me. I found myself smiling back. Then I suddenly laughed aloud, a startling sound in that utterly silent place. I was feeling quite pleased with myself. After all, I, Zaia, child of the city, had come on the forbidden road through the dangers of the desert and was sitting without any fear in this wild place, naked and all alone. I thought of Melanthia's words that I had heard in my head, that my body was my own and that no one else had the right to it. The man on the road had tried to kill me and I bested him. He had wanted to use my body against my will and I had stopped him with one kick. "My body is my own," I said aloud and the bird-headed Goddess seemed to be nodding at me or perhaps with me.

Almost protectively, as if to assure myself that my body really belonged to me, I slipped my hands between my legs. This time, when I shivered, it was not with cold. A little tremor of pleasure went up through my body and another followed. I pressed my hands there harder and more deliberately and felt an answering warmth. When I glanced at the Goddess again she seemed to be nodding consent. Now there was a wave of heat coursing up through my body and with it the throb of desire. Hesitating only a moment longer I surrendered to it and began moving my fingers in a slow sensuous Dance of pleasure.

Gradually I slid down until I was lying flat on the sand, open to the night, with my head pillowed on my clothes. "My body is my own," I said aloud, moving my fingers faster and feeling the answering sensation coursing up through my body in waves. At last, with a groan, I spread my legs wide and thrust both my hands between them, rubbing in an agony of pleasure until my cry filled that lonely place, echoing strangely among those stones. Afterward I felt as if I had fallen back into the beginning of time with only those old stone pillars for company, the Goddesses of another world.

Finally I came back to myself. Sweaty, sandy, cold, smelling of body heat and sex, I got up, brushed off the sand and wrapped my naked self in my warm cape. When I glanced at the bird-headed Goddess she seemed as remote as when I had first seen Her, ancient and eternal. There was no sign of that smile of permission I was so sure I had seen on Her face. With a shrug I added a few more twigs to my tiny fire. Then I sat far into the night, long after the fire had cooled, watching the stars shift in the sky. I had never before been so alone, in a place so silent and so far from other humans. But I didn't feel lonely. The night itself seemed full of presence, pressing in all around me, keeping me company.

It took two more days to cross that dry, brown valley, mostly walking in the morning and late afternoon and finding some sort of shade at midday. Then it took another day to make my way through a low set of rocky hills on the other side before I came to human habitation again. There were just a few scattered farms at first as the land turned greener. When I began to see people, I stopped and put on my Dancer costume to cheer myself up. I had indulged in enough gloominess over that man on the road and was ready to be done with it.

CHAPTER 7
Galaina

In the first town after the hills some combination of festival and market seemed to be under way. There were booths and stalls, flags and banners. People were dressed in bright clothes. Everything had a gay and colorful air. My dark mood forgotten for that moment, I walked about delighting in it all, saying good-day to strangers with a smile on my face. When they asked if I planned to Dance for the festival, I answered vaguely, "Not today. Tomorrow perhaps or the next day." Not ready to Dance, I thought of concealing myself by hiding my Dancewand and covering my bright clothes with my black cloak. In the end, I did neither. Instead I wandered about enjoying my own bright plumage in that multicolored throng. It was a pleasure to be able to feel safe among people again and to put behind me that encounter in the woods, at least for the time being.

Soon I noticed that a crowd of townsfolk had gathered at the center of the market square, and so I went in that direction to see what drew them. It was the music that pulled me as much as my curiosity. Undulating, hypnotic, unfamiliar and yet deeply known, I felt it in the bottom of my belly and it tugged at my heart in a way I could not explain.

At the center of this crowd I could see a woman dancing on a raised platform. She seemed to fill the entire space with her energy and power. The sight of her amazed me. She looked nothing like the Temple Dancers that I knew. A big woman, wide as well as tall, she seemed like a moving mountain with her huge breasts and belly. She was untrained or at least not trained in Temple ways. Instead of the Dancer costume I was accustomed to—the vests and skirts and sashes—she wore a long, dark shift of some shimmery fabric that clung to her, revealing rather than concealing her form. The cloth was shot through with red, orange and yellow as well as many threads of gold so that as she moved the illusion of flames flowed up her body. This was the Mother-Of-All-Things Herself, come to life among us.

I stayed well back, not wanting to be noticed. Sometimes I even had to peer around other heads to see at all. This Dancer did not leap or whirl about the stage. Her feet scarcely moved though she kept turning, rotating so that she faced everyone in turn. All the movement was in her body itself, rippling, rolling, undulating. I had never seen such power in a human body. Not even

Melanthia had such force. The whole crowd around me had begun swaying and moaning with her motions, caught in a spell of sound and movement.

I too was caught in her spell. To me it seemed as if she were the Goddess, Dancing the very world into existence with her big round motions, Dancing the universe into being in a vast spiral of movements. It felt like an incalculable blessing to be there at the beginning of time, a speck of dust watching the creation of all things. I was totally lost in her Dance when she suddenly raised her arm, pointing a finger directly at me. "There's a skinny little Temple Dancer out there watching. Come up here and show us what you can do, Girl." Her tone was mocking, almost contemptuous.

The music stopped and the way parted for me. Shocked out of my trance, I went forward reluctantly, unable to understand how she had seen me through the crowd. All eyes were on me now. When I reached the platform she beckoned me up as if I were her puppet to do with as she pleased. Then she reached out her hand. I ignored the proffered hand and leapt up beside her. She looked me up and down while I struggled not to lower my eyes before her bold stare. There was a long moment of absolute silence as if the crowd held their breath. Then she grinned and nodded. "Come on," she said roughly, "We'll give them a show like they've never seen before. It's not often a Temple Dancer and an Earth Dancer come together like this. In this town I'm called Galaina. Do *The-Dance-of-the-Changing-Moon* for us, Girl. Dance around me like the moon around the earth. Use your agility for something useful. I can't move my feet very fast but as you can see I can move everything else well enough."

I was staring hard at her, trying to gauge whether or not she mocked me, when a voice in my head said clearly, *Don't turn away from this. It's a great chance in your life.* I hesitated only a moment longer, then I said, "My name is Zaia," and gave a nod of assent. She, in turn, nodded to the musicians. That wonderful music started up again, weaving through my mind, flooding my senses and filling my belly. Though I had had no chance to prepare I moved into the Dance of the moon changes with ease, floating on that sensuous music. I started slowly in order to find my footing on that unaccustomed stage, but soon I was moving faster and faster. I spun around Galaina, leaping and twirling while she rotated inside my orbit, turning in all directions and undulating her body like a snake. I Danced with all the skill and agility I possessed, but I modified the Temple Dance so that I always remembered to pay homage to the Mother-Of-All-Things who turned at the center of the Dance like a great engine of power at the core of life. Golden threads flowed between us in a vast web that seemed to contain the universe with all its spinning stars.

I Danced and Danced. It was as if I had been set upon a course and had not the sense to stop. I might have gone on spinning around Galaina forever if she had not suddenly grabbed my arm and halted me on my way. "Enough now!" she hissed in my ear. "You'll wear me out with your madness, you little Dancing fool." Then she took a bow, forcing me to do the same with the pressure of her tight grip on my arm. We bowed in all four directions while the crowd showered the stage with money. The uproar of shouts and applause was deafening. I was dazed by it all. The woman beside me was breathing heavily, but otherwise she seemed very much in command of herself.

"Pick up all this money and put it in this sack of mine, not in your own pockets mind you. Then meet me at the feasting table." She spoke very grandly. Galaina strode off, leaving me to carry out her orders without ever asking my consent. Not even Melanthia was this imperious. I stared after Galaina angrily, my pride stung by her insult. Then my flash of resentment passed as quickly as it had come. I rushed through my little task so I could go sit by this amazing person and perhaps even talk to her.

Galaina had saved me the place next to hers at the table. When I handed her the sack of money she juggled it back and forth between her hands, weighing it with a look of pleasure on her face. Almost before I sat down there was a heaping plate of food and a glass of freshly pressed juice before me on the table. As I fell to eating with a ferocious appetite, people crowded around me with questions and praise and requests. Galaina kept shooing them away, but just as quickly they were back again. To my surprise, when a little girl came up to her and held out her hand, Galaina nodded and pressed three coins in it, closing the child's fingers over the money. My plate was filled twice more before I could object. Finally, I was shaking my head and trying to cover it with my hands.

"Turn it over." Galaina said in my ear. "That's the signal here that you're done." Quickly I did as she said. As I washed down that huge quantity of food with yet another glass of juice, Galaina poured out all the money on the table. She divided it into two piles, putting half of it back in her sack and the other half in a little pouch. Then, much to my surprise, she pushed the pouch to me. "Yours," she said with a satisfied grin.

I shook my head, quickly pushing it back to her. "Oh no, as a Temple Dancer I can't accept money, only clothes, food and lodgings. To take money is considered begging." I thought of my mother and how distasteful she would find this entire scene, especially the money. No, especially Galaina herself. It almost made me laugh.

"Take it, Girl. You've earned it and you might well need it down the road. Who knows what may happen in the future. The only certain thing about life is that nothing is certain, that much you can be sure of. Being on the road this way, your life will be an exciting one, full of surprises. Five years, you say? Well, that's a very long time to pledge yourself to anything. You won't always be so young and agile. Someday you may want a horse or who knows what else."

"But it's yours." I objected.

"No, you earned your share. That was much more than I would ever have had without you. Even dividing it that way I still have some extra profit from it. Here, take it."

This time when she shoved the little pouch in my direction I accepted. She was right. After all, who knew what lay ahead. The Temple would certainly not be there to protect me. As I put the pouch in my pocket I thought again of my mother and said with some bitterness, "So, my mother was right after all. Not only am I a Dancer, which she thought bad enough. Now I've become a beggar as well."

"Your mother does not approve of your Dancing? She should be very proud of you." Galaina sounded truly amazed and angry as well.

I shook my head. "No, my mother..." I started to say more, but just then the music grew louder and people got up to Dance, distracting Galaina and saving me from an explanation. As soon as I was rested I joined the others in a simple spirited Dance that they taught me with much teasing and merriment.

Later we slept in the Headwoman's house. She said she was honored to have us in her home and even gave us her own bedroom with a huge, many-pillowed bed. A narrow little cot was quickly added to the room. When the cot appeared, Galaina cuffed my arm in a friendly fashion. "For fairness sake, Zaia, we could flip a coin to see who gets the bed, but I think nature has already dictated the answer. Do you have any objections to that?" She was already settling herself among the cushions as she spoke. I shook my head. In truth I had no objections at all. That cot was much better than the hard ground of the night before, and Galaina had certainly earned the bed. As I sat down on it, preparing to undress, she winked at me and said with a sly smile, "Of course you could always share it with me if you fancied a little rolling about before we go to sleep." She sounded as if she would not mind at all sharing her bed for a little pleasure.

I shook my head again. "I'm not allowed. We take a pledge."

"Five years of celibacy! Now that's too much to ask! Not even for the Goddess Herself would I go down that road. Besides, I think the Goddess likes to see us have our little pleasures."

"I can't," I repeated.

She shrugged. "Ah well, you can't blame a woman for asking."

I was sorely tempted. I could feel the heat rising between my legs, my body hungering for her touch, reaching out hopefully. To change the direction of our talk I asked quickly, "Who are you, Galaina? And what are you? You are a great mystery to me. There's never been anyone like you in my life."

"No doubt! And there may never be again so you should fully appreciate this moment." She beckoned me over, patting the bed to show that I should sit beside her. "Temple Dancers are not known for mixing with Earth Dancers," she continued as I settled beside her. "It's almost as if we are a different species. You are trained in the Temple tradition and you have your ways. I'm a Kooreei, an Earth Dancer with a much older tradition, one that goes back to the days before the Temple. My mother and her mother before her and her mother before that were all big women, all the way back in my family, back to the beginning of remembered time. We chew ashi-root and we Dance. We Dance for the Old Mother who was before all things, the One who brought all things into existence, even your skinny little pretty-faced Goddess.

"There are few of us left now, fewer and fewer as the years turn. We are not Temple-trained and we carry no Temple wand. The Temple has contempt for us. They would not choose such as us to Dance. We are too big. We do not fit their mold. Every Temple has a grand statue of The Mother that they worship and revere, but they have no respect for her living representatives here on earth. We are reduced to Dancing at fairs and markets now, not holy places. People think it a show. Most have forgotten the old ways. You Dance for the Temple and your traditions are ancient, but ours are older still. We are the source, the origin, the beginning of Dance. We Dance the Dance that brought everything else into existence. But there are those, perhaps even in your own Temple, who would say we blaspheme against the Goddess and dishonor her because we do not Dance in the Temple style. They would have been very angry at seeing you Dance with me. Perhaps I should not have called you up there. My grandmother always scolds me for being so impetuous."

"It's hard to believe they would be angry." I said, feeling my own stubborn anger rising. "It was a fine Dance, Galaina, a wonderful Dance. We honored the Goddess together."

"Well believe that anger exists, Girl, and remember it. To know things like that is part of the wisdom of the road and will help keep you safe." Even as she spoke I thought about Melanthia and wondered if she would have approved. I had my doubts, though I think our other Dance teachers, Dhonir and Nekali, would have cheered me on.

After that we talked deep into the night, exchanging stories and experiences, though I think I did far more listening than talking. Galaina did not try to seduce me again. I might have been tempted if she had. On the surface there was a bluff good humor about her but under it I could sense a raging bitterness. She was so like Melanthia with her fierceness and her passion, her driving energy and force and yet so unlike her at the same time. Melanthia was deeply serious. Galaina mocked everything, even herself, even the Dance, even the Great Mother Herself. Melanthia was as tall as Galaina, but she had a tight, thin body, all muscle and will, no extra flesh. With hair that frizzed out wildly in all directions, Galaina was all curves and roundness, her power in her size—but they both burned with an inner fire and they both moved in that tall, proud way, dominating everything around them by their presence. I finally fell asleep that night at the edge of her bed and dreamt strange unfamiliar dreams. When I woke Galaina's arm lay heavy on my shoulder.

I traveled with Galaina for the next few days. She rode a brown and white spotted horse that she called Friend and indeed he seemed to be just that. "We always have a horse named Friend in my family. If one dies we name the next one that. Sometimes we have more than one Friend and it can get confusing, but we are seldom all home at the same time."

This Friend was big and solid, almost the size of a farm horse and seemed to carry her weight and her gear with ease. Moving grandly, placing one foot before the other, Friend went down the road at a steady, tireless pace. Sometimes I walked alongside, Dancing a little at times to keep up and sometimes I even rode. Galaina said Friend would not mind my added weight, "since you're so skinny and weigh almost nothing." But riding made me stiff and sore, so soon I would go back to walking again.

We even Danced together three or four more times before we parted company. In one place they threw flowers as well as money. Soon we were standing ankle deep in a sudden bright garden, our nostrils filled with the lovely fragrance of crushed flowers. "Here they remember the old ways," she whispered to me. In that village they had called her Undula, swaying together and chanting out her name. But in another place they shouted ugly names and curses and even threw stones, big enough to injure the spirit, if not the body. A small group of Temple Priests had been moving through the crowd, setting people against us. Those Priests seemed particularly enraged at me for Dancing with what they called a Babua. I heard that word shouted several times along with many other nasty and hurtful things.

When a scuffle broke out in the crowd between our attackers and our defenders, with much shouting and shoving on both sides, Galaina saw our chance. I had been frozen in place, staring in disbelief at the scene. She grabbed my hand and pulled me off the stage in the opposite direction. It amazed me how fast she could move for such a big woman. In no time at all we were both mounted on her horse and moving quickly down the road with me in front, held by one broad arm and cushioned against her soft breasts and belly. "You ride with me until we are clear of this mess," she commanded.

We set off at a fast, smooth trot. I had never ridden so fast, but it was not too bad since Galaina had me safely cradled in her embrace. I was very shaken by what had just happened and my whole body was trembling. Galaina, on the other hand, seemed calm enough after she caught her breath. She was even a little amused. "You see? That's what I said about life, full of surprises, one day flowers and the next day rocks. You can never tell which way the wind will blow."

"But it was Temple Priests who set those people off. Why would they do such a thing?"

"Don't ask me, ask the Goddess. I already told you it was possible. That's not my first encounter with Temple folk. The Priestesses can have sharp tongues, but it is the Priests who do real harm. They seem to think there is only one way to celebrate the Goddess—their way—when in fact there are many ways. They believe I mock Her while I know I honor Her, not the only way but the oldest way we humans know."

"How can you bear it?" I was amazed at her calm in the face of such viciousness.

"The hazards of the road," she said with a shrug. "If I wanted safety I would go home to my town and be a Babua there but I'm not yet ready to do that. The road is in my blood still, as it is no doubt in yours. You should understand."

"I think I do, though maybe not right now. After all that's happened I'm not so sure about being on the road. And what is this Babua they were shouting about?"

"When they shout it that way it's a sort of curse, an insult, a bad word, a bad thing to be. But among us, among my own people, being a Babua is an honor. A Babua is a wise old woman, a teacher of Dance and ritual, the one who raises the girls to be Dancers. My grandmother is the Babua for my daughters."

"You have daughters?" I asked in surprise. "Don't you miss them?"

"Yes, of course I miss them, but I also have another life. I see them when I can. I go home for a few months at a time until the road calls again. Back home it's my grandmother who raises my girls. That's how we do it among us. We need to make daughters so there will always be new Dancers, but we cannot stay to raise them. Later, when I'm older, when I'm weary of the road, then I'll go home to raise my daughters' daughters or their daughters. My mother is still dancing on the road and sometimes we meet. It must seem to you an odd way to do but it suits us well enough. I suppose your mother misses you. Does she think you strange for being on the road?"

"Oh yes, she thinks me strange. But she doesn't miss me," I said angrily.

"Ah, I hear a story there. This time we won't be interrupted. Now tell me about this mother of yours." And so we spent part of the day with me retelling my old woes, which helped take my mind off our present ones. I sounded so grief-struck I almost had myself in tears.

"It saddens me that she's not proud of you," Galaina finally said after my dreary recital.

"She wanted me to be something else, something that I couldn't be. I would be miserable trying. How is it with you if your daughters do not do as you wish? If they aren't Dancers? Would you be angry?"

"I would love them, bless them and let them go. I don't own my daughters, Zaia. They are a gift from the Goddess. Only She and they can decide what they should be."

"But how do you really know? What if one of them wanted to be a baker instead?"

At that she burst out laughing. "I know because I have three daughters. Two of them want to be Dancers more than anything in the world and the other one, the youngest, is already in love at the age of sixteen. She wants to marry the village baker and so she will be a baker herself and probably have many children. Maybe she will even raise her sisters' daughters. I do not love her any more or less than the others, only differently, but then I love them all differently."

"And if you have a son?"

"Then he goes to live with his father's family," she said curtly. I sensed some pain there and asked no more questions in that direction.

We stopped early at a roadside tavern as the ordeal had wearied us. We certainly had not been feasted that day but we made up for it now. Galaina ordered everything in sight. When I protested, she laughed. "The rule of the road is to eat everything you can when you have the chance. You never know when you will find your next meal." She also ordered a bottle of sweet wine. When I hesitated she gave me a friendly nudge in the ribs. "Drink up, Girl. You're all grown up now, not a Temple thrall any more. You're on your own. You should celebrate that. Here, let's celebrate it together." She raised her glass to me.

I tried the wine and found that I liked it. Tasting like sweet crushed fruit, it sent a rush of warmth to my belly and made a pleasant little humming in my head. She didn't have to persuade me to drink another and then a third.

Galaina told me more of her stories, and as the evening wore on I found myself telling her about the man in the woods who had tried to take me down. Suddenly her eyes turned hard and dark. There was an angry set to her jaw. "Thank the Goddess you knew how to protect yourself. That Temple Dance may have some uses after all. I don't think I could Dance a man down. If you left him dead then it's good riddance in the world. Predators like that shouldn't be allowed on the public road." Then she looked at me in silence for a long time with a strange unreadable expression on her face. At last she said in an altered voice, "There will be more of them, many more. My way is coming to an end. Yours will end also, though in a very different way. Enjoy it while you're young. Dance for your life. It may be all you have."

"What...?" I started to ask, wanting to know more.

"Enough of this gloomy talk," she said abruptly. Then she waved to the serving boy. "More wine, we need more wine for this young Dancer. She's too serious by far." And so she distracted me with more wine and tales. At that moment I was only too willing to let her charm me. Later I was sorry I had not questioned her more carefully for she had traveled much, going all the way to the far north and then south until she reached the sea. But, at the time, I was delighting in my freedom, sitting among adults, drinking, eating and talking with nothing on my mind, no task or responsibility, at least for that moment. I even had my own money in my pocket though Galaina would not let me spend any of it, not a single coin. Each time I tried to she would knock the money out of my hand and put it back in the pouch. "Time enough for that later," she would say. She even paid for our beds at the tavern when I had drunk so much I could barely sit upright and had to be helped to bed by the serving-boy. Galaina came and sat by me on my bed and began stroking my arm with hypnotic repetition. "Sorry to see you're not feeling well. It seems a shame to waste this little time we have." This time it was easier to refuse her. My head was spinning and my body felt wretched. It was not just the pledge. I had no taste for loving at that moment.

I woke the next morning in a foul, loathsome mood. Each time I moved, my head throbbed and my stomach lurched. I wasn't even sure I could keep down my night's meal. When I complained to Galaina she laughed and said gaily, "That's the effect of the wine. It's always better the night before than it is the next morning."

"In that case I'll never drink that way again."

"That's what they all say, but they forget soon enough," she answered mockingly.

"*I'm not they.* I'm Zaia and I won't forget, I promise you that." I replied rather sharply. Galaina could laugh if she wanted to, but I knew I would never willingly inflict such misery on myself again.

Later in the day, as we went along with me walking and Galaina riding, my mood lifted. I began to play the little hand drum my cousin had given me and we even sang a few songs together, though we knew very different versions. In that way we came to a Y in the road. I was about to take out my map when Galaina said abruptly, "This is where we part. Your way is straight ahead and mine lies to the south. All this talk has made me hungry to see my daughters again." I wasn't ready for such an abrupt separation, but Galaina slid from her horse's back and reached out her arms. "Say a quick goodby now, Zaia. That's the best way when you're on the road." I stepped forward and found myself totally enveloped in her soft, voluptuous hug. I could have stayed a long time in the luxury of that embrace and began to wonder if I should have been so quick to refuse her offer, but she soon pushed me away. "No use postponing the inevitable. We will meet again if the Goddess wills it. Meanwhile, I thank her for the gift of your company. Who could have imagined that a Temple Dancer would be my companion of the road?"

"Can't we go on a little longer as we have been? Perhaps I could come with you and visit your town."

"No," she said sharply. "We're too different. We would pull each other off course. You would bend me to your ways or more likely I would bend you to mine." Saying this, she led her horse over to a rock and was on his back faster than I could have imagined. With one quick wave she rode off down the southern road without a backward glance, though she was still singing the song we had begun together. I stood watching her out of sight and feeling strangely bereft. Then, with the pleasant weight of those coins in my pocket, I turned and took the road east.

Almost a year had passed since I last Danced with Galaina. Since that time I'd Danced in many places, almost more than I could remember, meeting innumerable people along the way and walking through every sort of weather. Still, I thought of her often and watched for her everywhere, hoping we'd cross paths again. Twice I just missed her, Dancing in a town only a few days after she had been there. I was sure we would meet again somewhere on the road. Even if we didn't, I knew I'd never forget what she taught me: that Temple ways are not the only ones, that the children of The Mother Dance for Her in many ways...

CHAPTER 8

Making a New Dance Court

Well before I reached the town of Shoma, I stopped to undo my hair. For the first time since I'd earned my Dancer's Knot, I took it out and hid it away in my pack along with my Dancewand. I'd always worn it with pride, putting it on first thing in the morning and not taking it off except to bathe and sleep, but now, after two years on the road and more Dances than I could count, I suddenly felt weary—deeply weary. This time I wanted to come into a town as just another traveler, just an ordinary woman, at least at first.

The awe and admiration with which I was always greeted as a Dancer had been thrilling at the beginning of my journey, but just behind it I had sensed the wariness, the distance, the awe, the fear of my difference. Though it was subtle and unintended, it had started to hurt. Also, there were the enormous expectations, the excitement the moment I appeared and with that the frightening responsibility that I carried. After all, I was a source of magic, a connection to the sacred, the divine. I was their link with the Goddess. In fact, while I Danced I was the Goddess Herself in earthly form, not something to be taken lightly. After a while it could even become a burden.

How little of all this I'd understood when I set out so boldly and bravely from the Temple of Kernoss. Melanthia had tried to warn me, but the young always have to learn for themselves. No one could have explained it to me then. Besides, I would have still taken my pledge, though I might have been more fearful and less bold. Maybe it's for the best not to know what lies ahead along the road. "Forgive me Goddess," I said aloud as I undid my Dancer braids. "Just this one time I need to do this, to be like other people." I wound up my hair so that it looked shorter and straighter and changed my Dance shirt for a plain tunic with no sign of my profession. Then I checked with my little hand mirror to make sure there was nothing in my appearance that would betray me.

When I went on I was feeling freer and lighter, though a little guilty, almost as if I had betrayed a lover. *Forgive me Mother, but I'm only human. The burden of always being holy and carrying the needs of others was weighing me down. I hope you can understand.* Legend has it that when the Goddess came to earth She came in the form of a Dancer. One story even told of how, after a while, She'd disguised Herself in ordinary clothes just that same way because She'd grown weary of people's entreaties. Perhaps She would understand.

The morning air was still cool and moist, pregnant with possibilities. The newness and softness of spring was all around me, things budding and flowering with the faith of renewal. I was walking along at a good pace. My disguise, which was in fact no disguise at all but only the most ordinary of clothes, made me feel light-hearted and adventurous. When a man in a horse-drawn wagon drew alongside me, I instantly accepted his offer of a ride and easily fell into talking with this stranger. After we had chatted companionably for a few minutes he asked, "Where are you from, traveler? Have you come to help us build our new Dance Court?"

"Dance Court?" I exclaimed, stupid with surprise.

"Yes, the whole town is out working there. You must be from far away to know nothing of it. Look ..." With that word he threw back the cloth that was covering his load. His wagon was piled high with turf, cut in strips and rolled into big mounds. "We've had a fine harvest for three years running and discovered a big vein of green clay that's making our potters famous all around the countryside, so we have much to be thankful for. We wanted to honor Her but up until now we've had no place for a real Dance. Those few Dancers that come through don't stay. They barely do a turn or two here, not a real Dance. Shomara said we should make our own Dance Court in the Lady's honor. We're building it down in the hollow, but who's to say that a Dancer will really come? We can hardly send messengers to all the Dance Temples to say that the little town of Shoma has finally built a Dance Court. Besides, it won't be a real Temple, only a court. Who knows if it will be fine enough for a Temple Dancer."

I felt a sudden ache in my throat. My silence thundered in my head, almost like a lie, but I kept my words locked behind my teeth until I had taken several deep breaths and could speak calmly. "I'm sure if you build it with love in your hearts, the Goddess will see and send you the Dancer you need."

"Do you know much of Dancers? Are you from far away?"

By now we were coming to paved streets and I could see Shoma was a fair-sized town. "Very far away, a farm near the city of Urshameel. I've had the luck to see many Dancers there, some of them very fine."

"And why are you so far from home?"

With no hesitation I continued, "My sister married the man I'd set my heart upon so I decided to walk off the pain of it and stay away from them for a while. By now I've grown so used to traveling, to seeing new things all the time, that I'm not sure life in one place would suit me anymore. She's welcome to him, but I will probably settle elsewhere. In the meantime, I enjoy the road." The lies flowed from my lips with such ease I might have been a storyteller rather than a Dancer. I wondered how my sister would appreciate this story and had to hide a guilty little smile. "Would you take me to this Dance Court? I'm very curious to see what you're making here."

"Gladly, I'm on my way there myself. You'll find most of the town already at the site working hard, even the Headman. What's your name, traveler?"

"Zendra. I've become a storyteller while on the road and sometimes I earn my bread that way. If this town has any wish to hear stories of places far away I'd be glad to oblige, but I'm also willing to lend my hand at any honorable work for my keep."

"Well, Zendra from everywhere, my name is Norus and you're welcome to come with me and see how the people of Shoma plan to honor the Lady. And I'm sure we can find a place for you. Kindness to travelers is also a way of honoring the Goddess."

The streets were near deserted. What traffic there was seemed to be flowing all in one direction. As we fell in with it Norus was greeted and called out greetings in return, saying that he had a traveler with him who wanted to see the Dance Court. By the time we arrived word was there ahead of us. I was met with a flurry of welcomes and questions, making me very glad that I'd kept my Dancer self well hidden. In no time at all I'd been offered lodging for the night in one house and my next meal at another. Soon I found myself with a shovel in my hands, digging a circular trench beside others from the town. As people questioned me, my little lie about my sister grew and grew into a story of vast proportions. At first I found myself enjoying it but after a while the sympathy I got for my sister's treachery was a little discomfiting. I set myself to digging in earnest to stop the questions.

Unaccustomed to such work, I was soon drenched in sweat. In no time my hands were sore and my back was aching. Finally I had to stop and rest a while, leaning on my shovel. When I looked around I noticed a carver perched up on a high scaffold, hard at work on the only column that was already set in the ground. This person had a broad back, gleaming with sweat and short cropped dark hair. With each powerful swing of the mallet a curl of dark wood flew from the chisel and gleamed for a moment in the light before it fell to land in the pile below. I assumed it was a man until the carver turned to talk to someone and I saw her bare breasts. That was the first surprise. The second was that I knew her. It was Ushain, the same Ushain who had been a sculptor's apprentice at the Temple and Kendrin's lover. If she recognized me now my story was exposed. I dug for just a little longer and then slipped away.

That first time I escaped, but I wasn't so lucky the second. She came on me while I was sitting by the fountain in the public square, cooling my feet in the pool and watching the sparkle of light on the falling water. "Zaia, so it is you. I thought I saw you digging at the Dance Court. What are you doing here, Dancer, and why in such drab clothes?"

As there were other people about I answered quickly, "You must be mistaken. We've never met before. My name is Zendra not Zaia, whoever she is, and I'm a storyteller." I looked hard into Ushain's eyes, willing her to believe me or at least to keep her silence.

She grinned at me, seeming unconvinced. "If you say your name is Zendra then it must be so, but you look very like a Dancer that I used to know." She gave me a conspiratorial wink at the deliberate rhyme. "Come to the Green Man Tavern with me, Zendra. I'll buy you some wine and you can tell me what you haven't been doing since I didn't see you last." Then she leaned over and whispered, "If I'm going to lie for you Zaia, I must at least know why. We can find an empty corner. I'll eat and listen while you talk."

"But I don't drink," I said quickly, remembering the last time.

"Come," she said impatiently, gripping my arm, "My curiosity is eating me alive." Her broad, strong fingers bit into my flesh. I wasn't so sure I wanted Ushain's company. She had an angry edge to her that had always made me uncomfortable. Besides, I always thought she was jealous of my friendship with Kendrin and that made her even sharper with me. At that moment, however, I seemed to have little choice.

Just as she said, we found a quiet corner. The tavern was almost empty as most of the town folk were at the Dance Court. Ushain ate a huge plate of food and downed three glasses of wine while I, true to what I had told Galaina, drank only juice as I leaned close to Ushain's ear and told her in a low voice why I wanted to remain Zendra, at least for a little while longer.

Ushain nodded, looking thoughtful as she chewed one huge mouthful after the other. Finally she said, "You'll have to excuse me, Zendra, but carving leaves me with a powerful thirst and hunger. Sometimes I get so absorbed in what I'm doing that I forget to eat altogether and then I have to make up for it." In a whisper she added, "I'll keep your secret for a while if you promise to Dance for these people before you leave. As you know, they're much in need of a Dancer."

"Done! You have my promise," I whispered back quickly. "I already intended to. Just give me a few days." With that solved I ordered a plate of food for myself. I would have paid for it with my own money, something that as a Dancer I didn't usually do, only Ushain had coins on the table before me.

"Just remember your promise," she said, giving me a warning look.

I answered her with a quick nod and then set to asking my own questions between hearty mouthfuls of food. "Have you been home? Tell me what's been happening at the Temple and in the city. What of Thesali? Have you seen her? Is she well? Does she sometimes think of me?"

She shook her head. "Slow down, Zaia, and give me a moment to answer." Then she took a deep breath and sighed before she started, saying, "I left shortly after you did and no, I have not been back since. Kendrin broke my heart by taking her pledge and going on the road. After a while it seemed pointless to stay on at the Temple when I could see no future there for my work, the other passion of my life. As to Thesali, her brother died and she's been helping Anyashu, his widow, to raise his two sons. When I last heard she'd left the Temple and wasn't Dancing any more. I think they've gone to live in her brother's village."

"Are they ...?"

"Yes, I suppose so. They've made a home together, if that's what you're asking. You can't expect someone to wait five years for your return, can you? After all, you're the one who left." There was a bitter edge to her voice.

"I know it's true, but it still hurts. And you? What of Kendrin? Is she still on the road? I haven't seen her, though I've asked for her everywhere."

Ushain shook her head. "I haven't seen her either and I also ask. I suppose she's somewhere on the road, Goddess protecting her. If not for that pledge of celibacy exacted by the Temple we could have traveled together, me to carve and Kendrin to Dance."

"But you can't carve in the same time it takes to do a Dance."

"It doesn't matter, we could have worked out something between us. She could have come back and forth to where I was working."

Yes, I thought, *and then you would have been the focus of her life, instead of the Dance and the Goddess being the focus of it,* but I didn't say it aloud. "I'm surprised you didn't stay carving at the Temple, Ushain. I thought you were well established there."

She gave a short, angry laugh. "Stayed at the Temple of Kernoss? Not likely! Whatever for? That was child's work and I needed to grow up. If I was lucky they would have allowed me to carve the toes on a foot on someone else's design, but I would never have been allowed to create something of my own. There are about ten old men and two old women who are the master sculptors at the Temple. Only if one of them dies does one of us, one of the apprentices, get to take their place, not likely me since I have a loose tongue and a bad temper. Besides, I'm a woman. I'm almost as unlikely to end up being a Temple sculptor as a man is to be a Temple Dancer. Until then I'm just a carver, someone else's hands."

"But you were so skilled ..."

"And it has nothing to do with skill or talent. I'm not too shy to say that I have plenty of that, more than enough. And most important, I have vision. I see things. I'm bursting with ideas. There's a force that fills me, that uses me. When I work on a statue for the Temple I'm only an apprentice, carrying out someone else's orders. Here *I'm* the tool, the power moves through *me*. There I would only be the tool of the tool." Her words were being pounded out as if she were hitting them with a mallet, or with her fist on the table. As she spoke her eyes stared intently into mine. Her face was flushed with passion while her hands moved constantly with her words, shaping them right there in front of me.

I knew the Temple carvers had worked for over a year on the huge statue for the procession, but I'd never seen it before it made its miraculous appearance. No one had been allowed to. "Did you work on the new carving of the Great Mother?"

She laughed again in that angry way of hers. "Yes, of course I worked on it. Just as I was saying, on that statue I was allowed to carve the left foot, the whole left foot—imagine that! I also did some of the roughing out on the back following someone else's clay models. Have you seen what I'm working on here? My carving of the Goddess? Here are *my* sketches, *my* design. She's coming alive under *my* hands."

"I didn't really get to see anything. I was too busy hiding, afraid you'd give me away."

"Do you want...?" She looked away, suddenly shy.

"Of course," I said, jumping to my feet. "Just remember that I'm Zendra, a storyteller from the countryside outside Urshameel and a good friend of your cousin Lerandi. We've just discovered all these mutual connections."

Winking at me she threw down a few more coins, took my arm and whispered in my ear, "I didn't know you were such an inventor of stories. You have quite a talent for it." Together we went out into the empty streets.

How can I describe her work? I stood below, looking up at it with awe and admiration. It had in it some of the bold forms, some of the fierceness and the archaic quality of the Great-Mother-Of-All at the Temple or the figures in the desert, but not so harsh and not so distant or so soft or pretty either, as most of the Temple figures—something in between, something full of power and yet protective and present, remote and yet compassionate. Leaning forward with great wings folded on her back, it was the Goddess, but more than the Goddess I knew. It was the Goddess in the present and the Goddess going back a thousand years. Rough like that, only partly formed, She seemed to be bursting out of the column and breaking into life.

There were tears in my eyes when I turned to look at Ushain. She had been watching me, expectantly. "She's magnificent," I whispered. Then I was shaking my head. "How is it that someone that I know, a mere girl really, could make something of such power and beauty, could create the sacred right before my eyes with a hammer and chisel?"

Her face broke into a wide grin as she leaned forward to whisper in my ear, "And how is it that you can Dance the Goddess into existence right before our eyes, Zaia? And could do so even when you were a child? Her spirit moves through us, Dancer. We're only the tools by which She creates and re-creates Herself in the world."

Then she straightened and threw her arms wide. "Here on the road I'm free, I'm my own person. This little town couldn't possibly afford a master Temple sculptor even if they could get one to come, which is doubtful, but they will feed me and clothe me for however long I work for them and look what comes out from my hands. Her energy comes through my hands and my mind just as it comes through your body. I *see* Her! I *see* Her! And that's what I carve. I carve what I see and feel, my own vision, not someone else's idea. She is ancient stone and present living flesh and I put all that into my work." We only had that one quick moment for admiring Ushain's work before others quickly surrounded us with questions and curiosity.

Smooth as silk, Ushain introduced me as Zendra to the young woman who seemed to be in charge and then introduced her to me, saying gaily, "This is Shomara, the one who has organized this project and tyrannizes over us all, giving the orders here."

Shomara blushed and shook her head. "No, no, it's not like that at all. Why do you say such things?" She gave Ushain a sideways glance of such love and longing that, for a moment, she seemed almost naked. Either Ushain didn't notice, or she chose not to respond.

To cover the awkwardness I asked quickly, "Your name is so much like the name of the town. Were you named for it?"

"Yes and no. In some ways you could as easily say the town was named for me. In every generation of my family there is a Shomara or a Shomar, sometimes both. It was a distant ancestor of ours who began this town. The name is thought to have some sort of sacred power for protection. There are special duties that go with it."

"So you were chosen for this?"

She shook her head. "It wasn't my birth name. It belonged to my aunt Shomara who was Headwoman here. When she died suddenly of lung fever that name was passed on to me and with it the keeping of this town as I was the only one left in the family. After a while of rebelling I have gradually come to accept the name and its burden and have grown into it. Now I live at peace with it, though not always comfortably." This was much more answer than I'd bargained for. She seemed very young for such a burden to be laid on her, though afterward, as I watched her move the work forward with a skillful combination of charm and will, I thought she carried it very well, even with grace.

However, when she looked at Ushain it was not the ancestor of power who looked out of those eyes. It was a young woman full of passion and desire. And I saw Norus, the man who had given me a ride in his wagon, watching Shomara in much the same way that she watched Ushain. He was not watching a sacred being—he was watching a woman he wanted with all his heart and wanted in the flesh. Suddenly I was seeing more than I cared to among these strangers and quickly returned to my digging.

Of course working didn't silence my mind. As I dug I thought of how Shomara was wasting her time or rather her heart. It was clear that Ushain couldn't return her affections because Ushain was looking backwards to a time that wouldn't come again and a love that was in her past. Though she and Shomara seemed friendly enough, talking and joking while they made plans for the court and the sacred statues, Ushain didn't seem to have eyes for any woman in the present.

For over a week I worked at the Dance Court, helping to trench out a huge circular drainage ditch around the central green, digging holes for the great posts, prying out boulders and loading river rocks on wagons. The green was like the bottom of a bowl, and we terraced the slope around it into a series of benches for seating that would later be faced with stone. Whenever Norus would appear with his wagon loaded with turf a crew of us would throw down our shovels and rush over to help unload. Together we would roll out the turf over the newly leveled earth, tramp it down and water it.

I delighted in being outside in the soft spring weather, feeling the sun and wind on my body. It was a relief to have no responsibility beyond the physical task assigned to me, to take orders, to do my work and to feel my muscles bloom with strength that even my Dancing hadn't touched. I found it a pleasure getting to know and work with the people of the town. I hoped they wouldn't be too angry later at my deception, but I felt as if I had no choice. Had they known I was a Dancer, they would have treated me very differently and they never would have allowed me to do such work. We often ate together in the town square, food that was donated by the taverns and came to us on huge platters. Invariably, someone would pull out pipes or drums or some stringed instruments and we would have a little music or even some singing before we went back to work. Often I joined in with my travel drum, but I made sure never to take part in the Dancing for fear of giving myself away. In the evening I would occasionally sit in the tavern and tell stories. The many coins I earned that way were quickly spent.

Norus was there almost every day at the Dance Court, laying the turf or helping Shomara to direct the rest of the work. When all the turf was neatly laid and the first of the great columns almost finished he began to fret, "If only we could find a Dancer to consecrate this part. It isn't altogether finished and may not be finished until next year or the year after if we wait while all the columns are carved, but this part is ready now for a Dancer to make it sacred and do a first Dance here. Zendra, you said you know something of Dancers. What should we do?"

"Make it ready just as you would if you had a Dancer. Do whatever ceremony or ritual you would do if one were about to appear and I promise you that she will be here."

"But how can you be so sure? Who would have sent a message to the Temples, and what Temple Dancer would come to this remote place? I'm afraid we'll have to fetch someone but from where? After all this work I fear Shomara will be deeply disappointed."

"Norus, you've asked me and I've told you. Ask no more questions. Do as I say and have some faith in the Goddess. If a Dancer doesn't appear then I'll Dance for you myself. I told you I know something of Dancing from having lived so near the city, but I doubt it will come to that."

He blushed, looking down at his feet in an agony of embarrassment and mumbled, "Begging your pardon, but we need a real Dancer with proper training to do this thing right. I'm sure you'd be a good enough Dancer in the tavern or the town square, but this is different..."

It felt cruel not to relieve his embarrassment and anxiety. Instead I laughed and said lightly, "Then I hope and trust it doesn't come to that."

Later that day I noticed that Shomara was watching me intently every time I paused in my work and her expression was far from friendly. I was pausing more and more often as my gentle hands had grown very sore. When those on either side of me disappeared on some errand I was startled to see Shomara approaching suddenly, obviously with some plan in mind. She stepped up next to me and whispered fiercely in my ear, "What's your real name, woman? Who are you and what are you doing here? You're no more a farm girl than I am. Hold out your hands." When I hesitated in confusion she shook my arm. "Drop your shovel and hold out your hands." It was a command, not a request. I did as she said. My palms were raw and lacerated, oozing with blisters. "Look at those hands. When did you hold a shovel last? What's the purpose of this deception? Why have you been lying to us? What are you here for, to do us some harm?" Her torrent of questions was coming so fast I could only shake my head. "Answer me!" she hissed in my ear.

I held up my hands, "I'll answer you, Shomara, but only if you give me a chance to speak." She nodded and I went on, "A deception, yes, but only temporary and no harm intended. I must ask you to keep my secret for a little longer. My name is Zaia and I'm a Dancer from the Temple of Kernoss." I saw her eyes widen when I said the word Dancer. "Don't say anything, let me finish," I added hastily.

As quickly as I could, I told her my story in a low voice while she listened in silence. When I finished she had a wide smile on her face. "Well, so we have our Dancer after all." Her voice was filled with relief. "No need to go chasing all over the countryside for her. Now I see how you could give Norus such assurances." Then a look of suspicion crossed her face. "You've told us so many stories. How do I know this one is true?"

"Ask Ushain, she can vouch for me."

"Ushain?"

"She knows me from the Temple."

"Ah yes, Ushain," she said dreamily. Then her tone changed again. "So even Dancing can become a burden. I thought a Dancer had the freedom of the road. Sometimes I envy Ushain. I've dreamt of picking up my pack and going with her when she leaves."

"Do you also envy her pain? Ushain has her own burdens. I see how you look at Ushain with eyes of longing, but believe me when I say that she'll never give you what you want. Ushain is a traveling artist. Her passion is all for her work and for a woman she can't have who's lost to her somewhere in the past."

She nodded, looking thoughtful. "Maybe it isn't Ushain that I love as much as the thought of escape. As a Dancer, you should understand what such a burden means, what it's like to be chosen and to carry the weight of that choosing. Since I'm the last of the Shomas it's even laid on me that I must make children to carry on that name. What if I don't want to make children? What if I don't choose to? What if it feels to me like a curse to pass on to a child rather than a blessing? What then?"

I didn't tell her that I'd chosen my burden with a passion, pursued it almost at the cost of my life. "I can't say you should pick up your burden, Shomara. All I can say is to look deeply into your own heart and find the answer there. It's between you and the Goddess."

"Ah yes, the Goddess, but does She care about our little mortal lives? She uses us as Her tools. That's what Ushain says. She speaks of it joyfully. For me, I'm not so sure."

"So then you'll leave this place?"

She was still for a little while, looking off into the distance, then she shook her head sadly. "Probably not. I doubt that I could run far enough to escape the memories. I'll probably stay and take care of Shoma, just as my family always has."

"Then you'll need someone strong and steady for a companion, some-one who can always be there for you. If you're going to bear children, Ushain would never have the patience for them or give them the love they'll need. For her, it's her work that comes first. That's her great love. You need someone who will love *you*. You're the flame and you need a hearth to contain your fire. I see how Norus looks at you, with devotion in his eyes. He's a good, steady man, a fine hearth to come home to."

"Norus?" she said with surprise. "Norus?" Then she threw back her head and laughed, her very serious face taking on a whole other aspect, full of mischief and merriment. "Are you trying to make a match here, Dancer?"

"A little happiness never hurt anyone. Besides, it's well known that Dancers are inspired with sacred sight. We give only good advice."

"More stories," she answered with a grin, shaking her head.

At that moment I noticed some of my shovel companions returning. Then I saw Norus coming toward us across the circle of new grass. "Don't tell him," I whispered quickly. "He's too eager. I don't think he could keep my secret for long, probably not for a minute." She nodded and put a finger to her lips.

Norus nodded to us both. His words were for me, but I could see his smile was for Shomara. "Only two more days and then we're ready. What do you think, Zendra? Will our Dancer be here by then?" Now he was looking at me anxiously.

"Do you really think the Goddess would fail us? Haven't you asked Her from your heart to send you a Dancer?" I answered quickly, replying to his question with questions of my own. As I turned and winked at Shomara I saw her turn her wonderful smile on Norus, that simple, humble man who so obviously adored her. He was twisting his hands with hopefulness. I wished him well as I slipped away, leaving them alone.

Ushain must have been watching it all. She was down off her ladder in an instant and followed me to the public square. "Well, did you tell them the truth? What did they say?"

"I only told Shomara. She already knew I was telling stories. I couldn't trust Norus to keep his silence. He says it's only two more days until they're ready for a Dancer. What about you? Is your carving finished?"

"Done enough for now. I have to buy some better tools for finishing and then do the painting, but that can wait until after the Dance. It's the Dance Court that needs to be consecrated now."

I thought I liked the Goddess better in dark wood than bright paint but kept my silence on it. "Ushain, what are we going to do? How am I going to suddenly appear? Who will dress me?"

"I will," she answered confidently.

"You?" I looked skeptically at her large rough hands.

"Don't you think I know how to dress a Dancer and do her hair? I've had enough experience. As for the rest, leave it to Shomara and to me. Together we'll think of a good way. Now, show me your hands."

Reluctantly I held them out for her inspection. "No! No! No!" She was frowning and shaking her head. "No more shovel work before the Dance. I have some salve here in my sack that's for quick healing. I use it when I've ruined my hands with too much carving." I winced at her touch as she put salve on my palms and wrapped my hands in soft cloths, but almost immediately I felt a cooling relief. "Now stay here with the flowers for the afternoon. No more hard work for your tattered hands." She left and I wandered about the gardens, looking at all the beds of bright flowers and thinking, a little sadly, of my father who was so very far away.

The day of the Dance, Shomara gave me the use of her house to prepare myself. An ancient stone structure at the far edge of the town, it was beautiful but much neglected. It had been her aunt's and her grandmother's before that. As the last remaining member of her family it had passed to Shomara, though it looked as if she was seldom home. That day she was at the ceremony to bless the new Dance Court. I regretted my absence, but I needed a time of silence after all the bustle of the work. I closeted myself in her bedroom for the morning, and Ushain met me there in the afternoon to help me make ready.

Ushain was right about her skill. Though at first she was so excited that her hands were shaking, she soon steadied herself and began moving her fingers through my hair, lightly and deftly, making the multitude of Dancer braids. "So these people will have their Dancer after all and the Goddess will have her Dance. What a wonder that you came at just this time, Zaia."

"Came or was called," I answered gaily as I proudly replaced the Dancer's Knot in my hair. I looked at it this way and that in the mirror, glad to have it back where it belonged. Then she helped me into a new purple vest and skirt, both with wide bands of red and gold embroidery along the edges. Some of the girls of Shoma had made new clothes as a gift for the Dancer when she came, and Shomara had laid them out on the bed for me. With my own sash and beads and the face paint Ushain applied, I saw the transformation happening right before my eyes. In the mirror was the sacred being and I, Zaia, only inhabited a little corner of her.

After that Ushain went through the town beating on a drum and shouting, "The Dancer has come! The Dancer is here!" A shiver went up my back as I heard others take up the call so that the word *Dancer* seemed to be echoing through the town. Shomara came for me alone. She helped me mount a huge gray horse borrowed from Norus and decked with ribbons, bells and flowers. Thank the Goddess that he was a quiet and patient creature since I was unfamiliar with horses. Except for that short ride on Friend, held in the safety of Galaina's arms, I hadn't been on a horse's back since I'd left my family home for training at the Temple.

People began pouring from their houses, filling the streets and calling out to each other. They were full of noisy excitement but fell silent and bowed with awe and respect as we passed, not recognizing me in my transformed appearance. Then the crowd fell in behind in a huge boisterous procession, with drums and horns and clamor swelling in back of us. It was glorious to sit high up on that horse, floating on a river of sound and energy with Shomara's steady presence to keep me safe.

The raw new Dance Court had been transformed as well, turned into a thing of beauty and magic. Huge pots of flowers filled the holes that had been dug for the other columns. Flares had been lit that gave everything a shifting golden glow. The smell of incense was sweet and heady on the air. People were filing down the bank from all sides, dressed in their brightest clothes. With Shomara's aid I slipped off the horse's back. She threw my dark cloak over me and I stood still and silent as a shadow until people were seated. The Lady in all Her majesty was directly across the circle from me. At the base of Her column was an altar heaped with flowers, greens and lit candles. People added to it as they passed, saying their words to Her, touching their fingers to their lips and then to the carved wood.

Finally, the music began. Never taking my eyes off The Lady, I lifted the cloak from my shoulders, raised my arms and dropped it in back of me like a puddle of darkness. As I stepped out on the new turf, a collective sigh went up like wind passing over long grass. Gathering myself at the core I turned and bowed in each of the directions. Then, with my eyes on the statue I began the Dance for The Goddess, the purest form of the Dance, the one we first learned at the Temple, simple, powerful, elegant, but I did it in my own way and with my own passion. I took what I had learned from the Temple, from my time on the road, from Galaina and from the dedication of the people who had built this place. Sore hands and sore muscles forgotten, I Danced like a flame for them that night, giving them everything I had. I also Danced for all the Dancers who had ever Danced on the road before me and all who would come after me. And, most of all, I Danced for The Goddess. The Lady was no longer a thing of wood made by human hands, made by a woman I knew. Her folded wings seemed ready to open at any moment. She had become a thing of power and mystery, moving in the flare of the torches, coming to life for me as I Danced in that circle. Power poured out of Her and into me. I opened myself wide and let that power carry me on and on until finally a voice in my head said, *That is enough Zaia. Any more is too much.*

With that I let the Dance wind down to its natural conclusion. When I glanced across the circle I saw that The Lady was, once again, a beautifully crafted thing of wood. Finishing to a storm of applause, I raised my arms high as if to gather it all in. Then I dropped to my knees, resting my forehead on the grass, pouring all that energy back into the ground, making this place sacred in the best way I knew how.

Later, still in my Dance clothes, I went with a crowd to the Green Man Tavern. With me were Ushain and Norus and Shomara and several of the people I'd made friends with while working on the Dance Court, along with a score of others. We were barely able to fit around the biggest table. Shomara and Norus sat together opposite me and I noticed that she had slipped her hand over to cover his.

Clearly my little time of being anonymous and ordinary was over. As we sat around together I saw that look on people's faces, that look of awe and love and admiration and distance that gave me joy and cut my heart at the same time, the "burden" Shomara spoke of. They toasted me loudly with wine and hard cider while I stayed with my glass of juice. Through all this, Norus seemed to have something on his mind. Finally he was able to get up the courage to speak.

"It's very hard to ask this of you Dancer, but are you really...? Were you Temple trained or were you ...?

"In plain speech, what you want to know is am I a real Temple Dancer or only a country girl who got inspired by a wooden Goddess." I stood up to answer. It was time for the truth. Speaking loudly to be heard over the noise of the tavern, I said, "My real name is Zaia. I was trained at the Temple of Kernoss in the city of Urshameel and, putting aside false modesty, I was probably one of their best Dancers or at least that's what they always told me. I've taken my five-year pledge to go on the road and Dance wherever The Goddess calls me, but I needed for a little while to be only an ordinary woman. So I'm sorry for speaking untruths before, but I can tell you that your Dance Court has been truly blessed and consecrated and that The Lady was here among us.

"Perhaps you called to me just as I said you should call a Dancer. Perhaps I was the one The Goddess sent and Norus was Her tool when he gave me a ride in his wagon. He was the one who brought me here and told me of the new Dance Court and inspired me to stay and Dance. And Shomara was the one who held my secret and Ushain the one who made me ready. However it all happened, I have to say that working here among you for this week was one of the great experiences of my time on the road and one I will always treasure." I bowed to Norus and then to the others and finally sat down to a thunder of applause.

Full of apologies, Norus bowed in return and said with great humbleness, "Oh, but if only you'd told us you were a real Dancer, we never would have let you dig holes in the dirt with a shovel."

"I know that," I said with some sadness, "And that's why I didn't tell you. I hope you've forgiven me. I meant no harm." They were all smiling and nodding. Many reached out their hands to touch me. They would have forgiven me anything at that moment or given me anything I wanted. It was right then I vowed to myself that I would also go on to the next town as a plain woman, wearing no Dancer signs and see what adventures The Goddess sent me.

Turning to Shomara I said, "I think you should choose from among your young women two or three who are the best Dancers and send them to a Temple for training, so when your Dance Court is complete you will have your own Dancers for The Goddess." Then to Ushain I added, "And I think you need to train some apprentices here to help you so you can finish this work before you're an old woman." Ushain glared at me, but the others nodded in agreement and even offered some names. Then Ushain leaned over and said in my ear, "Perhaps, Zaia, it is time for you to be on the road again."

I'd been feasted and toasted and honored and praised and asked to stay longer and begged to Dance again but I was ready to go. My feet were itching to be back on the road, though I would never forget this place and its people where I was allowed for a little while to be an ordinary woman and set down the burdens of being a Dancer.

CHAPTER 9
The Sculptor and the Storm

I was sitting on a bench in the town square, looking at my map with Ushain leaning over my shoulder. Except for that remark about it being time for me to leave soon, she had been surprisingly friendly with me since the Dance. I have to admit I was somewhat flattered by her sudden attention. Back at the Temple, whenever she found me spending time with Kendrin, she had treated me like an annoying in-the-way child rather than an equal. Now she seemed to take a real interest in me. In fact she was actually being quite charming, something I would not have thought possible. Though I felt a little wary, still I allowed myself to be charmed. "Where are you going to next?" she asked with what appeared to be kind curiosity.

"In that direction," I said pointing to the little dot that marked the town of Anthrin, "But there seems to be a long, tiresome loop in the road before it."

"I know a much shorter way through the woods," she offered. "You can come with me if you like. I'm going that way myself to buy some better tools for finishing my work here."

"Why not?" I answered with a grin. After my adventures at the Dance Court I was feeling carefree and daring. Besides, I liked her bold manner and was glad to have her company for a while longer, though somewhere under this I felt a little current of unease.

Shomara and Norus walked with us to the edge of the town. Then they stood, hand in hand, waving goodbye. When we were out of sight Ushain nudged me with her elbow. "They seem to have gotten very friendly all of a sudden. Did you help that along?"

"I told her she was wasting her hopeful looks on you."

"What looks?" Ushain asked with false innocence. Then more seriously she added, "It was probably for the best."

We only went for a short way on the road before we turned off on a little path into the woods, a path I never even would have noticed had I been alone. Certainly I would never have ventured there on my own. The little current of unease returned, stronger this time, but the cards had already been dealt as my aunt Veraine would have said. Now it was up to me to play out my part of the game.

That morning I saw a different side of Ushain, gentler, more light-hearted, less driven. Following her through the woods was a magical experience. So much of it was new to me. Though I'd been on the road two years now I was still in many ways a child of the city. Traveling between towns and villages, I slept by the side of the road if I had to, but I much preferred sheltering under a roof. This was the first time I'd ever entered the deep woods by choice rather than necessity. Ushain seemed very much at home there.

She rambled along, telling me whatever came into her mind about everything we saw, sharing information about healing plants and entertaining me with stories about the animals she'd lived with as a child. "My family isn't from the city like yours and Kendrin's. Before I came to apprentice at the Temple I lived in a little house at the edge of woods much like these. My father cut wood for the village. It's from him I learned the use of tools." I think she knew the name of every tree and rock and plant and wildflower and bird and creature in those woods. I tried to learn as much as I could from her, asking questions and gathering little samples in my pockets.

The day had started sunny and clear, full of promise, but by noon there was a heavy cover of gray clouds and the sound of far-off thunder. When we came to a small stone shelter by the path Ushain said it was time to stop. We laid out some food and shared it between us. Then we sat on the stone bench for a while trying to decide whether or not to go on. I was uneasy and favored staying, though who knew how long that would be, waiting there for the storm to come and then pass. Ushain was for going on, but with speed in our steps. "I'm sure we can reach Anthrin and shelter before nightfall and it looks like the storm may hold off until then." With that I nodded and stood up to go. She was the one who knew the woods and I certainly wasn't going to stay there alone.

For a while it seemed as if we'd made the right choice. The rain waited and the sky did not get any darker, though there was an occasional rumble of thunder and a few flashes of lightning in the distance. Singing in time to our steps, we walked along at a good pace with no more stories or questions. Then, about an hour or so after we left the shelter, a terrible loud wind came up, the sky turned dark as dusk and a sick, green light spread along the horizon.

"Now we're in for it." Ushain muttered. "I don't like the looks of this. We'd better find some shelter fast."

"Where?" I asked fearfully, looking all around us. We were deep in the woods with nothing but trees in every direction and a faint little path winding between them. No use reminding Ushain that it was with her assurance that we'd left our last shelter more than an hour behind us.

The sound grew louder and I could see the wind coming, see the trees in front of us bending. They were creaking and groaning with the force of it, their branches whipping about like frenzied arms. When it reached us we were almost knocked off our feet. Right after that the rain came, not a gentle little rain but torrents of water beating down on us, hitting the ground and bouncing back up, soaking us through and instantly turning everything to mud. "Which way?" I shouted frantically over the noise.

"This path goes over a bridge. We better cross now before the water comes up and we're trapped on this side," Ushain shouted back. With that she set off at a run down the path. I did my best to keep up, trying to force my way against the wind and rain. In all my time on the road I'd never been out in such weather and here I was trapped in a place where there were no towns or villages, not even the chance of a farm house, following someone I scarcely knew.

We made our way across the bridge just in time, our feet clattering on the loose planks. As soon as we reached the other side there was a terrible roar and we turned back to see a solid wave of brown water coming toward us carrying logs and all manner of debris. It washed over the bridge and rushed on, instantly making the creek impassable. The storm must have started upstream from us to make such a rapid flood. Water began quickly spreading out and rising. There was no bridge to be seen anymore. Some of the planks had been upended in the rush of water and were swiftly floating away.

Ushain stood there shaking her head, staring silently at the place where the bridge had been. She looked almost as frightened as I felt. We could so easily have been on that bridge at the instant the water hit. "Thank You, Mother," I whispered, grateful for our momentary safety.

After a moment or two Ushain seemed to gather her wits by an act of will. "We better keep walking and see what's ahead. We won't stay any dryer by standing here." The water was beginning to rise toward our feet. I understood by the gruffness of her tone that she had no more idea than I did about where to go for shelter. I only followed her because there was nothing else to do.

As we set off the wind died back for a little bit, giving us hope. Then, with sudden renewed fury, it gathered its force again, blowing even more fiercely than before, only now it was coming from all sides, driving rain into our faces no matter which way we turned. Leaves, torn from the trees, were swirling around us along with twigs and bits of moss. The ground had turned slippery underfoot. My wet pack was becoming an agony of weight with the straps sawing into my shoulders. Peering through the rain at Ushain's hunched gray form in front of me, I saw that she appeared just as miserable. All around us I could hear the crash of falling branches. I went forward with my head bent low, expecting to be hit by one at any moment.

Suddenly, there was a terrible loud sound of ripping and tearing. I stood frozen with fear, unable to understand what was happening. Ushain turned back and leapt at me. "Move!" she shouted, grabbing my arm in a grip of iron and dragging me forward with sheer force. Together we went slipping and sliding out of the way as a giant tree came crashing down just where I had been standing. It was so close I felt the wind from its branches as it fell and twigs scratched my arm. "By the Goddess, don't you have any sense, Dancer? When a tree starts to fall you move, you get out of its way as fast as you can. I don't know what they taught you at the Temple, but they certainly didn't prepare you for life in the world. You could have gotten us both killed."

"And if you're so clever in the woods then why are we caught out here in this storm? I warned you back at the hut that we shouldn't go on." We glared furiously at each other for a moment. Then lightning flashed close by, illuminating everything in its flat eerie light.

"Come on!" she said, grabbing my arm again. "Even if you're right we can't stand out in this storm arguing like two fools about how we got here. We have to find some shelter."

I shook myself free. "You go and I'll follow. You know more about this place than I do."

Soon we were climbing up a steep slope away from the roaring creek. "Maybe...shelter...there..." Scraps of her words came back to me over the howl of the wind and the rush of the water. Before us, gray bluffs rose out of the gloomy light like a solid wall. We appeared to be headed for the base of them. Certainly we couldn't be expected to climb over them.

"I'm looking for a cave or an overhang," Ushain shouted back at me with a quick turn of her head.

I could see no hope of either. The bluff came straight down to the slope in a sheer rock face. Boulders had fallen from above and were scattered about, some of them huge. It seemed a very dangerous place to be, but then everything at that moment was dangerous. I could never have made my objections heard over the noise—and besides, what did I really know?

As I was despairing of any hope, we came around a corner of the bluff where it curved inward. Just as Ushain had said, there was a cave-sized opening right in front of us. But there were also several huge slabs of flat rock that had fallen from above and were blocking the entrance. The biggest of them was right in the middle, pinning the others in place.

We threw ourselves at it, desperate to get in, but no matter how we tried we couldn't force our way past the slabs, though it was possible to peer between them and see what appeared to be a large dry chamber on the other side. My fingers were bleeding and my breath was coming in ragged gasps. In despair, I slid down to the mud with a groan, sobbing while water poured down on my head from the ledge above. I think I had resigned myself to dying there in that wild place.

"Get up and help me," Ushain said impatiently. "We can't stay here and I can't do this alone." When I didn't respond immediately she kicked me, shouting over the storm, "Get up, I said!"

"Ushain, leave me alone. I don't care what happens. I can't go on."

"We're not going anywhere. We're staying right here. Now get on your feet, Dancer. I need your help in moving this rock."

Before she could kick me again I struggled to my feet, protesting, "There's no way we can move it."

"Here!" she said, thrusting a big branch into my reluctant hands. It had been ripped from a tree by the fury of the storm. "You go on that side, jam the pole between the rocks and pry with all your strength, using the other slab for leverage. I'll do the same on this side. Wait until I give the count." When she counted to three we both threw our weight against our poles, groaning and straining with all our might while water poured down our backs. Lightning struck close by and thunder roared all around us, shaking the ground under our feet. Nothing moved, not even an inch, though we tried again and again. "It's no use," I finally yelled to her over the noise of the storm. I was exhausted beyond hope, ready to sink down again and die right there.

"Do it again!" she shouted, adding contemptuously, "What good is a Dancer who can't even save her own life?"

Her words stung me into action. "As good as you are, Carver!" I shouted back. My anger must have given me a little added strength. The next time when she counted and I threw myself against the pole there was a torturous grinding noise and a slight shift.

"More! More!" Ushain shouted. "It's moving! We almost have it!"

"Help me, Mother!" I called out in despair and suddenly found strength I didn't even know I had. With a harsh grinding sound the slab fell outward as we both jumped to either side for safety. It did one flip forward, bounced up on its edge, spun sideways and began rolling down the hill at incredible speed. Looking like a giant wheel, it went careening noisily into trees and rocks until it came to a halt with a final resounding crash against a huge boulder down by the creek. The sound of its passage was still echoing from the slope on the other side when Ushain grabbed me in a huge hug, then quickly pushed me into the shelter of the cave.

Groaning with exhaustion and relief I slung off my pack and glanced around. The place had a high ceiling. It was as big as a good-sized room or a small hut and surprisingly dry. Before I could think of what to do next to ease my misery, Ushain was tugging on my arm. "Now help me with the next slab and then we're done."

"What for?" I shouted in exasperation.

"So we can see the storm, of course."

I was too weary to protest this madness. It was easier to help. This smaller slab had been pinned in place by the other and was not nearly so hard to move, especially with both of us pushing from the inside. It soon toppled and fell outward with a great splash. A sudden gust of wind rushed through in its place as well as more light. "There, you see, much better," Ushain said with satisfaction. I thought it had been better before but kept my silence on the matter. She was busy examining the roof of our shelter in this new light.

"Look at this!" she said with a wide sweep of her arm. "This place is a wonder, all carved by the water, or if you prefer, by the hand of the Goddess—all more intricately shaped than any human hand could possibly master."

The woman amazed me. We had barely managed to escape with our lives and yet here she was going on about the beauty of the cave as if we had just been out for a little stroll and this had been our destination all along. When I could catch my breath and look around I had to admit that it was a glorious sight. Full of wondrous subtle colors, soft shades of rust and rose and mauve and maroon, the whole ceiling had been sculpted by an ancient river whose restless movement had left complex swirls, pinnacles and spiraling ridges. But I was too cold and wet to care much about beauty or natural marvels at that moment. Before I could say anything Ushain added quickly, "Ah, I can see by your expression that you're far more concerned with warmth than beauty at the moment. A fire, that's what we need first."

The floor was littered with old dry leaves and broken branches. She gathered up piles of them and then, working with her flint, she quickly had a little fire going. Once it had become a goodly blaze she made a few mad dashes out into the storm to gather some green branches with the help of her big knife. With these and some vines and the cleverness of her quick, skilled fingers, Ushain made a frame of bent wood to dry our clothes over the fire.

I had been too paralyzed by fear and cold to be much help with any of this. Besides, she moved so fast I couldn't even think of what to do. At first she didn't seem to mind, but when the frame was finished she looked over at me and said impatiently, "Take off your wet clothes, Zaia. Undo your pack and lay your things out to dry. I can't do everything for you." The sharpness of her tone got me moving again. Soon her little frame of bent, green wood was all decorated with the bright colors of our clothes, though she made sure we left enough space clear to warm ourselves.

Steam rose from our clothes and blankets, tinted pink by the firelight. It filled the cave with a sudden warm fog. In spite of the fire I was still cold, shivering so that I could hardly stand, my teeth clacking in my jaw. Ushain pulled a large flat rock over by the fire, sat down on it and beckoned to me. "Surely the Temple can't object to our keeping each other warm in this storm," she said. There was a tone of mockery or challenge in her words. With no hesitation I sat down on the rock beside her. She wrapped her arms around me. We shivered together. Our wet, naked bodies were pressed into each other for warmth, while outside the storm roared and howled. At any other time I certainly would have felt shy sitting next to this stranger, body to body, but for that moment the elements ruled our lives and dictated our manners.

"Did you know this cave was here?" I finally asked when my teeth stopped chattering enough so I could speak again.

"No, but I know this country well and there are often caves or overhangs at the base of these limestone bluffs."

"I've never seen such a storm," I said with a slight tremor in my voice. Just then another flare of lightning filled the valley.

"Neither have I. Magnificent, isn't it? Think what a Dance you could make out of this. Thank you for helping me with that other slab so we could really see."

I would have been just as happy for the shelter of that other rock and had no wish to witness any more of nature's fury. Ushain, on the other hand, had settled herself to watch the storm as if she were attending an exciting Temple drama. Outside, the trees were bending back and forth in the fierceness of the wind as if they were no more than reeds. Water, full of rolling boulders, was rushing down the hillside to join the torrent of the creek. Repeated lightning flared over the scene with its startling brilliance. Finally, a tree was uprooted right before our eyes. With a monstrous sound it toppled and crashed in front of our cave, almost blocking the way again. I watched all this in a trance, unable to look away and desperately wanting it to stop.

At some moment Ushain reached over to touch my pendant, which was the only thing I was wearing, the one my father had given me. "May I see that?"

With some reluctance I slipped off the thong and laid the pendant in her hand. I never took it off while on the road, not even for bathing. She turned it round and round, holding it up to the light and looking at it from every angle. "A beautiful image of the Goddess as Dancer, done by very skilled hands. Someday I'll carve a full-sized figure of Her for the Temple of Kernoss." She slipped the thong back around my neck and carefully laid the little gold and silver figure in place between my breasts, lightly brushing my skin with her fingertips as she did so.

Soon after that, Ushain stood up and began clearing the floor of debris. She broke all the wood into smaller pieces, stacking them by the fire. With some of the stones she made a long oval shape and filled it with leaves. The rest of the stones she pitched out into the storm, except for a few of the largest, which she arranged against the back wall like a row of seats.

When I offered to help she shook her head. "Stay by the fire and get warm. You'd only be in my way. The energy of the storm is in me. I'm driven by restlessness and can't sit still for long." She finished her work by breaking a leafy branch from the tree that had fallen in front of our shelter and using it as a broom to sweep out the rest of the litter. Then she stood the branch against the wall as if it were a real broom and brushed off her hands. "There, a nice orderly home. Who could ask for a better shelter from the weather?" Caught by her enthusiasm, I clapped as for a grand performance and she bowed. Then she gave me a funny sideways glance. "Well, Zaia, I've done several things I'm skilled at that are useful to us both and now you must do something in return. I want you to Dance for me so that I can draw. I think I may have some dry paper at the bottom of my pack."

I stared at her in surprise. I'd never Danced naked for anyone, not even Thesali. I'd only Danced naked once before in my life, that time at the ancient Dance Court above the dry valley. She noticed the expression of distress on my face. "Come now, I didn't know Dancers were so shy and modest. I'll only look at you as an artist looks at a model. Besides, what more can I see that I haven't already seen?" More seriously she added, "It would be a great gift for me. You don't have to do a formal Temple Dance. I'd much rather you didn't. Just go through some steps. Maybe you could even stop in a pose. I'd be very grateful and Dancing might warm you even better than the fire."

I nodded and shrugged. "Alright, why not. It will serve us as entertainment in this place. I think the storm means to keep us here for a while." Besides, I owed her something. At risk of her own life she had saved me from an awful death, and I hadn't even thanked her.

While she went to fetch her drawing materials I got to my feet and began to go through the stretches that warm the body for Dancing. Soon the Dance began moving through me, gathering force and energy, reflecting the storm. After a while I lost my awareness of her watching from her stone seat, though sometimes she would ask me to stop and take a certain pose. The only music was the screeching and howling of the storm, the moaning wind and the raging water, but after a while I found myself moving to those sounds. Soon the Dance so captured me that I was startled by the sudden sound of her voice. "Come closer, Zaia. Do you think perhaps I could touch you as you move, feel the muscles under the skin? So much of my work is done by feel."

I though of objecting and then it seemed pointless. I would only end by consenting anyway, so I nodded and Danced over close to her. I could see skilled drawings in charcoal scattered about on the dirt. She reached out and ran her hands up and down my body when I came near enough. Those hands where broad and had a roughness to them from using tools. Their touch sent little chills all through me and then a rush of heat. "Go now so I can see you again at a distance," she said, pushing me away.

After that I alternated Dancing close enough to put myself within range of her touch and then whirling away again to Dance by the fire. She was right that the Dancing warmed me, but not all of that warmth was from motion. My body had its own fire. It burned each time she touched me. It was becoming harder and harder to move away again. Warning bells were going off in my head. One part of me knew perfectly well I was playing with fire, risking my pledge. Another part didn't care and had already surrendered to the wildness of night, the force of the storm, the strength of Ushain's will—as if what was happening was not my fault. I suppose I really wanted this to happen but did not want to be the one responsible. It was easier to blame Ushain or the storm.

When Ushain finally said, "Stand still so I can get both hands on you," I found myself complying as if I had no will at all in the matter. This time, as she ran her hands up and down my body, they left a trail of heat in their path. It was not the artist touching me now, it was the woman and she wanted far more from me than modeling for her drawings. I could feel the demanding hunger in her touch. When she finally thrust a hand up between my legs I melted and could hardly stand. As I slumped forward she fastened a hungry mouth on my breast and cupped my rear in both her hands, pulling me down to sit straddling her leg. We stayed locked together that way while I rocked and moaned, taking pleasure from the eager and insistent pressure of flesh on flesh.

Then she suddenly thrust me away, saying, "Let's do this thing right." That was it. That was the moment when I should have honored my pledge, when I should have said no and stopped things in their course. Instead, with no more thoughts of my pledge or the Temple, I became her willing accomplice. We rushed to the fire, grabbed our blankets, threw them over her bed of leaves and fell among them in a tangle of legs and arms.

It had been so long since my body had known any loving that my hunger was enormous. Hers was the same. We grappled with each other there, grabbing, thrusting, sucking, sliding on each other's moisture. At some moment I could feel her wet hair slapping against my naked flesh. The weight of her broad body was pressing me into our bed of leaves that crackled with each motion. With a roar, I flipped her over and fell on her so that our breasts pressed together and my open mouth covered hers, my tongue thrusting hungrily inside. At first she responded willingly, surrounding my tongue with eager lips and sucking hard. Then, not to be outdone, she rolled me back with one fierce motion and drove her hand up between my legs. I groaned and pressed my thighs hard against her fingers, wanting to draw them all inside. In passionate response I grabbed for her, needing to feel the soft dampness of her sex in my grasp. My own fingers drove inside her, reaching deeper. At just that moment lightning flared in the cave, lighting our strange struggle. Only an instant later a roar of thunder shook the ground beneath us. Our wild shouts of release joined the noises of the storm.

Then with hardly a pause we started again, only this time we went slower, looking, stroking, licking, exploring, sucking nipples, cupping rears firmly, spreading open the core of passion layer by layer with fingers and tongues, taking time to enjoy each other's bodies and revel in our own responses, feeling the fullness build and mount into an agony of pleasurable tension that spilled over again into the fierceness of the storm. Over and over again we brought each other to that place.

Finally we slowed down, panting and sweating, our bodies glued together, melting into each other's every crevice as if we were one body. When our breathing at last returned to normal Ushain said thoughtfully, "The Temple makes a hard claim on its children, or at least its Dancers on the road. If not for that, I have no doubt that Kendrin and I would still be together. To me it all seems much the same, Dancing or carving or loving, all a celebration of the Goddess in our lives. I can't think She much cares which we are doing. Why should the Temple care?" There was a bitter edge to her words.

"They say that it would distract us from our Dancing, that many short couplings would drain away our sacred energy and that a love attachment would create conflict and keep us from following our own way on the road. They say that when we take the pledge we are Hers for that time."

"They say this and they say that," she replied contemptuously, spitting out the words. "But is it Her will or the will of the Temple? Their way of keeping control even at such a distance? And what will happen now? Do you really think the Goddess will punish you for taking pleasure in the midst of Her storm? Could it not just as well be the will of the Goddess that brought us together in this way?"

Lying in my pool of guilt and pleasure, I was surprised to find that there was far more pleasure than guilt. I had broken my pledge of celibacy. I should feel dreadful. Instead, my body felt soft and languid, as if it had just been given something it very much needed and was relishing it with utmost pleasure. "Who knows?" I said lazily as I pressed up against her body. "We'll see what tomorrow brings..." After that we slept wrapped in each other's arms for warmth and comfort.

Sometime in the night I was awakened by the tap-tap of her carving mallet. That, the crackle of the fire, and the rush of the creek were the only sounds. The fury of the storm had all died away. She had lit a flare and was carving something on the cave wall. I watched for a while in silence, feeling little quivers of pleasure run up my belly as I saw how skillfully her broad strong hands moved with the tools. Then, before I could speak, I was gone again into sleep.

When I woke next it was morning and the sun was shining in through the leaves of the fallen tree, making a shifting, dappled pattern on the cave floor. Ushain had the fire going again and was folding clothes, repacking her pack. On the wall past her head I could see the rough carving of a woman's profile, a combination of my features and the features of the Goddess from my pendant. It was outlined in a circle of black soot. The slanting morning light painted it with a warm rose glow that gave it a semblance of life. All around it, sketched on the wall, were charcoal drawings of wildly Dancing figures, all leaping, turning and whirling in different directions. They were filled with such energy it seemed they might Dance right off the wall at any moment and go whirling about the cave.

"Well, do you hate me this morning?" Ushain asked when she noticed I was awake. There seemed to be real concern in her voice but there was also an edge of mockery. Actually she appeared to be quite pleased with herself.

"Not nearly as much as I should. My mind may be wrestling with the issue, but my body has no questions at all. It's full of gratitude and feeling quite content. I see the storm is all gone."

"That's the way with storms, they can cause a lot of trouble, but they never last very long."

I got up and went to stand at the edge of the cave, very conscious of her eyes on my naked back. The storm had passed, but its damage was everywhere. Tree limbs and whole trees were strewn across the slope. Some were tilted against each other at crazy angles. In places, the earth was gouged in long, jagged runnels with water still running in them. Torn green leaves carpeted the ground. The storm was over and last night's passion had gone with it. All I felt now was a kind of cool remote emptiness. I had broken my pledge of celibacy, or rather I had let Ushain do it for me, almost as if I had no will in the matter. Now what would happen? Would I still be able to Dance or would that be taken from me? Would I still hear Her voice in my head?

We ate quickly and in silence, bread that had gotten soggy in the rain, some cheese, and an apple that Ushain divided between us with her knife. Then we made ready to leave, both of us impatient to be on our way. As I moved about, I glanced at her a few times. I suppose I was hoping for some look of recognition for what we had shared. She seemed to be avoiding my eyes. On the surface she was friendly enough, underneath there was a strange distance between us, as if she had gotten what she wanted and now she was done with me. I felt some anger or perhaps more like a smoldering hurt. And yet there was nothing I could fault her with. I had been an all too willing participant. I suppose I was hoping she would spare me a kiss or a hug by morning light, but then where would that lead? Perhaps it was better this way.

With a nod to each other we hoisted our packs and set off, first having to force our way past the clutching branches of the fallen tree that blocked our shelter. It took a while to pick our way through the debris of the storm, but once we reached the path it was easier going with only an occasional fallen branch to navigate. We went mostly in silence, walking fast, each deep in our own thoughts. I had a soreness between my legs to remind me of the night. It sometimes made walking difficult, but I had no wish to share this information with my silent companion. After two hours or so of hard traveling we came back out on the road. In another hour we were in the town of Anthrin.

Within a few blocks, Ushain stopped on the street and turned to look at me with some odd, unreadable expression on her face, a mixture of sorrow and anger and longing and much more that twisted her features. "There's a Temple here where you can claim shelter. Just follow River Street to the end. I have a friend I need to find. Thank you for your company on the road, Zaia." We might as well have been casual acquaintances, strangers of the road. With no touch of farewell and no mention of what had passed between us, she turned again and walked off swiftly in the other direction, leaving me standing bewildered in the streets of Anthrin.

I didn't claim shelter at the Temple for the night. Still sore from forbidden loving, I would have felt like an impostor there. Instead I went to a tavern where they would not let me pay one cent for my keep. They said it was an honor to have a Dancer staying with them, that my presence would bring them many blessings and would also be good for trade. As I sat there—dry, warm and safe from the weather with my bed and my food assured for the next few days, I thought about Ushain and how she had used me. If she wanted tools she easily could have ridden to Anthrin, or gone by wagon, or sent someone else to fetch them. No, she had had her own purpose in coming through the woods with me. Though she could not have called down a storm, it certainly had been advantageous. In fact, it could hardly have been better planned or more useful. It was clear to me now that I was her tool of vengeance against the Temple. And in all honesty, I had to wonder if I had not used her as my tool to pry myself free from their strictures. Who knows, really, if it had been lust or revenge against the Temple or the wild energy of the storm or the loneliness of the road or because I reminded her of Kendrin whom she so sorely missed or all of those combined that had kindled her passion. One thing it had certainly not been was love. My body was satiated, but I felt a strange sort of emptiness at the core. On top of that, I felt fear. I had broken my pledge. What if the Goddess abandoned me? What if I could no longer Dance and there was only cold, endless silence in my head when

I called to her? What if...? *Hush Child. That is enough now.* As the Voice
resonated in my head I clapped my hands over my heart and felt a rush of
warmth all through my body.

*Later, I found that I wasn't at all sorry for what had happened. I was
more sorry to know that Ushain and I were going our separate ways and that
this pleasure wouldn't be repeated, just the sort of longing the Temple had
warned us against.*

*For months afterward I carried the fear that the Goddess would punish
me in some way for breaking my pledge of celibacy. As time passed and
I went from place to place, Dancing and living my life with nothing bad
happening, I began to think that the Goddess and the Temple had a somewhat different understanding about life. My only punishment seemed to
be the sense of loss and longing I was left with, the emptiness I sometimes
felt. There were moments when I thought that was punishment enough, but
mostly I enjoyed the memory. Though I wasn't very tempted to repeat it, I
didn't regret the encounter.*

*Weary from my constant wandering, I found myself longing to be still for
a while and so I headed for the city of Parth, hoping I could beg shelter at the
Temple and rest there until the road called to me again.*

CHAPTER 10

Dance Contest

T he closer I came to the city gates, the thicker the crowd grew. Finally, there was hardly room to press forward, even on foot. It seemed as if the whole countryside had emptied itself out and was pouring into the city all at once. Colorfully dressed, noisy and quarrelsome, these people seemed short-tempered and impatient at the delay. As there was no festival that I knew of at that time, at first I thought it was a market crowd I mingled with, but such a market as I had certainly never seen, even in the city of Urshameel. Of course Parth was a much larger city than Urshameel, the largest city, in fact, in that whole region.

I had planned to go to the Temple, ask for shelter and request permission to Dance there. Now I wondered if I would be able to reach the Temple at all. It would be a challenge if the crowd grew any thicker in that direction. Turning to the man next to me who was struggling with his oxen, I asked, "What is happening in the city of Parth?"

"The great Dance contest, you fool. Everyone knows that," he answered rudely. "Now if you would help me with these oxen instead of asking me witless questions then perhaps I could get there and set up my booth in time to watch."

"Of course, no trouble," I said with a grin, feeling suddenly less tired. "Can outsiders take part in this contest?"

"Whoever can Dance can take part in it. Where are you from that you know so little?"

"From Urshameel to start with and from many other places since," I answered gaily. "I have never been to Parth before today, though I have heard of the glories of its Temple."

I was wearing my road clothes, but when I moved between the oxen to coax them forward he saw my Dancer's knot and my Dancewand strapped to my pack. "But you're a Dancer yourself," he blurted out, much embarrassed. "Pardon my rudeness, Lady Dancer. I didn't know. Truly I meant no harm. I'm just cranky from struggling with these stubborn beasts in such a thick crowd. You can rest yourself and ride the rest of the way in my wagon if I can get these animals moving forward again."

"No harm done and thank you for that kind offer, but I think I can move faster on my own two feet. I wish to go pay my respects at the Temple." As soon as I had the oxen both going in the same direction I stopped to slip my Dancewand into my pack. Then I gave the man a nod and set off again with renewed energy, though I found that making my way through the crowd took considerable patience and all of my Dancer agility.

Once past the gates the crowd seemed to spread out, leaving the city streets more passable and making walking a little easier. There was no need to ask the way to the Temple. I could see it crowning the first hill. Glad to be free to move again, I walked on rapidly, my well-trained legs making the climb with ease. Though I looked around at everything, full of interest and curiosity, no one in that bustling street gave me more than a passing glance. Wearing my road clothes I was just another dirty, dusty, ragged traveler in a city full of voyagers, nothing to make heads turn and mark me as being a Dancer. I hoped that the customs were the same here as elsewhere, that a traveling Dancer could go to the Temple and beg food and a bath, and perhaps some new Dance clothes as would befit this grand occasion.

I was halfway up the hill and already dreaming of scented soap and a deep tub full of warm water, when I sensed a presence next to me. A young man was keeping pace with me, though he glanced away quickly each time I looked in his direction. When I speeded my pace he did the same. And when I slowed, he matched my step. I felt angry at being intruded upon in this way and his rudeness shocked me. Suddenly wary, I stopped and turned on him. "My name is Zaia. I am a stranger here. Do you have some reason to think you know me or is everyone in this city just rude by nature?"

He shook his head and flushed a deep red. The look of grief on his face was such that I felt myself quickly go from anger to pity. "What is it then? Why are you following me this way?" I asked more gently. "Do you really think you know me? Truly, I have never been in this city before."

He was silent for a long moment, staring down at his feet. Then, his voice ragged with pain, he burst out, "You remind me so much of my sister Neoshi. She was also a Dancer. You are very like her, in appearance and in the way you move. She would have Danced in this contest if she had not been killed on the road coming home, murdered by a gang of men, strangers in these parts. She was more than murdered, she was...People from the city came on them while they were..." He stopped speaking, unable to say those terrible words, but I heard the truth in his silence. There were tears running down his face and he was twisting his hands in front of him as if to break his fingers.

Quickly I put a steadying hand on his arm to quiet his trembling. In the midst of the crowd we stood in silence and stillness that way for a while. People had to step around us. Finally he put his hand over mine and asked, "Are you Dancing in the contest, Zaia?" There was a strange eagerness in his voice.

I nodded. "If I'm not too late."

"Then you are no doubt on your way to the Temple to seek shelter and perhaps a new Dance costume there." I nodded again, trying to understand the intensity that lay behind his words.

"I must ask you a great favor," he went on quickly. "When they brought back my sister's body they gave me her pack with her Dance costume in it, the one she would have worn today. It would be a great honor to me, and to her as well, if you would consent to wear it for the contest."

I thought of my own worn and shabby Dance clothes and how I had planned to ask at the Temple for new ones. This might be a good solution. But still, wearing a dead woman's clothes seemed to carry an obligation I might not be ready to take on. I hesitated, wanting to say no, yet the pain in his words tugged at me. Much to my surprise I found myself saying, "I would be proud to."

The young man's face broke into a sudden smile of pleasure and he embarrassed me by bowing low before me. "They are very busy at the Temple now as several of the Temple Dancers and the Dance Mistress herself are entering the contest. Though my home is small and humble compared to the Temple, it is close by. I would be glad to offer you a bath and a meal as well as the Dance costume."

Suddenly aware of my weariness, I nodded. "Show me the way," I said with a sigh. "It might feel much better to appear at the Temple already dressed and bathed than as a beggar at the gates in my dusty road clothes."

"My name is Jovin," he said simply as he reached out for my pack and shouldered it. I followed him in silence as he turned up a narrow side street and then up a cobbled path that led to the door of a small, white stone house set all around with flowers. He opened the blue door and motioned me in ahead of him. Though the inside of the house seemed cramped and narrow, I saw that the back of it opened wide into a well-kept yard with a sweeping view of the city.

"This was our grandmother Anyi's house. We grew up here. Our parents died when we were very young and she raised us. We went to live in the city of Garthain so Neoshi could Dance in the Temple there. When Anyi grew too ill to take care of herself we came back to care for her. I apprenticed to a potter and after a while we opened our own small shop. I made the pots and Neoshi did the selling. After Anyi died, Neoshi and I lived here together."

Jovin set my pack carefully on a bench and I followed him to a wooden tub on the deck outside. It was surrounded and screened by huge potted plants. Steam was rising from it. It was already filled with warm water as if he had been about to bathe himself, or as if it had been waiting for me. He poured in soaps and oils and laid out towels and a scrubbing sponge. Then he went back into the house with a strange look of joy and grief combined on his face.

When he came back he carried a shirt of flame yellow that darkened at the base of it to bright orange and a blood-red skirt that darkened at the hem to a deep red. He laid these reverently on a chair. Then he beckoned to me. With a shock I realized that he must have been his sister's dresser and that he intended to be mine. In the Temple only apprentices act as dressers for Temple Dancers. On the road I had been forced to accept whoever was willing and had able hands, though it had always been women, never a man. I hesitated for a moment, but I could sense no bad intentions there. Now that I had come this far I thought, *What harm can there be?* Having been gone from the Temple for so long, I found myself doing many things differently from the strict rules that governed our conduct there.

In a few quick gestures I stripped off my road clothes, dropped them in a pile and stepped into the hot tub, all the while trying to master my awkwardness at being naked in his presence. With gentle expert hands Jovin began to scrub my back. Then he had me lean my head back while he washed the dust from my hair. Finally, he handed me a thick towel saying, "I would like to leave you to the pleasures of the bath. You have certainly earned it, but there is not much time before the contest." He turned away as I stepped out of the tub, wrapped the towel around my naked body and dried myself. At least he had not offered to do that for me.

Next Jovin helped me into his sister's clothes, turning me this way and that while he smoothed and adjusted everything. When he was done and I was dressed to his satisfaction he gestured that I should sit in a chair. I leaned back while he brushed out my hair before expertly braided some of it in Dancer braids and leaving the rest to hang loose. He kept shaking his head. "So like her, so much like her. How is that possible? And that you would suddenly appear here today of all days..."

As he worked I puzzled over what he had told me. "Why didn't your sister live at the Temple or at least get her training there?"

"Dancing was her life, but she could not Dance for the Temple here though she was a better Dancer than any of them," he said with great bitterness. "We are poor ordinary folk, not born of rich families. Here you need to be sponsored by one of the wealthy and prominent families if you are going to be a Temple Dancer. She had to go elsewhere for her training, all the way to the city of Garthain. I can tell you that there are people here who have some angry feelings about her treatment by the Temple. Then we had to come back here because Anyi got so sick."

"If Neoshi was such a good Dancer, why would no house sponsor her?"

"Usually it is their own girls they sponsor, a daughter or a niece of the house or every once in a while a serving-girl if she has great talent, but you have to pledge your allegiance to the house as much as to the Temple or the Goddess. It is as if in some way the house owns you and you are their person. Neoshi couldn't do it. She was too outspoken, she had her ways."

"I never heard of such a thing," I said indignantly, sitting up so suddenly that my hair was pulled. "In my city those who had the talent went to the Temple to learn and were treated just alike, no matter what their family connections. My family were rich merchants and believe me I was treated just the same, no better, no worse. I had to do all the same work, no matter how distasteful, for the sake of being able to Dance. I learned to scrub floors and wash dishes just like girls from poor families. What you are saying goes against fairness and against sense as well. What does the gift of Dance have to do with the size of one's parents' purse? Talent goes where the Goddess chooses."

"Easy for you to say. You're from elsewhere. My sister is dead because she went to the city of Garthain to see if they would let her come back and Dance again for the Temple there. She went even though they had told her she could never come back if she left. Not being able to Dance, she felt as if her wings had been clipped or her legs broken. I wanted to go with her, but she said to stay here and mind the shop, that someone had to. 'I won't be gone long,' she told me. 'And when I come back I'll Dance in the contest and I'll win. Then those fools will see what they're losing.' We were twins. We had never been apart. And now...Oh, if only I had gone with her none of this would have happened." With that he began to weep again.

"Yes and you might both be dead," I said with more harshness than I had intended.

"I might as well be," he said bitterly. "Some part of me is. Some part of me died with her. When they brought back her poor mangled body I wanted to throw myself on my knife, I just lacked the courage. Things are all shadows now and have no color. We had never been apart and now my whole life stretches empty before me."

Suddenly I understood what he was telling me. "She was more than a sister to you. She was a lover as well and that is what you mourn."

He lashed out furiously at me, "How dare you say such a thing? What do you know?" Then his face suddenly crumpled with pain. "Yes," he said softly. "Yes, that is the truth of it, that was our secret. Though others might think it a terrible thing, I am not ashamed. I loved her and she loved me. She was my twin, my other half and there will never be anyone like that for me in my life again."

Bells began to ring and Jovin suddenly came back from the pit of grief that had swallowed him. "It's time to go. We don't want to be late. Your name must be entered in the roster."

"But I am not ready," I protested. "This is all happening much too fast. I have to prepare my body and my mind. Is there anywhere I can stretch and move and start to warm my muscles?"

"This way, but we only have a few minutes to spare." He led me into the small yard. For Dancing purposes the space was tiny, but it would have to do. I wondered now if I should have gone on to the Temple instead. Too late. Jovin stood in the doorway to watch, his eyes so filled with longing and hunger that it frightened me. Wondering again if I was doing the right thing, I waved him away. "This is between me and the Goddess," I told him sternly. "I need a little time alone with Her." He turned away with obvious reluctance.

As I began stretching and bending to limber my body I whispered, "Is this right, Mother? Should I Dance today in Neoshi's name?" The answer came instantly, *Dance and win!* With it came a rush of heat and power surging up my body so forcefully it threw me off balance and almost brought me to my knees. I was not sure if the answer came from the Goddess or from Neoshi herself, but it was not a command I could ignore. I had my answer. Now I had to concentrate on my breath and movement. All too soon Jovin was calling in a gentle, anxious voice, "It's time, Zaia. We must find you a place in the procession. They are gathering at the City Plaza."

The streets were even more crowded than before, with everyone moving in one direction now. Some people turned to stare at me with open-mouthed surprise. "Neoshi, back from the dead," one woman said with shocked awe. "No," Jovin said loudly. "Zaia from the city of Urshameel to Dance in her place." Now more people turned to stare. I heard the words "Zaia" and "Neoshi" and "Urshameel" echoing through the crowd. Still more people turned to look at me until I felt as if I was the focus of everyone's eyes and wondered again if this was not a mistake. As Jovin hurried me forward, people called to each other to let us pass. The way parted before us, but many reached out to touch me as I passed and it made me nervous. It was hard not to flinch away. Harder still to deal with the expectations, the sense that someone else's will was moving me about. The moments leading up to the Dance had always been under my control, starting in my own time and with a chance to connect with the Goddess. Now I felt as if I was being rushed into something that was out of my control and out of my hands.

There was a platform in the center with several richly dressed personages on it who seemed to be issuing orders and many people coming and going from it. The noise was intense and I shivered as a sudden chill of premonition went through me. Not only was I wearing a dead woman's clothes, I was wearing her mantle as well. And I was carrying all of her brother's hopes, as well as the hopes of many of the common people of this city who were angry at the Temple for not acknowledging one of their own. I, who had been raised in the Temple and thought of it as my home, would now be Dancing against the Temple on behalf of the poorer people of this city. It all seemed very strange—that I should arrive in this town at just this moment and look so much like a dead Dancer.

On the platform there was a woman in a long blue robe with green trim and next to her, a tall imposing-looking man in a purple and silver tunic with several gold chains across his chest. "Monyal, the High Priestess and Lord Korvian, Protector of the City," Jovin said in my ear as he maneuvered me up to the platform. Monyal looked down at us with obvious annoyance and said loudly, "It is too late to add any more Dancers to the roster. It is full and we are about to line up for the procession. You should have come forward long before this." At this there was a rumble of angry mutterings from the crowd around us.

"She is taking my dead sister's place and I know Neoshi's name is on that list. She registered well before she left the city."

"Her name is already crossed out. You should have done this before, Jovin. Now it's too late." Monyal sounded unyielding and very determined.

"Zaia just got here this morning from the road. She barely had time to dress. She is from the city of Urshameel and will honor the city of Parth with her Dance."

"It is against custom for one Dancer to Dance in another's place. This has never been done before."

The mutterings from the crowd grew louder and more insistent. Some even started calling out, "Let her Dance! Let her Dance! Zaia, Zaia, let her Dance!" I also heard them shouting Neoshi's name. Monyal's eyes hardened and a flush spread up Lord Korvian's face. The words of the crowd were threatening to become an angry chant.

Before things could get any worse, Lord Korvian leaned over and said something in Monyal's ear. She nodded, looking grim. Then she held up her hand for silence. It took a while for the crowd to still. Monyal spoke loud enough for those at the far corners of the plaza to hear. "Though it is very irregular, Lord Korvian agrees that we should make a special exception and let Zaia Dance in Neoshi's place. This is a way of honoring Neoshi's skill and mourning her death." Then she leaned forward and asked in a hostile voice, "Where are you from and why are you here on this day of all days?"

"My name is Zaia and I'm a Dancer from the Temple of Kernoss in the city of Urshameel. Over two years ago I took a pledge to go on the road for five years and Dance wherever I was needed. That I am in the city this morning is accidental, not intentional, unless She had a hand in it. Jovin asked me to Dance for his sister, and the Goddess let me know very clearly that I should accept." I was not sure if that last part was altogether true, but it seemed to impress Monyal. She straightened and addressed the crowd. "It is done. Zaia's name is on the roster. She will Dance in Neoshi's place." At those words a cheer went up from the crowd and the atmosphere of rising hostility seemed to ease. Lord Korvian looked pleased. He beamed at everyone, even me. I don't think he wanted to be forced into making a very unpopular decision.

The procession was indeed forming as we got there. The musicians were at the front led by a single trumpeter. A band of drumming Dancers fanned out behind them. They were followed by the Dance contestants, led by a woman Jovin told me was the Dance Mistress of the Temple. A tall, beautiful woman. No longer young, she carried herself with elegance and grace, and she radiated power. She looked like the Goddess herself walking at the head of the Dancers. "Jaidira is the best Dancer in the city or anywhere around. She won the competition last time and the time before. It's likely that this is the last event she will compete. That's the one you'll have to beat if you're going to win."

"She looks very formidable."

"She is indeed, but you are younger and probably in better shape from being on the road so long. Besides, you're wearing Neoshi's clothes. How can you lose?"

He found a place for me in the line, and the others looked at me curiously. Jaidira turned just once and I met the full force of her stare. If a look alone could decide the outcome of the contest, I had already lost. Those around me also turned to stare. I feared I would soon be besieged with questions and comments, but at just that moment the musicians started to play and words could not be heard. Anything spoken was lost in waves of sound. Then, much to my relief, the line began to move.

It was a wonderfully colorful procession that wound its way through the city streets and then headed up the steepest hill. Glancing back, I was rewarded with a magnificent view of Parth spreading out below us. Ahead of me I could see many flags and banners flying at what appeared to be the top of a hill, but when we gained the rise what I saw before me was a huge green bowl. The Dancer next to me told me it was the top of an ancient fire mountain that had burst ages before and left a shallow crater. Now it was all grassed over with the greenest grass I had ever seen. The tiers of seats had been carved directly into the black volcanic rock and rose steeply on all sides, giving an excellent view. This was by far the biggest Dance Court I had ever seen, unroofed because it was too large. The people of the city flowed up into their seats while the Dancers and musicians gathered at the edge of the grass.

When everyone had settled, the High Priestess, Monyal, walked to the center of the court and said in a loud, commanding voice, "This is not a day for gaming and wagering, so put away such things. This is a holy day dedicated to the Great Goddess Herself. Everything you do here today is in Her name." After that she turned to the Dancers. "May you all Dance your very best in Her honor." Then she intoned some holy words and poured out a libation of wine on the ground.

In spite of her clear instructions I heard the men in back of me making bets, and I even heard my own name. "I'll make a wager on that one called Zaia who's wearing Neoshi's clothes. My bet is that she wins her first round. After that I have to see if I put any more money down in that direction."

"You'd be a fool to bet on her when you've never even seen her Dance, but I'd be only too glad to take you up on it. I have no trouble taking money from a fool." They went on to argue about the sum of my worth as they moved out of hearing. It gave me a strange, prickly sensation to be wagered on that way, like being a fancy race horse or a prize hog.

Though Monyal had said this day was dedicated to the Goddess, I did not feel Her presence in the midst of all this pageantry and commotion. Nor could I find Her in the silence of my mind. This was one of those moments when She seemed as cold and distant as the stars. But I was Dancing for Neoshi and all those who mourned her death, and for now that would have to do.

Besides Jaidira, there were thirty-six Dancers competing, about half from the Temple here, a few from the city itself and the rest from other places, some far away. Because she had won the last time, the Dance Mistress would not take part in this first level of the competition, so the rest of us were divided into six groups of six. As I was to be in the fourth group I sat in a seat in the tier set aside for Dancers and watched the others, something I was seldom able to do. I must say I was not overly impressed. Some of them were quite good in places and at moments, but they didn't have the stamina and consistency to maintain that level of excellence. As I watched, I found myself feeling increasingly grateful that Melanthia had trained us so ruthlessly. During the Dance the watchers shouted, clapped, cheered and booed. They even yelled out the names of their favorites, something that had certainly never happened when I had Danced for the Goddess in other places.

The judges, meanwhile, kept up a lively, noisy discussion among themselves that sometimes seemed about to erupt into an argument. Then they would suddenly all nod to each other in agreement and call the next Dancer. I wondered how they could maintain a level of fairness if they were all from Parth, but one of the Dancers explained to me that more than half of them came from outside the city.

I avidly watched everything that was happening, and when I finally stood up to Dance I had few doubts about winning this first round. It was the next round that frightened me. We were each asked to step forward when our name was called out, along with the name of the city or Temple or house that we Danced for. When it was my turn I did not hear the voice of the Goddess in my head, either to encourage or to forbid. I called to Neoshi instead and felt her presence deep in my core—waiting and watching. We had been told to Dance a portion of the Dance we did best and I chose the Dance of the Returning Geese because although it had difficult and intricate steps, it did not demand huge exertion. I needed to save my energy for later.

Coming forward, I bowed to the judges and moved with confidence into the familiar steps. Though I knew I was Dancing well and Melanthia would have approved, there was no great joy in it. I was Dancing with mind and body only, not with heart or soul or spirit. I found myself carefully measuring what I needed to do to win and giving nothing more. It felt odd to Dance with such detachment and I wasn't sorry when I was given the signal to stop. What surprised me was the enormous cheers I got for my efforts. The strangeness of that sent shivers up my back.

Next we were all called to come out on the field together and told which steps to Dance. The others were eliminated one by one until I was the only one left standing, all alone in that huge Dance Court. I had felt Jaidira's eyes watching me intently the whole time I was Dancing, no doubt taking my measure and studying my moves, feeling for my strengths and my weaknesses. Since the Goddess was silent, I had found myself Dancing for Jaidira as well as against her, rising to the challenge. I could see that she would be a formidable opponent. Besides, not having Danced this round, she would be better rested when I came up against her. Also, she would know far more about me than I did about her. I bowed to the judges and stepped back as the next group was being called.

When that first part of the contest was over there were seven of us left, the six winners of those first contests and Jaidira. This time the judges had us Dance in pairs and, in one case, threes. They shifted us about frequently, telling us what steps to Dance, testing our strengths and weaknesses against each other while people shouted noisily for this favorite or that. I still felt confident of my own powers except for the brief moment when I Danced against Jaidira. That was where the challenge was, where the real contest remained. One by one the others were eliminated until only Jaidira and myself were left facing each other in the Dance Court. The noise of the crowd was deafening now and Monyal had to shout several times before she could make herself heard. "Rest a few minutes and catch your breath. This is the last part of the contest. The one who wins this round is the winner today and gets to take home the Golden Dancer and keep her for the next four years."

We stood staring at each other, not with hostility but with a kind of wary respect. I was trying to take Jaidira's measure. She had certainly had enough time to take mine. She would not be easy to beat. I knew that from the brief moment we had Danced opposite each other. Now she was panting, but then so was I. I was younger and perhaps stronger; she was more experienced. I had the noisy part of the crowd cheering for me, but this was her city and her Temple that she was Dancing for. Ultimately, most of these people gave her their backing as one of their own. Besides, I was more tired from having already Danced another round. I found myself wishing we were Dancing this part the next day after a good night's sleep.

The instructions from the judges surprised me. They did not ask for a specific Dance or even specific steps. Instead we were to meet at the center, bow to one another and then begin to Dance in opposition to each other, each in our own style until they chose a winner and called a halt.

This was what I had waited for, planned for, saved my energy for. This was where I would win or lose. And still I did not Dance with passion. I watched Jaidira's every move and countered it, striving to do better, Dancing with cool, skilled precision, trying to remember all of Melanthia's training and to put it to good use. We were almost a match. We started slowly, watching each other intently, move and counter-move, leap and turn, like Dancing with a mirror. Gradually the tempo increased, gained in intensity, but for me there was still no passion in it, none of the ecstatic trance that filled me and possessed me and carried me forward when I was Dancing for the Goddess. This time the Dance was not Dancing me, I was Dancing the Dance and in a very calculated way. This was a job I had been asked to do, the assignment I had accepted when I put on those clothes. I would do it to the best of my ability. My movements were all thought out and deliberate, driven by will, not joy.

At some moment, we passed close to each other and I heard myself saying, "I will beat you this time, Jaidira." Those were the first words that had passed between us. Where had that come from? What did that mean, *this time?*

Jaidira quirked an eyebrow and gave me the slightest nod of acknowledgment. "Maybe, maybe not. We shall see," she said softly. Then she smiled, a wolfish smile that said, *I will eat you alive and enjoy it. I will win again as I always do. You are nothing and I am Dance Mistress here.* Or, at least, that's what I read into her smile.

In that instant something in me shifted and a sudden rage burned up through my body—red rage. I even saw red. I had heard that spoken as a figure of speech. Now I saw it was real. Everything around me turned red as if I had blood on my eyeballs. I had never had such an experience in my life, not even when I fought the man on the road. For a moment I thought I would not be able to Dance at all since I couldn't see past that field of red. Then my vision cleared and there was indeed passion, but passion of a very different kind, a passion of anger—a passion of hate, not love. I began moving faster and faster, Dancing on the force and fury of it, countering Jaidira's every move with a terrible concentrated speed and energy.

At that moment the crowd grew louder. The sound of it became a constant, much like the roar of a river in flood or the howl of the wind in a winter storm. I sucked it into myself, Dancing on its power, using it as fuel. I was moving in a flame of fury so hot it could burn the world, a flame that left me cool, almost cold, watching each move, flowing into each space, taking lethal advantage of every opening, balancing on the sharp blade of anger that fed that fire.

I had seen the look of shocked surprise on Jaidira's face at my sudden change. When my Dancing shifted, she had been unprepared for the onslaught and was having a hard time matching my pace. I had the advantage of her surprise and I pressed it hard. My Dancing became like an attack, driving her back, commanding the space. I could see she was tiring and would not last much longer. It was just small things in her timing that someone else watching might not have noticed, but things that I saw and fed on. I was like a hawk getting ready to dive, a cat circling for the kill.

The thought suddenly burst in my head, *I will win! I have to win even if it kills me! Even if it kills her!* At that moment a very different voice in my head said, *Zaia, is that really how you want to use the Dance? To use your power? Use your body?* In that instant I stumbled. A pebble? A twig? And just that suddenly I came back to myself. I was no longer Neoshi, Dancing for vengeance. I was Zaia, abruptly drained of anger and weary beyond measure, hardly able to catch my breath, scarcely capable of moving my feet much less lifting them in the steps of the Dance. Emptied of every ounce of energy, I could hardly breathe. Colors began swimming before my eyes in great meaningless swirls. Blackness started closing in from the edges of my vision. Dizziness took hold. I staggered and might have fallen if Jaidira had not reached out at that moment to steady me.

With her strong grip on my arm my vision cleared once more. I looked at her and in that instant I saw, not an enemy, but a woman I admired, one who might even have been my friend had the world moved in a different way. Did I really want to beat her in her own city? Did it mean that much to me? Either way it didn't matter. I was done. For the moment there was no more Dance left in me. I could not have gathered my strength and gone on even if my very life depended on it. My body was trembling all over. I was gutted, emptied. "Yours," I said to her in a hoarse breathless whisper. "It is over. You have won."

Instead of being glad she was angry and pushed me away. "You threw me the contest at the end," she hissed. "Threw it away as if it were a thing of no great value or importance. How am I to think that I won fairly?"

I shook my head. "Not true, Jaidira. Neoshi possessed me. She was Dancing me into the ground without mercy. She would have won. She would have beaten you even if she had to kill me to do it. When I stumbled I became Zaia again. I suddenly felt the full weight of my weariness and could not go on. You beat me fairly." Still panting and gasping for breath, I could hardly get out the words.

Jaidira was also panting. Sweat was pouring down her face and soaking her clothes. She gave me a shrewd look. "Is that the truth? Do you swear it?"

"The truth. I swear it by the Mother." With those words her expression changed and softened, but I was not finished. "Now, tell me why you let such a talented Dancer go elsewhere for training rather than studying in her own city and Dancing for the Temple here? What a shameful waste! In Urshameel we would not think to do such a thing. We never send our gifted Dancers away."

Now her expression changed again and she looked both angry and very sad. "Because that is how it has always been done here and it took a Dancer as good as Neoshi to challenge our ways. Because I listened to those who have more power than talent. I can't help but think that if she'd been allowed to Dance here, she might still be alive today. The guilt of that is mine to carry with me for as long as I live. You're a very good Dancer, Zaia. I have never Danced so hard in all my life." With that she gave me a little smile and made a slight bow.

"Nor have I," I answered. "Thank you for the contest." I gave her a bow in return. Then I lifted my eyes to meet hers. She held my gaze and something more than words passed between us in that look—peace, forgiveness, a settling of old scores.

At that moment the Head Judge stood up to speak for the others. He intoned loudly, "We declare Jaidira, Dance Mistress of the Temple of Nuldraith, to be the winner of this year's contest." At that there was a roar of cheers and applause that was also well peppered with boos, jeers and groans. It drowned out the rest of his words.

Jaidira nodded, turned to me and said in a low voice, "Well, Dancer, you have lost, but you have also won. Now you will get what you Danced for. Come." She reached out her hand to me. Puzzled and too weary to resist, I allowed her to draw me toward the edge of the grass just as Monyal, the High Priestess, stepped into the Dance Court and came toward us. She was holding up a necklace of flowers and leaves, intricately woven together and was followed by Lord Korvian bearing the beautiful gold statue of the Dancer that flashed brightly in the late afternoon sun. When she reached us, Monyal held up the necklace as if about to put it around Jaidira's neck. She started to speak, but Jaidira quickly interrupted her, "No, put it in my hands instead. It is not really mine to wear. It is for Zaia to wear in honor of Neoshi."

Monyal looked shocked. "Is that really what you want?" she asked in surprise.

Jaidira nodded. "Yes, that is what I want."

"Are you sure? After all, you're the one who won at the end. The judges all agreed."

"Yes, Monyal, I'm very sure. And yes, I'm the one who was left standing at the end if that's what you mean. I doubt if I am the one who won. A grave wrong has been committed here. This is a beginning to setting it right." From the way they looked at one another and the tone of their voices, it felt as if this exchange was part of an old, ongoing argument between them and that these two women were close, intimate adversaries, sisters or good friends or perhaps even lovers and that somehow I had gotten myself caught in the middle of it.

Jaidira took the necklace of flowers from Monyal's hands. Turning in all directions, she held it high for everyone to see. Then in a graceful ceremonial gesture she laid it over my head and arranged it around my neck. I opened my mouth to protest, but she spoke over me, saying loudly, "This is for Zaia to wear in Neoshi's stead. She Danced better than anyone I have ever met. But Neoshi should have been the one to Dance here today. Instead she died on the road at the hands of evil men because she went to see if the Temple at Garthain would take her back. Never again will one of our Dancers find herself shut out of the Temple of Nuldraith for lack of a wealthy backer. I personally will see to it." This time the roar of cheers and applause was not tainted by boos and hisses.

Now Lord Korvian stepped forward. He looked uncertain and confused. Clearly this was not what he had expected. When he held out the statue his voice was hesitant. "This is yours, Jaidira, to keep until the next contest four years hence." I had the feeling there was a much longer formal speech to be made, but Jaidira took the statue and said quickly, "Thank you Lord Korvian, but this also is not mine to keep." Then she called to Jovin to come forward. He came with a look on his face that was such a mixture of grief and pride and anger. It made me want to cry. "I know that nothing in the world can make up for your terrible loss, but I give you this in memory of Neoshi to keep in a place of honor in your house."

Jovin stepped up and took the statue, caressing it with a look of wonder on his face. Then he mumbled, "I thank you in Neoshi's name," made a slight bow and quickly stepped back. Now the roar was deafening.

As Jaidira and I stepped out of the circle, we were quickly swept forward in a rush of people that threatened to crush us, all going in the direction of the Temple. There a grand banquet had been spread out in the Temple courtyard for all the Dancers and their families and sponsors, as well as the Priests and Priestesses and the city dignitaries—in other words, a very large number of people. I wanted more than anything at that moment to be away from people, to be alone to think and maybe reconnect with the Goddess. I wondered if She would still speak with me after my use of the Dance, which now seemed a betrayal of all my training. There was little chance of escaping from this mob of people. Since I was still shaken from my experience in the Dance Court and a little unsteady on my feet, Jovin took my arm. I allowed him to guide me.

Soon I found myself seated in a place of honor right next to Jaidira, with Jovin on the other side. The moment everyone was seated Lord Korvian raised his glass and made a lengthy toast to the most exciting Dance contest he had ever witnessed. Then Jaidira made a salute to Neoshi's spirit and after that several others made toasts to my extraordinary Dancing and to Jaidira's. Then Monyal toasted all the Dancers who had come from other places to be with us that day. And so it went, on and on and on. It seemed as if this making of toasts was going to continue forever and we were never going to eat.

Though much of this talk was in my honor, it mattered little to me. I was weary beyond belief, dazed with boredom and faint with hunger from having burned up everything I had in the Dance. Also I felt as if I had fallen into the middle of someone else's quarrel. I had been raised in the Temple—it had been my home. Today I had Danced against the Temple and for the common people of the city. It had left me confused and lonely. I didn't feel comfortable in this company, and yet I could not imagine how to extricate myself without outright rudeness. It was promising to be a very long and tiring evening. Then I glanced at Jovin and realized that he was trying to get my attention. At that moment our eyes locked in silent communication as clear as any words, and I knew what I needed to do. Closing my eyes, I let my head bob forward with all the weariness I actually felt and had been trying so hard to resist for the sake of politeness.

I heard Jaidira's startled exclamation, "Look to our Dancer. I think she's about to faint."

Jovin said quickly, "No, I think she's just very tired. It's been a long day for her and a long walk before that."

"Yes, just tired," I echoed in a dreamy voice. "Long walk, long day, never Danced so hard in my life. So sorry for my dreadful rudeness, but Jaidira has Danced me to exhaustion."

The company laughed appreciatively at that and Jaidira herself said kindly, "Perhaps you need to go rest now instead of listening to all this long-winded talk. I'm sure there would be a place for you at the Temple..."

Jovin stood up and actually interrupted, "All her things are at my house. She can rest there."

I stood up too, holding on to the table and swaying slightly on my feet. "Thank you for all your kindness. I apologize again for my rudeness, but I should go. It would not do to fall asleep with my face in my plate of food. I would disgrace my Temple. You would think the people of Urshameel had no manners."

Several of them laughed good-naturedly at that. Jaidira reached across the table, laid her hand over mine and looked me in the eye. "Thank you, Zaia, for the most challenging Dance contest I have ever taken part in. It is the last time I will Dance in it. It is for those who are younger now. And thank you for teaching us something we needed to learn. If you ever come this way again, you will always be welcome in the city of Parth and at the Temple of Nuldraith." With that she gave me a little private smile that told me she knew perfectly well we were trying to make our escape. Then she turned to Jovin. "I am more sorry than I can say for your loss. I know nothing in this world can possibly compensate, but the Golden Dancer is yours to keep. Neoshi herself would likely have won it."

Waving aside offers of a carriage ride, saying it would do me good to walk off the Dance, we finally made our escape. I left sighing and leaning heavily on Jovin's arm, but as soon as we were well out of sight I let go of it. With a nod and a wink he took my hand and we began to run down the hill, laughing breathlessly at our escape. People waved and called out to us as we passed. Jovin held up the gleaming statue like a trophy.

When we reached Jovin's neighborhood, we found that his neighbors were making ready their own feast. They had set up tables and chairs in the middle of the street with bunches of wild flowers at the center and bowls of steaming food all up and down the length of the boards. It seemed we had run away from one feast and right into another, but somehow I thought I would be more comfortable here. At the sight of us a loud cheer went up. They rushed forward to greet us and to make me welcome. Jovin set the statue in the middle of the table with a loud thump and said proudly, "She is ours to keep. She will never leave here again." They all cheered again, and for a startled moment I thought he meant me rather than the statue.

That was without doubt the jolliest meal I have ever taken part in. Wine flowed freely and many toasts were made, but they were more likely to be raucous and bawdy than long-winded and dignified. People sang and played stringed instruments and danced in the streets. They kept filling my plate with food and I kept eating, making up for my time on the road, storing up for the next long walk. Finally, with much tugging and teasing, they got me to my feet. I discovered I was not so weary after all, and soon I found myself Dancing in the street with the others while they clapped and stamped and cheered and shouted. It was wildly exhilarating, Dancing for the pure pleasure of it with no responsibilities and no expectations, but finally fatigue really did come to claim me and it was actually time for bed.

As we walked back to his house Jovin asked, "What happened today in the Dance Court? It looked as if you were winning and then suddenly you lost. Was that intentional?"

"No, it was not," I said sharply. "I have no idea what happened. I Danced my best and I lost and that is the end of it."

"I'm sorry. I was only trying to understand. It seemed as if..."

"How can I explain something I don't understand myself? What happened happened and now it's over. At least some good came of it." I nodded in the direction of the statue in his hand. "What happened to Neoshi will not likely happen in this city ever again. I don't want to talk anymore about it, not now, not ever." I especially did not want to be discussing the Dance contest with Jovin. The memory of being possessed by Neoshi's angry spirit sent shivers up my spine. Jovin ducked his head and looked hurt, almost wounded, but he said nothing more on the matter. I wondered if that was how he looked when Neoshi scolded him. I pictured her as having been self-willed and very forceful, the strong mistress in their home.

By the time I stepped over the threshold to Jovin's little house, I was stumbling with weariness, ready to lie down that very moment. But when he drew back the sleep curtain I was dismayed to see only one bed there. He saw the look on my face and said quickly, "You can have the bed. You have certainly earned it today. I will sleep on that mat over by the door."

I protested, but not for long. I was only too glad to shed my Dance clothes and the bed was so wonderfully comfortable that I actually groaned with pleasure when I sank into it. At the sound Jovin said quickly, "Let me rub your sore muscles. I always did that for my sister."

I was about to refuse and then I thought, *He has already washed my naked back. What harm can there be in this?* I nodded and tried to relax as he rubbed some fragrant oil onto my back and legs. Under his practiced hands I could feel all the aches and stresses of the day melting away. I sighed and let myself go with his touch, drifting out into a world of semi-dreams.

When at last he patted my back and gently covered me, I was not at all sure I really wanted him to stop. He had awakened some unexpected flutter of desire in me. It came alive when he kissed the back of my neck and said softly, "Sleep well, Dancer."

I whispered back, "Thank you Jovin, that felt wonderful." At the same time I lay very still, trying to give no sign of my feelings. Soon after that he blew the candle out and I heard him sighing and settling himself down for the night.

I lay awake for a while trying to quiet the sensations the touch of his hands had roused in me. When I finally slept I dreamt of a huge Dance contest with everyone in the city taking part. I Danced and Danced and Danced myself to exhaustion. Then suddenly I was Dancing with Thesali and holding her very close. Somehow we had found each other in the crowd. In the next moment it was night and we were Dancing in a Dance Court all by ourselves. And then we were naked and Dancing horizontally with the stars spinning overhead. The Goddess was laughing wildly, only she looked just like Jaidira.

I woke suddenly feeling Jovin's hands on my body and his warm body pressed up against mine. My head told me I should shout and push him away. Instead my body swelled with pleasure and turned slowly in his arms. The instant he knew I was awake, he stopped touching me. "You're not angry? I thought you would hate me. But I just had to see what you felt like. You are so like her and I miss her so. But it was inexcusable of me to take advantage..."

He was right. It was inexcusable. I silenced his words by covering his mouth with a kiss. The heat and hunger in me could not be denied any longer. I had been safe when there was no temptation, but Ushain had opened that door and now Jovin was walking through it. The kiss deepened as he ran his hands up and down my body. I felt myself falling into the voluptuous sensations. Then I suddenly drew back, afraid. "But I have never been with a man this way before."

"I understand," he whispered. "I will not try to enter. I only want to touch you and give you pleasure."

With those words I relaxed again and threw myself open to him with hardly a moment of guilt, barely a thought for breaking my pledge a second time. After what I had done today, the way I had used the Dance, this seemed of little consequence.

Jovin was very skilled at pleasuring a woman, very caring and gentle, but under the pleasurable sensations that flooded me, in some separate part of myself, I could feel the weight of his terrible sadness and his need. After I had come in a glorious burst of ecstasy, he let me touch and caress him but not to completion. "Enough," he finally said. "Time for sleep now."

Moments later I fell asleep in deep comfort with a stranger's arms wrapped tight around me.

I woke the next morning, aching all over and very confused. It took a few moments to remember where I was and all that had happened. Then I blushed furiously, the heat of it rushing up through my body. Jovin was already up, fussing at the stove. When I looked at him it was with a certain amount of embarrassment, also with a feeling of sadness and loss. I knew I was leaving. Already I could feel the loneliness of the road waiting there for me but also drawing me on. The voice I heard in my head at that moment was not the voice of the Goddess. It was Melanthia saying with her mixture of sternness and humor: *And that is why sexual encounters on the road are forbidden. It can only cause you unnecessary heartache and your attention ends up being drawn away from your real purpose.* In my head I answered, *True enough. And I don't regret any of it.*

When Jovin felt me watching him he also blushed deeply and could not meet my eyes. I quickly slipped into my own clothes, then went over and hugged him. He drew away, shaking his head and muttering, "I'm deeply ashamed and embarrassed that I behaved that way to a guest in my house."

"No need for all that. I wanted it as much as you did or, believe me, it would not have happened." He seemed to relax somewhat with those words and even started humming a little as he went about his work.

After Jovin laid out my breakfast, he took his own plate and sat down opposite me. We both ate in silence for a while, but I could tell he had something heavy on his mind. He eventually laid down his fork with a nervous clatter and said, "You could stay here for a while and rest from your time on the road. I know you are weary. I would enjoy the company, and I'm sure you could Dance at the Temple. After all that has happened, they would be glad to have you."

I could tell he was trying to speak casually and not let all his terrible grief and longing pour out on me, but I could feel it just under the surface, pulling and pulling at me. It was true that I was deeply weary from all my walking and some part of me was actually tempted, but I knew the price.

"Jovin, we have different destinies to work out. Yours is here in this city, mine is out there on the road. I can't be the sister you lost and I certainly can't be the lover you need. It's really women that I love in that way. Besides, I am pledged to the Goddess and pledged to the road, a five-year pledge of celibacy that I have broken twice now in a short time. If I stayed I could not be a Dancer here, not even if the Temple invited me. The Goddess does not speak to me here. And if I could not Dance, it would be as if someone had cut off my feet or broken my wings. I would be useless and bitter, and we would end by hating each other. Let me go with love and leave room for someone who can love you the way you need and deserve."

"Only a little while," he pleaded. "Then I promise I will send you on your way."

I was tempted again. I could actually feel myself weakening, but I knew where it would lead. I shook my head. "We would still get to this same place of parting, and then it would be even harder and more painful."

"Let me at least walk you to the start of the first hills." I shook my head again, harder this time, and stood up suddenly, pushing my chair back so hard it screeched on the floor. "No, it will be no easier to part there. Better to let me go now. Understand that I am both flattered and tempted. It is only that I can see what would come of it."

He snatched up the flame-colored Dance clothes and thrust them at me saying, "At least take these. They are certainly no use to me. They are only a cruel reminder."

I pushed them back into his arms. "No. I cannot take them. I can never Dance in those clothes again. I almost lost myself wearing them." On sudden impulse I took his face between my hands and kissed him on the mouth. "Oh Jovin, I wish I could take away your pain, but I cannot stay here in your sister's place."

"Cannot or will not?" he asked with some bitterness.

"In this case it is all the same. Please give me your blessing and let me go with love."

He sighed in resignation. Then he leaned forward and kissed me on the forehead, his eyes closed in pain. "Good roads to you, Zaia. Her blessings on you and may She keep you safe wherever you wander—always." There was a little sob in his voice and he turned away so I would not see the tears.

With a practiced gesture I swung my pack on my back. Then I walked quickly out of his house and started down the little street toward the hill, my neck aching painfully with the effort not to turn and look back.

That night, camping alone by the side of the road, I renewed my pledge of celibacy, not for the Temple, not even for the Goddess, but for myself, because I finally understood the cost of such entanglements and wanted no more of them.

After the Dance Contest in Parth, I steered clear of large cities and Dance Temples for a while, preferring to Dance in villages and small towns. People there seemed simpler and more direct. And somehow the Goddess seemed more accessible and present in such places. Sometimes there was too much pomp and pretension in the Great Cities. Ritual and ceremony there seemed to be more about form than spirit and I felt a need to reconnect with spirit.

CHAPTER 11

At the Crossroads

I stood at the crossroads, turning my map round and round, first in one direction, then the other. I had set down my pack to do this. No, this spot was definitely not on the map, no matter which way I looked at it. I sighed as I refolded the map and replaced it in my pack. I had copied my Dance map over many times when it grew too creased and worn from use. Now I wondered if I had made some error or if I had truly reached the end of mapped territory. I had not expected it so soon. I had been heading east and this would be my sign to start south, so I could eventually circle around and be heading back west toward Urshameel at the end of my pledged time.

I felt a shiver of excitement. I was tempted to go on past this invisible boundary for at least one more Dance. And why not? What could be the harm in it? I might discover something new, some information I could take back to the Temple when my time was up, a gift for the mapmakers. Perhaps I would find a wonderful city with a great Dance Temple that no one in Urshameel knew of, not even the old Temple Mother herself.

There was not even a sign on the post to say what lay ahead in any direction. Someone had chopped the sign down and then tried to burn the remains, as if in anger. Looking at it made me want to turn back, thinking some danger might lie ahead, but under the fear there was a much stronger tug of curiosity. I stood there indecisively, shifting from foot to foot. At last I decided on a toss of the coin. If the profile of the Goddess came up, I would turn back and retrace my steps until I found a road that led to the city of Chandairi. That at least was on the map. And if the coin landed Dancer-side up, I would continue walking forward into the unknown.

Having tossed the coin high in the air I watched expectantly while the shiny copper flipped over and over, flashing brightly in the sun as it came down. It landed with a soft pouf on the road, sending up a little cloud of dust. When I bent to look, there was the image of the Dancer shining in the dirt, standing on one foot, arms raised, the other foot lifted in a pose of readiness. I was glad. Somehow I was not ready to turn back just yet. Something was drawing me forward, on down the road. With no further hesitation I picked up my pack and set off.

It was early enough for the summer morning to still be cool and fresh. The excitement of adventure made my spirits soar. I began gaily singing some little scraps of song. I even played my little travel drum that had kept me company so well on this journey. My mood carried me through the early morning, but when the heat began to rise my spirits started to fall. It seemed like something more than heat or fatigue dragging at me. I had been passing mostly through farm country and had hoped to ask someone what lay ahead, but no one passed close enough. The few people I saw were far out in the fields. They didn't even wave back to me. I thought of the burnt and broken sign and began to feel a little chill of premonition.

Soon afterward I smelled smoke. Coming around a curve in the road I saw a burning farmstead ahead of me. All my fears coalesced, counseling me to go back, but I had come too far. It felt as if fate were drawing me on, even against my will. I approached warily. The buildings seemed to have been carelessly torched. Parts of the house and barn were still burning while other parts smoldered. There were dead animals, some charred and blackened, even a whole cow down on its side. Beyond the cow were bloody mounds that seemed vaguely human. I could see scraps of bright fabric quivering in the wind. The barnyard mud had been churned up by the hooves of many horses. I shivered and took a few hesitant steps forward, thinking there might be someone in need of help but also afraid that whoever had done this could still be lurking about—though the silence made that unlikely.

Before I could go very far I felt some force, almost like an invisible hand, press itself against my chest. It stopped me in my tracks. Then a voice in my head said, *Too late for this place. Go where you are needed.* The message was very clear. I backed up hastily, turned away from the scene of destruction, and set off down the road again, trying to shut from my mind whatever dreadful things had happened there. As I went on it was with a deep sense of foreboding, my gay mood from the early morning completely dissipated. Whatever lay ahead, I knew now that it would not be something new and wonderful.

When I came to the edge of the village I found the streets as deserted as the road had been, but again it seemed as if some disturbance had just occurred. Wagons and market stalls appeared to have been recently over-turned. Their contents were spilling out into the street. And there was the harsh smell of burning in the air. Seeing the empty streets sent a chill up my back, but I knew not everyone there could be dead because I could hear loud, excited voices in the distance. Trying to imagine what horrors I might find, I went reluctantly in that direction. Suddenly I heard screams. Then a terrible wailing began, mixed with angry shouts. With no more hesitation, I set off at a run toward the sounds.

It seemed as if all the people of the village were gathered at the central circle watching some dreadful living drama being enacted there. Several rough-looking men on horseback with swords flashing in their hands were patrolling the edges of the crowd. Most of them had the light skin, yellow hair and soulless pale blue eyes I associated with northerners, but others were of dark complexion and looked more like the villagers they were guarding. The armed men and villagers alike were so engrossed in what was happening before them that no one seemed to notice me. Certainly no one attempted to stop me as I squeezed between them, propelled forward by the same strange urgency that had brought me to this village in the first place. Trying to make my way to the front of the crowd, I felt invisible, even with my Dancewand in my sash.

The wailing went on and on until a man's harsh voice finally shouted, "Stop it! Enough of that cursed noise! All of you stay where you are or you'll get the same thing!"

At that the howling stopped abruptly and a momentary silence fell over the scene. Just then I reached the forward edge of the crowd and gave a gasp of shock at the sight before me. It was all there in front of my eyes, just like the dramas I'd seen enacted in the theater square in Urshameel, only they were never so violent and I was sure this one hadn't been planned and rehearsed. It was stark and harsh and I had no doubt that it was real: a broad, stocky man with a bloody sword raised in his hand and a much younger man lying at his feet, still as death and covered with blood. There was an old woman in the robes of Headwoman standing alone on the central platform, staring down in horror. I found myself instantly caught up in a storm of conflicting emotions.

The moment of silence soon ended and the sobbing began again, this time even louder than before. At that, the man turned instantly to wave his sword in a threatening gesture at the people behind him. "All of you stay back until this is over!" he roared. "Or you can have a taste of my sword and end up like Tyne." Next, he turned back to the old woman and said in a voice full of menace, "I've been standing here long enough, waiting for you to come to your senses and do what has to be done. Now I'm finished with waiting. One more time Tekla, give me the robes of office from your own hands and the token from around your neck, or you can be lying there next to your grandson who was fool enough to challenge my sword with his bare hands."

Tekla shook her head. There was no sign of fear on her face, only grief. When she answered, her voice sounded incredibly weary. "You've already killed my future, Murdock. Tyne was the only family I had left. Now he is lying there in his own blood, murdered by you for trying to protect me. I'm old. Death holds few fears for me, in fact I talk to it everyday. I care nothing for this robe and would gladly hand it over to another. But not to you, Murdock!" She raised her arm and pointed her finger straight at him. "Not to you! Especially after what you've done here today! I was chosen by my people and will only pass this on to the next person freely chosen by them."

The man she called Murdock, who seemed to be the source of all this pain and trouble, growled in anger and took another step forward. He raised his sword even higher as if he meant to finish his bloody work at that instant. But then he paused and lowered the sword slightly, seeming uncertain as to how to proceed. Tekla went on as if he hadn't taken that step and wasn't looming right in front of her, sword ready. "If you want this robe you'll have to take it from me by force. I won't willingly hand it over in front of my people. Let them witness my killing and remember you as my murderer every time you stand before them in the robe of Headman. My blood will be on it."

I couldn't see his face yet, but Murdock appeared to hesitate at her words, shifting nervously from foot to foot. It was as if this role was new to him and, in spite of his bold words, he wasn't yet sure how to play it.

A man from the back, one of the northerners by the sound of his speech, shouted, "Get on with it, Murdock! Enough of all this talk! That's not what we're here for. You said this would be quickly done." At that, there was an echo of angry mutters from some of the other swordsmen. Clearly his men were growing restless and impatient. I couldn't imagine what Murdock had promised to bring them south to this little dirt village, but this was probably not what they had been anticipating.

Glancing at the villagers around me, I could see smoldering anger under their very evident fear and confusion—see it and feel it. There was so much tension in the air that it thrummed painfully in my head and made my chest ache. If these villagers were like others I had met in my time on the road, they were independent farmers used to being in charge of their own lives. They were certainly not cattle that could safely be herded and contained that way. They were all scowling and many of them were holding pitchforks or shovels or axes gripped in their hands. Tyne's death must have been sudden and a shock. They hadn't fought back then, but I couldn't imagine they would stand still for Tekla's deliberate murder, happening right in front of them. That would likely be the spark to ignite the fire. As soon as one villager moved against these invaders, a bloody battle would ensue and there would be no stopping it. The villagers far outnumbered the intruders, but even if they were to win in the end, it would be at a frightful cost. After all, they were not trained fighters. I could see no good outcome here, only terrible disaster.

Murdock seemed oblivious to all the feelings swirling around him. Apparently he was too caught up in his own drama, the one in which he was the only person of importance, the only one that mattered. He didn't turn to answer his men or even seem to have heard them. Instead, he appeared to be gathering his resolve. Stepping over Tyne's body he reached for Tekla. She stepped back quickly and held up her hands.

Murdock shook his head in frustration. "Tekla, give over the robe and don't force me to take it! You'll give these people dangerous mistaken ideas if you make them think they can stand up against a sword. "

At that Tekla leaned forward and dropped her voice as if she were speaking just to Murdock and no one else. "Murdock, put down that sword and stop all this craziness. Do you really mean to kill me? Think on it, I've known you since before you were born, helped you into the world, fed your mouth, changed your messes and sung you to sleep. I can't say you were a wonderful child, even then. You were always surly and discontented, out of sorts with the world. Even so, you were a decent person until you went north and had your mind poisoned by madmen and barbarians. Now you've brought their ways here among us! And look at how this has affected those men of your own village who rode out with you, hoping for an exciting new life. They've done terrible things. Now they've come back to us, confused and ashamed."

Suddenly she held out both arms with her hands palm up, as if beseeching him. "Murdock, what did they do to you in the northland? What spells did they cast to twist your mind this way?" Then she dropped her arms with a sigh. "Even now, if you repent and spend this next year making reparations for harm done, then perhaps we can find forgiveness for you and a place in our hearts again."

Murdock gave a roar of rage. "You old fool! I don't want a place in your hearts! I certainly don't want forgiveness here! And I have no intention of making reparations. I want to be Headman and to use that as the beginning of my campaign. I have plans and ambitions that go far beyond the boundaries of this dusty, forgotten little place." With those words he made a wide sweep of the hand that held the sword. Those nearest to him leapt back with cries of alarm. Ignoring them he went on in a thunderous voice, "I intend to be Chief in this region and then King. I've seen how it's done by men bold enough and clever enough to make their claim. Now hand me the robes and the token of office. You can see that I'm serious." He gestured at Tyne's body.

Though he could easily have taken what he wanted by force, I sensed uncertainty under the bluster of his words. Clearly he wanted Tekla to grant him legitimacy in front of "his" people. I thought it likely that much of his fierceness was only bluff, posturing to impress his followers and frighten the villagers. Tekla's jaw was set and her face very serious when she said, "Then you must take them from my dead body because you won't have them from my hands." Though her hands shook slightly, she stood straight and firm, seeming to stare death in the face with no fear.

"I warned you, old woman!" Murdock snarled. He raised his sword again, clearly about to make his move with no further talk.

With my heart pounding wildly in my chest, I found myself leaping up on the platform next to Tekla. "Stop! Don't touch her!" I yelled, holding up my hands as if to ward him off. My voice sounded strange to my own ears. The instant before I had held no thought of doing such a thing.

The villagers instantly came to life. "A stranger!" "A Dancer!" "Where did she come from?" "Why is she here?" "Did she drop from the sky?" "Did the Goddess send her to save us?" The sound of voices swept back through the crowd like a sudden wind rushing through a field of wheat. Everyone was staring at me. Even Murdock had jumped back in surprise, though he quickly recovered. "Who are *you* to tell me to stop? An unarmed woman doesn't give orders to a man with a sword in his hand."

I shrugged and shook my head. "A sword isn't everything in the world," I told him as I drew my Dancewand from my sash and pointed it at him. He shrank back a little, giving me a look of fear mixed with rage.

At almost the same moment Tekla said wearily, "Don't do this for my sake, Dancer. If this is how the world is going to be, then I'm not at all sure I want to stay in it."

"The Goddess brought me here." I told her quickly, never taking my eyes from the sword in Murdock's hands. "I do Her bidding. Why else would I have followed a road that was off my map and with the sign burned down?" Then I turned to Murdock and said sternly, "What has happened to you? Is your soul sick? Have you no respect for the Goddess? For the women who nurtured you? For your own mother who gave you life? It was women who suckled you and women who tended your most personal needs and women who saved your tiny life a hundred times over—otherwise you wouldn't be standing here alive to speak such foolishness." In the face of his sword I tried to sound strong and confident, very sure of myself. Inside, in spite of my anger, I felt a shudder of fear.

Now Murdock turned to focus all his anger on me. "Anyone who thinks this is foolishness can talk to the end of my sword. Besides, why should I care about the Goddess? What has she done for me lately? Two years of drought and one of flood. All that work for nothing. Barely enough to stay alive. Then my land stolen by my cousins and their thieving kin. And Tekla made the judgment that allowed such an injustice.

"Besides, I'm a man. Why should I bow down before women? In the north they taught us to worship Homat, the great Sky King. Homat teaches men to take what they want with a sword, not beg the Goddess for mercy as women do. Those not brave enough or strong enough to defend what they have will fall like leaves and be trampled underfoot." Since his words grew much louder and more forceful towards the end of this little speech, it felt as if he were speaking past me to everyone assembled there.

Just then I saw another old woman pushing her way to the front of the crowd. People were hastily stepping aside to make way for her. I heard the word "mother" being murmured as she passed. Her face was drawn in deep lines of sorrow, but there was also fierceness and determination written there. When she reached Murdock she put up her hand and tugged hard on his sleeve, calling out in an anguished voice, "My son! What terrible thing have you done here?" He whirled to face her, then he looked back at Tekla, then turned to his mother again, his face a study of anger and confusion.

The old woman went on, "Cronin escaped from your men to come and tell us you raided your cousin's farm and killed everyone there. Six of your own people have died because of you, and now a seventh is lying here in his own blood. And perhaps there are even more. Please, I beg of you, set aside your quarrel. I'm speaking to you now as your Mother, the woman who brought you into this world and gave you life. Now you have blood on your hands and that blood lies heavy on my heart. Listen to me, Murdock, I have a Mother's claim on you and I'm calling it in at this moment. Before the Goddess Herself I say to you, END THIS MADNESS NOW!"

Though the woman was small, almost frail-looking, and Murdock was a big man, at that moment his face turned gray and he appeared to shrink in the face of her anger. His shoulders slumped. The wind seemed to go out of him. He even lowered his sword slightly and looked almost embarrassed. Seeing that, I had hopes for a peaceful settlement with no further bloodshed. Then a man, perhaps the same one, called out from the back again, "Enough of all this fool talk! Get on with it Murdock! Are you going to let some woman tell you what to do? Are you going to *obey your mother* or stand up and be a man? We need to get finished here. We have other things to do."

At that, Murdock shook himself as if shaking off a spell. Then he straightened his shoulders, stood up to his full height and sucked in a big breath of air. "My mother!" The word exploded out of his mouth with such forceful contempt it made me flinch. "What does that matter? What are you to me now? You have no claim on me. You're just the person who gave birth to me forty years ago, nothing more. That doesn't give you the right to talk to me like a child. What did you do for me when my cousins stole the land that should rightfully have been mine? You talked and talked. Nothing came of it. What use are women's words? Some things can only be settled with a sword. The men who ride and fight in the north have no ties to mother-sister-daughter—not even wife. They take the women they want and no one tells them what to do. They are brave and bold, free men in a wild, free country." As he spoke, he seemed to be looking past this little village into another world, a world much wider and grander than this one.

Though he appeared to enjoy wounding his mother with words, I noticed he didn't turn his sword on her. Apparently, the habit of treating women with respect was not so easy to overcome. He glanced about uneasily and I thought I could see the old ways struggling in his mind with these new ideas from the north.

As his mother went on and on, alternately demanding and pleading with him, one of the villagers at the front said impatiently, "Is there no way to be rid of this sword without using a sword?" The man looked angry enough to jump at Murdock and challenge him with his bare hands. I could feel the rage vibrating under his words.

A man directly in back of him answered, "Don't be a fool, Pavron, nothing made of flesh can stand against steel. What do you suggest?"

Hearing those words, I suddenly remembered my encounter with the man on the road. Seeing Murdock occupied with his mother, I whispered something in Tekla's ear. Tekla wrinkled her brow and shook her head vehemently. I persisted. Finally she nodded agreement, but only after I told her, "I've done this before. I know I can do it." Then I stepped forward to stand in front of Murdock.

"Murdock, I have a proposal to make you. With the consent of Tekla, and if we can get agreement from the people of this village, I'll make a bargain with you. If I can take your sword from you using no weapons of my own, then you must agree to ride away and not come back and take with you all those who want to live by the sword. On your honor, you must promise to go north and leave your own people in peace."

His men began laughing at me, especially the northerners, laughing, pointing and shouting. "That skinny little thing is going to best a man with a sword?" "Maybe she's going to use her Dancewand on him." "Don't kill her when you're done, Murdock, I might find some pleasure there."

Somehow I felt called to answer that one. "When this is over I'll make sure to arrange for a little private Dance just with you." I smiled with no friendliness. If I had fangs they would have been showing.

Murdock laughed an ugly mirthless laugh that was half mockery and half uncertainty. "And if I best you with my sword and you end up like Tyne, then what's in it for me?"

"If you can bring me down with your sword and keep me there for a count of a hundred or kill me, whichever way you choose, then you can rule here as you please, be Headman, use these people for whatever purposes you want and have them all under your orders. Tekla herself will hand you the robe."

At that there was a storm of protest from the villagers. Some might have been worried for my safety, but I thought it likely that most were afraid for their own future. I looked around for Murdock's mother, thinking she might have something to add, but she seemed to have vanished into the crowd. Tekla and I let the people talk themselves into silence. Finally Tekla said into that silence, "This young woman has put herself forward and risks her life to help us. She says she can do this. If any of you have a better idea, now is time to put it forward."

Though the villagers did considerable muttering among themselves, no one stepped forward. I took that moment to look around and try to assess this situation that I had just thrown myself into so recklessly. There were about twelve to fifteen armed men guarding the crowd, more than half from the north. They held their swords where they were visible and threatening and kept a watchful eye on the crowd. I saw how they glanced at Murdock for guidance. Clearly he was the leader there and they wouldn't make a move without his signal. In the circle there were seventy to a hundred armed and angry villagers, all visibly tense and ready. For now there was a precarious balance, but I knew it could turn to violence in an instant.

When the silence had stretched on for a while I stepped up on a bench to make myself more visible and said, "It's not as bad as it seems, not the end of the world. I am not really risking my life or your future. I'm a very good Dancer. What you will see is the Whirling Dance, usually only done for the end of harvest and the beginning of the winter storms, but today I will do it for you in mid-summer. Believe me, it is faster than any sword. I'm betting my life on it. I wouldn't do that if I weren't sure. This man will not even come near me until I'm ready to take away his weapon." I spoke very deliberately, hoping to convince the people and prod Murdock's pride and anger at the same time and with the same words. I knew that his anger would be my best ally. "Or perhaps you're afraid that my hands and my feet are better weapons than your sword?" I added with a taunting smile and a nod in his direction. It felt as if I were speaking out of both sides of my mouth at the same time.

Murdock stared at me with disbelief. His jaw was working in anger. If rage could kill, the rage in his eyes would have struck me dead where I stood. I thought he was not going to answer. Then something in his mind seemed to shift. With a sudden eager grin he shouted, "Yes! I accept! I will bring you down! After that I will be Headman here, and then I will go on to be Chief in the region. That will be only the beginning of my rise to glory. I plan on being King in this part of the world. Tekla, when I have taken down this Dancer, will you hand over the robe and token to me with your own hands? Do you pledge me that?"

"Yes, Murdock, you have my word on it," she said with a weary sigh. "If you win, I will give you whatever you want with my own hands. I will declare you Headman and even hold a ceremony in your honor." Now there was more muttering from the villagers, louder this time, as well as some protests from Murdock's men.

"And if you don't succeed, Murdock, will you leave?" I persisted. "Will you promise that on your honor? Otherwise I do not Dance with you today, and everything is as it was. Are you afraid to pledge this? What can you lose? Or do you secretly think I'm a better Dancer than you are swordsman?"

"Yes, I pledge to leave if you can take away my sword," he growled.

"Leave and not come back, Murdock?"

"Yes, yes," he said impatiently, "Leave and not come back. I pledge it on my honor."

"And your men?"

"My men will do as I tell them." Having heard some of their mutterings and seen their looks, I was not altogether sure of that, but Murdock seemed to have no question. He went on impatiently, "Now let us begin so we can be done with this soon. You have only a short while to live. I'm looking forward to this ceremony and there needs to be a good feast to go with it."

I nodded. "Agreed, let it begin. I'm getting hungry too, since I never eat before I Dance."

"Come down here where I can fight you."

"You can fight me easily enough here. For my part I plan to be Dancing, not fighting." I stood very still on the bench, facing him and holding my arms straight out from my sides, a perfect target. I was breathing deeply, trying to connect with the deep calm, the core of stillness from which the Dance grows. Instead I was battered by a tumult of feelings, waves of grief and pain and anger surging at me from the people all around and my own feelings rising in response. *Help me Mother!* I called in the silence of my head, but nothing came back, no reassuring voice, no answer from Her. I even recited the Dancer's Prayer in my head—still nothing. Well, so be it. I was on my own and there was no going back now. This was not the way I was used to Dancing, but I had been summoned. I had made my challenge and I had pledged myself to these people. I would Dance by will and training alone if spirit did not come. That would have to be enough.

Murdock was watching me intently, shifting from foot to foot again. "It's hard to run you through unarmed. I'd feel much better if you had a sword, Woman."

"But I would not," I answered instantly. "It would only get in my way, hamper my movements. What is so hard about killing me, Murdock? You've killed others who were unarmed with no concern. Besides, I'm a stranger.

You had no trouble killing those of your own people who opposed you and would have put your sword through this old woman for a few yards of cloth. Come on, I'm standing right here in front of you. What's bothering you now? I say, let the Dance begin!" And when he still would not move I added, "Besides, I am armed, better armed than you are. Are you afraid that my hands and feet will outshine your steel? Try it and see."

With a howl of rage he lunged at me, sword straight out before him and aimed right at my belly. There was a gasp of shock and a warning shout from the crowd. I was standing directly in his path. Then, at the very last minute, I wasn't there. I had leapt over his sword, landed lightly on the ground and whirled about. "You see, not as easy as you thought," I said with a mocking grin when he had spun around to face me. "Are you ready to leave now or should we play some more for these people, give them a good performance?"

His face was flushed deep red with anger now. "How did you do that? I should have had you easily."

"With the help of the Goddess and my good Dance teachers. Yes, you should have had me, but you were much too slow. This time I'll wait longer for you." He lunged at me once more. Again I waited until the last instant and suddenly was gone. I was watching his movements intently, judging, weighing, learning his responses. Each movement of his was a lesson for me, a lesson I needed to learn—and learn quickly. I saw that he handled the sword well enough, but not like one trained from childhood as I had been trained with the Dance. In truth, he seemed to be driven more by anger than skill.

This was like the man in the woods all over again, only now I was three years older, stronger, better trained and more confident. Also, I was not Dancing for myself alone. I was Dancing for the peace and freedom of this little village.

"Now I'm done with playing and I'm ready to Dance," I said abruptly, making a slight bow. With those words I suddenly leapt into motion and became like a whirling wind, twisting, spinning, twirling, now here, now there, hard for the eye to follow, a blur of moving color. This was the fastest of the Dances and, in terms of sheer exertion, the hardest. No Dance demanded swifter footwork or better balance. Spinning around him so that he had to keep turning to keep me in sight, I used my anger to fuel the Dance, feeling so full of fire I might ignite at any moment.

Confused and frustrated, Murdock was lunging in all directions, shouting curses at me. Somehow his anger was feeding mine. Remembering the young man lying dead on the ground, I couldn't help but feel some pleasure in Murdock's helpless rage. I purposely drew him away from Tyne's body. Out of the corner of my eye, I saw two women and a man slip in and carry him off. Finally Murdock stopped, panting and shaking with anger. "Stand still you coward and fight like a warrior! Fight like a man!" he shouted at me in frustration.

"But I'm neither a warrior or a man." I answered mockingly. "And I didn't even say I would fight, only that I would Dance and that I would take away your sword, which I will do in my own good time." I had stopped at some distance from him, too far away for him to suddenly lunge at me. I wanted to catch my breath and judge the condition of my opponent. He was breathing hard, much harder than I was. I caught the flicker of uncertainty in his eyes. In his plans I should already have been dead, or at least begging for mercy. By now Tekla should have been handing over the robes of office. This was probably the first time he understood that he might actually lose, that his sword might not settle everything in his favor.

"You have a strong arm, Murdock. No doubt you do very well with cutting down unarmed villagers but probably not so well with trained swordsmen. You're hopelessly clumsy against a Dancer. Do you want to lay down your sword now and surrender honorably, or do you want to push this to the very end?"

"I'll have your life," he growled at me. I had him now, hooked by his own rage, barely under control. His rage was a cord that tied him to me, a cord I could pull on as I wished. His desire to kill me hummed in the air. Things seemed red around the edges, as if blood had suddenly erupted into that space. I whirled off in the other direction and twice more came close enough that he struck at me, each time with less skill. He was tiring fast and beginning to falter. I could see that he had considerably less skill and stamina than my first opponent.

Suddenly, I was weary of it all. Weary of tormenting this man and ashamed that my own anger had so easily turned to cruelty, weary of this Dance that was not really a Dance and not really a battle, weary of this village that was brimming over with fear and grief and anger. I wanted to be gone from there, to be back on the road again, going some place where I would Dance a real Dance for people full of joy and spirit. I longed to feel the Goddess working through me again. This town was infected with fear, and this man trying to kill me was the source of the sickness. I had let that sickness into my being with my own anger. Now I wanted to be done with it—and quickly.

I stopped in the midst of my whirling, pausing on one foot, instantly materializing from spinning color into flesh again. "Look to your sword, man," I told him calmly. "You are about to lose it." I felt a strange compassion for this man who was so full of pride and high ambition. I was planning to bring him down in front of his own people. He wanted so much to impress them with his power and I was about to take that all away.

Murdock was sweating rivers, his wet tunic clinging to him like a second skin. His breath was coming hard and his eyes were bloodshot. He was ready for the fall. He snarled back, "Look to your life, Woman," but there was little energy behind his words. It was desperation, rather than strength, speaking.

I shook my head, almost with pity. His words couldn't touch me now. I was clear again, all my anger gone. Only the Dance was left, the lines of light, the ways of moving my body in relation to the movements of his body. It was time to finish this. I took a deep breath and started whirling again, but this time very close so that he had to spin harder to keep me in sight. At one moment I came close enough to tap him on the shoulder and leap back. He roared with rage and whirled around. When he struck with his arm fully extended, I had already dodged away and was in back of him. With one quick upward kick to his forearm I sent his sword spinning through the air, flashing bright and dangerous in the sun.

I watched intently. At the exact right moment I reached out with swift precision, caught the hilt in my hand and raised the sword high above my head. I could hear the roar, the villagers shouting and cheering, their power restored to them and their freedom assured, but my eyes were on the figure before me. He had turned to find me, stumbling about, blinded with sweat and rage, holding his hurt arm with his other hand.

"Stop and sit down, Murdock. It's over now. You need to catch your breath." He stumbled a few more steps and then sat down abruptly, leaning against a tree and cradling his injured arm.

"You win this time, Dancer, but I think we will meet again," he whispered hoarsely.

"Perhaps, but it will have to be in another place. You are pledged to leave here now." At the sound of my voice he started to rise again, anger overcoming his weariness.

I shook my head. "Take care, Murdock. Don't come at me again. I could have broken your arm or your leg or even your neck for that matter. I chose not to do so, not in front of your mother. Remember that I spared your life. When I first left the Temple a man attacked me in the forest, thinking to use my body against my will and I left him for dead. I'm not a killer but I can be. I would rather not be forced to do that again."

One of Murdock's men rushed forward. I turned quickly and held up my Dancewand, thinking I would need to defend myself. He threw up his hands and a look of fear crossed his face. He said quickly, "I only came to see if he was hurt and if I could help."

"Then look to him," I said wearily and turned away. The cheers and applause from the villagers went on and on. Relief was like a visible presence in the air. It was over. Suddenly everyone was in motion. There were people rushing forward to thank me, reaching out to touch me, wanting to talk to me, offering me food, clothing, gifts, lodging in their house for the night or the week or even the year, if I would honor them with my presence. I wanted nothing more than to be left alone in stillness and silence, but I smiled and nodded and tried to be gracious, absentmindedly eating food that was offered and then regretting it when my stomach rebelled. Usually I was famished after Dancing but not this time. This time I felt sickened.

Behind me I heard Murdock proclaiming loudly, "So this is not to be the beginning of a bold new story after all, only the end of a tired old one. If there's nothing here for me I'll ride north again, go where the land holds promise for bold, strong men ready to take what they want. Who will go with me?"

I had to admire the man. Even in defeat he was not defeated. Perhaps he would be a king after all, whatever that might mean. At Murdock's words there was more commotion. Three of the village men had decided to go back north with him, in spite of the loud pleas of their families. The rest of the men who had returned were choosing to stay in the village, saying they would rather make reparations than ride with Murdock again.

The youngest of them, Jandru, seemed especially contrite for what had happened. "I didn't kill any of them, I swear. I couldn't have. None of the men from here did. All the way back Murdock talked of how he'd been cheated out of his land and I believed him. I thought he just meant to confront his cousins, maybe frighten them a little. But when we got there they laughed at him. The whole family was out in the farmyard. They must have heard us coming. Orin stood there with his hands on his hips and said, 'Well Murdock, did you need to bring back an army to try and claim this land? It's not yours anymore. Tekla already decided that.' And then he laughed. They all did. With that, Murdock went wild. He was like a crazy man, shouting, 'Kill them! Burn this place! Tear it down!'

With no hesitation, the northerners did as he said. It was like a terrible madness, blood everywhere, people screaming, animals being slaughtered. It happened too fast for any of us to stop it. They killed all of them, even the children, even the baby." As he said that he started to cry, big choking sobs, bending forward with his hands over his face. At that, a young woman who looked enough like him to be his sister came and led him away. Some of the villagers seemed to feel a little sympathy for him—not me. He had been riding with Murdock for a while now. *What other terrible things had he seen and done?*

Now that everything appeared to be settled, I found myself weary beyond belief, yet too restless to sit still. I was uncomfortable with all the gratitude being heaped on me, feeling like a fraud or an impostor. It had never really been a contest. The outcome had not actually been in question, at least not in my mind. And while I was moving about, smiling and talking and eating and trying to appear at ease, I was also keeping a close eye on Murdock. I didn't totally trust the man to leave, not without trying to do some damage first. After all, he had not made that bargain in good faith. He was sure he would win and had been tricked into this mock fight by someone who knew what the odds really were. By now he might be feeling cheated and thinking of ways to get out of his pledge—or ways to get even. I thought the sight of this Dancer following him about might help facilitate a smooth departure with no further violence.

When I heard his voice raised in anger I rushed to see what was happening. I spotted Tekla hurrying from the other direction. Murdock was berating a woman with little children clinging to her skirts. She was crying and shaking her head. An older child, dry-eyed and angry, was tugging at the woman's sleeve and saying insistently, "Mother, don't let him make you cry that way."

Murdock towered over the woman. He was shouting, "Leave the children with your sister, I tell you! They'll only slow us down. We can come back for them later." Then in a softer voice he added, "When I have power, when I have proved myself, I will raise you up and make you my queen. Anything you want will be yours, Ashell."

She shook her head again, keeping her gaze down at the ground. "They're too young, Murdock, I can't leave them."

"You're my wife! I command you to come with me! Get your things ready now or leave with nothing! We ride out of here before nightfall."

Now she looked up. Though her lip was trembling, she was able to keep her voice steady. "I can't leave my children. It's out of the question. Besides, why would I want to live in a place where men are so full of hate? I would rather stay here with my own people."

He raised his hand as if to strike her and I suddenly appeared at her side as if by magic, having come up silently while Murdock was shouting. "Why would she want to go with you to that harsh place? It would be hard for any woman to live in a place where the Goddess isn't honored."

"No harder than for a man to live in a place where She is." The terrible bitterness in his voice froze my heart. It seemed far more dangerous than his clumsy sword play. That had never really threatened my life. This seemed to threaten my world—especially when some of his men began nodding in agreement.

Ashell was crying again. "Why do you have to do this? What's happened to you, Murdock? I don't understand. You were never like this before. How could I ever trust you again after what you've done?"

Murdock reached for her arm but I stepped between them. "You promised to leave peacefully. Are you going back on your word?"

"She's my wife! I have a right..."

Tekla interrupted, "Murdock! She's a person, not your property. Is that how women are treated in the north?"

Just then the man named Pavron thrust himself in front of me so that he was facing Murdock. "Leave her alone or you'll have to answer to me!" he shouted at him.

With a roar, Murdock raised both his fists. Now I was sure our fragile moment of peace would be shattered. There would be a bloody fight after all, with the villagers defending Pavron and Murdock's men coming in with swords swinging.

Before anything more could happen, a young woman sprang forward and grabbed Murdock's arm, distracting him. I was afraid he might hit her. Instead he stayed his hand, staring at her in surprise. "I'll go with you if she won't. Will you take me, Murdock? I want to see more of the world than this dreary little dung heap. *I* could be your queen."

She was so young and eager and foolish it made me want to laugh or cry—or maybe scream. With her unlined face and lovely body, she had just presented herself to him as a gift. An act of foolishness surely, but I stepped back and breathed a sigh of relief. She had just saved us from disaster, though I very much doubt that had been her intention.

Murdock stared at her for a long moment, amazement written plain on his face. Then his sullen expression changed to a grin of pleasure. "Yes, Naldeen, I'll take you with me. Why not? Since my wife has abandoned me, why shouldn't you go in her stead? My gain. You are younger and stronger and prettier by far, and I will not have to listen to her endless crying. Yes, indeed, why not? You will have all the robes and jewels my sword can win. Get your clothes and your horse ready. We are leaving this place as soon as possible." Then he spit on the ground in front of Ashell. "And you are not my wife anymore. I renounce you!" After that he turned his back on Pavron in a deliberate gesture of contempt. Ashell was standing frozen in shock, staring after him. Pavron scooped up one of the children, took Ashell's hand and quickly pulled her out of the way before Murdock could change his mind or anything else could happen.

Naldeen's mother ran out to stop her daughter, but Tekla blocked her way. "She's not a child anymore, Hadil. You don't own her and you can't really stop her, but you can make it a bitter parting. She has her own lessons to learn."

"But he will mistreat her," Hadil wailed.

Naldeen turned on her mother. "Why should I stay here and listen to your endless complaints about how badly I wash the clothes or stir the pot? If I stayed, I would just end up marrying some cowardly dog-belly like Jandru. Better to ride north and see something of the world."

"Well, well," Tekla muttered in my ear. "A lot of spirit in that one and very little sense."

Then Murdock turned to me and said boldly, "Give me back my sword, Dancer. I'll have need of it in the north country."

I could hardly believe his words. "Now I think you are truly mad, or else you take me for a total fool. Do you actually expect me to give back the sword you just tried to kill me with? No, it's mine now. I won it fairly. It came into my hands right out of the sky."

"But how will I get another?"

"I don't care if you make one or buy one, steal or beg one, or find one along the way. That matters little to me, but I tell you it will not be this one. This sword is mine now. I may even learn to use it. You say we shall meet again. Well, perhaps I will need it by then."

His anger flared up again. "How did you do that? What did you do to me? I'm a strong man, much bigger than you are. And I'm good with a sword. I should have had you easily. What kind of spell did you cast on me?"

"You can believe that if you want to, if it makes you feel better, but the truth lies in training, not magic. I've trained as a Dancer since I was ten years old, trained with sticks since I was twelve. For these last three years I've done nothing but walk and Dance. I was a formidable opponent and you mis-judged me. You saw a skinny woman in front of you and thought it would be no contest but in truth you never had a chance. I could have taken your sword much sooner, I was just waiting for the right moment to make it fall into my hands."

He gave me a menacing look. "In the north women like you are called witches. They are not kindly treated. Men there know how to deal with your kind."

"I wish I had access to witch powers," I threw back at him angrily. "It would have been much less work to Dance you down, and I wouldn't be feel-ing so tired now." I spoke with some bitterness. I felt both weary and empty, empty in a different way. Usually the emptiness I felt after Dancing was full of peace, my whole being relaxed and spent, almost in a trance. Instead I was feeling tense and sour, caught in a strange sort of soul-weariness. Talking with this man was making it worse.

As I turned to walk away he made a grab for my arm, saying threaten-ingly, "If we ever meet again, Witch, I'll..."

I whirled at him. "Don't!" I shouted, with my eyes flashing fire. "Don't ever grab at me that way again. I told you what I can do. Don't force me to it. Next time you may come away with more than your feelings hurt. Next time I'll break your arm or your leg for you and then maybe your neck."

Murdock stepped back with a snarl, but there was a flicker of fear in his eyes as well as anger. He turned away and did not look back. In less then an hour he was gone, taking ten men with him and one young woman. Pavron shook his fist at their departing backs and said angrily, "For all the harm he has done here, I'm glad to see the last of him. May his road be full of rocks. May he never pass this way again."

At that, Ashell began to weep in earnest. "Naldeen went with him instead of me. Now that he has her, he'll never come back to me."

Pavron shook his head. "Ashell, listen to what you're saying. How can you weep for such a man? It's Tyne you should weep for, dying at his grandmother's feet. Murdock has caused the death of at least eight of his own people and yet seems to feel no remorse. What kind of a man is that? Who could want him? How could you even let him touch you?"

Tekla said gently, "Ashell, the man you mourn for is long gone. The man who came back is not the same man who left for the north. It is as if an evil wind entered him there or as if he ate spirit-poison."

Pavron added, "Or perhaps this is his real self and he has kept it hidden from us all this time."

When Ashell went on shaking her head, Tekla said more sharply, "Listen to what I'm saying. You are well rid of this man and so are we all. He's a killer. As to Naldeen, she's young, hardly more than a child. She acted on impulse and will soon regret it. She has much to learn. He will not treat her kindly. He's too full of anger. I predict she'll be back before the year is up if she's not already dead by then, or trapped in that life with no escape. Pity her, don't envy her. Be glad she went in your place." Since Ashell could not seem to stop weeping, Tekla finally told Pavron to take her and the children back to their home and stay with her there until she was calmer.

As I stood watching Murdock and his men ride off I wondered if he was right and we would cross paths again. Not something I looked forward to. I didn't think him sick or crazy as some of the villagers kept saying. I wished I did. Instead I thought him different, profoundly different. He viewed the world in another way, a way that was both a puzzle and a danger—a way that threatened everything I knew. Even if I didn't meet with him again, I knew I would probably meet with others of his kind.

After Murdock was gone, there was a wide mix of feelings among the villagers—joy that they were safe, terrible grief for those who died and a strange uncomprehending sorrow for those who had left with him. They were men who had been their brothers and fathers and sons and even husbands, now suddenly turned into strangers, enemies to be feared and hated.

Some of the young people began to gather, planning to go to the raided farm to assess the damage, bury the dead, tend to the animals that were still alive and bring them back. They were very set on doing this but Tekla blocked their way, strongly advising against it. "Too soon, much too soon. How do we know if Murdock is really gone or just lying in wait, hoping to exact vengeance, thinking that is just what we are likely to do? Then we would have more dead to grieve and more of our people to bury. Hard as it may be, it's better to wait a day or so." There was some grumbling and sullen looks and a few half-hearted arguments but they knew she was right. Besides, she was the village leader. It would be hard to go against her word, especially at this moment.

People started to scatter, probably heading for the comfort of their own homes. After a while only one figure remained, unmoving. Wrapped in a gray cloak and sitting on a gray rock, Murdock's mother was hunched forward in an attitude of grief. Still as the rock she sat on, she seemed more like an ancient statue than living flesh. I walked over to her thinking to say some words of comfort. The face she turned toward me was deeply carved with sorrow, and tears were running down her creased cheeks, but her eyes, when they met mine, blazed with anger. By the slightest shake of her head she signaled me away. I left her alone with all my well-meaning words unspoken.

I wasn't sure whether to be glad or sorry I had chosen to come in this direction from the crossroads. The voice in my head had been right. I had stopped a bloody slaughter with my Dancing. Also I knew more than I did before, but it was not a great city or a wondrous Dance Temple I had found. Still, it was information of value. *What sort of people were these northerners that they could kill with no feelings of remorse? And why would anyone choose to go live among them?* I needed some answers to these questions.

Out of all the offers of shelter for the night, I accepted Tekla's. By staying with the Headwoman I did not risk offending anyone. In fact I was doing them an honor. Most of the houses in the village were long buildings of rough stone, some large enough to contain several families. They were built in several loose circles around the central meeting circle with the platform, but Tekla's house was off by itself, a small stone and wood structure at the far edge of the village. When I asked her about that she told me, "I only agreed to be Headwoman if they promised to build me my own little house away from all the fuss and commotion of family living. There was no way I could listen to everyone's needs and squabbles all day long and then in the evening as well. I needed some time alone to be able to think clearly."

Exhausted and deeply troubled by the day's events, I was very grateful for the peace and quiet of her house. I thought maybe she would want to talk about her grandson and share her grief with me, but when I offered she only shook her head. "Thank you, Dancer, but it has all been more than enough for one day."

She made our evening meal with quiet efficiency and then gave me a cup of tea. When my head began to droop over the cup, she took it out of my hands. Then she led me to my bed like a child, and I fell asleep the moment my head was down.

CHAPTER 12

Dance Lessons

My intention had been to rise early and be on my way down the road before the villagers were up and about. Instead I woke late with sunlight already streaming in the windows. I could hear Tekla moving softly around the kitchen. The cot where I had slept was just off to the side of the stove so she noticed instantly that I was awake.

"I trust you slept well, Zaia. You exhausted yourself yesterday for our sake. I didn't want to wake you, but I needed to make some food. Some of us sat up with Tyne's body last night to keep him company on his last journey and now we must eat." She didn't cry, but her eyes were red-rimmed and there was a quaver in her voice. I could see how tired she was. Her shoulders were hunched over and her wrinkled old face was set with deep lines of grief and weariness.

"So you fed me and saw me to bed yesterday evening before sitting up all night with your grandson? You are too kind, Tekla."

"Kind? You think me kind? Dancer, you saved my life yesterday, saved many lives. Actually, you saved our whole village. We would do anything for you. In fact, they are all waiting just outside to thank you."

I groaned and shook my head. "Just what I'd hoped to avoid. I had planned to slip away early this morning."

"Too late for that, I'm afraid, far too late."

"Well, I suppose I must go face them, then I can be on my way."

"Not so simple. There is something they want to ask of you."

"What would that be? I don't have it in my heart to do a Dance, not after all that's happened."

She shook her head and turned away, muttering, "No, not a Dance, more than a Dance. Best you go ask them yourself. I can't speak for them anymore. They will have to choose someone else to say their words. I have resigned, set aside the robe and token."

I raised my eyebrows and gave her a quizzical look.

She didn't meet my eyes. I could sense there was much she wasn't saying. "Yesterday you would have given your life to defend those things," I said softly.

"No! Wrong! It wasn't for a thin disk of metal and a few yards of cloth that I risked my life and faced Murdock's sword. It was so my people could have the right to choose who would lead them. There's a difference. Now go see what they want before they knock down my door with their impatient gratitude."

I shrugged, picked up my pack by a strap and went to the door. When I opened it I saw what looked like the entire village gathered in front of Tekla's house. A cheer went up at the sight of me. Then slowly they fell silent again, struck shy. It was an awkward moment. I had no idea what to say to them nor what they might want to say to me. All I knew was that I wanted to be away from there.

Since no one was speaking, I thought this might be my chance to escape. As I bent to put on my pack I felt a sudden chill and looked up to find a girl blocking the way. Sunlight shining through her hair made an aureole of reddish-golden light around her face. The girl was beautiful in her own fierce way, but her expression was hard and stiff, set in lines of determination. There was no smile of welcome there. "Lady Dancer, you can't leave yet, not before you teach me the Dance. I need to know how to do this thing. We all need to know. You can't leave us defenseless this way."

This was the same girl who had been tugging on Ashell's sleeve, telling her mother not to cry while Murdock was berating her. She could not have been more than twelve and had attracted my attention the day before with her bright red hair and bold, forthright manner, so different from the shy deference of many of the villagers. The oldest of Ashell's children, she was the only one who didn't cry when Murdock was shouting at her mother and threatening to leave again. Instead, she'd tried to comfort the others.

Equally determined, I shook my head, swung my pack onto my back and made ready to pass. "I can't stay in your village. I have to get back on the road. There are places I need to go. I should never have come here in the first place." Not a very gracious speech to people who had all assembled to thank me.

The girl was undeterred. She didn't move to let me pass. "Three days, give us three days, you owe us that much," she insisted. "How could you bring something like that here and then take it away again without sharing it? How else will I learn? I need this in my life. Murdock is a dangerous man."

"What's your name, child? I noticed that you were the only one who didn't cry when your father left."

"My father!" The words exploded out of her mouth, filled with derision and disgust. Then with a rude gesture she spit in the dust. "My name is Natchul and that one is not my father. Dougal was my father and now he is dead. Murdock found an excuse to kill him even before he went north. He said Dougal attacked him with a knife and he was only defending himself,

155

but I know the man is a liar, a liar as well as a killer. I would certainly shed no tears for him—nor he for me. And I think we are not done with him. If you don't teach me your Dance how will I be able to protect myself? To protect my mother? Should I learn to use a sword?"

"But I can't possibly teach you to Dance in three days. In the Temple we learn from the time we're little children. Even as adults we train and practice all the time."

"Then it won't be a fancy Temple Dance. It will only be a Dance of protection. Teach us all you can in three days. After that we can teach ourselves and each other."

"Natchul, if they come back with horses and swords you won't be able to stand them off with a Dance."

"I'm not a fool. I can see that clearly enough. But teach us what you can. At least we will have that much to protect ourselves."

I looked around helplessly. I was surrounded now by a circle of children who had come forward to stand near Natchul. They stayed back a little, shyly kicking in the dust, but nonetheless holding their ground and giving me furtive expectant glances from under their eyelashes. Beyond them was a circle of adults all looking at me hopefully. Now others began nodding and calling out, "Yes, teach us, teach us." "Please, Lady Dancer, teach us how to do that." "Show us how you Danced Murdock down." They sounded so much like the chorus in *The Dance of the Spring Frogs* that I had to struggle not to laugh.

Finally, with a sigh of surrender, I shrugged out of my pack and set it down on the dirt. Instantly a little boy ran forward, picked it up respectfully and hung it with care in a tree. *Well, why not?* I thought. *After all, what are three days out of a lifetime?* Perhaps that was why I had come here to this place that wasn't even on my map. "Three days then," I said sternly. "Three days and no more. That is all I have to give. But I warn you, in those three days you'll work harder than you've ever worked in your lives. You'll find yourselves begging for mercy. You'll become familiar with every muscle in your body and they will all ache. At night you'll go to bed groaning and cursing me.

"Now I need to make this clear: while I am teaching I'll give the orders and you'll do as I say. The rest of the time I'm yours to command. Three days, only that and no more, then I'm gone from here. Now make a space ready and let the Dance begin. We have no time to lose."

Tekla had been standing in her doorway, listening to all this. With a big smile on her face she beckoned me in and set some food on the table. The three who had carried Tyne's body away also came in. While we ate, the people of the village set about clearing the platform and the benches out of the central circle, filling in the fire pit and tamping down the earth. Afterward, they swept the ground with stiff brooms made of branches. In less than an hour, a crude Dance Court had been made ready and there was hardly a pebble to be seen.

When the people of the village had all eagerly gathered around me I had a moment of despair, staring at this great variety of untrained bodies. Goddess, how on earth was I to teach them to Dance the Dance that I had learned with great discipline from the time I was ten years old? At least they were hard-working farm folk and not lazy house-bound city people unaccustomed to using their bodies. I had just three days to create an effective force for the defense of this village. Not possible! I shut my eyes for a moment and said into the dark silence of my mind, *Goddess, if You brought me here for a purpose and You mean me to do this thing, please help me now.*

When I opened my eyes again and gave them all one more quick glance, I could see that nothing had improved. Well this was what I had been given to work with and I would have to make the best of it. With a shrug I opened my mouth and just let the words come as they pleased. "I don't want to be responsible for your deaths. If you find yourselves short of breath, step back and watch until you can breathe normally again. Don't push yourselves past good sense. Don't do more than you're able. Whatever you miss, the others will teach you later. It's more important to last through the three days than to show off your prowess on the first one."

It seemed as if everyone was there—from young mothers who left their babies on blankets in the shade to sleep or entertain each other, to old women like Tekla whose bodies were stiff and slow and whose movements seemed determined by will rather than ease. The one person who did not join the circle was a dark-cloaked figure who was seated on a distant bench rocking back and forth and chanting mournfully. Murdock's mother was mourning her son as if he were already dead. Aside from that, even Ashell was there and this time she didn't cry. Instead she held herself very straight and tall. Even Pavron came, though at first he looked bored, impatient and superior. Soon enough he was sweating and panting just like the rest of us. Even those of Murdock's men who had come back from the north and decided to stay in the village showed up to learn how to meet steel with the skill of the Dance, though at first they just stood back and watched as if judging my worth. They called themselves "The Returners" and seemed particularly able, perhaps because they had already learned the skill and discipline of swordplay. Of the four, Jandru was by far the most adept and eager to learn—he was also the most repentant. As I watched, my heart began to soften toward him.

I saw how the other villagers looked at the Returners, saw the wariness and hostility on their faces. These men had done terrible things, even killed people. But there was also some grudging admiration in those looks. After all, the Returners had been daring enough to go north into unknown places.

They had gone through experiences the rest of them could scarcely imagine. At first some people objected to their presence at the Dance lessons, but after the Returners all swore before Tekla an oath of loyalty to the village and promised they would never go north again they were allowed to stay. This was good because they had very valuable skills to share.

Just as I was about to start, Murdock's mother stepped out of the crowd and came to stand right in front of me, fixing me with her fierce stare. "Thank you for saving this village, Lady Dancer. And thank you for sparing my son when you could have done much worse to him. I grieve for him and I carry the shame of what he has done, but I still love him. It's a mother's lot, though I hope never to see him again in this lifetime. Now, if you will teach me, I want to learn this Dance of defense."

She startled me with her little speech. The words rang loud and clear as if they had been well rehearsed. Looking down at her small form I said the first thought that popped into my head. "Mother, it may be too hard for you." Instantly I knew that was the wrong thing to say.

Her eyes flashed with anger. "After what happened yesterday, nothing is too hard. Are you saying you won't teach me?"

I made a slight bow and said quickly, "Forgive me my hasty, thoughtless words. Of course I'll teach you."

Then it was time to begin. The first thing I had all my eager new students do was breathe together. I told them to find the core of their being in their breath, not a concept they were familiar with. Then I had them start moving by stretching in different ways until they had made acquaintance with every muscle in their bodies and each became achingly familiar. Soon there were groans and complaints. If not for the lash of pride, some might have been ready to quit. Natchul, the girl who had set all this in motion, was certainly not among them. Instead she was vibrating with impatience to move faster. I could read it clearly in her every motion. At last, unable to keep silent any longer she burst out, "When are we going to stop all this playing and really begin the Dance? We have only three days. At this rate we'll learn nothing at all."

I glared at her. "I'm the Dance Mistress here and you will do as I say. That was the promise. Stretching is all part of the Dance. It wouldn't do to have everyone lame and crippled by the second day because their bodies had not been properly made ready. The agreement was that if I stayed to teach, you would all do as I say. Natchul, if you think you can teach better, then perhaps you should be teaching and I should be learning from you." Natchul flushed and made a face, but she was silent after that, at least for a while.

At noon we ate a light meal, took a short rest and then began again. After a few stretches to warm them up, I did begin teaching them some real

Dance steps, but very slowly so they could see how the steps connected with each other and how each flowed into the next. I was teaching the Dance of the Guardians. After that I would have them do a Stick Dance. They would have a few bruises to show for it, but it would improve their skill and agility very quickly. On the last day I would teach them the Whirling Dance, much harder, but much better for confusing an enemy.

Natchul seemed to learn everything instantly as if she already knew the steps. Again I could feel the tense, insistent hum of her aggravation. She resisted saying anything for a while, biting her lip to keep silent. Finally she was unable to hold back another moment. "This might be a lovely salute to morning, but how could we ever use this to bring down an armed enemy?"

I groaned. That was enough. It was time for a very different kind of lesson. "Pick up a stick," I said sharply. She did as I told her, looking a little worried now that the others had all stopped to watch and she was the center of everyone's attention. "Now attack me with it." She shook her head. "Do as I say," I commanded. When she still didn't move I shouted, "Now!"

"If you say so," she growled. With that she ran at me with the stick raised to strike, ready to put all her rage and grief and frustration into that one blow. I moved in front of her with deliberate slowness using the steps I had just been teaching. At the last minute she found herself flat on her back, gasping for breath. The stick was in my hands.

"When you can do that, then you'll be ready to teach the rest of them. Until then, leave the teaching to me. Those were the very steps I've been teaching you, just a little faster." Then I turned to the others. "Did you notice how I used her force and her speed against her? In this next day or so you will learn how to do that. Thank you for this demonstration, Natchul." I gave her a nod and a grin, then reached out my hand to help her up. Ignoring my hand, she got to her feet on her own, dusted herself off and glared at me. I stared right back at her. There was total silence from everyone watching. When she finally shrugged and gave me an answering grin, I said, "You're very good at this, Natchul. Soon enough you'll be teaching others. But first, have a little patience with my ways and learn all you can while you have the chance." Then I bowed to her and added very seriously, "To a great future Dancer."

She bowed back and said with equal seriousness, "To my teacher." Natchul gave me no more trouble after that. In fact she quickly became my best and most attentive student.

I worked them hard for the rest of the afternoon and was quite pleased with their progress. They were doing far better than I could have expected. They had learned how to shift their bodies quickly to counter each other's moves, how to fall, roll away and be on their feet again instantly, how to use their hands and feet, arms and legs in ways that were totally new to them, how to control their breathing and how to keep a constant watchful eye on their opponent. Soon I would have to see how they did with sticks.

As soon as the day's lessons were over some of the villagers gathered to go to Orin's farm and bury the dead. This time Tekla made no objection, assuming that Murdock was already well on his way north. After a shared meal, the remaining villagers were planning to bury Tyne and do a ritual to see him on his way. I was not sure if I was expected to attend the burial and was just looking to Tekla for advice when Natchul grabbed my arm and tugged on it. "Zaia, stay and work with me," she begged. "There's no need for you to be at the burial. Please!"

"But what about you? Out of respect for Tyne?"

"We can do this out of respect for Tyne. He died for us. In his name we can learn how to stay alive. He would be proud of us. Besides you are only here for this short while and I can put a rock and flowers on his grave later." This girl was certainly very persuasive. She had an iron will. As she grew older, if she survived, she would no doubt be a power to be reckoned with. I glanced at Tekla. She gave me a shrug and a weary nod. "Why not?" she said, her voice thick with grief as she walked away.

And so, to the wails of mourning and the rhythm of the death chant, Natchul and I began again to move in the steps of the Dance, only much faster this time. Turn and strike and kick and move in and whirl about and dart away again. We were moving faster and faster and she was matching me move for move, watching me intently with bright unblinking eyes. I had to keep reminding her to breathe, showing her again how the breath was part of the Dance, the very source of it.

Now, instead of opposing me, she hung on my every word, eager to do exactly what I told her. I thought wistfully what Melanthia could make of such raw talent, such passion. In her skilled hands Natchul would be a Dancer in no time, one of the best, as eager and hard-working as I had been. But now was not the time for such things. These people could not afford the luxury of a Dancer. This girl would be their defender. I was training the child to be a fighter, not a Dancer.

After a while we were both sweating profusely and I was actually panting harder than Natchul. "Fast enough for you?" I said through my teeth as we whirled again to face each other. She only nodded, her eyes glowing with excitement, her teeth gleaming in a big grin against her dusty face. She seemed to know just what to do and how to move, as if the information had just been stored in her body all these years. It was like seeing myself all over again, the way I was when I first came to the Temple.

Finally, with a groan, I sank to the ground. She stopped instantly with a look of concern, almost fright, on her face. "Did I...? Are you...?"

I shook my head, grabbed her wrist and pulled her down next to me. "No, Natchul, you're very good for someone just beginning, good—but not that good. It will be a while before you can bring me down that way. It is exhaustion that felled me. I am only human. Even a Dancer has her limits. After all, I have been at this the whole day. And the day before I Danced against Murdock."

Her face suddenly flushed and she mumbled, "I'm sorry I was so rude today. Now I'm ashamed of myself. It was only that I was so eager to..."

"Yes, yes, no need to apologize. I understand, only do not interrupt that way again. I must be allowed to proceed in my own way. In the Dance Temple that would have earned you a good scolding—or worse."

"Tell me about the Temple please." Her eyes were glowing with eagerness again. This child was certainly hard to resist. And so for the rest of the time until the others returned I told her stories of the Temple and of my time on the road.

When I heard the rest of the villagers coming back from their sad task, I leapt to my feet and went to get Murdock's sword. I had hidden it under the cot in Tekla's house. As they all gathered I held the sword high and Tekla signaled for silence. She and I had already consulted on this. I turned toward Jandru. "Next to Natchul, you are the one most skilled at the Dance and you know already how to handle a sword. You're the one who should have this. It is certainly no use to me."

"No, no, not me!" he said quickly, stepping back and putting up his hands as if to ward it off. "I have pledged never to use a sword again. I have seen first hand the harm it can do. I even tried to break my own sword with a big rock before I threw it in the river."

"Jandru, you will have to unmake that pledge for the sake of your people. I don't believe you've seen the last of Murdock. I think he'll be back. If not, there may be others like him who are just as bad or worse. You need to be able to defend yourselves. Not only must you take this sword, but you and the others who went north with Murdock must teach these people how to use swords, even if at first they just start by learning with sticks."

Jandru's face looked stricken. He was still shaking his head but he glanced at Tekla. Even without her signs of office she was still the leader there. Tekla nodded. "What she says is true. Things are happening now that we could not have imagined just a short while ago. Everything is changing and we must change or die. For myself, I'm not sure which I prefer, but I'm old and my life is finished. Many of you have your whole lives ahead of you. Take the sword, Jandru. Whether or not you would wish it to be that way, you have a job to do. And perhaps you're the best one for it because you're reluctant, rather than eager."

Murdock's mother, whose name I later discovered was Balyan, had joined the circle. Now she came to stand next to Tekla and said decisively, "You're the right one to have it, Jandru. Perhaps some of the harm done can be repaired by using it in the defense of your village."

Jandru nodded as if Balyan's words had decided for him, as if her approval made it possible for him to hold a sword again. When he stepped forward to take it there were tears in his eyes and his hand was shaking. "You have no idea the things I've seen," he told us with grief choking his voice. "You have no idea what swords can do."

There was a chorus of rising voices. Tekla raised her hand for silence again. "While we are all gathered together here and not Dancing or eating, it's time to take care of some unfinished business. I'm not Headwoman anymore. I can't carry that burden any further down the road. You must choose a new Head as soon as possible, tonight if you can. It's too dangerous to leave that place unfilled. I know it is your choice to make, but I would like to put Jandru forward because he knows best what we are facing and can help us prepare for it." There were many nods and voices raised in agreement but also some loud opposition. Jandru was shaking his head furiously. Pavron was looking like a thundercloud. I suppose he had expected to be chosen. In a voice husky with anger, he muttered, "I think I'm better suited for that post and know far more about how things are done here than some young fool who ran off to the north with Murdock."

Jandru's expression changed. He didn't look so frightened any more. "What Pavron says is true. Day to day he is far more capable than I am. Do it with me," he said turning to Pavron. "We can share the burden and consult with each other. Right now it's too much for one person alone. I can work on defense and you can keep the village running smoothly through the seasons. That's the only way I'll accept, if we can do this together."

Pavron shook his head, still glowering. He was shifting from foot to foot, muttering angrily, "Never been done that way before... No way could I work with that young fool..."

Ashell came up and put a hand on his arm. "Do it, Pavron. It's the best solution." He hesitated, looked around at the others and saw their nods of approval. Then he turned to Ashell and a sudden smile lit up his face, making him look much less threatening. "I'll do it for you," he said, taking her hand. "Why not? Might as well. No real harm in it."

Jandru gave Tekla a questioning look, still needing her approval. Tekla shrugged, looking thoughtful. "We have never done such a thing before, never that I know of, but these are new times and new times require new solutions. If you both are willing. Do any stand against it?"

This time there were cheers from the villagers and much waving of hands. When no one spoke against it, Tekla went into her house and came back with the robe and the token. She made both men stand in front of her. Her hands shook and there were tears in her eyes as she put the robe on Pavron and the chain with the token around Jandru's neck. "By the will of this village, I, Tekla, daughter of Madra, daughter of Adaila, pass on to you the responsibilities that have been mine for these past many years. May you carry them well. May you not be overly burdened. May you work together using all the skill and wisdom you each possess." Then she put a hand on each of their heads and kissed their cheeks. "Now you are both the Headmen of the Village of Avrin." It was the first time since coming there in the midst of that violence that I heard the name of the village spoken aloud.

Afterward the other villagers all crowded around, congratulating the new Headmen, hugging them, clapping them on the back. Jandru looked a little stunned and dazed, but in a short while he was talking with Pavron and three or four others about the best way to get more swords. "There's no metal here but perhaps we can collect all the pots that need mending, those that are very dented and full of holes. We can take them to the village of Rashlin where they work in metal and see if they will make us swords in trade for some of our best pottery plates and bowls. Besides, we need to let other villages in the valley know what is happening. Perhaps someone should even ride to the city of Morainsha with word of things in the north." Others came crowding around to make suggestions. Watching how easily he worked with people, weaving a web of agreement among them, I thought, *Maybe Jandru will make an alliance for defense between the villages along the valley and the nearest cities. Maybe this reluctant Headman is the one who will become the chief in this region because it is nothing he wants for himself.* Tekla was right, things were changing. Something new was happening in the world, certainly nothing I would have chosen or could have predicted.

Later, those who had gone to the farm to bury the dead came back in a strange, sad little procession, leading some cows and a few horses. Their faces were pinched with pain and their eyes glazed in shock. One of them grabbed Tekla's arm. "It was terrible, worse than you can possibly imagine. We should never have let Murdock leave here alive!"

"We hardly had a choice," Tekla said dryly. "If not for this Dancer's skill and courage and very timely arrival many more of us might have ended that way." Then others crowded around them asking questions. Soon they all moved off to put the animals out to pasture, and I didn't hear any more.

The next morning, after lessons in breathing and some stretches, we started all over again, moving faster and working harder. This time, when Balyan joined us, I was surprised at how quick and agile she was in spite of her age. By that afternoon I had all of them working in pairs, some using sticks, others just hands and feet and bodies. By that evening they all had skinned knuckles and a decorative rash of bruises, even Tekla and Balyan, but they were visibly improving, their movements more fluid, their kicks and punches more forceful and decisive. I was the one who had to call a halt. Almost giddy with pride and excitement, they would have gone on until they dropped—or I did.

That evening as we ate around big common tables set up in the Dance circle I found myself sitting next to Natchul, or rather she wormed her way in beside me. She kept looking up at me proudly as if I were her new pet or her prized belonging. When there was enough conversation going on around us to mask my words I asked her, "Why did Murdock kill Dougal? What was the real reason?" I had been wondering about that ever since she told me.

"I don't know why Murdock was so angry and jealous and hated Dougal so. After all, my mother chose to live with Murdock, though it's hard for me to imagine why. He was always ambitious and hard-working, I'll give him that, but certainly never very kind. She said Dougal was too much of a dreamer, a free man and a wanderer. How could she ever hope to raise children with such a man? But Dougal was good and kind even if he was restless. He would have taken me with him the next time he went on the road. He had promised me that. And then Murdock left anyhow, so what did my mother have after all? Three little children clinging to her skirts that now she's raising all alone. It's clear Murdock cares nothing for them. I think maybe Dougal was flirting with her and that enraged Murdock. He had a bad temper. I know. I was often enough on the other end of it. But Dougal flirted with all the women. It didn't mean anything, it was just his way. No need to kill him for that. I know Dougal never went at Murdock with a knife. It was all a big lie! I think that's why Murdock went north after that. Too many people didn't believe him and they blamed him for Dougal's death."

Natchul told me all this as casually as if she was just telling me some old village gossip that had little to do with her, as if this was not the story of her own family. But just under the surface I could feel the hum of her terrible grief for Dougal and her burning rage at Murdock, feelings almost too great for a child to contain, feelings that she had been pouring into the Dance.

Our last day! Everything went smoothly at the beginning. People moved into position, ready to start. They seemed to know what to do. After breathing and stretching I worked them in pairs again, attacking and repelling attacks, moves and counter-moves, back and forth. It amazed me how skilled they had become in such a short while and I told them so several times. Even the children had learned quickly, far more quickly than new girls at the Temple. Fear is a harsh teacher. The shadow of Murdock lay heavy over the village of Avrin. Even Melanthia never drove us that hard.

When we stopped for lunch I was assuming that things would run just as well for the rest of the day and I would have no more trouble with anyone. Then a young man named Dardrin stood up suddenly, turned to look at us all and said in a challenging tone, "I'm done with this foolishness. If you really think this Dancing will protect you from what's coming then you're all fools. This is child's play, good for women and children. I'm a man and a man needs a sword. Best to give me Murdock's sword, Jandru. I am going to find him, join his men and go north with them. I was an idiot not to leave when he did. If these northerners are coming as surely as the rain and if they are as powerful as everyone says, I might as well join them, learn their ways and get some profit from it, rather than staying here to be killed by them like sheep in the pasture—which is what will happen to the rest of you, no matter how well you Dance."

This was followed by a storm of shouted arguments, everyone hoping to be the one who persuaded him to change his mind. I could tell that was not about to happen, he had already decided. Tearfully his mother and sisters pleaded with him. His father shouted that he was the fool. Dardrin kept shaking his head. By now the villagers sounded like a pack of barking dogs. He shouted back at them that they were all fools. "I'll go to find some glory in a place better than this little dirt pile, somewhere far from here. Naldeen was right. There's a bigger world out there and Murdock knows the way."

Full of anger, his father finally said, "If you change your mind and decide you don't like it out there, don't come back here. The door of forgiveness is closed. You have been warned. Now go without our blessing. You go to do evil work."

Dardrin ignored his father's threat and did not even look at his weeping mother. "The sword," he said again, coming right up to Jandru in a threatening manner. "I need Murdock's sword." Perhaps he thought to gain some advantage with Murdock by returning his sword.

Jandru stood up and faced him. "It's not Murdock's sword any longer. Zaia won it fairly and she passed it on to me. I am not handing it to you to do Murdock's work. You can leave without it or you can stay, but you cannot take it with you."

Pavron burst out, "But how can we let him go? He will inform Murdock of everything we're doing here."

"And maybe that's for the best," Tekla said. "Maybe Murdock will see that it won't be so easy to come back here and take over our lives. Besides, how can we stop Dardrin? Since we can't persuade him and we have certainly tried, I see only two other courses open to us if we want to keep him from leaving. We can kill him where he stands, or we can hold him in chains. And I don't think we have come to that place yet, at least I hope not."

As Tekla was speaking I saw Dardrin make a dash for his horse. Then I noticed the horse was already saddled and bridled. There were packs hanging from the saddle loops. So he had planned for departure well ahead of time and had just stayed in hopes of getting the sword from Jandru. With everyone shouting for him to stop he vaulted into the saddle, flung some curses at the rest of us, kicked the horse hard and was galloping down the road before anyone else could mount. There were some who wanted to give chase, but Tekla shook her head and Pavron said loudly, "No use. Tekla is right. The only way we could keep him here would be as our prisoner and that would hurt us far more than letting him go."

Dardrin's mother and sister were wailing as if for the dead and his father was staring after him, stony-faced, standing still as a statue with tears running down his cheeks. I had planned on teaching them the whirling Dance that afternoon, but Dardrin's sudden departure had thrown a pall over the village almost as if someone had just died. It felt as if a storm had passed through, leaving devastation and despair in its wake. People spoke in low voices and moved about listlessly. I could feel their hopelessness infecting me and thought this might be as good a time as any to take my leave, since we would accomplish nothing more that afternoon. I was just plotting my escape when Jandru and Pavron beckoned me over. I had noticed them in earnest conversation with each other and thought this a good sign for the future of the village. We held a quick conference and I nodded my consent. "If you can get them to agree willingly. I'm not about to coerce agreement."

"We'll do what we can," Pavron said. Then he stood up, walked into the crowd and clapped for attention. "As your newly chosen Headmen, we urge you to be back in the practice circle as quickly as possible."

Jandru came to stand beside him. "We understand your shock and grief at Dardrin's departure, but you will have all the time you need to mourn for him later."

"Right now time is running out. We have only this last afternoon left to take advantage of Zaia's teaching."

"After that she is gone and we are on our own."

To my surprise people actually began assembling in the practice circle, not with much enthusiasm, but at least they were moving again. When they had all gathered I told them, "This will be something new, the Whirling Dance. With this you can seem to be in two places at once, or three or four. Your opponent will have a hard time knowing where you are or being able to reach you."

I Danced them hard that afternoon, hard and fast until finally Tekla shouted, "Enough!" and dropped down to the ground. One by one they dropped down around her, panting and gasping for breath and laughing. The Dance had broken the spell of gloom cast by Dardrin's defection, but looking around at them all I wondered if perhaps he was right and this had all been a mistake. If invasion from the north was inevitable then maybe it was better to join them or to surrender peaceably and at least stay alive. Then I pictured these strong, independent people having their lives run by men such as Murdock. I thought if that was the future, it might be better to die fighting beside your friends and loved ones than to live in such a world. *Not Yet!* the voice in my head said clear as a bell, *Not Yet!*

I raised my hands for silence. "You have all done incredibly well, better than I could possibly have imagined. To keep what you have you must practice every day, at least for an hour or so. Natchul can lead you almost as well as I could. Jandru can train you in the use of the sword. Now I have done all I can do here. I need to go wash off this dust and rest in the shade for a while."

That night they made a feast in my honor. As if by common agreement, we did not talk about Tyne's death or Dardrin's departure or Murdock or the men from the north, though their shadows hung heavy over us all. Instead we ate and laughed and chatted, sharing tales of our lives. They were very curious about the world out there and wanted to hear about the Temple and the city and my time on the road. They pushed me into telling story after story. In turn, I wanted to hear more about their village, since country life still seemed mysterious, almost as foreign to me as the city was to them. Afterward instruments were brought out and people sang. It was the first time I had heard these people make music for pleasure.

Clearly they were accustomed to singing together. Some of their voices were very sweet and clear, others deep and resonant. Ashell sang a song with her sister. Then she and Natchul sang together, their voices weaving through and around each other's in a lovely harmony. When they finished I smiled to see Natchul leaning back against her mother and Pavron, on the other side of Ashell, with his arm around her shoulders. Perhaps this time she would find a better protector than Murdock. The rest of her children were asleep on a blanket on the grass. After a while, others either spread out their blankets beside them or slipped away to their houses.

By the time I crossed Tekla's threshold I was staggering with fatigue. I dropped into bed exhausted, feeling as if I had used up all my strength. I thought I would fall asleep instantly. Instead I tossed about restlessly, my body aching and my mind in turmoil with all that had happened and what it might mean for the future. When I finally slept, I fell into ugly dreams of cities burning and vast numbers of armed men clashing with each other on a bloody field.

When Tekla woke me in the pre-dawn darkness as we had agreed, I felt as if I had hardly slept at all. My eyes were gritty and my mouth felt dry. I got up groaning with weariness and struggled into my clothes. She fed me a filling breakfast of morning porridge with nuts, berries and honey. "That should hold you for a while on the road," she said as she served up my steaming bowl. She had gotten up even earlier to cook for me and stuff my pack with food. As we ate we hardly spoke, each caught in our own thoughts and the stillness of the morning. Afterward she walked me to the far edge of the village, each of us covered by a dark cloak so as to not draw notice, two moving shadows in the gray dawn light. I had told her I couldn't stand any more outpourings of gratitude.

Finally she said, "This is as far as I go." When I turned to face her she took my face in both her hands and kissed me on the forehead. "Thank you, Zaia. I will never forget you. You saved us and gave us back to ourselves. May you travel with joy in your heart and safety on the road in these times of trouble and turmoil."

"And thank you, Tekla," I said, kissing her on both cheeks. "I hardly had a mother. She wanted me to be something I couldn't be, and when I became a Dancer she disinherited me, drove me from her house and never spoke to me again. I take you as the mother of my heart and will carry you with me wherever I may go." Then we embraced and I turned to leave, setting off down the road just as a red sun began to crest the purple hills. I looked back several times and she was still standing there, watching, a dark shape against the morning light.

Tekla had drawn me a map with her village on it and showed me how it connected to my map. She'd marked the spot where I'd lost the way, or rather misplaced myself. She said with a smile, "I'd already decided that I'd had more than enough of exploring and adventuring." I no longer wanted to go on. What I wanted now was to go back to the crossroads and start over, going south from there to the city of Chandairi, which was clearly marked on my map as having a Dance Temple.

I'd left without saying good-bye to any of the villagers except for Tekla. The burden of their gratitude was too heavy for me to carry. Instead I said the words silently in my heart, wishing them well, wishing them safety and asking the protection of the Goddess for them all. In truth I was only too glad to be gone from there.

CHAPTER 13
Following the Stream

I hurried past the raided farm, moving as fast as possible. The acrid smell of burning still hung in the air along with the stench of death. I was trying not to look in that direction or dwell on what had happened there. Even so, I caught a glimpse of the bloated cow with black-feathered carrion birds dancing around it. The sight sickened my spirit.

A mile or so after that I came to a little stream with a narrow plank bridge across it. I had crossed it on my way there and hardly noticed. Now it drew me. The clear, rushing water promised to wash away the ugliness I had witnessed. Birds, flowers, leafy trees, it all spoke of a peace I didn't feel in my heart but found myself longing for. Flowing under the bridge, the stream pulled at me, calling and calling for me to follow where it led, burbling its music and beckoning as it wound its way into the woods. For a while I watched its lovely motion sparkling in the sun, mesmerized and almost tempted. Then I thought to myself, *You are pledged to the Dance and this is just a mindless diversion, an escape.* Besides, I was still too close to the village. It might not be wise to linger there. Even so, it was an effort to tear myself away.

When I set off again, I was deep in thought, mulling over everything that had happened and what it meant for the future, paying little attention and barely watching where I put my feet. It was the smell of smoke and cooking food that warned me and most likely saved my life. I was walking through a stretch of deep woods with no houses about and could smell meat cooking. I stopped short, instantly alert and watchful. Then I heard a horse nicker and another answer. Someone was camping nearby, well hidden from the road. Was it just a band of travelers stopped in some pleasant little glen, taking their ease, travelers that had nothing to do with me? Or was it Murdock and his people waiting for me with sentries posted? Had they already seen me walking along unaware and foolishly distracted? Hard to imagine that he would be here after all this time but it was still better to be safe.

In front of me was a sharp bend in the road that could be hiding anything. Best not to go any farther. Soundlessly, I slipped off the road and made my way through the woods toward the smell, watching all around me for any movement, all my senses totally alert now. They weren't hard to find. The aroma led me there just as surely as a trodden path. They were camped in a sheltered little hollow, hidden from view by giant boulders and a thick stand of trees. It was Murdock's people alright, but the man himself wasn't there, nor were another three of his men. The rest were lounging by the fire, taking their ease while Naldeen roasted some big chunks of meat on a spit of green sticks.

Observing this scene, I was sure Murdock and the three others were hidden near the road, probably watching and waiting for me. A few more steps, likely just around the next curve, and I would have walked right into their hands. I had no doubt that this was Murdock's plan. I had bested him and he needed his revenge. The others probably had little interest in me.

So he was practicing his skills of leadership and learning to be a king by killing an unarmed Dancer on the road. And they would kill me this time, of that I had no doubt. No matter how fast I Danced, there was no way I could stand against four armed men, especially if they were on horseback and ready for me. Likely the others would join them at the first shout. If they didn't find me, would they break their pledge and go back to the village to search for me? Try to force answers from the people there? I shivered. Ah well, I had done what I could for the folk of Avrin, taught them as best I knew how. They would have to manage on their own. There was nothing more I could do for them. Now I had to think about saving myself.

I could not go forward. The road ahead was a trap. Even if I managed to slip past the watchers they would be behind me, able to catch up to me at any moment on their horses. I certainly didn't want to go back to the village. There was no safety there and I would only endanger the villagers as well as myself. In that instant I remembered the little stream that had beckoned so invitingly only moments before. Now it seemed like shelter, like the possibility of safety if I could slip away unseen from this dangerous place. As I watched, one of the missing men came back into camp. With a few words another left to take his place. I heard the first one mention Murdock's name. The other said angrily, "Curse it all, he won't leave until he has her. I'm ready to move on. We can't afford to take another cow from around here. People may get angry and come after us." Then he turned to Naldeen and said roughly, "Here girl, give us some of that! You're taking much too long."

She looked up at him with a sullen expression on her face and backed away warily as he took out his knife to cut himself a bloody chunk of meat. Her face was bruised and swollen, and there were dark marks on her arm. Even in such danger, I suddenly felt torn between pity and amusement. Was Naldeen practicing to be a queen, whatever that might be, by squatting, soot-covered and half naked, dripping with grease, cooking haunches of stolen beef for men who held her in contempt? They would probably have bedded her there in the dirt, roughly and against her will, if not for their fear of Murdock. Well, she had lessons of her own to learn on this journey—if she survived. There was nothing I could do for her now.

If they come after me this time I'll go for Murdock first and kill him if I can, break his arm or his leg to start with and then neck. That may cool their ardor. Even if they kill me I'll have chopped off the head of the monster and made it less dangerous for others. Oh Goddess! Even at such a distance they were training me in their ways. A week ago I couldn't have imagined such thoughts. *Mother, help me, protect me, be with me now. Please!*

As silently as I had come, I slipped away from my viewing spot and retreated back in the direction of the stream without going anywhere near the road. It wasn't easy finding my way through the woods or trying to be quiet in that rough terrain, but as I got closer the sound of running water became my guide. By the time I reached the stream my heart was pounding wildly and my breath was coming in hard little gasps. I stood very still, listening intently, hoping that I hadn't already been observed and that they were not playing some cruel game with me. Hearing nothing but the rush of water, I dipped my fingers in it and daubed my forehead in a rough blessing. Then I squatted down and scooped up handfuls to drink.

After that I set off again. Going as rapidly as I was able over slippery rocks and fallen branches, I followed the water wherever it led me. It was a while before I could slow down a little and longer before I could actually bring myself to stop and rest. My breath was still coming in ragged gasps. With a deep sigh I unfastened my sandals and slipped my sore feet into the cool water. When I looked about me I realized I was deep in the woods with no human sounds from any direction, and no idea what lay ahead or where I was or where the road could be. At that moment I felt a very different sort of fear.

Now that I thought myself lost the woods no longer seemed so welcoming. I could see that they had grown darker, denser, more tangled. As I tried to continue on my way it became more and more of a struggle. Thick branches hung with moss hunched low over the ground, forcing me to duck my head. Thickets of briers often blocked my way. Or I would suddenly come up against house-sized boulders that must have rolled down in the far past from some unseen mountain. All this forced me to zig-zag away from the water before I could make my way back to it again. I was trying to hold on to the stream as it was my only path or guide in that wild place, not an easy thing to do. I hoped it would eventually bring me out of the woods again or perhaps cross another road. Without it, I was afraid I might find myself going around in circles as people sometimes do when they are lost, finally growing weak and dying of starvation.

I had just forced my way through a dense thicket of low-growing trees and stopped to listen for the sound of water when the noises began. Low and strange at first, they quickly became louder and louder. The rustling and snuffling soon turned to moans, growls, roars, howls and loud crashes that sounded like some huge terrifying beast, or rather beasts, as this uproar seemed to be coming from three sides. I looked about frantically and could see nothing at all, but the din was getting louder and more threatening and plainly coming closer. I think I might have been able to gather my courage for facing a visible adversary, but this unseen monster was too much for me.

With a scream I broke and ran in blind panic, going in the only direction that was relatively free of noise even though it was the opposite way from where I thought the stream to be. Nothing mattered now but to get away from that dreadful din. It seemed to be swallowing up the world. It was like a switch laid on my back. I fled, stumbling and falling and struggling up again, crying out in fear when branches whipped across my face, tangled in my hair, or snagged my pack. Roots caught at my ankles and rocks twisted underfoot. Running on with the breath aching in my chest, I had no thought in my head but escape until suddenly a path opened up before me, a green way in the dark, tangled forest.

As soon as my feet reached the mossy path the noise behind me lessened and began to fade away until at last it was nothing but a distant murmur like wind in the leaves or running water heard from far off. The woods seemed less hostile now, more benign. I could hear birds singing again. The huge trees that bordered the path seemed to lean over it pro-tectively. Suddenly my terrors felt foolish, almost groundless. I slowed to a walk and followed the path as it wound between the trees. It was clearly human-made and would take me somewhere. Anything had to be better than trying to go back the way I had come. Gradually I caught my breath and felt a sense of calm settling over me. Whatever lay ahead I would try to meet it with a brave spirit, with a Dancer's center of stillness. I felt a little ashamed now of my earlier panic.

Coming around the corner I stopped with a sudden gasp of surprise. There in front of me, rising out of a clearing in the forest, I saw what appeared to be the ruins of an ancient Temple, vine covered stone walls still partially intact. In places there were holes in the stonewalls and small trees grew in those gaps, but through the vine cover I could see the giant columns of the outer walls. These columns were carved in the likeness of enormous Goddesses, half beast, half human, some even with the heads and wings of birds, like nothing I had ever seen in any Temple. Wondrous and fearsome and very old, they had some semblance to the figures in the ancient Dance Court in the desert, but they were clearly from a later time, far more detailed and realistic. There were also monstrous stone heads with bulging eyes, serpent hair and protruding tongues guarding the corners far above my head, as well as curious fragments of animals and humans carved on the broken walls. Brilliant flowers were blooming on the vines that tangled everywhere, scenting the air with a heady perfume. Brightly scaled lizards ran about the walls and darted up and down the vines. I walked forward as if pulled by an unseen hand. Strange as it all was it didn't frighten me.

Without hesitation I went under the remains of a great archway and followed the path into a central Dance Court. Though the ruins were clearly ancient, someone had been there recently, keeping a path open by cutting back the vines and shrubs that otherwise would have blocked the way. The Dance Court itself was carpeted in moss rather than grass and must have been kept cleared of debris by human hands. I looked around but there was no one to be seen. Not wanting to offend, I called out several times, thinking there might be a keeper there. Only the echo from the old stones answered me.

I was alone there. Refuge, sanctuary, the place felt sheltering and welcoming. All my fears gradually began to fade away. I wanted to walk around, to examine everything in this amazing place, but I was much too weary. Instead I slipped out of the burden of my pack that was still miraculously with me after my panicked flight and pried my sandals from my raw, swollen feet. Then I went to the center of the Dance Court and with a groan knelt down on the moss, my body collapsing forward in exhaustion. When I rested my forehead on that thick green carpet the coolness of it went all through my body. It was like a cool hand on a fevered forehead. *Thank You, Mother,* I said softly. The scent of the flowers flooded my senses and made me drowsy. Utterly alone and at peace, I stayed that way a long time, not asleep but drifting in a deep, peaceful trance until sudden booming, angry voices shattered the silence.

"Intruder!"

"Vandal!"

"Mocker!"

Instantly I leapt to my feet, looking around fearfully. Three large women had surrounded me and were advancing furiously. Though they were of different ages, they all looked much like Galaina and had her massive build. Each had a long knife fastened in the belt of her tunic, and none of them looked friendly.

"What are you doing here?"

"You have no right in *our* sacred space! This is *our* Dance Court where *we* Dance for the Goddess."

"Be gone from here!"

All my fears returning in an instant, I threw up my hands in front of me protectively. "I didn't know...I didn't mean..." I stammered, trying to speak in my own defense. They went right on talking as if I weren't speaking at all, taking threatening steps forward with each burst of words.

"This is a sacrilege!"

"You'll be sorry you did this!"

"Your Temple can't protect you here, little Temple thrall." The third woman to speak, who seemed the oldest of the three, raised her fists menacingly. My eyes blurred and I couldn't tell if she held a rock or knife or nothing but anger in her closed fist. It seemed I had fled from one peril straight into the arms of another.

"Do you plan to kill me?" I asked as calmly as I could, trying this time to keep my fears in check. They had me surrounded and were coming closer all the time. I didn't think I could Dance them down as I had with men. They were too wide and had a much lower center of gravity, but I thought I could use my speed and agility if I moved before they could close the circle and lay their hands on me.

At my question the youngest of them took a step back in surprise and then threw back her head and laughed, a deep, rich, warm laugh that was full of mockery but with no menace in it. Another of them said quickly, "Why should we bother, little skinny-bones, the wind will blow you away soon enough." And the third finished indignantly, "Kill you!? What do you take us for? We are Dancers, not assassins. We are Kooreei, the Earth Dancers, and this is our most sacred place that you have invaded so rudely. Now answer my question. What are you doing here? Did the Temple send you to spy on us?"

My fear fled and anger rose in its place, sharp and hot. "I'll try to answer if you give me a chance to speak and stop advancing on me in that threatening way. If you keep interrupting, I'll turn silent as a tree or a rock. You won't have another word from me." With that I turned slowly, staring at each of them. They each gave me a nod, planted their feet and crossed their arms in front of them, clearly showing they were waiting in silence for my words.

"This has nothing to do with the Temple. I was being hunted by a group of armed men. They were laying in wait by the road to kill me. I fled into the woods for shelter and followed the stream. For a while it was very peaceful there. Then, suddenly, there were terrible sounds that seemed to come from all around, though I could see nothing. I began running, lost the stream and found myself on a path to this place, just as if I'd been led here."

"Ah, so you were frightened by the Booli-Booli?" said the youngest of them with a wicked little smile. I gave her a questioning look. She shook her head and said nothing more.

"How could our sacred place call to you, a Temple Dancer?" asked the oldest of them with contempt.

"What manner of armed men? What is your quarrel with them? Where are they from?" asked the middle one at the same time. "Did they follow you here?"

"Which of you should I answer?" I asked looking from one to the other.

"Me!" they all said at once and suddenly all three of them were laughing.

Not feeling very humorous, I turned to the middle one and said angrily, "First of all, I may have been trained at the Temple, but I'm a Dancer for the Goddess, just as you are, even if our ways are different. I've taken a five-year pledge and have been on the road three of those years. It's been that long since I've seen my Temple or spoken to any of the Temple folk there. In that time I've Danced in many places, met many people and learned many things that the Temple never taught me and certainly didn't prepare me for. I spy for no one. I'm not a Temple thrall. I'm my own woman with my own mind and I Dance as the Goddess moves me to, just as you do. And yes, I was drawn here, as if to sanctuary, by some very powerful force." I let the sparks of my anger fly from my eyes as I looked at each of them in turn.

"As for your other question," I went on, "Some of those men are from the north. Others, including their leader, are from a village by the road, but they have been north and gained dangerous new notions about the use of weapons and power, also about the use of women. They've left a trail of destruction wherever they've gone, burned-out farms and dead farmers. I tricked their leader, Murdock, into pledging that he would leave his village in peace and take his men away and so they..."

"Wait," the oldest of them said. "We need to hear everything you can tell us in this matter of armed men, every detail. It might be better to do this seated comfortably rather than standing here like enemies."

As if at a signal they all sat down on the moss and indicated that I should take my place as the fourth in their circle. I sat warily, but after that rude beginning I didn't sense that they meant me any harm. When I began talking, looking from one intent face to the other, I was struck again by their resemblance to Galaina. On impulse I interrupted my narration to ask the middle one, "Do you know Galaina? You look enough like her to be her sister."

A look of shock and surprise bloomed on each of their faces. "How do you know of Galaina?" the oldest of them asked harshly, leaning forward with her jaw jutting out, full of suspicion again.

"We Danced together in my first year on the road. We spent over a week traveling together and Dancing. We had money thrown at us and flowers and even rocks in one place where the people were driven to mischief by some Temple Priests."

"So you're Zaia, the one she spoke of when she came home. No wonder you found your way here. You were supposed to!"

"Yes, I'm the one. I hope she spoke well of me. She taught me much and I would gladly have gone on with her and perhaps become more than a friend, but she said we would pull each other off center, change each other too much. I've looked for her ever since, twice just missing her. How is she? Where is she? Is she well?"

Speaking at the same time they said with one voice, "She is dead!"

The terrible finality of those words struck me like a blow. "Oh no!" I cried, doubling up with the pain of it.

"She was killed on the road by armed men, just a little to the north of here, perhaps the very ones you tangled with."

I looked at them all with tears running down my face. "I'm so very sorry. I always thought I would find her on the road again. It's hard to imagine the world without Galaina Dancing in it somewhere."

"That's why we're here. We were to meet her at the bridge and all come here together to do a Dance and a celebration for Spring-Crossing."

"Instead we have come to her favorite place to say goodbye to her in a fitting way."

"I *am* her sister, you guessed right, her younger sister. My name is Jorain. We were only two years apart."

"And I'm her oldest daughter, Alea."

"And I'm her mother, Thurga. Go on with your story, Zaia. Tell us everything you remember. We need to know. Clearly we have work to do."

"First you must tell me, what are these Booli-Booli that made such terrifying noises and frightened me so?"

"They are the spirits of the forest." They all said together.

"But are they human or animal?"

"We said they are spirits. You can't see them, but they keep the forest safe," Thurga said firmly. "We have an understanding with them from the far past."

"I didn't feel very safe, I can tell you that much." Even through the grief I could feel my anger returning. I was tired of being frightened.

"You weren't supposed to feel safe. You were an intruder here. You were supposed to be frightened. But I promise they won't bother you again. Now let's not speak of them anymore. It is wiser so. To speak of them calls them to you." Thurga spoke with a decisiveness that silenced me. Her words sent a chill of remembered fear up my back. "Now tell us exactly where those men are hiding and what they look like and what sort of weapons they have."

As the day grew darker around us I told them everything I could think of while they listened intently, occasionally interrupting with a pointed question.

I even told them of my former encounter in the woods and any stories I had heard of such men in my travels. Thurga asked again for an exact description of Murdock's hiding place in relation to the bridge and drew some lines in the dirt with a stick. When she was satisfied she nodded and made a sign to the others of a hand across the throat. "You plan to kill them? But how? You are only three and they are many, ten I think, not counting the girl."

"Not yours to know," Thurga said sharply

"But you said you were Dancers, not killers."

"We do what we have to do," Jorain answered.

I shook my head. "Besides it is such a long way back. Perhaps they will have left already."

"No chance. From what you say they will still be waiting there for you, a matter of pride and a display of power for that Murdock you spoke of. After all, you disgraced him in front of his men. Such an insult must be avenged. Anyhow, it's not as far as you think, Zaia, no more than an hour's walk at most. There are many ways back to the road that are much shorter than the winding stream and we know every one of them. We've been familiar with these woods since childhood."

"This is no longer your business," Thurga said in a voice of authority. "We have work to do. Don't put yourself in the way of it."

"Spare the girl if you can," I pleaded. "She is only with them from ignorance." I found myself liking these women in spite of our rough start, but they also frightened me. I thought Murdock's luck might be fast running out, that no matter how many men he had with him he was not likely to reach the north or become king.

"As the Goddess wills it," Alea answered. "Remember, that girl is also weaving her own fate."

With that I shrugged and fell silent on the matter. I could see it had already moved out of my hands. Next they asked me many questions about my meeting with Galaina and our time together, probing hungrily for every detail. In exchange, with much tears and laughter, they told me wonderful stories of her life while I nodded and asked my own questions, their attentive audience of one. In this way we brought her back to life with our words, at least for that moment. After a while they even told me of her death, as much as they knew of it, and how they had found her at the side of the road, stabbed and violated. Those men had not concealed their kill but rather made a show of it. At the end of that terrible recital we all cried together and those tears formed a further bond between us.

Finally Thurga gave a nod and they all stood up at the same time. "It grows dark. It's time to make the fire for the ritual and the Dance-of-Parting. We'll also do a Dance-of-Vengeance. You can't Dance with us, that would not be proper, but as a great favor you will be allowed to watch, though only because you were Galaina's friend."

I nodded and made a slight bow as I rose wearily to my feet. "I'm very honored. And thank you for not asking me to Dance. If you had asked, begged even, I could not have done it. Not even for Galaina, not even to save my own life could I have Danced this night. I'm too weary from all that has happened in these last few days."

"Good. Sit there by that column and keep your silence no matter what you see, do you understand?" I nodded silently. Thurga's voice sounded harsh and grudging, but I could see from her face that she was struggling to keep her grief under control. Without another word I took my blanket from my pack and settled myself to watch at the far edge of the circle with my back resting against a column.

They started by sharing a cup of something, passing it around and around and emptying the last few drops on the ground. "Ashi-root mixed with water," Jorain explained. "It gives visions, helps open our inner sight to bring the Goddess close." After that they set about their own pursuits and ignored me. First they painted their faces with wild designs in bright harsh colors. Then they began adding layers of colorful, noisy clothing, all of it sewn with coins and little bells: sashes, belts, shawls, scarves. They fastened circlets of little bells to their wrists and ankles so that they made a musical sound with every movement. After that they created a little altar by one of the columns, made a fire in the center of the court and lit some flares since it was already beginning to get dark.

When they began to wail the hair on the back of my neck stood up. The sound was so wild, so dark and inhuman, so full of ancient grief, it made tears run down my face. It went on and on, filling the night. After a while, I'm ashamed to say, my fatigue overpowered me. I started to doze even before they began to Dance.

I was awakened by their fierce chanting. The words, sung in an unknown language, were beautiful. They were also terrifying. Rage hummed in the air. When I opened my eyes I saw them Dancing around the fire in a close circle, massive dark shapes caught momentarily in the light. The gold and silver threads in their tunics flashed in the dark like flames or lightning. Their features appeared, suddenly highlighted, then just as swiftly were shadowed again. They moved round and round, leaping, whirling, swooping, as light on their feet as any Temple Dancers but with a very different kind of force and power. Finally, with a shrill wild cry, they all pulled their knives from their belts at the same moment and passed the blades through the flames. Then they lifted their arms together and began to do an intricate Dance with their raised knives. Soon their steps turned to stamps and it sounded like drums beating. The ground shook with it. Their blades flashed wildly in the light of the fire and the torches. A shiver went through me when I thought I saw blood dripping from those knives. It must have been a trick of the light or some wild imaginings of my weary brain. Now I understood Thurga's exhortations to silence. "Vengeance" they had said, and I could feel it gathering in that ancient Dance Court like the darkest of storm clouds. Chills ran up and down my back. I felt as if I was watching a scene from two or three thousand years back, from a time way before the existence of the Temple of Kernoss.

CHAPTER 14
Shadow Dancer

I must have slept again. When I woke I found myself lying on that soft carpet of moss. Someone had carefully covered me with my blanket. Patches
of sunlight were slanting in through the leaves, dappling everything around
me in a restless pattern of gold and shadow.

Shaking my head groggily I sat up and looked about for my companions.
They were gone, of course. Only the faint smell of fire and a thin wavery line
of smoke rising from the little pile of ashes in the center of the Dance Court
gave any indication of their presence. Otherwise there was no sign that the
Kooreei had ever been there and were not some creatures of my imagination
who had come to life in this strange place. They had slipped away without a
sound and left me there.

Vengeance! They had gone to exact vengeance! I shivered, wondering if
Murdock and his men and perhaps even poor silly little Naldeen had slept to
their deaths in the pre-dawn darkness.

The Kooreei had left me a handful of ground ashi-root wrapped in a leaf.
I stared at it for a long time, wondering if I should take it. They said it gave
them visions. Did I need visions? I had never done such a thing. It was not
allowed in the Temple, at least not for Dancers. But this was not the Temple, or
rather it was a very different Temple, one that no doubt had a very different set
of rules. I looked around at the columns, all fearsome Goddesses, half woman,
half beast, totally different from the grand and solemn images of the Goddess
in the Temple of Kernoss. Staring back at me with their bulging eyes and their
strange distorted features, they seemed to be saying, *Why not?* I shook the
ground roots into a cup of water, stirred it quickly with my finger and drank
it all down in two gulps, afraid I might change my mind. I expected a sudden
rush of energy, a jolting change, or at least interesting visual distortions. I was
somewhat disappointed when nothing much happened.

With a yawn I stood up and stretched. Very slowly I began to Dance,
doing a Salute to Morning, a Dance full of joy and hope. I was chanting as I
moved. Then something in me shifted suddenly and I found myself Dancing
my sorrow for Galaina. My mouth opened. I heard moaning, then wailing
and howling, the sounds of grief pouring out of me, filling that place and
echoing back. After a time and with no will of my own something shifted

again and I was dancing my anger, rage at those men who were changing our world with their bloody swords. My feet pounding loudly, my hands slashing, I was roaring out my fury into that ancient space. Then, just as suddenly, the joy came again, filling me up and moving my feet in a different rhythm. And so it went, shifting round and round, from joy to grief to rage and back again, turn and turn about, a wild new Dance that came from that particular place and, without a doubt, from the ashi-root.

At some moment I chanced to glance at the columns. I was shocked by what I saw. Without leaving their places they were moving, dancing with me, all of them, their mouths opening and closing, grinning, grimacing; their tongues darting out from between stone lips, or stretching out fully, or curling about; their eyes squinting, winking, opening wide and then closing again; their heads turning from side to side as they watched me Dance. Even their hands were moving, gesturing and beckoning. Everything was rippling and in motion. The old gray stone actually took on colors, changing in a constant flow of patterns that shimmered across the surface. I was terrified and fascinated. I tried to tell myself it was only the ashi-root, yet it seemed all too real. Longing to touch the stone, I reached out toward a column. Then, at the last moment, I drew back my hand, afraid. As I Danced from one emotion to another I saw the expressions on those stone faces change with my feelings. They even lashed their tails and extended their claws if they had paws instead of hands.

I Danced on and on until my energy finally ran out and I found myself exhausted, drenched with sweat and panting for breath. With a groan I sank to the ground and pressed my forehead to the cool moss. It took some time for me to catch my breath again. When at last I raised my head to look at the statues they were totally still, impassive and gray, their stone eyes staring straight ahead, their stone mouths frozen in place. With a sigh I shut my eyes and lay back on the moss, feeling as if I had been on a long, tiring journey to places I couldn't possibly understand.

When I opened my eyes again I could see by the slant of the light that it was well past noon. Time to leave. Before I could go on to the city of Chandairi I had to go see for myself what had happened. I would never feel safe on the road until I knew the truth of the matter, whether those men were still waiting there for me and my new friends were all dead, or if it had gone the other way. If I were a betting person I would have wagered on the Kooreei but I had to be sure.

I found my way to the stream without too much trouble and followed it back since it was the only way I knew. Armed with foreknowledge I was determined not to be afraid of the Bouli-Bouli. This time I was ready for them, but of course this time they didn't come. When I got close enough to the road to see the bridge, I stayed in the woods, watching intently, trying to sense any sound or movement that might mean danger. There was nothing to hear but a little breeze rattling the leaves and the sounds of the rushing water. Reassured, I made my way through the woods to Murdock's camp. Well before I reached the place I could hear the raucous crowing of the death-birds.

It was a hideous sight that met my eyes, bodies strewn about where they fell, some still in their sleep sacks with the rusty stains of blood on everything and death-birds fighting over the grisly feast. There were no weapons, no horses and no sign of the Kooreei. I wished them well on their road wherever it might lead, no doubt enriched by this little raid. I hoped I could count on them as friends. I would certainly never want them for enemies.

I had no wish to go any closer, but even from where I was standing I thought I could count eight bodies. That was all of them then—dead. Murdock's ambitions to be king ended there in those woods. If he had not been lying in wait for me he would have been on his way north. I was much relieved not to catch sight of Naldeen's slender young form in the midst of that carnage, but of course it wasn't possible to be sure. Though she may have been a fool, she certainly didn't deserve to die that way. It was hard to imagine what her life would be like now. Would she go home to mockery and disgrace? Or find herself another man with a sword? Or would she travel for a while with the Kooreei if they really had spared her life?

Suddenly the ghastly smell of death caught in my throat. It filled the air, leaving nothing to breathe. I turned away and was sick on the ground, losing all the breakfast I had eaten. After that I backed away quickly and then ran to the road. I kept running even when I reached it, running until I could no longer hear the greedy cry of the birds, and the air once more smelled sweet and fresh.

I didn't reach the city of Chandairi that night. I had started out much too late. Instead I found myself in the little town of Undrin. There was no Dance Temple of course and the Dance Court was small, but the grass was soft and green and it seemed well tended. Indeed the whole town was well tended. It looked prosperous and safe, very far from burned-out farms and the men who traveled with death in their hands. I was glad to be there and I found instant welcome. The Headman, Bernair, was kind and courteous. He assigned a woman named Hathi to care for me because she had been a Dancer and he thought she would best know what I needed.

As I was following Hathi to the baths I noticed that she had a tremor in her hands and arms. I assumed it was Dancer's shakes—what is sometimes called Dancefever. Since she made no mention of it I hesitated at first to speak of the matter. After we reached the bathhouse and she was unable to manage the latch, I asked.

She whirled on me. "Oh yes, I have Dancefever," she said bitterly. "Any fool could see that. Sometimes it's just my hands and arms that shake, and sometimes my whole body so I can hardly walk. They say it's staying too long on the road and being burned by Her power. The Goddess has used me up and thrown me away like a worthless old stick."

"But why not go to the Temple of Raimarth for a cure? Chandairi is not that far away."

"The Temple?!" She spit in the dirt. When she glared at me her eyes had a hollow, shadowed, haunted look that was startling. "Raimarth was my Temple, Chandairi my city. When they found they could not cure me, they abandoned me as useless trash. Oh yes, they would have fed me and let me work sweeping the courtyard, but I was a Dancer and I was the best of them. How could I stay there, watching others Dance, doing what I could no longer do and had once done better than any of them? How could I stay and see the pity and contempt in their eyes? There, if you're not a Dancer, you're nothing, less than nothing, dirt underfoot. So I came here, and now that fool Headman thinks I'm the one who should care for you because I used to be a Dancer. He knows nothing, understands nothing. He's a fool, no better than a block of wood."

"He seems like a good man to me," I said sharply, feeling called to defend him. I was angered by her tone and stung by her words.

"And no doubt you're also a fool," she said spitefully, abruptly turning all her anger on me. "You probably believe in a Goddess who's all kindness and love like the pretty statues in the Temple, the all-nurturing Mother or the lovely ever-youthful Maid. I know a very different kind of Goddess. Maybe you haven't seen Her face yet, but you will. She uses what She wants then destroys what's left. She used me up. I burnt out my core in Her service. And now, for thanks She mocks and torments me. I dream at night of Dancing as easily as birds float on air, Dances more beautiful than any I ever did in this waking world. Then I awake in the morning into this useless, crippled body—and I curse Her! I can almost hear Her cruel laughter when I rise and try to walk.

"The Priests at the Temple talked to me about accepting the mysteries of the Goddess' ways, may their tongues rot out and their members fall off. Fat, arrogant pigs! What do they know of Her ways? And the Dance Mistress, that pompous cow, she said I was too proud, that I set myself above others and this was to teach me humility. May she be taught humility. May her vulva fill with snakes. May she give birth to a dog that slits open her belly."

I quickly stepped back, profoundly shocked by her words. They were like the pounding blows of a hammer against my heart. I'd never heard a woman speak that way, with such venom and bitterness. She sounded like Murdock. "Don't wish for such things," I said in a horrified whisper. "You have no idea what you're calling down in your anger. There are already terrible forces out there on the move." Thinking to touch her heart I told her about the violent men I had encountered in the village of Avrin. I finished with the tale of the man who tried to ambush me on the road, wanting to use my body.

Her eyes narrowed and her face took on a pinched, crazed look. "Good, let them come! A curse on the Temples and on the cities that spawned them! Let those men come in their hundreds with their swords drawn and bloody. Let the cities go under. If I were inside the Temple and they were in the streets at this very moment I would draw back the bolt, open the gates to them and invite them in."

"And the first thing they would do is kill you."

"Good. Then I would be rid of this wretched, useless body. I don't have the courage to do it myself. And I hope they would burn it in a huge fire that would swallow everything. Everything!"

Now I was furious. "That's enough! That's more than enough! You were asked to show me to a bath, and all you've done is spew out your anger on me. I won't stay in your presence another minute. Being with you is like drinking poison. Go! Leave me! I'll find my own way to the Dance Court."

Her face underwent a sudden drastic change. In that instant she must have understood that she had said too much, gone too far. "I beg your pardon, Dancer, for my sharp tongue. Sometimes it runs off with me. I'll show you the Dance Court now and will speak no more of such matters."

I wasn't sure I could trust her, but after that alarming outburst she seemed quiet and subdued, almost contrite. Hoping for the best, I followed as she led the way. The Dance Court was very lovely, with the half moon casting a quivering silver light and the shadows making a pattern of velvety dark. I stood at the edge of it picturing the Dance, feeling it rise and fill my body.

I was so absorbed I almost forgot her presence until she startled me out of my reverie by speaking very close to my ear. "Dance with me, Zaia. Let's do the Dance of the Broken-Winged Bird together. That one I can surely do."

At that moment she sounded wistful instead of bitter. I felt encouraged. "I suppose there's no harm in that." Coming off the road that way I would rather have bathed first. I wasn't dressed to Dance, but this was a Dance that didn't require much in the way of costume. I nodded and we stepped into the circle together, side by side. Gradually we stepped apart as we began the movements, swooping low, rising and then drooping almost to the ground. It was an easy Dance, one I had learned in my second year at the Temple and it came back with its comfortable familiarity, though I hadn't done it in years. It was also a good Dance to do with another Dancer. Hathi stayed with me and for a while all went smoothly.

Her feet were steady and there was hardly any tremor in her hands. We moved in unison and then in opposition, rising and falling, swooping and turning, circling the Dance Court, creating this Dance together. By some trick of the light it seemed as if I was Dancing in the light while she was always in shadow, dancing the dark side of these movements, my reflection, my shadowed self.

After a while I began to actually feel hopeful. Maybe I was the one who could cure her. Maybe her body would finally heal so she could find her way back to the Dance and away from bitterness. I even smiled my encouragement. When she saw my smile her face suddenly went dark with anger. Perhaps she thought I mocked her. At that moment she stumbled and almost fell. Indeed she would have fallen if I hadn't grabbed her arm in a firm grip. Instead of thanking me she shook off my hand in a fury and hissed through her teeth, "You see the kind of games She plays, letting me have my one moment of pleasure and then smashing it all for Her own amusement." Then, she raised her arms in a ritual gesture and thundered in a voice full of hate, "Here on this Dance Court, consecrated to Your worship, I curse You!" Then she swung a pointing finger toward me. "And I..."

"No!" I shouted, raising my Dancewand in front of me for protection. "You will not curse me! You will not say another word! That Dance was a gift. You don't see it because your anger has blinded you. I can't be near you a moment longer. I'll find my own way to bath and bed." I turned quickly and left her standing there, but her pain followed me, slicing at my heart, and her anger lodged itself between my shoulders with the sharpness of a knife blade. That night I lay awake a long time in that comfortable, clean bed, tossing about as if I were sleeping on rocks under a cold sky.

The next day it was not Hathi who dressed me for the Dance. It was two girls from the town who were all aflutter with awe and embarrassed me with their devotion. They told me Hathi had vanished without a word to anyone. "She was very strange, that one. We never knew where she had come from and now we don't know where she's gone."

I shivered as if from cold. One of the girls quickly wrapped a shawl around me, but it was not that kind of cold—it came from within. I probably knew more about Hathi than the good people of this town because she had been willing to talk to me, or rather spew out her sickness on me. I thought she might as well be out on the road somewhere, looking for men with swords, hoping to open the gates for them so as to bring our whole world crashing down in ruins. Of course I said nothing of this to those two young women who were so sweet and innocent.

When I was dressed and perfumed, face paint skillfully applied and my hair piled high in Dancer's braids, I walked between them to the Dance Court. Would I be able to Dance this time? I thought of Hathi's near curse and our interrupted Dance. I could feel the fear rising, but I used all my Dancer training to keep it under control. In the stillness of my mind I said the Dancer's Prayer, giving weight and meaning to each word and gathering some comfort there.

While I waited for the musicians to begin I took deep breaths to clear my mind and open my spirit. Then I bowed all around and stepped into the circle with seeming perfect confidence. In the inner stillness I asked the ritual question, instantly found myself answered and felt my body begin to move into the Dance of the Eight Trees, a lovely spring Dance for blessing the land and its people. Relief and gratitude spread out from me and filled the space. I Danced as if on air. Afterward the grateful townsfolk showered me with praise and gifts. They wanted me to stay and Dance for them again since there were several ritual days coming, but I politely declined. I was feeling called to go on to the city of Chandairi and to the Temple there. I needed the shelter of a Temple to heal from the wounds of Hathi's anger.

Before I left Bernair drew me aside. "I'm sorry if Hathi wasn't helpful. She's so full of pain and bitterness it seems to eat her up. I had hoped being with another Dancer might bring her some comfort. Now I see I was mistaken. I fear for her, what might happen to her, what she might do to herself. Wherever she's gone, she won't be nearly as safe as she could have been here. I had hoped that in time she would mend, that the spirit of this town would cure her, but I see I was mistaken in that also."

Bernair was no fool. This was a caring and humble man who had tried to do a good thing. I thanked him for all his kindness. I even tried to reassure him but I was also afraid, far more afraid *of* Hathi than I was for her. I left the town of Undrin refreshed and rested, laden with food and gifts. As I went down the road my pack was considerably heavier. And so was my heart. I kept hearing Hathi's words echoing over and over in my head, *Let those men come in their hundreds with their swords drawn! Let the cities go under! I would draw back the bolt and open the gates to them!* I could not rid myself of those words. They kept time to my steps all the way to the city of Chandairi. I was to hear them for a long time afterward. Later, I came to better understand their meaning.

I made my way to the city of Chandairi and stayed for some healing at the Temple. The people there were kind and considerate and treated me with

*care, but when I mentioned Hathi's name strange looks passed between them
and a heavy silence fell over the place. I didn't repeat that mistake or ask any
questions. It felt as if I had stepped in a stinging ant nest of bad feelings.*

*After my healing I stayed on to rest and to Dance at the Temple. Then
I headed south for a while. Encountering no more men like Murdock nor
even any talk of such men, I walked through peaceful country. It was as if I
had come into a different world. My memories of what had happened began
to fade like a bad dream. I Danced in many towns and villages and finally
headed for the city of Khoberah because so many along the way spoke of its
beauty. I grew curious to see this jewel of a city for myself and find out how it
compared to my own beloved city of Urshameel.*

CHAPTER 15
Khoberah

On my way to Khoberah I met an old woman with a terrible story. It was a crisp, fall day. The trees on either side of the road had turned golden yellow and leaves carpeted the road. I was walking in a tunnel of gold, humming to myself with my heart full of joy, when I noticed far ahead of me an old woman trudging along with a sack over her shoulder. Hurrying to catch up, I called out, "Let me help you with your burden, Mother."

Much to my surprise, she whirled on me, saying angrily, "Stay back! I have a knife. Just because I'm old doesn't mean I'm helpless. I can defend myself well enough. Don't think it will be so easy to take an old woman's belongings." Her face was all twisted with fear and anger. Brandishing her knife, she did indeed look ready to defend herself.

Startled, I took a step back and threw up my hands. "Look, my hands are empty. I meant no harm. It was only that you looked weary and I thought to help."

She looked me up and down quite thoroughly and finally put her knife back in her belt. I could see her expression change and soften as she saw my Dancewand tucked in my sash and realized I was a Dancer. "Forgive my rudeness, Lady Dancer. The roads are not as safe as they used to be. Things have happened in this last year that I never would have imagined before." She was shaking her head, looking as if she might cry at any moment. "Yes," she said suddenly, "Some help would be welcome. I've walked a long way." She held out her sack to me.

Walking up slowly so as not to frighten her, I took the sack from her hands and swung it over my shoulder. As we set off, I slowed my steps to match hers. "Where are you from, Mother?"

"From the north and before that from the village of Halduir, west of here. My name is Rashem and now I'm coming home to stay. Curse me for a fool if I ever leave again. I have relatives in Khoberah that I plan on seeing, a nephew and his wife and their children. Also, I have a message for the authorities here. After that I'm headed down the road to Halduir. And you?"

"I'm Zaia, from the city of Urshameel, but I've been a Dancer on the road. This is my fourth year, so now I'm from everywhere and nowhere. I must say, no one has ever greeted me with a knife before." As I said those words I realized they were not true. A sudden chill went through me as I remembered the man in the woods. And then I thought of Murdock and his men. I was curious as to what would make an old woman feel she had to defend herself with a knife. Before I could ask, a farm wagon came up behind us and the farmer stopped to offer us a ride into the city. Rashem gave me a questioning look and I nodded to show I would come with her. I helped her up and we sat in the back on sacks of potatoes, since the farmer had her small children on the seat beside her.

While we rode together Rashem told me some of her story, a story so bloody and frightening I was glad when the wagon stopped in the market square so we could get out and go our separate ways. I needed to get away from her. Her harsh voice had started to grate on me. Now, even in her absence, it was difficult to regain my good mood of the morning. I kept hearing her bitter words, ragged with anger, and seeing the pictures of death and destruction she had painted all too vividly before my inner eye. I had thought all that was behind me, and suddenly it was filling my head again.

Finally, as I wandered about the streets, her words began to fade. The spell of the city took hold of me and absorbed my attention. I began to look around me with pleasure. After all, this is what I had come to see. The city of Khoberah was so exquisitely beautiful it made Urshameel, that I had always thought quite fine, seem dull in comparison. The grand buildings of the city were mostly of white stone, worked with such intricacy it almost looked like lace. Everywhere I turned there were wide avenues as well as endless gardens, fountains, archways and winding walls built in decorative, openwork patterns. It was indeed lovely but so delicate it made me somewhat uneasy. It hardly seemed real. It looked fragile as a shell and, like a shell, it could easily have been crushed. Should an earth tremor or a violent storm pass through much of that beauty would come crashing down. My pleasure and admiration were strangely mixed with discomfort.

After a while I began to feel tired and dirty and made my way to the Temple. There I was greeted with a bath and fresh clothes. The Dance Mistress, Lurian, was excited to meet a Dancer from Urshameel. She invited me to come watch her Dancers rehearse. They were to do the Harvest Dance for the Fall Festival that evening in the Temple and also the next day at the Grand Ceremony in the city square.

The Dancers were all young, thin and beautiful. They were skilled enough and went through the steps perfectly, but they seemed to Dance without spirit, without force, as if something was missing or had been stripped away. Without saying anything, I gave Lurian a questioning look. She nodded as if answering my silent question. "They've been working very hard on this. They're newly picked to be the lead troupe. My brother, Jarvon, the High

Priest of this Temple, has chosen them himself. He said my Dancers were not graceful enough, that they were too big and too ..." She hesitated as if searching for the right word. What came to my mind was 'powerful.'

Before I could stop the words I found myself saying, "In the Temple of Kernoss only the Dance Mistresses have the right to choose the Dancers, not even a High Priestess has that right, and certainly not the Priests."

She sighed and looked away. "Though there have always been Priests in this Temple, until just a short while ago they shared the power with the Priestesses. Here, too, only the Dance Mistresses would decide such things, but everything is changing now. My brother says the people of the city prefer Dancers who are young and graceful and pretty."

I felt a rush of anger going up my back. "But is that what the Goddess prefers?"

The Dancers had come to the end of that set of steps. Lurian clapped her hands and called out. "That is enough for now. You are doing very well. Go wash, eat and rest for a while. Meet back here at two hours past noon." They looked surprised but did as they were told, rushing off in a twitter of girlish voices.

My question still hung in the air unanswered until they were gone out of earshot. Then, she turned and faced me. In a low voice, so as not to be overheard, she said, "These days pleasing the Goddess seems to matter less and less and pleasing the Priests matters more and more. I probably should not be saying these things to a total stranger, but for some peculiar reason I feel I can trust you more than my own people. You come from a city that, I have heard, keeps to the old ways. Tell me more about your Temple and how things are done there." She sounded hungry, desperate even, for news from elsewhere. When I nodded she quickly led me to a bench in an alcove in the garden where we could talk in comfort. Before we sat down she looked in all directions as if to make sure no one was near.

I told her about the Temple Mother and how she had final say at the Temple and yet always listened to the opinions of others and always expected them to speak truthfully. I told her about Melanthia and the other Dance Mistresses and how our Dancers were chosen. While I spoke I found myself suffering from terrible homesickness, a longing to see all those loved familiar faces again. Every time I answered a question she eagerly asked another. I kept having to remind her that this was how it had been when I left and that I had been gone for four years.

"Will you Dance for us tomorrow at the ceremony in the city? I want people to see, I want them to remember what the Dance was like, what it could be like again. But not here tonight. If my brother saw you Dance here today, he would never allow it tomorrow."

I found myself consenting, though it seemed a dangerous game to play. What was I agreeing to do? There was something strange going on under the lovely surface of this city and by Dancing I was about to step right into the middle of it. But how could I resist Dancing for the Goddess in a place where She was being pushed aside? We had agreed on the time and had just stood up to say goodbye to each other when I heard a commotion coming from the entrance to the Temple compound. A look of alarm crossed Lurian's face. She set out at a run in the direction of the noise. I followed right on her heels.

Soon the shouts were loud enough to hear the words. "And you're a blind fool, an idiot, if you think invasions are not coming here just as they have come to the northern cities. I have seen it! I know! It's my duty to warn the people of Khoberah." Instantly I recognized the voice of the old woman, Rashem, the one who had been my companion that morning. Her voice was becoming louder and more shrill with each word. Then another voice thundered out, deep and full of authority, "Put her out of the Temple courtyard and bar the gates." In a very different tone he shouted, "Shut your mouth, you crazy old woman! Not another word!"

"You're the one who's crazy if you think that spells and incantations will keep this city safe! If you won't listen, I'll go from place to place, shouting it in the streets of the city. Someone has to hear me, someone has to pay attention so people here are not caught unaware like the people of Zir and Yairnith. You cannot silence me! This is too important!"

"No! Stop! Take her instead to the cell behind the orchard. Put a gag in her mouth if she won't be silent any other way."

With Lurian just ahead of me I rushed around the corner to see Rashem struggling with two strong young men while the High Priest shook his fist at her, his face blazing red with barely controlled anger. There was not a moment to lose and no time at all to think. Without an instant's hesitation I rushed up, pushed one of the men aside and grabbed Rashem's arm, shaking her hard. "Grandmother, Grandmother, stop this at once! You're having one of your crazy spells. I told you not to come to the city with me, but you wouldn't listen. Now look at all the trouble you've made." Then I turned to the men and said tearfully, "I need to take her home to her village. The city brings out the madness in her. There is too much happening here all at once, too much for her old brain to deal with. It makes her crazy and she has delusions. Once she gets started this way it's hard for her to stop. She doesn't really mean all those things she said. She's not in her right mind. When she's back home with the cows and the goats she'll be just fine. Let me take her off your hands right now."

I could see the High Priest weighing his choices. If he put her in the cell then he would either have to kill her or he would have to feed and care for her.

She wouldn't be easy to silence and keep under control. He hesitated and I thought he was about to let her go into my hands. Then he started to shake his head and Lurian said quickly, "Let me take care of this, Brother. I'll walk them to the edge of the city and make sure that they're gone down the road. Then they won't bother you anymore. Surely you don't want all the trouble of putting this mad old woman in a cell and then trying to keep her there."

Meanwhile Rashem was struggling in my grip just as she had struggled with those men. She started to say indignantly, "I am not..."

I gripped her arm even harder and shook her forcefully. "Silence, Grandmother!" I shouted, desperate to keep her quiet. "That's enough. You've already caused enough trouble here."

"Get her away from me! Now!" Jarvon yelled, almost out of control with fury. "Go with them, Lurian! You two as well," he ordered the men, "Do not let them out of your sight. See that they are really gone from the city and shut the gates behind them."

"This way," Lurian said. "Follow me."

I could feel Rashem resisting. I gave her arm a jerk and muttered in her ear, "Not another word. For the sake of your life we need to be out of here as fast as possible." I think she finally took note of the danger she was in because she nodded and stopped pulling against me. Instead, when I started walking, she hurried her steps to match mine. As soon as we were through the Temple gates they shut behind us.

For a while Lurian hustled us through the city streets in silence. When we were out of sight of the Temple she slowed her steps a little.

"Is she really mad?" she asked me.

"No more than either of you," Rashem said tartly. "Though with all I've seen it's a wonder I'm not. I have not told the half of it. If the little I said got me in that much trouble why should I say more?" Her voice began to rise in anger and the two men stepped forward, alarmed. They seemed ready to take hold of her again.

"Leave us," Lurian said imperiously. "I think your presence agitates her. I need to do some healing to calm her mind and I cannot do it with the two of you looming over us."

"But Lord Jarvon told us to stay with you, not to leave your side for a moment."

"I'm quite able to manage. I've worked with people like this before. After all, I am a healer as well as a Dancer, and I don't need your help in the matter. Here's some money. Go to the market and buy yourselves the meal you're missing at this moment. I'll call if I need you." She thrust some coins in their hands and they backed away, looking reluctant and confused, torn between two masters.

"Good, now we can talk in peace." Lurian fastened her large, sad eyes on Rashem. "Tell me what you've seen and what you were doing in the north. I at least will listen even if the rest of this city won't."

Rashem nodded. Very eager to talk, the words came tumbling out of her. "I left my village of Halduir to go live with my granddaughter and her husband in the city of Yairnith far north of here. Her mother died in childbirth so she's been like a daughter to me and begged me to go with them. Her man was a skilled silver worker and had found a good place at the Temple there. They had a nice house on the Temple grounds with enough room for my little garden. It was all much nicer than my small, windowless hut in Halduir. I felt blessed. The city was beautiful and we were welcome there. And soon I had two great-grandchildren to help care for while their mother helped her husband with his work. Life in Yairnith was good until suddenly refugees from Zir began pouring into the city, turning everything upside-down. Zir had been invaded and everyone who had not escaped had been killed or enslaved. I heard stories then that could make the stones weep.

"There was a lot of talk in the city about whether we would be next and what we could do to protect ourselves, talk and talk and talk, but nothing really came of it. In the end people would not believe it could happen to them. They wouldn't dare invade Yairnith. We are too large, too powerful. We are under the protection of the Goddess."

"The fools! Much good the Goddess did them. The raiders came at night when decent folk were all sleeping. They came screaming and howling, riding fast, carrying torches and armed with all sorts of weapons. Though there were far more of us, we never had a chance. They killed everything that moved and set fire to everything that didn't. By morning light it was over. The city was overrun and in flaming ruins. They cut down anyone who tried to escape. I lost everyone that night, my whole family, everyone I loved, even the little ones. I saw them die right in front of me. I only survived because I was in the loft at that moment fetching some herbs and the killers were in a great rush as they swept through our house. I was watching through a crack. They never thought to look up there."

"And afterward, why didn't they kill you?"

"I think they were too busy looting and gathering spoils and fighting with each other. Old women probably seem harmless to them. Sometimes they killed us for the fun of it, for sport, sometimes they ignored us. We were no more to them than stray cats. I had a dark shawl and kept myself all hunched over and so I got overlooked. Since I escaped from Yairnith I have been making my way south, avoiding cities, wanting to come to Khoberah and sound the alarm since I have family here. I haven't even had a chance to see them and now I'm being hustled out of the city."

"Better than being hustled into a cell," I reminded her sharply.

Lurian looked thoughtful. "If things are so bad in the north, why haven't they already raided in the south?"

"Good question, Lady. I think it's because right now they have no leader. They fight among themselves, struggling for power, stealing plunder and women from each other. Each time one of them gets a little higher the others drag him down in a fit of jealous rage. They have no rules or laws. They are as likely to kill each other as to kill the rest of us. It doesn't make them any less dangerous to others, but it certainly limits their range. If one man rises to power and succeeds in becoming their leader, then the cities of the south will fall within the year just as surely as some cities in the north already have. And believe me it will matter little what prayers you say, chants you sing or animal sacrifices you make. The Goddess did not protect the city of Yairnith or the city of Zir. She will not protect the city of Khoberah either. Unless you have a force to stand against them, they will slice through this city like a hot knife through butter. Look at this place. It will crack open like an egg."

"Why did you go to the Temple?" Lurian asked.

"I wouldn't have gone to the High Priest first. In truth I have little use for such men and don't trust them. I went to talk to Yavodosha, the city Guardian, who I knew from the past to be both wise and clever. I was sure she would listen to me. But she's dead now and her granddaughter sits in her place like an empty painted doll. She wouldn't notice danger if it was standing right in front of her with its claws out and its fangs dripping blood. All she could tell me was that the Temple was taking care of everything, saying it over and over as if they had wound her up to speak such foolishness. True, she is much prettier than her grandmother and wears fancier clothes, but she is certainly not fit to rule a great city. She has no brains. Why on earth did they choose such a one? How can they have made her Guardian? I could as well have been talking to a bird or a cow."

"The Temple chose her. They said they did it out of respect for her grandmother, but I think it was because she is easy for them to manage. The people did not oppose it. They fear the Temple, though none of them would admit it."

"What happened to Yavodosha? How did she die? No one wants to talk about it."

A look of pain crossed Lurian's face. "Because they are all afraid. She was perfectly healthy one day, then the next she died quite suddenly and in terrible pain. It sounds to me like poison; it has the smell of it. It was looked into, but nothing was ever proved."

Rashem nodded. "So now the power has shifted to the Temple, and that's why I went to talk to the High Priest—to argue with him, as it turned out. He tells me he's done all the right things, said the right prayers, made the right sacrifices, held the right ceremonies and so the city is safe. He and the other Priests have made it so. That's when I lost my temper and my calm and started shouting like a madwoman, telling him he was a fool. They are all fools, all those Priests if they think that pious nonsense will protect them. But it's true that my angry little speech won me no willing ears. In fact, if not for this Dancer, it would have gotten me a trip to the dungeon.

"Listen to me, Lurian, what I say is true. An invasion is coming as surely as I have two hands. Whether it happens this year or next or the year after, armed men from the north will be coming here and this city is wide open, ripe for the picking. But there is nothing more I can do. No one will listen to this crazy old woman. See if you can persuade your brother to at least think about it, maybe send some spies north to see what is happening there."

Lurian shook her head and said sadly, "Not much chance. I doubt I can persuade my brother of anything. He doesn't listen to me anymore. I'll be lucky if I can keep my own head on my shoulders. Things are shifting and changing in this city, control is moving and my brother is at the center of a new web of power. Yavodosha's death has altered everything. Women are slowly being pushed from power and out to the fringes of things. You probably think, *but why does she sit by and do nothing?* Because it is all being done so subtly and skillfully that if you sound the alarm, you are made to look like a fool. If you make too much noise on the matter you are declared mad and might easily end up in one of those cells that you barely escaped today. You would not likely get out. After a while in there you really *would* be mad. Who knows where it will end. At great risk I say all this to you, because there is no one here I can safely talk to and I have to talk to someone."

I was puzzled and interrupted to ask, "Is there no Council for the city? Do you just have a single ruler?"

"Oh no. As well as a Guardian, there's a Council made up of the heads of the ten first families, the heads of the guilds and the upper Priests of the Temple. You notice I say Priests because the Priestesses no longer have power there. We have been relegated to keeping house, tending to the day-to-day running of the place and not making any of the decisions that matter.

"Actually this talk of invasion is nothing new. Everyone has heard rumors about the north. This city hums with fear, but the Temple says it has been taken care of. The Priests say that the people have only to make more donations for more sacrificial rituals and then all will be well. No one is ready to challenge the authority of the Temple. They're too afraid. Anyone who objects or refuses is regarded as an enemy of the city and a danger to its people."

"But that's evil." Chills went up my back as I said those words and my mouth felt dry.

"Evil?" She raised an eyebrow at me. "My brother may very well believe he is right, or at least he's been able to convince himself of it, since it's all so greatly to his advantage. I know he doesn't see himself as an evil man. He thinks he does nothing but good. He would have locked up this old woman to silence her for the good of the city and felt pleased with himself for having averted a great danger."

I shook my head and burst out, "But this is madness, real madness!"

"Hush," she said quickly, glancing around. "Understood," I lowered my voice before continuing, "But when everyone is mad and has agreed to the madness, how do you keep your sanity? How do you not appear to be the one who's crazy?" Then she turned and gave me a sharp look. "Perhaps this is all a trap to draw me out. Who are you, Dancer, and where are you from if she's not really your grandmother?"

"I told you the truth about all that. I really am from the city of Urshameel. I trained as a Dancer in the Temple of Kernoss and took a five-year pledge to go on the road. In the name of the Goddess. That is the truth. I met this woman just this morning on my way into your city. You had best credit her story. I have no doubt she tells the truth. I have seen enough such men in other places."

"I have no doubt either. There have been rumors for a while now. Perhaps when this is all over, if any of us are still alive, I'll come and visit you there in your city. How much longer do you have on the road?"

"This year is almost up and then I only have one more. I would like it very much if you came to Urshameel. There would be welcome for you there. If I'm still away, ask for Melanthia at the Temple. She would be glad to give you shelter in my name."

Her lip quivered and she whispered, "Thank you for your kindness, Zaia."

At that moment I noticed the two men coming back. Rashem saw them as well. She quickly got to her feet. "Enough of all this talk," she muttered. "Let us be out of this city before the High Priest changes his mind and decides it would be better to have me locked up after all, for the good of the city. First I must go warn my nephew. He lives on Haslan Street."

"No! No time!" Lurian and I both said at the same instant. Then Lurian added, almost in a whisper, "It would mean your lives and probably mine as well and maybe his also." With those words she stood up and her whole manner changed abruptly. Speaking to the men, she said in a very different tone, "I have done my work here and was about to call for you. It's time for these two to be on the road. I've wasted enough time today and need to get back to my Dancers."

After that she marched us through the city at a fast pace in silence. I noticed that this part of the city was not nearly so grand and elegant. As we went farther it became quite poor and shabby, built of old wood and rough stone, in a state of disrepair such as I had never seen in Urshameel. The people also seemed poor and shabby. They were dispirited and not at all like the fancy, well-dressed crowd I had seen in the center of Khoberah.

We were soon at a gate that Lurian said would lead to the road west. She signaled to the men to stay back. Then she took Rashem's arm in a firm grip and walked her through. Very softly she said, "Thank you, Rashem, for risking so much to try to warn us. I'm sorry if it was of no use. I'll do what I can here, though I have little hope. At least I'll try to talk to your nephew and tell him you were here."

Then she raised her head and her face took on a cold, haughty, arrogant look, and she said loudly to me, "See that you never let her come back this way. The old one is not welcome here with her mad tales and neither are you, Dancer. Your grandmother is a disturbance in the city. Take her back to her village and give her something to calm her ravings so she's not a danger to herself or others. It is only due to my brother's great kindness and generosity that she's not sleeping in a cell this night."

In a whisper I said to her, "Lady, you are safely outside the city gates. It might be better for your health to just keep walking and not look back. There are many other places to live in this world."

She shook her head and whispered back, "But not better for the health of this city. I do what I have to do. The rest is in Her hands."

She was turning to leave. Behind the mask of arrogance that hardened her face I could see the depth of her grief and despair. I wanted to reach out and touch her, to grab her hand and beg her to come with us. I did nothing. I let her turn away without a word of comfort. Anything I did or said would only endanger her more. I wanted to cry. I heard her say to the guards in that same harsh voice of command, "Shut the gates so they don't wander back in now that we have just gotten rid of them."

Little chance of that, I thought as I heard the gates closing behind us. I was so glad to be out of that city it was all I could do not to run down the road shouting with joy. Rashem muttered to me, "Those gates are not much protection for a city. An angry mule would have them down with a couple of kicks."

"Not our business anymore," I said, taking her arm in a firm grip and moving her on down the road before she could say anything else to get us in trouble.

"When they come this city will shatter like a glass dropped on the paving stones."

"True enough—and there is nothing we can do to change that."

She nodded. Then she gave me a sideways glance. "You let him call me a crazy old woman and said nothing to defend me. You know I'm not crazy."

"Maybe you are a crazy old woman. Only someone crazy would talk that way to the High Priest, calling him a fool and an idiot to his face."

"But he is a fool and you didn't even give me a chance to speak for myself."

"Goddess give me patience!" I felt myself flushing with anger. "How can you think to talk to me that way? Only by the quickest of thinking was I able to extricate you from a very dangerous situation. I likely saved your life and at no small risk to my own. You should be thanking me on your knees rather than berating me."

She gave me another of those sideways looks. "Well…" she said skeptically. She did not continue. I thought that was probably all the apology I was likely to get.

There was no one else on the road at that moment, but I was just starting to feel uneasy. I started to think that we might best keep out of sight and then she gave a deep sigh and said, "I'm so weary I could just lie down by the side of the road and sleep for a week."

"Not here and not now!" I said sharply. "I'm not at all sure the High Priest is finished with us. It might be better to stay off the road for a while and walk at the edge of the woods."

This time she didn't argue. She followed as I led her toward the fringe of trees. Almost as soon as we got off the road we heard the sound of horses being ridden fast. There was only time to crouch behind some boulders and pull my dark cloak over us both, a rock among the rocks. From where we were hiding we could see five or six men from the Temple riding fast and looking from side to side. As soon as they had passed we made haste away from there and were well into the shelter of the woods when we heard them riding back again. I didn't think either of us would ever see the city of Khoberah again. As the sound of the horses faded away, Rashem put her hand on my arm and said, "Thank you Dancer, thank you for saving my life one more time."

What happened in the city of Khoberah had frightened me deeply and left me with many troubling thoughts. The idea that a Temple could be a place of danger rather than shelter had shaken me to the core. From Khoberah I turned back toward Urshameel, taking the shortest way in hopes of reaching my own city shortly after the end of my fifth year. I suddenly found myself longing for home in a way I hadn't at any time before, thinking constantly of the city and the Temple and worrying about what I might find there. If such things could happen in Khoberah, what might have happened in Urshameel? Five years away is a long time. Melanthia and my aunt and my cousin, and especially my father, began coming into my dreams. I longed to hear their voices and see their faces again. I even held long conversations aloud with Thesali as I walked along. But my most pressing reason for going back was my hands. They had begun to shake. It had started even before Khoberah, but at first it was so slight that I could deny it, pretend it wasn't real. After a while it began to get worse each time I Danced. It would have been wiser not to Dance again, but it was so hard to resist.

CHAPTER 16
The Prophetess

I was trudging along at dusk, trying to find a good place to camp and wishing I had stopped sooner, when I glimpsed the light of a fire. As I came closer I saw that a lone woman sat by it. Yielding to sudden impulse, I stepped behind some trees to watch her instead of calling out a greeting as I should have. I was full of curiosity but also feeling a little guilt for spying on her in that way. A large woman dressed in rich, town finery that was ragged and tattered from travel, she was sitting cross-legged on a blanket with cards laid out before her. Touching the cards or turning them, I heard her intoning some words aloud, but I was too far away to understand or perhaps she was speaking a different language. I thought her totally absorbed in her cards when she suddenly looked up. With her stare fastened on my place of concealment, she said loudly, "No need to go skulking around that way, Dancer. Come out and talk to me, if that is what you want."

I stepped out of hiding and came over to her fire, somewhat embarrassed at having been caught that way in my spying. "How did you know?"

"I have the 'othersight.' I'm never sure if it's a blessing or a curse, but at least it's hard for anyone to sneak up on me, even on silent Dancer feet. I saw the image of your presence in my mind well before you saw me." At those words she looked me up and down with a quick sweep of her eyes and I found myself blushing. "Now that you're here you might as well sit down on my blanket and share my evening meal. Sometimes it grows lonely on the road."

"I'm sorry. I didn't mean to intrude on you that way."

"Too late now for sorry, you've already intruded," she said brusquely as she scooped out a bowl of food from a big pot by the fire. When she handed it to me her eyes met mine. The grief in them shook me so deeply that I almost dropped the bowl, but when she spoke her tone was light and mocking. "In payment for intruding on my solitude this way you have to tell me your story. But first, eat. You're probably hungry."

The smell was wonderful. I drew in a deep breath of it and gave a sigh of satisfaction. I ate the first bowl without a word and didn't begin to talk until I had almost finished the second. Then I told her my name and some stories of my travels while she nodded encouragement for me to go on. When my voice finally grew weary I asked, "And what of you?"

"Me?" She shrugged and shook her head. "Not much to tell. My name is Jekartha. My mother was a Temple servant in the city of Theranin. I grew up in the Temple where my talent for 'othersight' was quickly spotted. They trained me to be the Temple Prophetess. I could have held a high position there, a position of honor and power that would have made my mother proud, but I saw too much in that city, said things that might better have gone unsaid, especially about those who had power in the Temple or the city. I could no more keep my mouth shut about the truth than I could avoid seeing it. Speaking is part of the gift, though I have learned since then how to moderate it somewhat. Also I knew too much about those I loved, things that would happen to them that I would rather not have known. It was hard. Sometimes people were angry at me for what I saw, as if I were the cause of all their misfortunes. Often they didn't believe what I told them and so they walked right into life's traps, in spite of my best efforts to warn them.

"Despite all that, I might have stayed if I had not become aware of some very irregular dealings between the Temple and the head of the Council. Of course, I talked. After that my place at the Temple was no longer assured and I was too uncomfortable in the city of Theranin to remain there. I even felt as if my life might be at risk. They wanted the truth from me but not that much truth. Since then I have wandered from place to place, never staying long. At first I'm very useful and people beg me to stay, but soon my truth-seeing becomes a nuisance and an embarrassment and so I move on. By now I know that there's no hope of settling anywhere, so I don't grow too attached. It no longer breaks my heart to leave. The things I see...the things I know...that's what breaks my heart."

"Can you read hands?"

"Of course, but I'd rather not."

"Read my hands," I said impulsively as I held them out to her. As I did so I shivered.

She shook her head. But then, moving as if she couldn't help herself, she slowly took my hands, opened them, stared into them and held them up to the firelight, turning them this way and that with a puzzled frown on her face. "Not what I would have expected," she muttered as she traced the lines with the fingers of one hand. "Strange...you will be a leader of people but not as a Dancer. I see..." Suddenly her voice shifted into trance mode and she spoke in that strange, dazed way seers sometimes have, "I see you surrounded by women, I see weapons, I see much blood and danger, I see many dead bodies, I see..." Suddenly she shuddered and shook herself. Then she said in her normal voice, "The vision has faded. Sometimes it happens that way." With a strange look on her face she cupped my hands in her own and pressed them between her breasts. "Goddess bless you, Dancer, on your journey through this life—wherever it may take you."

"Please, Jekartha, tell me what you saw." I was wide-eyed and trembling, staring into the seer's face.

"I told you all I saw. Now it's gone dark. Don't ask me what it means. The Mother didn't see fit to tell me that. She only gave me glimpses."

What could it mean? I knew I was not being told the whole truth, but it was clear I would get nothing more from my questions. I tried to put some coins in the woman's hand, but she refused them with a shake of her head. "I told you nothing worth paying for, Dancer. I'm very tired, perhaps it was only a waking dream. It's late now, time for sleep. If you're also going to Norshell you can accompany me in my wagon. I'll be reading fortunes at the market tomorrow and you no doubt will be Dancing at the festival of Yanteerin for the good folk of that town. They will probably try to get you to stay for longer than you planned."

"You've been here before?"

"Yes, several times." There was some sort of warning in her tone, but I couldn't get her to talk more about the town either. She just yawned widely, threw ashes on the fire and began to unroll her bedding, saying, "We sat up too late talking and now tomorrow will come all too soon."

The next morning we made a quick breakfast of tea, cheese and trail bread. Jekartha did not change out of her ragged clothes. She merely added some bright scarves and sashes to cover the damage, but she encouraged me to dress in my Dance costume. "I've always found it pays to advertise your wares," she told me with a broad wink.

Watching Jekartha with her horse, the way she petted his neck and whispered in his ear, the way he rubbed his head against her arm and snuffled his nostrils in her hand, I realized that this was her life companion, probably the only creature in the world she could really trust. She was humming to herself as, with quick, skilled hands, she got the wagon hitched up and ready. I saw that the wagon was well maintained and brightly painted, the harness oiled and all the rings and buckles on it shiny. This was her rolling home and clearly she took pride in it.

The moment we entered the town people rushed over to greet "The Dancer" until there was quite a crowd around us calling out, "We have a Dancer for Yanteerin!" "Thank the Goddess, she came just in time!" "Someone run quickly and tell Zorkan." I was used to some excitement when I first appeared in a place but this seemed extreme. It was almost as if I were a prize or a trophy to be claimed. "I warned you, didn't I?" Jekartha said mysteriously—though of course she hadn't warned me at all. "Don't let them sweep you off your feet or bend your will." The moment I was out of the wagon she winked, waved, turned her horse down the street and was gone, leaving me in the hands of these overeager town folk.

"Will I see you again?" I called after her departing back.

"Look for me at the market," she shouted back as her wagon disappeared around the corner.

At almost the same instant, a man pushed through the crowd, saying he had been sent to escort me to the Headman's house. He was very courteous almost obsequious and, though I kept refusing, he offered several times to carry my pack. The crowd of people followed us down the street, all talking excitedly. I heard the town of Palmuri mentioned several times. It seemed as if there was some sort of rivalry in progress between the towns and I had suddenly become the focus of it. My guide kept saying, "Zorkan will be so pleased that you're here. We've been praying to get a Dancer before Palmuri did."

The Headman's house was a large imposing stone and brick structure with many intricate wooden embellishments that seemed more for show than beauty. He was standing in the doorway with a big grin on his face, waiting to greet me. "Welcome, Dancer. Welcome to Norshell. You are the answer to our prayers." With those words he immediately took charge. Dismissing the crowd as well as my escort, he ushered me inside with that same overblown courtesy. With a flourish, he introduced himself as Zorkan and asked my name and the name of my Temple. Almost in the same breath he offered me food and drink. In no time he had me sitting at his table with a large glass of cider, which he kept refilling as soon as I had taken a few sips and eating a huge bowl of porridge with cream, dried fruit and nuts.

While I ate, he promised me a hot bath and a very comfortable room— meanwhile he plied me with questions and rushed me with plans of his own. "So you have been trained in one of the great Dance Temples. Even in this far corner of the world we have heard of the Temple of Kernoss. We are very flattered to have you here among us. How long do you plan to stay? The Festival of Yanteerin is two days from now so I assume you will Dance for that, but the Day of Remembrance is in less than two weeks. Could you possibly bless us with your presence for that long?"

Soon he left me there, eating under the watchful eye of his cook, Urdra, while he rushed out on some important business. I was relieved to have him gone. He asked too many questions and wanted too many quick answers to things that needed some thought. Urdra, on the other hand, made no fuss at all over me beyond setting down two little honeycakes by my plate. Because of this, perhaps I felt I could trust her. She was a short, stocky woman of indeterminate age, almost as wide as she was tall. She had a penetrating gaze and gave off an air of easy competence as she moved about her work. She kept bustling around in the kitchen until I finally persuaded her to join me at the table. "Urdra, what is happening in this town? These people all seem very excited to have a Dancer among them, yet they appear to have forgotten the real reason for the Dance."

She pursed her lips and looked at me in silence for a while, as if trying to judge whether or not it was safe to speak. Finally she gave a nod and said dryly, "Quite right, Dancer, they have forgotten that the Dance is sacred and holy, not a weapon for stabbing the town of Palmuri in the back. This rivalry has been going on a long time now, too long if you ask me. Last year Palmuri had four Dancers and Norshell only had one—and not a very good one at that. But the year before it was just the opposite. When will it end? Personally, I've seen more than enough of this and care nothing for who wins, though I'd rather you didn't mention my views to the master of this house."

"Perhaps I should leave and not Dance here at all?"

"And what purpose would that serve? Would that please the Goddess? If you know the real purpose of the Dance and keep that clear in your heart how can it be corrupted? I for one would be quite disappointed not to see you Dance."

"How is Palmuri to know how well I Dance in Norshell?"

"You may be sure they will have judges here watching your every step." I didn't like the sound of this but said nothing more on the subject.

When I tried to fall asleep that night I was in a turmoil of indecision, wondering whether to stay or go. One thing was clear to me, I would not stay past Yanteerin. As soon as I Danced I would be back on the road again. I wasn't even sure if I could stay for the two days of processions, the feasting and street-dancing that would follow, though they would surely expect me to take part in all the festivities. But if I left now I would probably not be able to Dance for Yanteerin at all. Palmuri was the only town that was close enough and I had no desire to leave one rival and rush into the arms of the other. In the end I got very little sleep and woke next morning tired and out of sorts, not a good way to prepare for a Dance.

To better my mood I decided to explore Norshell. As I walked about, what I saw of the town appeared to be orderly, solid and well-built. Most of the houses were made of stone and large dark timbers. In truth, it was not very interesting, with little there to excite the eye or entice the spirit. These structures were nothing like the magnificent gardens in Urshameel or the intricate and delicate stonework in Khoberah. In fact I found myself rather bored and I wandered aimlessly until I came to the market. Then my mood shifted instantly. Here everything appeared to be in a state of noisy lively confusion. It looked as if the life and color missing in the rest of the town had all been gathered here. Soon I was in a much happier frame of mind, munching on apples and little cakes while ambling up and down aisles brightly colored with fruit, flowers, vegetables and crockery. People fussed over me, paying compliments and asking questions, reaching out to touch my clothes or my hair. It was impossible to pay for anything. For luck they each wanted me to have something from their booth.

When I found myself at an herb seller's stall I remembered my bad night's sleep and thought to get myself a packet of tea that would relax the muscles and the mind. This booth was all hung with bundles of drying herbs. Shelves on all three sides were crowded with bottled tinctures, salves and other remedies. It was run by a woman and her nearly grown daughter. The herb seller was ingratiatingly polite to me, bowing deferentially and calling me Lady Dancer. In painful contrast, she ordered her daughter about in an angry, spiteful tone as if the girl could do nothing right. "More string, Chandri, any fool can see that packet needs more string. Hang that bundle back up where it belongs and don't be breaking off all the leaves with your eternal clumsiness."

Hearing this made me cringe inside. The pained look on the girl's face went right to my heart. On sudden impulse I asked, "Could your daughter show me the Dance Court? I haven't seen it yet and don't know the way."

Very pleased, the woman bowed again. "Yes, Lady Dancer, whatever you wish. It would be an honor. She can show you around the whole town if that is your pleasure. Look sharp to it, Chandri. Take the Lady Dancer wherever she wants to go and don't be lazing around."

As soon as we were out of earshot I leaned toward her and said, "My name is Zaia, not Lady Dancer, and I have just bought you a day of freedom." A sudden, dazzling smile was my reward.

We went first to watch Jekartha who had spread her blanket under a huge flowering tree in the middle of the market. She had quite a little crowd waiting for her skills. She grinned and winked at us but was much too busy to speak. As we wandered out of the market, sharing my cakes and apples between us, I noticed two young men who seemed to be following us like shadows. Once we were clear of the stalls Chandri called them over and introduced them to me. "This is Denaldi," she said nodding toward a tall, thin, very dark young man. "And this is Avron," she went on, gesturing at the shorter, wider one. "They are my only real friends, but my mother doesn't like them, so in the market, they keep away from me."

"We don't have to go to the Dance Court, Chandri. We can go wherever you please."

"I'll take you to my favorite grove of trees," she said with that same heart-melting smile.

When we had all settled in the shade of some ancient trees with widely spreading branches, Denaldi produced a round of cheese, a loaf of bread and a knife from his pack. Avron pulled some pears from his pocket while I contributed the rest of my apples and cakes, and Chandri put out some candied fruit slices. I gave her a nod. "Now, in trade for your day's freedom, you have to tell me why your mother is so angry with you."

She shook her head, and I saw tears brimming at the edge of her eyes. I was about to tell her to forget my question when she began speaking intently. "I'm a seer. I prophesy and sometimes read minds. When it's happening I have to speak, I have no choice. What I say frightens people. They think me strange. My mother wants me to stop altogether or else use it for money, do what Jekartha does, but I have no control. It's something that just comes on me when it wills and uses me to its purposes. Some call it a gift, but I think of it more as a curse. It has certainly poisoned my life. And it's the same for Denaldi and Avron, only their families have already put them out."

"You should talk to Jekartha, her story is much the same."

"Oh, no, she's a real card reader. That's very different."

"Not so, she's just like you only she uses the cards to mask and channel her gift. Talk to her. You'll see."

Chandri shook her head, hopefulness and fear and pain mixing in her face. "Maybe," she said doubtfully.

After that we talked of many things. I told them of the great cities I had seen and entertained them with tales of my life on the road. In turn they told me stories of their lives. We even sang some songs together and shared some poems. Altogether it was one of the most pleasant days of my life and certainly one of the freest.

Later all three of them took me to see the Dance Court. Then, with some flowers in hand, we went to pay our respects to the Goddess. She was represented by a huge, polished, dark-stone figure sitting on top of a mound in the center of Norshell. A brooding presence, Her features were nearly worn away by the attack of the weather and the touch of many hands. When it was my turn to lay my flowers down at Her feet I asked for Her blessings on my Dance. All that came back was profound silence, dark as the stone itself.

When I finally went back to Zorkan's house Urdra told me he was quite frantic and had been looking for me everywhere, wanting to take me to a meeting of the town council. Hearing that, I was doubly glad for having spent the day under some trees in the company of those charming young people.

It was time. I had done all the proper things and still, somehow, I didn't feel prepared, though this was one of the easiest of all the Dances and one of my favorites. I kept trying to find that core of stillness inside, and it kept eluding me. I wondered, much too late, if I should have stayed in a different house and perhaps found more peace there. Yet how could I have done that without giving offense and being very rude? And my hands still shook. There was no denying it anymore. When I was moving about it wasn't so obvious, but when I held them out in front of me I couldn't keep them still.

It was Urdra who helped me dress and did my hair with deft, skilled fingers. She also kept me entertained with her dry wit and irreverent observations. She had none of that cloying, fawning deference that was beginning to sicken my spirit. Instead she made shrewd, wry and insightful comments about everything: my appearance, the town folk in general and some of them in particular, life in the Headman's house, Zorkan's self-importance, her own wide stature. Nothing was spared by her sharp tongue.

The people of Norshell had given me a new Dance costume, a very beautiful one in shades of blue and purple with red and gold trim at the edge of the vest and the hem of the skirt. It was much needed as my old ones had grown shabby from use and were in dire need of mending. When she was done Urdra turned me this way and that for a critical appraisal. She patted a few things into place and then nodded her approval. "Not bad. The Lady should be pleased." Then she brought me my dark cloak and laid it over my shoulders. "Better to wear this in the street and keep your bright colors covered. Otherwise the crowd will eat you alive. They'll each want a little piece of you to take home." Then, to my surprise, she pulled my head forward and kissed me on the forehead. "Good luck, Dancer. Goddess give you strength to bear up under the weight of all those expectations."

When Zorkan appeared just before dusk to escort me to the Dance Court I wanted to cry out, It's too soon, I'm not ready, though of course I did no such thing. Going down the street we soon acquired a sizable procession of town folk cheering us along. A few of those that I passed were glowering at me. I thought they must be from Palmuri and was very glad for the protection of my dark cloak. I could feel Zorkan's pride swelling as he walked beside me. Bowing while he ushered me along, he kept saying to people, "This year we will have a better Dancer than Palmuri, much better. This one is from the famous Temple of Kernoss in the City of Urshameel."

Somehow this all felt wrong and strange, but it was happening too fast and I couldn't think how to change course. A Dancer is not any man's possession, nor any woman's. We belong only to our own selves and to the Goddess, yet Zorkan was acting as if he owned me. He seemed to be taking personal credit for my presence in Norshell. In your hands Goddess I said in the silence of my mind and tried to hold Urdra's blessing close to my heart.

There was a huge noisy crowd at the Dance Court. Everyone in Norshell must have been there. It took a while for them all to find their places and longer for them to silence themselves. Still wearing the cloak, I waited quietly by a pillar, a shadow among shadows. After the musicians had played for a few moments, I slipped out of the cloak and stepped onto the Dance Court. Instantly there was a flurry of exclamations. While Zorkan tried to hush the crowd, I stood there breathing deeply, trying to find the stillness inside as I waited for silence. Then I raised my arms, took the first step forward and asked in my head the ritual question, Goddess, am I fit to Dance for you tonight?

I was expecting that familiar, sudden, miraculous lift into Dance, that amazing transformation from being a creature of mortal flesh with all its limitations to being an instrument of divine will. Instead, my next step was just an ordinary step that quickly brought me back down to earth. I took one more very ordinary step and then stopped altogether. No! Not here! The voice had spoken! It was like being hit by a fist! I staggered back with those words thundering in my head. I stared at my Dancewand and saw no colors moving there, no guidance. Frozen in place, unable to move, I looked about me in bewilderment. Soon the crowd began muttering and after a few minutes the musicians stopped playing. Everyone was staring at me, first with amazement—and then with hostility. They had all been waiting for me to Dance and it was clear I was not Dancing, that I was probably not going to Dance.

This was the moment every Dancer dreaded, the moment when the Dance failed her. Melanthia had told me it happened at least once to every Dancer on the road, sometimes more than that. "It is the will of the Goddess and something you have to accept," she had said. But nothing could have prepared me for the shock of it, no words could have softened the blow. I felt like a bird whose wings had suddenly been cut off just as she was rising in flight.

Trembling all over, I bowed deeply. With my voice cracked and shaky I managed to say, "Forgive me, people of Norshell, I cannot Dance for you this night. The Goddess does not will it." This was followed by a wild clamor of angry voices.

"After all we've given her..."

"...food and clothing..."

"Deep insult to our town..."

"Maybe she's a fake..."

"...not a Dancer after all..."

"An impostor from Palmuri..."

"...took advantage of our good will."

And mixed in with the angry voices from Norshell I could hear gloating voices from Palmuri.

"...even worse than last year."

"They won't get any prizes for this one."

"Wait until I tell Yozzin that his prayers have been answered. That'll teach Zorkan to be so arrogant."

Tears stung my eyes. It was through a sort of fog or haze that I heard the hostile mutterings of the people and saw them milling about. Though I didn't really think they would attack me or do me physical harm, almost by instinct I raised my Dancewand as if to defend myself. There was no color moving in

its depth, only different shades of gray. Dizzy, disoriented and very frightened, I was swaying on my feet while the scene before me swam in my sight.
The lights of the torches began to spin wildly and then, just as everything
started to go black, I felt a hand on my elbow. If I still had any strength left
I might have flinched away in fear, but her grip was strong, strong enough
to hold me. It was Jekartha. With a fierce whisper she said in my ear, "Come
with me, Dancer. You need to be away from here and quickly. Maybe you
even need to get a little food in your belly."

I nodded and breathed a sigh of relief. Leaning heavily on her arm, I
allowed her to lead me away. "Move! Out of the way! Let us through!" she
barked out gruffly as she pushed her way forward and made a path for us.
People actually gave way before her with a look of fear on their faces. We
went as quickly as I was able to walk, while the shouts and mutters faded
behind us. Finally I thought to ask, "Where are we going?"

"To Three Brothers Inn. An old friend of mine owns it. You will get fed
and be safe there." I made no objection, but when we went in I looked around
fearfully, half expecting some attack. We sat at the table closest to the kitchen
where the light was dim. Some of the townsfolk had followed us there.
Though they didn't cross the room to bother us, I could see them all talking
excitedly. I was sure the innkeeper already knew my story when he came to
take our order. He was a big burly man with a broad, friendly, bearded face.

"Hello, Jekartha, good to see you again. You will have to put up with
my poor service as everyone has deserted me for the Dance Court." Then he
thrust out his hand to me. "My name is Nagail and any friend of Jekartha's is
welcome here. I hear you foiled their plans for beating the town of Palmuri.
Zorkan must be livid. He was counting on you to be his tool in this work."
Unlike the others of the town, he appeared to be amused rather than angry.
Indeed he seemed to take some pleasure in this turn of things.

I shook my head. "Either way it was no intention of mine. I had no wish
to be any part of his plot, but it was also no choice of mine not to Dance. I
think it was the Mother's will that stopped my feet."

"Well that's fine if you believe in the Goddess, and being a Dancer I
suppose you have to. Me, I'm a practical man. I only believe what I see right
in front of my face. I thought they just pushed you too hard, but in truth I'm
just as glad it happened as it did. Serves them right. I want no part in this
rivalry with Palmuri. My two brothers live there and so does my old mother.
Why should I care about beating the town of Palmuri? Of course there are
fools there who would have tried to use you for their own ends, just that
same way if you had gone to Palmuri instead. So, the Mother's curse on all of
them I say—if you believe in that sort of curse."

I started to say, "It was only a flip of the coin that brought me here, two out of three. I could as easily have ended in Palmuri..."

At the same moment, Jekartha said impatiently, "For heaven's sake, Nagail, stop prattling and bring us some food. Can't you see she's about to faint?"

"What would you like? We have..."

Jekartha interrupted again, "Whatever you have that's hot and good and ready to eat right now. A lot of it and quickly."

While he went to fetch our food, I looked around nervously. By now the inn had filled with people. They were muttering and grumbling, gossiping avidly among themselves, obviously about me. Some were even pointing in our direction but at least they kept their distance. I think I owed my safety to Jekartha, or perhaps they were just afraid to attack a Dancer. I laid my Dancewand across the end of the table and the colors in it swirled darkly in wildly agitated patterns.

The food, when it came, was indeed good and plentiful. In preparation for the Dance I had eaten nothing since our meal under the trees, so the smell of it made me dizzy with hunger. Nagail obviously wanted to stay and talk, but Jekartha waved him away. "Leave her some peace. Can't you see she's already shaken and distraught. She can't answer a lot of foolish questions right now."

Seeming not at all offended by her rudeness, he grinned and went off, whistling to himself, while I gratefully plunged into my portion of food. When I was finally satiated I leaned back and asked what had been on my mind the whole time, "You knew, didn't you? That's why you were ready for it. You knew that I wouldn't be able to Dance."

"Of course I knew. I'm not head-blind. I do have othersight."

"Then why didn't you tell me, give me some warning?"

"Would you still have tried to Dance?"

"Of course, but if I'd known I might have been better prepared. I might have been able to overcome it."

"Overcome the will of the Goddess? Do you really think so?" She gave me a quizzical look.

"I suppose not. How can you bear just to watch things happen when you already know?"

"Sometimes I can't." That terrible look of pain crossed her eyes again.

I sighed. It was all such a strange tangle. "Jekartha, why are you helping me? You hardly even know me."

"Let's say I know what it's like to be treated that way, to have people suddenly turn on you like that. You're not sorry are you, to be seen with me? If I hadn't come forward you might have fainted on the Dance Court and still be lying there. I doubt if any of those cowardly fools would have risked the wrath of their fellow townspeople by coming to your aid."

I was about to thank her when she said urgently, "Watch yourself, here comes trouble. I see he finally got up the courage to come pester us." I looked up to see a big man crossing the room in our direction. There was a table full of men over by the door and they were calling out encouragement to him. When he reached us, Jekartha looked up at him and said coldly, "Hello, Thanton, we're busy right now."

Not at all discouraged by her deliberate rebuff, he planted his huge hands on the table and leaned over. "I see the fake prophetess and the fake Dancer are old friends. Have you made an alliance to rob this town of its rightful place in the world?"

"We made an alliance to eat a meal together because we were both hungry. Whether we're friends or not is really no business of yours. Now go back to your comrades and leave us in peace."

"Not until you lay out your cards and do a reading for this town. I want to know what the future is for us now that the Dancer, if she really is a Dancer, has failed to Dance. I want to know what it means." His voice sounded threatening as he slammed down a large coin on the table.

"No!" shouted Jekartha, leaping to her feet so fast she knocked over her chair. She seemed afraid, not so much of the man as of what he asked. Almost instantly Nagail was at her side. She pushed some coins at him, saying quickly, "Thank you, friend, that was very good. We have to go now."

With one hand Nagail scooped up the coins and slipped them in his pocket, while with the other he grabbed Thanton by the neck of his tunic. "Go back to your table and behave or I'll have to ask you to leave. You can't go bothering the other customers here." The two men were of about the same size and weight. If it came to blows it would have been a dangerous contest, probably very damaging to everything and everyone around. I had no wish to be witness to it.

Jekartha ducked under Nagail's arm, grabbed my hand in a grip of iron and quickly pulled me out to the street. "My horse is at the stable on the corner. I think it's time for us both to leave this town." With some coins in hand she sent a boy to fetch her wagon and horse. While we waited, a hostile crowd was gathering. To deflect their anger, Jekartha pulled a tiny stringed instrument from the pocket of her wide skirt and began singing an old country song to her own accompaniment. That seemed to be a sufficient distraction. As soon as she stopped someone called out for another and after that one still another. In this way we passed the time in relative safety until the boy drove up with the wagon.

Jekartha was quickly seated and trying to help me up. Ordinarily I could have leapt up beside her with ease, but since being unable to Dance my legs seemed to have momentarily lost all their strength. Just then Thanton appeared before her, blocking the way. He grabbed the horse's reins so we couldn't make a sudden escape, and tossed some coins on the seat of the wagon. "You will tell our future before you go. You owe that to us, to the people of Norshell. Lay out the cards." Instantly there were others tossing coins on the seat, shouting, "One hand of cards! Just one!"

As I slumped against the wagon, she whirled to face them, very angry now, too angry for caution. "You ignorant fools, you don't even know what you're asking for. Do you think I really need those stupid cards to tell the future? If I want to see the future I only have to shut my eyes and ask, but I don't plan to do that because you wouldn't really want to know. It's so much worse than any of you can imagine." With those words she turned toward me again.

Just as she was reaching out to help me up, her head jerked back and her eyes shut involuntarily. Her whole body jerked a few times and then went rigid. As if under a spell, her face distorted, her mouth opened and a terrible wail filled the night. Then words began spewing out: blood... dead bodies... many men with weapons... fire and death... burned ruins... nothing left... Her limbs were convulsing spasmodically as if in the power of something much stronger.

Suddenly she tumbled off the seat and crumpled on the ground, raving incoherently, foaming at the mouth. Her eyes flew open and rolled back so that only the whites were showing. She was tossing about so violently I was afraid she would do herself some harm. Then, abruptly, she went still, so still I thought her dead. I sank down to feel her pulse. At that moment the Headman pushed his way up to us and said imperiously, "Put her in her wagon and drive away from here. Both of you need to be gone right now before you bring any more harm to this town, or before you yourselves are harmed. I can't be responsible for your safety here after what you've done to us."

"But I don't know how to drive a wagon. It's dark and she's sick. We have no place to go. She needs care. She may die."

"You should have thought of all that before you refused to Dance for us after all our generosity."

I pulled myself up, suddenly strengthened by some anger of my own. "I didn't refuse. I went to your Dance Court to Dance. I prepared myself with all the proper rituals. It was the Goddess who refused because you turned her Dance from a sacred thing into a contest with the town of Palmuri. It was your own greed and malice that blocked the Dance."

His face turned dangerously red and his eyes were bulging. "My greed! You've eaten my food, slept in my house and after all my kindness you have the gall to call me greedy? Don't stand here arguing with me, Woman. There's no roof in this town you could shelter under this night, certainly not mine. Get her in that wagon and get yourselves gone from here."

My moment of anger quickly faded into fear. With Jekartha unconscious I was very much alone there. The grumblings were getting perilously loud. I put my hand over my pendant for protection and in the silence of my head called out to the Goddess for strength. Zorkan was probably right about our safety resting in a quick departure, but I could not lift Jekartha's large stiff form by myself. I could barely stand on my own feet without something to lean on. "I'll go now, but I need someone to help me put her in the wagon." I spoke sharply, trying to cover my fear with a tone of command.

Zorkan shook his head. "I wouldn't touch her," he said spitefully, putting his hands in his sleeves and spitting off to the side. Those who were closest to me looked away as if I could not possibly be speaking to them, while others even took a step back. In despair, I slumped against the wagon again. I almost envied Jekartha lying there unconscious, with no worries and no decisions to make. "Someone has to help me," I called out despairingly. Suddenly Nagail was at my side. He tossed a large sack on the front seat. Then he unfastened and rolled back enough of the canvas side to give us room and said in my ear, "If you can steady her head and arms I think I can lift the rest of her."

I lifted her head and as much of her torso as I could manage while he lifted the rest of her stiffened body. Together, grunting and straining, we managed to slip Jekartha's rigid, unconscious form into the back of the wagon, though not as gently as I would have liked. As we stood up together he whispered in my ear, "I regret that I didn't speak to shelter you, but I was afraid they might burn the inn down over our heads. Go by the West Road. There's a little stream there where you can set up camp. I don't think they'll follow you that far. They are too afraid of whatever power they think you possess. There's food for a few days in that sack. Tell Jekartha, when she wakens, that I wish her well and will be thinking of her often. I wish things between us could have been different in this life." Then he gave me a hand up.

Totally unfamiliar with the skill of driving a horse and as shaken as I had ever been in my life, I snapped the reins and we set off into the night. I knew there was no help to be had in that town and was much relieved when the aggressive crowd parted for the wagon. I'd been afraid they would hit the horse or begin throwing things at us, but beyond shouting a few insults they seemed far more intent on having us gone than in doing us any real harm. It was good that the horse was docile and gentle and didn't choose that moment to rebel in my inexperienced hands. Soon we were rolling toward the edge of town, going, I hoped, by West Road. Luckily there was a little moonlight, for by now night had really come.

At some moment I heard hoof beats behind me and looked back fearfully, but it was only Urdra, Zorkan's cook. As soon as I saw who it was I pulled back a little on the reins to let her catch up. "I thought you might need these," she said breathlessly, "And I knew he would just burn the lot."

She had gathered up all my belongings from Zorkan's house and stuffed them in my pack, all those things that would have been sorely missed later when I remembered, things that I might not have been able to replace. "Thank you more than I can say, Urdra. And Goddess bless you."

She dropped the pack on the seat beside me. "Well, the Great Mother certainly takes care of things in her own peculiar way. Good luck, Zaia, and Dance well in some other place. I have to go back quickly before anyone notices that I'm gone. This is not an errand I'd want to explain to Zorkan. You aren't very popular right now in the town of Norshell." Then she was gone into the night and I was alone again with my burden.

I'm no healer. Jekartha's condition frightened me. There was no one to turn to or consult with, no help to be had anywhere. I wished Urdra had been able to stay. Somehow I thought she would know about such things. I didn't dare take Jekartha to another town for fear they would take one look at us and drive us away too, perhaps with violence. Besides, the next town was too far.

As I drove I could hear her groaning in back of me. Every time I looked back she was either thrashing about in a way that frightened me or in some stiff distorted pose that terrified me even more, thinking her dead or dying. I went as fast as I could, trying to avoid jouncing over rocks and holes. Finally I found the place where a little stream went under a bridge and turned off into a grove of trees. Perhaps this was a trap. If so, we would just have to die there. I had no energy left to go on and certainly none to fight.

Instantly I slipped down from the wagon and stumbled back to tend to Jekartha. As I said, I am no healer and had little notion of what to do. She was still foaming at the mouth slightly, her eyes were still rolled back and her breath was ragged and sporadic. I mopped her sweat away with a clean cloth and cold water from the stream. Then I called her name over and over, but with no result. I might as well not have been there at all. There seemed little hope of bringing her back. Finally I made a tiny twig fire and heated some of the soothing tea I had bought for myself at the market. Hanging a lantern from the cross piece, I clambered into the back of the wagon to raise her head and get her to drink some. Most of it spilled out, but some must have gone down and had an effect. After a while she seemed to relax into a more natural form and her breathing returned to normal. When she finally dozed off, looking more like herself, with her eyes closed and her limbs relaxed,

I unrolled my mat on the ground and fell at once into an exhausted sleep, much too tired for fear.

When I woke up it was morning and we were still unharmed. Looking around I was surprised to see the three young people from the village standing at the edge of our camp, Chandri from the market and the two young men who were her friends, Avron and Denaldi. They were leaning close together, conversing in whispers and looking anxiously in our direction. For a moment my fears of the night before returned, but I quickly realized they looked far more frightened than frightening.

The moment she saw I was awake, Chandri rushed over while the other two hung back shyly. I struggled to rise to my feet. By the time I was up she had already reached the side of the wagon and was looking down at Jekartha with concern. "Is she alright? Will she survive? Perhaps I can help with her healing. I know something of herbs and cures." By that time the other two had drifted over so that when Jekartha opened her eyes there were three anxious faces peering down at her. "Go away," she croaked harshly. "Go away and leave me alone. I don't need you added to all my other troubles." She tried to turn her face away, but she could scarcely move.

"We can help you." "We want to travel with you." "You won't have to be alone anymore." They each spoke quickly in turn.

"I don't want your help. I don't need your help. I've been alone a long time. It's what I know. It's what I do best. I want you to go away."

Denaldi burst out, "But that's just it, we have no place to go, no one wants us. We're all seers and we all see too much. We thought we could travel together and have someone to talk to, someone who would understand, someone who was older. We also thought we could help you get well again. And we could find food and protect each other and ..."

"Don't beg, Denaldi, it's shameful," Chandri said sharply. "It's no use. You can see she doesn't want us either. It's alright, we can take care of each other just like we always have."

"Yes, go home where you belong. I have nothing to offer you. You can see that. Go now. You'd leave me soon enough anyway. Go away!"

"I thought we might have something to offer you but now I can see we don't." Chandri's voice was sharp with bitterness. "As for going home, I have no home anymore. Because you came to Norshell, my mother drove me out of her house. Denaldi, Avron, come on, we're not needed here." As Chandri turned to leave, the very air around her was vibrating with raw pain. A few more steps and she would be at the edge of the camp and then on her horse and then gone, leaving despair on both sides, also leaving me to care for someone when I had no idea what to do. "Wait!" I shouted, reaching out and grabbing Chandri's wrist, forcing her to turn back. "Don't be so quick with your pride."

Then I looked down at Jekartha. At that moment I wanted to shake her. "Your pride is even worse. You're older, you should know better. So easy to send these young people away with a few sullen words. They offer you healing and companionship. They need someone older and more experienced to talk to when the seeing gets too painful and drives them to the brink of madness. But of course you have offers like this everyday, so you can afford to turn this one down. Who does that leave to take care of you? Me! The person who has no skill or knowledge for it. Also, I have my own work to do. I'm a Dancer, not a healer, and the road calls. What right do you have to tie up my life in this way because you're too proud to look at what's being offered to you?"

"Help me sit up," Jekartha ordered in a strange hoarse voice. I released Chandri's wrist and was about to go to Jekartha's aid, but the young people were there before me. They gently and carefully propped her up with pillows and lovingly wrapped her blanket around her legs. Then Avron quickly brought her a jug of water.

"Don't go yet," Jekartha said softly. "I need a chance to look at you. I need some time to think about this. It's all too sudden." There was a long silence while she stared at the three of them. They stood very still, not fidgeting under her gaze. When she began to speak again the words came out slowly, as if each one was very heavy in her mouth. "You have to understand, it's been a very long time since anyone wanted to be with me for myself, longer still since anyone chose to stay. No matter how much I love them, or how much they say they love me, sooner or later everyone leaves, usually sooner. What I see... what I know... it's just too much... It drives others away. I've grown accustomed to sending people away before they themselves leave, before I can get too attached. I've also grown hard and bitter. Now tell me again, what is it that you want from me?"

Chandri stepped up next to Jekartha. She seemed to be the spokesperson for the three of them. As she began, I breathed a sigh of relief. Now at least there was a chance. She also started by speaking slowly and thoughtfully. "We, too, have been outcasts among our own people, seeing and knowing too much. They think us freaks. Lately the things we see have gotten worse, terrible nightmare visions of death and destruction. No one wants to hear such ravings. We have only each other to talk to. We can't even warn people—they think us mad. Besides, we don't know what to tell them to do, how to protect or defend themselves. And yet I know what we see is true. It's coming as surely as the rain. We aren't mad to see such things, but the seeing of them may make us mad.

"Yesterday I understood for the first time that others besides the three of us saw such things. I was there, I heard you. When my mother drove me out of her house I went to find Avron and Denaldi. Together we made some plans. We thought perhaps we could travel with you and share what we see. Who else can we talk to? We also thought we could help to cure you and be of assistance if such a fit ever came on you again. Not such a bad proposal, something to give and something to gain. Besides, we can't stay in Norshell any longer. It isn't safe for us there now."

"You want to travel with me, is that what you're saying? You want us to take care of each other?" Jekartha was shaking her head in amazement, her voice choked with emotion.

Chandri began nodding vigorously. Avron said quickly, "Not forever of course, but for a while at least, or until we mutually decide to part."

"We won't desert you suddenly because you see something strange," Denaldi added. "We'll probably be seeing the same thing."

"How did you find us?" I asked suddenly. "There are many roads out of Norshell. Why did you take this one?"

"Because Nagail told us. He cares for you, Jekartha. He knew we meant no harm and only wanted to help. But even without his words we would have found you. With that much pain pouring out, we could have followed your trail easily enough. It's like following a scent or a sound."

"Will you let us go with you?" Denaldi was anxiously watching her face with his large dark eyes.

"Do you want us?" Avron asked with painful eagerness.

Chandri kept her silence. There was a deep frown between her eyes as she stared off into the distance, careful not to stare directly into Jekartha's face. She had a proud disdainful look, but she was chewing nervously on her lip.

Jekartha shrugged, then she nodded slowly. "I suppose, for a while. It can't do any harm. As you say, it won't be forever. It might be a relief to be able to speak of what I see without having people back away in fear. Now come up here by me, Chandri, and tell me what happened to you last night."

As she clambered into the wagon, Chandri called out orders to her friends with the careless casualness of long habit, "Avron, make a good fire. And Denaldi, help him with gathering wood and then get out our lind-bark tea. The sooner she drinks some the better. After that, we need to make them both some breakfast." Then she settled herself comfortably beside Jekartha and began to talk. "I saw everything that happened in front of the Inn but I didn't come forward to help. I was a coward. The people of Norshell already think me strange. I was afraid they would drive me out too and then where would I go, alone, a beggar in the world? As it was, I might just as well have had courage because in the end I had nothing else.

"When I got home it turned out that my mother had been there too, seen everything. As if I'd been the cause of it all, she quickly turned her anger and fear on me. She began shouting, 'I want you out of my house! Now! You're already so strange you frighten away some of my customers. Soon you'll end up like that one, raving and foaming. I should have beaten you more when you were little, when it all began. Then maybe it wouldn't have come to this.'"

With those words Chandri's face crumpled and she began to cry, huge wracking sobs that shook her whole body. Jekartha watched for a moment in silence. Then, very tentatively, she put an arm around the girl's shoulder, and after a slight hesitation, drew her close. Chandri quieted gradually in that embrace. Finally she sat up and looked straight at Jekartha. "'Pack your things. It's time for you to leave!' Those were the words that welcomed me home last night. I packed everything that mattered. She's said things like that before, many times, but this time was different, this time I knew she meant it. So now here I am with nowhere else..."

Hearing all this, I turned away to gather my things together. Now that I knew Jekartha would be cared for I was free to worry about myself. I had been harboring a growing terror that I would never be able to Dance again, that something had been broken irreparably in Norshell. I needed to get to the next town and try again, any town but Palmuri, of course. I chose the city of Korshi where there was a Dance Temple and perhaps I could find some healing for myself. I planned to be on the road again as soon as we had eaten, ready to put some distance between myself and the good people of Norshell. As I was consulting my map, I felt Chandri's hand on my arm.

"Dance for us, Zaia, before you leave. Please! I would so love to see you Dance. Please!" Now Chandri herself was begging. There was so much pleading eagerness in her young voice and in her eyes that it went right to my heart. Then the others joined her, even Jekartha. I shook my head. I was about to protest that there was no Dance Court and no music, and besides, I was not even sure I could Dance at all. Before I could say the words I started to feel the energy gathering and rising, strength and power coming back into my legs, the Dance wanting to move itself through me. It seemed I had no choice. Just as I was about to take my first step I saw a flash of color at the edge of trees and realized Urdra was standing there, watching us. I gave her a slight nod of recognition. When I glanced down at my Dancewand it was coming alive. As I watched, bright colors began swirling through the gray. In the next moment I found my body moving with a will of its own.

This was not a formal Dance such as I had learned at the Temple. It came of itself. I didn't know the next step until it was already happening. For that rapt audience of five, I Danced joy and pain and loss and courage and fear and hope and love, on the rough uneven ground and over rocks and humps of grass. Whirling, leaping, twisting, bowing low and rising up again, in this wild place I remembered that even if I couldn't Dance for Zorkan or the people of Norshell, I was still a Dancer for the Goddess.

Entering the Dance Court the next time, I found myself tense and nervous after my failure to Dance for the people of Norshall. But when I Danced effortlessly that time and several more times afterward, saying the ritual words and feeling that wonderful familiar lift into Dance, I regained my confidence. Dancing, however, was not the real problem. The real problem was the tremors, which were getting worse every day. So far they left me each time I began to Dance, but I was sure it wouldn't be long before the Dance itself would be affected by them.

I knew it was time to be back at the Temple of Kernoss for a healing, but I wanted to do one last Dance, one that would be truly memorable. I was nearing the end of my fifth year, the end of my time on the road. I had intended to go to the town of Shamuiri. That had been the next place on my map where there was a Dance Temple. My hope had been to get there in time to Dance for Ghalshamain. Instead, I'd lost my way in a tangle of roads and ended in the little village of Margail. I had only meant to stop long enough to beg some food and get clearer directions to Shamuiri. Much to my surprise, the whole village had poured out into the streets to greet me, beating on drums and shouting joyfully, "The Dancer is here, the Dancer is here, the Temple Dancer is here already." It was as if they had been expecting me. They were so eager I didn't have the heart to shatter their excitement with the truth.

CHAPTER 17
The Last Dance

L *ast Dance. The last Dance.* Those words resonated in my head as I kicked off my sandals and shivered from the chill of the cold stones under my feet. *This would be my last Dance on the road.* Giving a deep sigh of weariness, I began to strip off my dust-encrusted road clothes. I felt nervous and fluttery, all too much my limited human self, with little of the assurance of the Dancer in me at that moment. Later the calm would come or, at least, I hoped it would—that incredible, all-enveloping calm that made me feel as if I were the one still point in the whole whirling universe. Then I would Dance.

My clothes fell in a colorless, gray heap at my feet, looking more like a limp unsightly creature than like any clothes a decent person might wear. It had been a long dusty walk this time and getting lost had made it doubly wearisome. Now I had to be gracious and get over my disappointment that this was not Shamuiri and that I was not to Dance in that city. Perhaps the Goddess Herself had guided me here. How else could I have found my way to this little back-road village that was not even a dot on my map?

Walking into Margail, I had been given a truly memorable and amazing welcome. People had rushed out to greet me, shouting, "The Dancer! The Dancer! The Dancer is here!" Then the Headwoman had pushed herself forward between them to be the first to speak to me. A stern, powerful-looking old woman she seemed very flustered and confused at the moment. Bowing with reverence, she said a little breathlessly, "Be welcome among us, Lady Dancer. This is only a humble little village, but we have a newly built Dance Court. We are deeply grateful that you have come all the way from Shamuiri to grace it with your presence. If only we had known you would be here so soon, we could have prepared a far more fitting entrance for you."

Children quickly surrounded me, thrusting flowers into my hands, and people began crowding around, trying to give me little gifts. I had looked around at them all in bewilderment, shaking my head. Thick-witted with weariness, smiling foolishly with my arms full of flowers, it had taken me a while to understand that the people of the village had just sent someone to petition the Temple at Shamuiri for a Dancer to consecrate their new Dance Court. Seeing my Dancewand strapped to my pack they had mistakenly assumed I was the answer to their prayers—an answer that had certainly arrived with miraculous speed.

For the sake of honesty, I had made a few feeble attempts to explain that I was not who they thought I was. They had no ears for my words, so I finally surrendered to being their "Chosen One," as they kept saying. And indeed, perhaps I was. After all, I had found my way to their village, on this day of all days. Often I had felt as if I were guided on my path. Sometimes I would even shut my eyes and let my finger choose my direction on the map, going where chance or the Goddess led me. But not this time. This time I had very deliberately set out for Shamuiri and ended up in Margail instead.

Well, what harm could there be in pretending for just a little while to be what these villagers so clearly wanted? After all, I really was a Dancer. That at least was no pretense. And it was not the first time I had been mistaken for another. I could consecrate their Dance Court as well as any Dancer from Shamuiri. I heard some of the old women muttering, "A Holy One, a Holy One come to grace us with her Dancing. Only with the help of the Goddess could the Lady Dancer have come to us so quickly."

The little girls pressed close, looking up at me with adoration, reaching out to touch me until their mothers called them back to give me room to move. It would have been cruel to tell them all that the Temple at Shamuiri would not likely have sent them a Dancer and certainly not so quickly. After all, Margail was only a tiny, insignificant village. With a shrug, I stopped trying to untangle truth from wish. Instead, somewhat embarrassed, I accepted their praise and their gratitude, hearing them say over and over how amazing this was, since Yorshan had only set out for Shamuiri two days before. They puzzled as to why he had not returned with me, but I only shook my head and shrugged, muttering something about his having found urgent business that kept him in the city. They would be even more amazed when Yorshan returned with his story, I thought, but by then I would be long gone down the road. Tonight I would have my chance and they would have their Dancer. I would Dance while the full orange moon rose in the sky as the full red sun was setting. In their honor I would perform *The Dance of the Sacred Sisters* for Ghalshamain, the holy juncture of the moon and sun and a very auspicious time for Dancing.

I was exhausted from my fruitless tramping around, searching for a city I couldn't find and my almost sleepless night by the side of the road. It might have been better to eat and sleep and Dance refreshed the next night, but how could I let such a special moment go by? *Even if I were under death's hand*, I thought, *I would still Dance this night*. I had expected to Dance at the Temple in Shamuiri on Ghalshamain. Instead, I would Dance here in Margail among these people who, in some strange way, had summoned me.

"By your will, Mother," I said aloud, and with another sigh of weariness I stepped naked into the tub of hot, herb-scented water they had prepared for me. When the water rose around my body, I groaned with that combination of pain and pleasure that only another traveler lost on the road could fully appreciate. "Thank You, Lady," I whispered as I settled back against the tub. The fragrant, pungent steam rose in my face, clearing the dust from my nose and throat.

From where I lay, soaking in the tub, I could see the grove of poplar trees—all tall, slim and straight, that surrounded the Dance Court. Among them, on the south side of the Court, was a huge spreading oak tree, the biggest I had ever seen. It was larger even than the two ancient oaks that flanked the Temple of Kernoss.

For a moment I felt a sudden ache of homesickness for my life at the Temple and for the women who had been my friends there. I remembered how some of them, especially Thesali, had begged me not to go. Of course Thesali had been more than a friend. I'd been almost tempted, but then I'd chosen a different path. Not chosen exactly. It was more as if this life on the road had reached out and chosen me, had laid its hand on me, or its mark. Altogether I had no real regrets, only sometimes a moment or two of longing.

What would it have been like, I wondered, if Thesali had waited for me. Ah well, one doesn't ask a lover to wait five years. When I'd heard from Ushain that Thesali had left the Temple and was raising her dead brother's children with Anyashu's help, I knew that was not a life I could have lived. I had no wish to settle down that way, nor any desire to raise two boys. It was better that we had set each other free before I left. Thinking this, I felt again that familiar tug at my heart, the old ache that I thought had long since healed over. Perhaps I was feeling it again because I was going home soon.

Home, I thought with sudden bemusement. After so many years on the road, everywhere and nowhere was home. *What will it be like to go back for good?* I wondered. *Will all the problems I had left behind still be waiting there for me?* I knew that seeing Thesali with someone else would not be easy, even after this long time away, and then there was my mother to be dealt with. Ah yes, my mother! There was a problem that lay ahead of me like a giant boulder on the road. Now that I would no longer be pledged to the road, my mother would no doubt increase her pressure on me to leave the Temple.

I sighed again and shook my head, trying to free my mind. It wasn't good to think such heavy thoughts before Dancing. I let my eyes wander. Beyond the grove of trees I could see the edge of the village. The village of Margail was a simple country place with only a few cobbled streets and the multi-colored patches of its fields stretching beyond them. The Dance Court they had shown me was not much bigger than a large barn, skillfully and carefully crafted out of the simplest of materials. The columns, that in a city might have been made of cut stone, were made of tree trunks and the roof was of a thick thatch, yet it was a place of humble beauty, that to my eyes rivaled any Temple Dance Court. At the entrance there was even a skillfully carved likeness of the Goddess-as-Dancer.

The walls of the bathhouse itself were low, no more than a few stones in height, so that I was in full view of any who might be passing by, though at the moment there was no one to be seen. Not that there was anything to fear in this place. After all, I was their Chosen One, set aside from such things. No one would think to bother me there. But what would my mother think of me sitting naked this way in a public place? "Ah, my mother again," I said aloud. "Why does she follow me even here? I thought I had finished with all that when I left five years ago."

In exasperation I pulled the travel band from my hair and flung it down on the polished stones. My hair tumbled to my shoulders and spread out around me in the water like feathery lakeweed. Taking the scented soap in my hand, I ducked under the water and began scrubbing with angry vigor at my matted greasy hair. All that was left above the water was my nose and the tips of my nipples. When I finally came up again with my hair full of soap, I found myself surrounded by a circle of giggling girls. They drew back instantly and regarded me in wary silence. Then, one of them, the tallest one who also seemed older than the others, stepped forward. She bowed and said with great seriousness and formality, as if the words had been well rehearsed, "Lady Dancer, we were sent to help you ready yourself for the Dance, if that is your wish."

This little speech was said so earnestly that I had to smile. Suddenly my mood lifted. My mother was far away, out of my life, and I was here, just where I wanted to be. With a laugh I swung my head around so fast that I spattered them all with water from my wet hair. When they fell back with shouts and squeals and bursts of laughter, I suddenly felt like a child myself among them. I remembered being a Dancer's apprentice before I became a Dancer and the mix of solemnity and high spirits and awe that had been my life then. In the Temple of Kernoss it was the apprentices who attended to the Dancer's needs and helped her make ready. On the road one took what one could get and was grateful for it. I swept them all with a sudden stern look. "Can any of you scrub a back or tend hair?" I asked. Many eager hands reached out to me.

For that while I was thoroughly attended to. As they worked, the girls chattered to me and to each other as well, all shyness gone now. Only one of them, the tall thin one who had spoken first, still seemed awkward and constrained, almost sullen. As if uncomfortable with their gaiety, she stayed a little apart from the others. Sometimes I found this girl staring at me intently.

After my back was well scrubbed and my hair was rinsed and dried they brought me a soft, warm robe, wrapped it around me and led me to a bench. There they buffed my nails and brushed out my hair, rubbing some kalien oil into it so that it gleamed darkly in the slanting afternoon light. "Lady Dancer, can we braid your hair?" they asked me eagerly. "Can we make the Dancer's braids?"

When I nodded, they all clamored around me, each tugging at some part of my hair. Instantly I realized my mistake. While I was still trying to think of some way to settle this, the oldest one stepped forward and said sternly, "Stop at once. This will not do at all. The braiding of a Dancer's hair is serious work and not a game for children." With that, she skillfully combed and parted my hair into separate sections. Then, setting aside the part that would be left to swing free, she assigned each girl a section to braid. "Work slowly and do it with care so you do not have to do it over again," she warned them.

I caught hold of her hand. "What is your name?"

"Margea," the girl answered solemnly. "It was my father, Jorahm, who had this Dance Court built. He did much of the work himself. It was my father who carved the largest statue." The pride in her voice was unmistakable, but there was something else in it as well.

"He must be a very devout man." I said, looking up at her as I spoke. There was something in the girl's tone, in her whole manner, that puzzled me, a sort of belligerence or challenge. Under it I sensed some terrible pain.

"He made it in memory of my mother," she answered gruffly. "She died last year. She drowned in the lake. Some say she meant to do it."

"I'm so sorry," I said softly, feeling the hurt of it go right to my heart.

"It's over now," Margea said curtly. "It happened a year ago. My mother always wanted to be a Dancer. She's the one who taught me how to do the Dancer's braids."

"Your father must be very pleased that the Temple is about to be consecrated."

Margea shook her head and gave a little shrug. "My father is a sad man. I think he wishes he had died when my mother did. He's only really happy when he's working. But yes, he's very glad you'll be Dancing tonight. Now tell us about life in the Temple."

While the girls braided my hair, working very carefully this time under Margea's watchful eye, I told a little of my time at the Temple, always remembering to say Shamuiri rather than Kernoss and hoping all the while that the Goddess would forgive me for my many little, well-meant lies. I also told them some stories from my time on the road. It was Margea who asked most of the questions. With unnerving persistence, she would follow each question with another. I described for them the Temple with its Dance Courts, its vast halls, its gardens and its fountains. I told them stories of my rigorous training and what it was like to be a Dancer. I even told them of old Estervan who swore she had once Danced with the Goddess Herself when she was young. "Some of the old women believed her, and the young girls often gathered around to listen to her stories, but the others scoffed at her, saying she was fire-touched."

"I would have believed her," Margea said with a sudden fierceness. "What do they know anyhow?"

After they were done with the braiding, Margea gave one of the girls a hand mirror to hold for me while she herself did the elaborate coiling and binding up of the braids into the Dancer's hairdo, doing it far more skillfully than I could have. Then she held it all in place so I could set in the jeweled bands and clips and combs that would hold my hair through the strenuous Dance. After that she placed the Dancer's Knot firmly in my hair. I was glad for the help as my hands were shaking and much relieved that none of the girls chose to comment on this. When they were finished some of the coiled braids looked almost like a crown of dark snakes raising high on my head. Others of them were wound around the long fall of loose hair that would swing out freely as I Danced and a few had been saved to loop around my ears. The whole hairdo flashed with jewels in sparkling colors and bright precious metals.

As soon as the last loops were carefully fastened the girls crowded around me, clearly full of admiration, clapping and bowing and exclaiming over my beauty. *Probably at this moment they all want to be Dancers for the Goddess*, I thought with amusement. Just then I was touched by a sudden sadness. What could they know of the hardships and the sacrifices? How could they understand what it meant to be on the road in all weather and have no fixed abode and no friends to count on? How could they possibly comprehend, at their age, what it meant to take the vow of chastity that the Dancer makes to her Goddess so that her energy will not be scattered in mortal loving? *Oh, but I would do it all again if I could,* my heart cried out as I looked at their eager young faces. I stood up suddenly. "Dance for me," I commanded. "Show me what you can do. There's a little time before I need to dress."

Instantly they were shy again, and Margea said with authority, "We cannot Dance in the Sacred Circle. It is forbidden. It is only for the Dancer herself."

"But I am a Dancemistress, and just this one time I give you permission in the name of the Goddess." This was not altogether true but I hoped it was close enough. Otherwise it would just have to be added to all my other little un-truths.

I wrapped myself in my dark cloak and went with them. I was afraid that someone from the village would see us and come rushing after us to forbid it, and though they passed at a distance no one came to interfere. As the girls stepped shyly into the Circle, I leaned on a pillar to watch. When they got over their fear they Danced well enough for village girls, all but Margea that is. With Margea it was different. She Danced with a passion, all her stiff awkwardness vanishing instantly in a flash of movement. She was the snake and the swan and the panther all in one. She filled the circle with the force of her presence. She Danced as if in a fever. I understood that fever well enough. In my own life I had often enough felt the heat of it burning up through my body. *That girl Dances as if it's in her blood and in her soul,* I thought as I watched her flashing movements. *She Dances well enough for any Temple. She should have her chance.* But would they accept her at the Temple coming from this poor simple village? I didn't know the customs of the Temple at Shamuiri. Not all Temples accepted girls from outside their city. Besides, how could I ask a man who had just lost his wife to lose his daughter as well? But if her father was willing, perhaps I could write a letter to the Temple of Ghalim and the Dancemistress there. I remembered how I had Danced at Ghalim once, Danced the *Great Dance,* the *Dance of Life,* and made quite an impression as I recalled. My letter should carry some weight.

Suddenly I felt very weary and in need of silence.

I clapped my hands and called out to them, "Thank you, thank you all so much for Dancing here for me. I feel honored. That was wonderful. You have given me much pleasure. Now I need to be alone with the Goddess for a while to ask Her for guidance." As soon as I said this, I knew it was true. The other girls scattered in an excited flurry of bows and good-byes, but Margea stood her ground, staring fiercely at me, clearly waiting for words of praise or condemnation.

"You're a true Dancer, Margea," I assured her, "A born Dancer, but I suppose you know that already. Do you want to go to the Temple at Shamuiri or perhaps even Ghalim for training? Maybe it can be arranged."

"When the time comes," she answered quickly. Then with a slight almost mocking bow she was gone, running after the others. I shook my head as I stared after her. I saw myself as a young girl again, caught in the grip of the Dance, driven by it, charged with all that terrifying and wondrous and irresistible energy that is so close to madness. "Goddess bless her and keep her," I said softly. "She bears Your mark, Lady."

As soon as there was silence again I slipped out of my cape and stepped out into the Sacred Circle dressed only in the bathing-robe I had been given. The grass was soft and springy underfoot, a good surface for the Dance. I took a few steps to test the feel of it and instantly a rush of energy surged up through my body. It was as if the power of the Dance lay in wait for me there under the soil, as if all the force of Earth Herself were focused in that place. Quickly I stepped out again, saying under my breath, "Too soon, Mother, I'm not ready yet. Let me prepare myself to meet You. Later we will Dance together."

I knew it would soon be time to present myself before the likeness of the Goddess. I needed to ask her blessing and make an offering to Her, but I had no wish to appear in front of The Lady in a bathing-robe. Quickly I went back to the bathhouse, having decided that for this last Dance I would dress myself, something I had never done in all my time on the road. The girls were very helpful but I needed silence, not their twittering admiration or, for that matter, Margea's intense stare that seemed to demand something of me.

The tub and all signs of the bath were gone. A large mirror was hanging on the wall with a table in front of it and a long bench in front of that. All my clothes had been lovingly laid out at one end of the bench. Looking at this humble arrangement, I thought with fond amusement how very different it was from the elaborate dressing rooms in the great city Temples. Then my eyes pricked with tears and I knew that this was where I was supposed to be.

Before I sat down I hung my hooded waiting-cloak on a hook by the door. Then, on the table, I carefully unrolled my djirha-cloth. Across the back of it I set my Dancewand, noticing how all the colors lay muted and dormant in the wand's glassy depth. In front of it I carefully laid out and arranged my jewelry for the Dance, as well as my pots and jars and bottles of face-paint and scent.

This djirha-cloth was the same beautifully patterned piece that Thesali had made for me. All those years on the road it had made a sort of instant traveling altar for me. Remembering whose hands it had come from, it never failed to touch my heart. Each time I saw its bright colors laid out before me I thought of her. "But not even for you could I have stayed," I whispered softly, running my fingers across its silky surface. Now I was ready to begin that familiar and yet awesome ritual of transformation that would change me from an ordinary woman to a Dancer for the Goddess.

As I raised my brush to paint the dark lines around my eyes my hand began to shake, making it difficult. The sacred shaking, a touch-of-the-fire, most of the best Dancers had some signs of it. Whatever it was called, I had a clear case of it. Much as I tried to ignore it, the tremors grew worse every time I Danced. "Yes, this is the last time," I promised the face in the mirror as I steadied one hand with the other to draw the dark lines back from the corners of my eyes. When that was done, I rubbed the blue-green nithra-paste on my eyelids. Then came the red focusing circle in the center of my forehead and the ritual markings to my cheeks. All the while I struggled to control my shaking hands. "One more good Dance, Goddess, just grant me one more and then I promise to go home," I whispered fervently. "Just let me Dance this one last Dance for Ghalshamain."

However much I might wish to stay on the road, I really had no choice now but to go back. I could hear my mother's mocking angry voice, "What a fool you are. How could you go and ruin yourself so young? Look at you, your hands shake like an old woman." For a moment it was my mother's face I saw in the mirror instead of my own.

"What does that matter anyhow? It will all be cured at the Temple," I said aloud to the reflection, but inside I felt a shiver of fear. Sometimes it could not be cured. Sometimes a Dancer bore the mark of it for the rest of her life. Sometimes it was so bad that, like Hathi, she could no longer Dance or do much of anything at all. Well, that was the chance I had taken. It was all worth it—the passion and the fire, the glory of the Dance. Actually, it had little to do with what I had wanted or not wanted. I had been called, it was that simple.

I leaned forward to peer at myself in the mirror. The slant of the late afternoon light reflected brightly in the glass. Even with my shaking hands I had done well. As always, with the ritual paint on my face, I looked like something more and also something less than my ordinary self, a human reflection of the Great One. With a shiver I stood up to dress. First came the red Dance shirt, thick with embroidery and encrusted with jewels. It was stitched all over with tiny mirrors that would flash in the torchlight when I Danced. The shirt covered my upper arms and back—it all but bared my breasts, pushing them up to fullness. I loved the way the bright red flamed against the darkness of my skin. Next came the skirt of a blue brighter than the bluest sky. The loose flowing fabric hooked on my hips and rode below the smooth roundness of my belly. After that I fastened on the sashes that would float out from me with each motion, moving as if on their own wind.

How strange, I thought as I had so many times before, that as the Dancer I was pledged to celibacy while the Dance itself was so full of sexuality, an invitation to the Great Dance of Life, a link between ordinary mortals and the realms of power. I knew that the watchers often went home to their beds afterward, filled with passion to do their own version of the Dance with each other. Ah well, celibacy had been my commitment and it was probably for the best. I didn't need a series of quick shallow alliances on the road, and I certainly didn't want another heart-tearing farewell like my parting from Thesali. My time of celibacy would be up at the end of my five-year pledge—and then what new turn would my life take?

I shook out my skirt and settled it over my hips. How my mother hated the blatant sexuality of the Dancer's costume. She always said, "Such clothes are not fitting for a woman of our house." But luckily my mother was not there with me at that moment. I needed to put her aside, out of my mind. *If only once my mother had tried to understand my life,* I thought with a sigh as I fastened on my long dangling copper earrings, *then maybe there could be peace in my heart and I would not be so fearful of going home.*

Suddenly, remembering Margea's story of her mother's death, another shiver went through me, this time of premonition. What if something had happened to Thea? "Maybe when I go back we can find some way into each other's hearts without fighting," I said to my reflection as I hung the pendant my father had given me between my breasts. Next, I coiled the snake brace-lets around my arms and slipped my rings on my fingers, kissing for luck the one Melanthia had given me as a road-gift. Before I left I re-wrapped all my things in the djirha-cloth with loving care and put it away in my pack, a habit from my years on the road. When I finally tied the bell straps to my ankles, it was the ritual end of my dressing. Now I was ready to go and meet the Goddess. I picked up my Dancewand, slipped it into my sash and walked to the Dance Court.

Circling the edge of it, I discovered that each outer column held a small image of the Goddess, either carved in the wood itself or set into a niche. The figures were crude and simple, made with more love than skill, but still powerful in their own way. All were newly painted in bright colors by caring hands. It looked as if many different villagers had helped in this work.

I saved the Goddess-as-Dancer for last. As I came up to Her, I drew in my breath in awe. She was taller than I had realized, more than life-sized and quite beautiful, obviously made by a very skilled hand. The crossed Dancewands She held high over Her head seemed to glow gold in the rays of the setting sun. With Her arms raised, She stood poised on the toes of one foot. Her other leg was lifted and bent at the knee, as if She were about to take the first step into the Dance. Clearly She was filled with power, but there was compassion in Her face as well, a face that came alive in that light. The features were almost familiar, a little like Margea's, but of course with none of her sullenness. Since the girl's father had carved this amazing statue, I won-dered if perhaps he had immortalized his drowned wife in this way.

With a sigh I sank down on the grass and gazed up at Her face. This form of the Goddess was the Lady-of-Changes, the patron of Dancers and artists and travelers, the One who brought mystery and surprise into human life, the One who received the offering of the Dance and wove it into the Great Dance of Life with the music that was always playing in the world. I set my little gift of pol-ished, brightly colored river pebbles in the offering bowl, saying softly, "Lady, Protector-of-Dancers, please lend me Your swift feet and brave heart for this Dance tonight. I wish to Dance in Your honor." Then I shut my eyes and bowed my head, staying that way for a long while and trying to clear my mind.

When I looked up again the change had come as it always did. This was no longer a thing of carved and painted wood that stood before me, made by human hands. It was the Goddess Herself. "Mother, You honor me," I whispered with tears in my eyes. At that moment the statue seemed to quiver and reach out to me. I gave a start. It was as if She were coming alive. Then I realized that someone had lit the evening flares and the movement was from the flashing of the torchlight.

When I stood up I saw that the other lamps had all been lit. There were huge brass bowls of flowers glowing at intervals around the outside of the circle and a ring of unlit candles along its stone rim. Fresh incense was burning in the holders. All this had been done quietly while I had been communing with The Lady. As I looked around I saw a black robed figure slipping silently out the other side of the Dance Court. Man or woman, I couldn't tell, but I wondered if perhaps it was the mysterious Jorahm I had yet to meet, acting as Temple Keeper for that night. The smell of flowers and incense together made my stomach clench with hunger. *Later*, I told myself sternly, *later I will feast, but no food before the Dance.*

Where the sun would soon be going down, the sky glowed red, pink and orange in vast, tattered banners of color. I could see an echoing glow from the other side where the full moon would soon be rising. I shivered again and drew my dark cloak around my shoulders, very carefully raising the hood to cover my piled and jeweled hair without disturbing it. I could see the villagers already making their way up from the village. Their voices sounded loud and eager after the silence of the Dance Court.

Watching them, I felt a sudden rush of warmth in my heart. The villagers and townspeople I served might seem crude and untaught to the city folk I had grown up among and perhaps they were, but at least their enthusiasm was real. They were not jaded by a surfeit of things in their lives. Their love of the Dance gave meaning to my travels. The only Dancers they were likely to see were those who were pledged to the road, since not many of them would travel as far as the city Temples. *If I had to stay in any one of these places for long*, I thought, *I might feel the heavy crush of boredom, but soon enough my feet are carrying me down the road so everything stays new and fresh to my eyes.*

Gathering my cloak tight around me for concealment, I went to stand in the Dancer's alcove that Margea had shown me earlier, a tiny hiding place built into one of columns of the inner ring at the edge of the Sacred Circle. From there I could hear people gathering without being seen myself. By the sound of it, everyone in the village must be on their way to the Dance. Soon the musicians came in, sat down opposite me and began to play—two drummers, a flute player and a young woman with a tzitha, a simple stringed instrument that sang like a bird in her hands. Along the horizon the sky behind their heads was beginning to glow, where only moments before it had been growing darker. Still hidden from sight, the full moon was beginning its ascent as the red sun was going down. I felt my heart pounding. My hands grew moist. It was almost time.

As I watched, the very edge of the huge orange moon began coming into view. There were exclamations of awe from the people who had assembled there. Then the musicians began to play the song of greeting for the sun and moon. Soon others joined in with their voices. At that same moment, the young girls who had helped me bathe came forward to light the candles that rimmed the stone edge of the circle. Margea was the one who was closest to me. Still in my cloak, I slipped out of hiding, and at just the same moment Margea finished lighting the candles. As she stepped away, she brushed against me with seeming intent. It was as if sparks were struck, power brushing against power. "Pardon, Lady Dancer," the girl said with a quick bow. Then she rapidly disappeared into the crowd, but I felt her waiting and watching from close by.

A troubled child, I thought, *but clearly filled with the Dancer's gift.* If I had the teaching of young ones like that it might not be so bad going back. I might be content to live at the Temple and stay in one place. Perhaps Margea should not go to Shamuiri after all, or even Ghalim. Perhaps She should come to Kernoss instead. Ghalim was bigger, but Kernoss was reputed to have the best Dance school in the entire region.

I gave myself a shake to clear all such thoughts from my mind. That was in the future. Right now I needed to focus all of myself on this Dance. The moon and sun were almost balanced now in their bright fullness. Ghalshamain! I took a deep breath and whispered urgently, "Please come to me, Mother, my heart is open to Your presence." Then I dropped my cloak so that it fell in a dark pool around my feet and stepped over the stone rim of the circle into the light.

It was as if I had appeared miraculously among them, light flashing from all the jewels and mirrors that I wore. There were loud exclamations of awe and excitement and then thunderous applause such as would never have been allowed in a city Temple. "She has come! She has come! The Lady is here among us." A few of the people began to chant these words and soon they had all taken it up. "She has come! She has come! She has come to Dance for us this night!" The words echoed from all sides.

For the duration of the Dance the Dancer is the Goddess Incarnate, Her representative in human form. I was trembling with the thrill of it, a thrill that was still fresh and new even after five years of Dancing on the road. I bowed to all four corners, as custom dictated, then took my Dancewand from my sash and held it pressed between my breasts, waiting for Her presence to enter. There was instant silence from those watching. The musicians stopped playing. Even the children had been hushed.

In my head and in my heart I asked the ancient ritual question, *Goddess, am I fit to Dance for You this night?* For heart-stopping moments there was nothing, no contact, no response. Though my heart clenched with fear, I tried to make my breathing slow and even and to keep my inner self steady. "By your will, Lady. Once more I have set myself in Your hands." I said softly.

I had been so fatigued that day, so preoccupied by futile arguments with my absent mother when I might better have been meditating on the Dance; maybe this was not to be my Dance after all. Perhaps I needed to be humble and wait for a less important night. Or perhaps I was going to fail again, as I had at Norshall. Then, just as I was thinking I might need to step out of the circle, I felt the answering warmth in my heart. When I held the wand out to look at it, I saw it was filled with glowing living colors, swirling in the glass. The moment had come.

I held my arms straight out so that I was pointing to the full red sun on one side and full orange moon on the other in their moment of shared glory. Now the stillness was total. Inside that stillness I could feel the energy gathering and gathering in a great spiral, a spiral of which I was the beginning point or the end point. It was inside that circle of stillness that I would do my fast whirling Dance. I lifted my foot, ready to step forward, ready to signal the musicians. Then, out of that stillness and with no warning, a stranger stepped into the circle, a tall woman I hadn't seen in the village before.

I sucked in my breath with amazement and set my foot down again. For that moment my concentration was ruined. If I stepped forward now I was afraid I would flounder and perhaps stumble. I felt a flush of anger rising. Didn't she know that it was strictly forbidden to step into the Sacred Circle when the Dance was about to begin? Or to interfere with the Dancer in any way? Even in such an isolated place, surely they knew this much. I expected an outcry from the watching villagers. There was nothing but the expectant silence and all those watching eyes.

I stared at the intruder, hoping to drive her away by the force of my anger, but the woman's face was shadowed by a wing of dark hair so that it was hard to look into her eyes. She was dressed in ragged clothing, clothing not at all fitting for the Dance. Obviously this was no Dancer—she didn't even carry a Dancewand. But in spite of her poor clothing there was power and authority in her bearing. She did not appear the least discomfited by my angry stare, but said in a low firm voice, as if speaking to me alone, "Let the Dance begin."

I was startled by the sound of her voice in the stillness. I couldn't imagine why the villagers hadn't leapt to their feet and pulled this woman out of the

Circle. Clearly the Dance was ruined now. As I was wondering whether to make the commotion necessary to have this intruder removed or whether to go on with the Dance in the company of a madwoman, I found myself raising my foot again as if the decision had already been made. The other woman raised her hands and one foot as if in readiness and stood poised. I took a step forward, the other one moved as well and suddenly the Dance had started. The musicians played again. Soon they were playing louder and louder, and people were clapping in time to the music.

After only a few steps I realized that no matter what her appearance indicated, the other one was clearly a Dancer and a Dancer of considerable skill. Perhaps she was one of those wild Dancers who did not go back when their pledge time was up, but instead roamed the hills, growing madder with each passing year. Perhaps that was why the villagers had paid her no heed. They were already used to her ways and knew better than to interfere. But then why had they needed a Dancer if they already had one of their own? And why had no one told me? Whatever her story, she was good and she was fast. She seemed to have perfect balance. I soon found myself mirroring the other woman's steps, straining to keep up with her.

The pace of the Dance grew ever faster, the leaps getting higher and higher, but always when I landed, there was that other figure before me, moving into the next step. No matter how fast I Danced, the other was faster still. I found I had no choice but to follow. Soon, sweat was pouring from me. My Dancer's legs, incredibly strong from five years of walking and Dancing, felt as if they were about to buckle under me. My heart began to pound like a hammer in my chest. My lungs were about to burst. I wanted to shout, *Stop! Please! I can't breathe, I can't breathe! I can't go on! I'm going to die!* But no words came. Instead I went on and on, twisting and turning and leaping, pulled or driven by another's will. I was Dancing far past my strength or skill, Dancing out to some dangerous edge where the earth might fall out from under my feet at any moment. *I'm going to die, to die, to die,* my heart was crying out.

Then, as if time had stilled, I could suddenly hear the drum beat again and could hook my heartbeat to its rhythm. Something had shifted. I had surrendered to the Dance and it had taken me. There was no longer any struggle. The Dance and I had become one thing. I regained my breath, began moving freely and easily. Now it was my Dance and the other one followed me willingly. It was as if I had been freed into the Dance, like a bird rising and taking wing. I spun my Dancewand so that the light rippling through it flashed colors in all directions. I set the steps and made the motions while the other followed me. Never, never in my life had I Danced like this, not even when I had Danced *the Dance of Life* in the Temple of

Ghalim, not even when I had led the Hundred-Year Procession in Urshameel. Power flowed from the ground up through my feet and power flooded out through my fingertips, and always there was the shimmering other in front of me, reflecting everything I did and drawing me on.

From somewhere in the crowd I heard a voice saying in an awed tone, "*The Dance of Life, the Dance of Life.*" In a sudden flash of comprehension I realized that we were not Dancing *the Dance of the Sacred Sisters*—we were Dancing *the Dance of Life*, the Great Dance, the high holy Dance that was only Danced once a year in the Temple at High Festival time. It was strictly forbidden to Dance it at any other time, but this Dance seemed to have a life of its own. I had no control over it. Even the tremor of fear I felt could not stop my feet from moving. The Dance was Dancing itself and it was Dancing me. If I was to be punished for that transgression then it would have to happen later, in some other life. For now, this Dance was everything. It was all there was in the world and it flowed through me like water, like fire. When I swung my wand arcs of light flared between my hands. There were moments when I was flying, looking down at the earth from above, seeing places I had never seen before. And then moments when this stranger I Danced with was like a lover and the Dance we did between us was an act of passion danced out before all these people with no shame, danced out before the world, before the universe itself.

Then, as suddenly as the Dance had begun, it was over, the moment of ecstatic union ended. The sun had set, taking with it the last glow of luminous pink. The moon already stood far up in the sky, flooding the Dance Court with silver light. Blinking in surprise, I found myself standing earthbound, panting, my sides heaving, sweat running from me like rain. I was swaying on my feet, my legs bending under my weight, barely able to hold me upright. Gasping for breath, I made a deep bow to my partner. As if that had been the signal, all those who had been watching leapt to their feet in a wild burst of clapping and shouting and stamping. When I looked up again, the other Dancer was striding out of the Circle. Without a backward glance the woman stepped quickly over the stone ledge and vanished into the crush of people. I wanted to call after her, but my throat was too dry to make a sound. I felt a moment of stabbing loss, as if this stranger was my beloved who was walking out of my life forever.

Hastily I made my bows all around to the villagers. Then, with quick words of thanks to the Goddess, I was striding across the Circle and out. I had to find this woman and thank her. Never, never had there been such a Dance. And to think that at first I had been angry at her. I had learned more of Dancing in this one night than in all my years at the Temple.

As soon as I stepped out of the circle the villagers came crowding around me, full of praise. I looked distractedly in all directions for some sign of the other woman, trying to see over their heads, but that one was nowhere to be seen. People were pressing so close I could hardly move, wanting to touch the hem of my skirt, my arm, my hand, my hair, to touch any part of me so some of the magic would rub off on them. I saw Margea's young face alight with awe and admiration, cleared at that moment of all her sullenness and pain. The other girls were pressing in around me, reaching for me, calling, "Lady Dancer, Lady Dancer, Lady Dancer," like a flock of little birds.

Usually I enjoyed the praises of the crowd. It was all part of the Dance. It made it doubly rewarding, a clear sign that I and those watching had shared in the experience together. Tonight I had no patience for any of this. I wanted to be free of them all, to cut through the crowd that clung to me like heavy mud.

While they kept saying I was the most wonderful Dancer who ever lived, better than any Dancer they had ever seen, even at a city Temple, I went on shaking my head. "Not me," I called out to them. "Not me. It was that other woman, the tall one. She is the one you should praise. She is the one who led the Dance." When there was no response to this, I turned from one to the other of them, asking frantically, "Who is she? Who is she? Is she from this village? Where did she go? Can you at least tell me her name?" They all shook their heads, looking at each other in bewilderment. When I finally shouted with exasperation,"Find her for me!" there was a stunned silence. Then the villagers began muttering among themselves and backing away from me. I felt a strange uneasiness. I saw the Headwoman push her way through the crowd until she stood directly in front of me. The old woman bowed her head slightly and said in her rough-edged voice that was so full of authority, "Lady Dancer, that was the finest Dance I have ever seen but I must tell you, there was no other woman there. You were the only Dancer in the Sacred Circle."

CHAPTER 18

The Old Woman of the Woods

S till believing I had come to them from Shamuiri, the villagers wanted to keep me for as long as possible, for feasts and praise and perhaps to try and persuade me to Dance again. Though none of them claimed to have seen the other Dancer in the Circle with me, still they knew they had witnessed something extraordinary. I, on the other hand, wanted to be gone as soon as possible from there in case by some chance the Dancer from Shamuiri really did make an appearance. I was not ready to struggle through that thicket of explanations and hurt feelings. Better to be an absent legend than an all-too present fraud. In any case, Margea's father would soon be back and he would surely know me for an impostor.

The village made a huge feast in my honor the night of the Dance and all the villagers came. Though they were full of admiration for my Dancing, still the old Headwoman kept watch on me out of the corner of her eye as if expecting more craziness. Meanwhile others praised me in speeches and plied me with food and drink until I could hardly stand.

After that I rested in the village for a day, staying at the Headwoman's comfortable little house. Profoundly exhausted, having Danced myself close to my limit, I ate and slept and could do little else. The people of Margail seemed eager to provide me with whatever I needed. They were kind and generous to a fault, yet shy of speaking to me—almost fearful. If I tried to meet their eyes with mine, their glances would slip away. They would stutter and stammer and quickly back out of the doorway. *Better to be alone, I* thought, *than to be treated with such wary politeness as if I were not quite human, as if I were something strange or other.* Ah well, who could blame them. They no doubt believed me to be fire-touched. None of them had seen the woman I claimed to have Danced with. Each time my mind touched on that, I shut it out and groped for sleep again. Sooner or later, however, I knew I would have to face it. The experience of the Dance was undeniable. I had no doubt of what I had seen and responded to.

Only the young girls who had dressed me for the Dance seemed untouched by this. They often came and sat by me. Margea stayed near me most of the time. When I woke I would often find the girl watching me intently. When she saw I was awake she would lay a cool cloth on my forehead or jump up to make me another cup of tea.

The second day I was already up, dressed and eating a bowl of fruit and porridge at the table when Margea came in. She looked flustered as if she had been caught away from her post. "Lady Dancer, I'm glad to see you feeling better," she said with a slight bow.

I looked up, smiled and beckoned her over. "I'm leaving this morning. I need to be on the road again. Come sit here and talk to me. It's good to talk to someone who will look me in the eye and not scurry away when I speak. And please call me Zaia. This Lady Dancer form of address is much too formal."

Margea bowed again and blushed. Awkwardly, she came to sit in the chair next to me. "Lady...Zaia, are you sure you're strong enough to go? You're only just on your feet again."

"Strong enough or not, I'm ready. It's not healthy to stay for long among people who think you mad. In time it's likely to *really* make you crazy."

Margea looked straight into my face for a long moment of silence and then said angrily, "They're all fools."

"Not fools, only afraid of what they can't see." Now I was the one who was silent, struggling for words. Finally, I put a hand over Margea's hand. "Tell me, did you...Did you see Her too?" My words were hesitant. I was fearful of the answer.

Now it was Margea who seemed afraid. She looked around the room quickly and asked almost in a whisper, "Is there anyone here?"

"No, Mother Ancora made me breakfast and left early to see to some village business."

Margea nodded, took a deep breath and leaned toward me. "Not always," she said softly. "Just at moments she would come clear and then fade away again. She looked..." Suddenly Margea's face glowed. The fear fell away and with it her sullenness. "She looked... Oh, there are no words..." She sat for a moment in a sort of rapture. Then suddenly her face changed again, turned pinched and angry. "Oh, I'm such a coward. I was afraid to say it to the others, afraid to defend you and say I saw her too."

"No, not a coward. It's better so. I'm leaving today, walking down the road. What does it matter to me once I'm gone if they think me mad. But you Child, you have to live among them. Believe me, they'll make your life miserable. I know. I've seen it already. Keep your silence on all this, at least for now. Later there may be time to speak." I pushed my bowl away and stood up. "Now for the road again, this time the road going home." There, in spite of any doubts, I had said it. I was going home.

Margea stood up too and said with a sudden burst of feeling, "Oh Zaia, I wish I were going with you. I can't ... my father ..." Suddenly she was crying.

I wrapped her in my arms. To my surprise she let me do it. When her crying had stilled I said with assurance, "You'll come when the time is right. Now help me gather my things and pack."

With the musicians leading the way, playing drums and flutes, the villagers accompanied me to the far edge of the village, almost to where the woods began. Shy as they were of me, they also didn't want me to leave. They showered me with still more offerings of food and flowers. They even offered me a horse for my trip home. After all, I had brought their little village a great gift. But there was only so much I could stuff into my travel pack. In the end the people made a pile of rocks as an altar and left most of it as an offering to the Goddess. Then Ancora, the old headwoman, came forward and said very formally, "Lady Dancer, in the name of the Village of Margail, I thank you for the great honor you have bestowed upon us by Dancing in our new Dance Court." She bowed and backed away.

When she turned the others all turned with her. Like leaves swept in the wind, or a flock of birds taking wing, they hurried away after her. Clearly caught between fear and admiration, they were as eager to go back to the safety of their village as they had been to escort me. All but the young girls who called out, "Goodbye, Lady Dancer," and kept turning back to wave as they followed the others away.

Puzzled and disappointed I looked for Margea, but she was not to be seen anywhere among them. As soon as they were all gone I knelt down by the crude altar of stacked stones, shut my eyes and said aloud, "Lady, let me accept whatever you have in store for me. Mother, I am in your hands." I stayed there for a long time, trying to find some peace in my heart. When I stood up at last, I found Margea standing at my shoulder. Startled, I asked rudely, "What are you doing here? Aren't you afraid of me? Why didn't you rush off like the others?" Instantly I was ashamed of the bitterness of my voice and the cruelty of my words. "I'm sorry, but there's something in the sight of people scurrying away in fear that makes one mean-spoken."

Margea looked away as if she could not meet my eyes. In a kinder tone I said quickly, "I looked for you. I was sad when I thought you had stayed back in the village and were afraid of me."

"I wouldn't have let you go without saying goodbye, but I didn't want the others to try to take me away with them. Besides, I have a gift for you—a gift for the road. Oh, how I wish my father could have seen you Dance! How is it that you came so quickly and he has not returned at all? Do you think something bad has happened to him on the road?"

I shook my head emphatically. "No, no, nothing like that." Knowing that I owed her the truth I went on, "I must tell you a secret, but for now it is another secret we must share, though the others will know soon enough. I never met your father nor spoke with him. I'm not really from the Temple of Shamuiri. I'm a traveling Dancer from Kernoss and have been on the road for almost five years."

Her eyes grew wide, but she said nothing and only stared at me strangely.

"Are you angry at me for my deception? I didn't know what else to do. Everyone wanted so much for me to be from Shamuiri that they wouldn't listen. It seemed a shame to spoil it for them."

Margea shook her head, took a step back and said with awe, "So you really were sent by the Goddess."

"Not you too, Margea. Please, I couldn't stand it. Don't pull back and look at me that way, as if I'm not really human. Come sit by me and I'll tell you how I found my way here. Or do you want to run off with the others?"

"No," she said resolutely. "I want to hear it all."

And so we sat down right there on the road by the little stone altar and I told her my story. I finished by saying, "If you want to come to Urshameel when the time is right, you would be very welcome at the Temple of Kernoss. I would speak for you. You're the best young Dancer I've ever seen. You would give me a reason to stay there and teach. Melanthia, my Dance teacher, would be very pleased with you."

With those words, the girl's usually serious face lit up as if by magic. "Maybe next year. I'll ask my father as soon as he comes home. Surely he won't refuse me." After that, for the next hour or so, we made plans and pored over my travel map together.

Finally I stood up, ready to move on. "So it's agreed, we'll meet again and in the meanwhile you'll work at your Dancing. When you come you may even have some new Dances to teach us."

Margea nodded, then shyly held out something wrapped in a scrap of bright cloth. I unwrapped it and a beautiful bronze pendant lay shining in my hand, a tiny copy of the statue of the Dancer her father had carved. I flushed with pleasure and then shook my head, "I can't take it from you. It's much too fine. I might lose it on the road."

"I have my own. My father made that one for my mother. It's been put away among her things. It needs to go with a Dancer. It needs to be worn by the living. Please, Zaia, please take it. I want to think of you wearing it, of it keeping you safe on the road."

Nodding, with tears in my eyes, I said, "Thank you, Margea, I'll wear it all the time. It will get me home safely." But when I went to put it on my hands shook so that I couldn't even fasten the clasp. The shaking was worse than it had ever been. That last Dance had been too much. I felt the girl's eyes on me.

"It's a hard clasp," Margea said quickly. "Let me help you."

I leaned forward and felt the chain drop around my neck, the cool metal of the pendant settling between my breasts, next to the one from my father. When I straightened again I saw Margea's stare fastened on my hands. She didn't look away as the other girls had done. "Your hands?"

"Let's be honest here. It's not that the clasp is hard. It's that my hands shake. The tremors are getting worse, Dancer's shakes. It's what comes of being on the road so long, Dancing in the full force of Her power."

"Will you...?"

"They'll cure it at the temple. That's part of why I have to get home soon. Now give me a hug goodbye."

With a cry, the girl threw herself into my arms in a bone-crunching hug, then just as suddenly she pulled back and stepped away, her look closed, sullen and as wary as it had been when I first saw her. I tugged the ring off my finger and handed it to Margea. "I can't give it to you forever because it was given to me by my Dance teacher, Melanthia, but wear it for now and bring it back to me when you come to Kernoss. It's getting harder for me to wear because my fingers are beginning to swell too much from the damp."

Margea stared at the ring in her palm then slipped it on her finger and looked at me with a nod. I swung my pack on my back with the practiced skill of five years on the road and said quickly, "I have to go right now or I'll stand here forever saying goodbye. Until we meet again at Kernoss, be well, Margea." With that, I turned quickly and strode off down the road. When I reached the bend and looked back, Margea was still standing exactly where I'd left her, not waving, but watching me intently.

By noon I was exhausted. Not even bothering to look for a better place, I sank down on the bank of the road with a sigh of weariness and began to spread out around me some of my ample supply of food, that amazing assortment that the villagers had pressed on me. Before I could even take my first bite a querulous voice, seeming to come from nowhere, said loudly, "I don't suppose you'd be generous enough to share some of your bounty with an Old Woman?"

Startled, I looked around. I had thought myself totally alone in that place and even now could see no one on the road.

"Here," the voice said impatiently. "I'm here. Are you deaf as well as blind?"

Turning in all directions, I finally saw an Old Woman sitting on a rock a little higher up the bank and off to the side, sitting in a place I could have sworn was empty when I had first stopped. She was all dressed in gray, as gray as the rock she sat on, as gray as the tree trunks.

"Come and share whatever you want, Grandmother, but you must come to me for I am much too weary to haul myself up that steep way with my hands full."

"Well, if that's all you can do I suppose I'll have to make the best of it," the Old Woman answered ungraciously. Then, with surprising agility, she came scrambling down the bank, squatted beside me and, without a words of thanks, began cramming food into her mouth. "Not quite ripe," she muttered about the apple as she cut off a big chunk and speared it with her knife before it vanished into her mouth. "Not nearly as good as my grandmother used to make," she said about the yoggel pudding she had just finished down to the last bite, before she reached for more bread and cheese. Food began disappearing at an alarming rate. I was glad I hadn't set out all of my stores, but I was too tired to object and could only sit staring at this voraciousness. It was like watching late-summer locusts descend on a field of ripe corn.

Finally the Old Woman slowed down, re-sheathed her knife, wiped her mouth with the hem of her long skirt and said sharply, "It's rude to stare when someone is eating, but perhaps no one taught you that." Before I could gather myself to answer, she went rushing on. "Ah, I see by your Dancewand that you're a Dancer. Well, Dancers are not known for their manners. Never mind, you can do a Dance for me to make up for your rudeness." She then cocked her head sideways as if she had said something so clever and irrefutable that it must instantly be obeyed.

"Old Woman, you've eaten most of my food without one word of thanks, insulted me several times, and now, on top of that, you're demanding that I Dance for you. Even respect for age has its limits. I don't Dance on demand. I Dance in honor of the Goddess. Besides, I Danced my last Dance in Margail. My five-year pledge is up and I'm on my way home to the Temple."

Immediately the Old Woman changed her manner. She turned wheedling and cajoling. "Please, I'm very old. I may not live another year. I may never see another Dance or meet with another Dancer. How can you deny me such a thing?"

I was beginning to feel as trapped as if some creature had landed on my back and was holding on tight with its claws. "I couldn't Dance for you even if I wanted to," I said quickly. "Look." With that I held out my shaking hands before her eyes.

The Old Woman nodded. "Dancer Fever," she said knowingly. "Well, I've seen worse cases. It's nothing a good Temple can't heal." She tapped my hand with her finger. "Even with that you can Dance well enough. After all, it's not the hands you Dance with, it's the feet." There was no sympathy to be had here.

"No!" I shouted in despair. "No! There is no way I would Dance for you!" Jumping to my feet, I hastily began to gather up my things and stuff them into my pack, all the while trying to control my wildly shaking hands.

"If you Dance for me I'll give you a great treasure," the Old Woman said in a wheedling voice full of cunning craftiness. "A very great treasure. Just the thing you need most in the world and that I have in abundance."

"No! I already said no! Besides I don't Dance for treasure. I told you I Dance only in honor of the Goddess. I don't Dance for jewels or money."

"Ah, the arrogance of youth, when you always think you have plenty of everything and all the choices in the world. I'll wager you're going back to the Temple with pockets more empty than a beggar's, hardly one coin to rub against the other, nothing to show for all those years on the road."

"Enough! That's enough! It's in the hands of the Goddess, not yours or mine. She's the one who commands and decides."

"Good," the Old Woman said quickly, pouncing on my words. "In that case, why not be silent and listen to Her will?"

With a groan I let my pack slip from my fingers. Too tired to argue any longer I sank down on the bank, shut my eyes and put my head in my hands. For a while there was absolute silence. It was as if the Old Woman had ceased to exist. I couldn't hear her breathing. After a while, I couldn't even hear my own breathing.

The silence deepened until I lost all sense of time and place. Finally, from far off, there came the cry of a bird. It came three times, followed by a silence and then another three times and another, each sequence of notes coming closer, the same notes the flute-player always played for *The Dance of the Wounded Bird*. Then it stopped altogether and there was total silence again. I sat for a while longer, slowly re-entering my body.

When I opened my eyes at last the Old Woman was hovering over me with a triumphant grin on her face. "Well?" she asked, "Wasn't that answer enough for you?"

With a sigh, I got to my feet. "I'll Dance, but for Her, not for you." *What madness,* I thought as soon as I heard my own words. I could barely stand, I had already Danced my last Dance, and yet I had just agreed to Dance there on that hard dusty road.

"Dance *The Dance of the Joyous Morning*. That's my favorite," the Old Woman said with greedy eagerness.

"No. That's not the message that came in the silence. I'll Dance *The Dance of the Wounded Bird*, nothing else."

"That's a Dance for funerals, not for a pretty noontime like this."

"Old Woman, that's what it's going to be," I said curtly. "That or nothing. If I'm forced to Dance for you here in the woods, at least it will be my Dance. *The Dance of the Wounded Bird* is what I'm going to do in this place, with this body, at this time. It's how I feel. If that doesn't please you, you don't have to stay and watch. You can go elsewhere for all I care. I'm not Dancing in your pay or for your treasure," I ended harshly, finally letting all my anger come through.

"Well if ... "

I raised my hand and interrupted, "And, if I'm to Dance, you must be silent while I prepare, totally silent. Not one more word. Is that clear?"

"It could hardly be clearer," she said with a sharp bite to her words. Then she sank back with a long elaborate sigh, but after that she kept her silence while I made ready for the Dance.

Very different from my usual preparations, I kept everything stark and simple. I did a brief water ceremony, then donned pants and a tunic of plain white-weave. Since I no longer needed my dark cape to cover my bright Dance costume and it had grown very ragged with travel wear, I ripped some strips up from the bottom edge so they would move like feathers with the slightest motion of my body. Then I pulled back all my hair and plaited it into one long braid. The only color in all this was my two-colored Dance sash of turquoise and magenta. My only jewelry was the pendant from Margea and the one from my father. I even left my Dancewand strapped to my pack. Dressed and ready, I went to stand in the middle of the road, wondering briefly what would happen if someone chose that moment to come riding through. Then I shrugged. "In your hands, Goddess," I said aloud. After that I shut my eyes, pressed my hand on the pendants that hung over my heart and waited for the stillness, the core of calm that is the center of the Dance. I didn't even ask the ritual question. The bird call had seemed summons enough.

This time it was not stillness that came but a wind, a forceful and insistent wind and with it a lifting, a strong and compelling upward pull. I spread my arms wide, stood high on my toes, leaned forward into the rising current and took the first step. The Dance had begun; there was no going back. I was the bird, dipping and tilting in the rush of air. I was fighting my way upward in the sky, struggling against the pull of earth and the drain of my wound. I knew I was flying my final flight, hearing for the last time the music of my own wings beating against the air. The road, the dust, the Old Woman, my weariness all vanished in the flight of the Dance. I swooped, turned, dipped, rose, caught the current and flung myself out on it. There was nothing in the world but that moment, which seemed as if it might go on forever.

Then, abruptly, the Dance ended. With no warning I found myself whirling, whirling, whirling down out of the sky on wings that could no longer hold me. The Dance Danced me down and down until I was finally flat on the ground. Exhausted, arms spread wide, I lay there stretched out like a broken bird on the breast of the mother, covered by her cape of tattered black feathers. Utterly spent, I made no attempt to rise and make the traditional bow. In fact, I fervently hoped the Old Woman would go away, simply melt into the woods, letting me lie there for hours or even days if need be.

All too soon however I heard the rasping, peevish voice over my own panting breath. "Not bad, not bad at all. Almost as good as at my sister's funeral. And there they had a whole troupe of Dancers and musicians too, as well as some very fine costumes. Yes, not bad at all for a road-Dance. Almost as good, I'd have to say."

With my face pressed in the dust, I felt a moment of choking rage. Then I understood that Old Woman had paid me a high compliment—or at least had meant to. Suddenly I began to laugh at the absurdity of it all. There I was, collapsed in the middle of the road and there was the old crone, who was my only audience, telling me I was almost as good as the whole Dance troupe at her sister's funeral. My laughter raised too much dust in my face. I coughed and spluttered as I struggled to sit up, but still I couldn't stop laughing. I rocked back and forth with my arms around my bent knees, laughing until the tears ran down my face, mixing with the dust and probably turning to mud.

"Enough! Enough," the Old Woman said impatiently, stamping her foot. "Nothing is that funny. Up on your feet now. It's time for the treasure. You have surely earned it. Yes, yes, almost the best *Wounded Bird* I ever saw."

Still shaking with laughter, I got myself up and began futilely brushing at my covering of dust. When I could speak again, I said as seriously as I could manage, "I already told you, I want no treasure from you. Save what you have. The Dance is its own reward. All I ask now is a drink of cool, clear, spring water. If you know where I might find that, it would be reward enough."

"Come with me," the Old Woman said insistently. "I know where to find the best spring in the forest. Come, come, don't stand there like a fool."

"But my clothes... my pack ... I need to ... "

"Leave it. Leave it all. No one will bother it here." She reached out, unfastened my tattered black cape and dropped it over the pack. Instantly everything seemed to disappear into the ground, turning into a shadow. "There, you see, no one will even notice." I nodded, much too tired to argue.

I was still panting, struggling for breath. "Why don't you just tell me the way? I'll come in my own time."

"Come now!" This was said in a voice as commanding as Melanthia's. She seemed suddenly to take on a very different aspect.

Without another word, she took hold of my Dance sash and began walking in a determined manner up the bank toward the woods. Not once did she even glance back at me to see if I was coming. Weakened as I was, I felt I had no choice but to follow. It would have taken more energy to pull myself free than to stumble up the bank like a donkey on a lead. Soon we were on a little path that was invisible from the road, walking faster and faster until we were finally going at a half-trot between the trees.

The trees grew larger in that part of the forest, as if they had never known the bite of ax or saw. The thick foliage shut out much of the sun and there was nothing green underfoot, nothing but a thick carpet of old brown leaves. The Old Woman kept to her pace, showing no sign of slowing. I thought we might go on this way forever, but soon I heard the sound of falling water and, in a few more steps, we came to the spring itself. It was a startling sight, an island of bright green in the middle of that somber, brown leaf cover. The water poured out from a crack or crevice high up in the rock face, falling into a small, almost round pool and then vanishing out of sight into what must have been an underground stream. All around the little pool, ferns and moss grew in lush abundance, watered by the splashing spring.

The Old Woman loosened her grip on my sash and made a broad sweeping gesture with her hand. "There, just as I said, the finest spring in this forest." She spoke as proudly as if she herself were responsible for this natural wonder. And indeed, just as she was speaking, a shaft of light broke through the leaf cover, turning the spray into a glitter of iridescence.

As soon as I was released, I collapsed by the edge of the spring. "Water, please give me some water." My lips felt caked and dry. My nose and throat were full of dust. With a quick practiced gesture the Old Woman took a gourd that was hanging on a tree, scooped up some spring water and handed it to me. I reached out eagerly, but when I held the gourd my hands shook so that the water sloshed out the sides. I couldn't even bring it to my lips.

"Help me," I said, near tears. The Old Woman took back the gourd, steadied my head with one hand and brought the gourd to my lips with the other. I drank deeply before the shock of the cold hit me. The pain of it caught me between the eyes and in the chest, leaving me spluttering and gasping for breath. And there was something more than cold in that water. There was some kind of force or energy that went all through me as if it contained a power of sorts. For just a moment, I wondered if I had been poisoned. When I looked up the Old Woman was leaning over me solicitously, saying in a soothing voice, "Just breathe deep and let it settle. You will be well, I promise you." She repeated the words over and over until I relaxed. Next she took a cloth that had been hanging by the gourd and dipped it in the water. With surprising gentleness she washed my face, cleaning away the dust and tears and, with it, some of the weariness. When she was done, she said brusquely, "Now put your hands in the water. It will refresh you."

I looked down at the dark water. It seemed impossibly far away. I felt dazed and without will. "I can't bend that far," I said plaintively.

"Do as I tell you!" The Old Woman ordered sharply with another of her abrupt changes. "You've taken enough of my time already." She spoke as one speaks to a foolish, stubborn child.

I wanted to make an angry retort. Then a shiver of fear went through me and I found myself leaning forward awkwardly to put my hands in the water. At the first touch, the cold of it bit into my bones and the pain raced up into my armpits. I gave a cry of distress and would have pulled out my hands instantly, but the Old Woman had a fierce grip on both my wrists. "Not long enough. Hold still," she hissed in my ear.

"Let me go! Let me go!" I struggled helplessly for a while, with tears running down my face. Then the pain began to abate, turning to numbness, and I felt myself surrendering a little to the other's will. Still, when I was released, I scrambled to my feet as quickly as I could. I found I was shaking all over, barely able to keep my footing on the steep bank. It was as if the tremors in my hand had infected my whole body. This was far worse than any Dancer's fever I had ever seen. "Why did you do that?" I shouted. "Who are you? *What do you want of me?*"

"All foolish questions, all of no importance," the Old Woman answered haughtily, getting to her feet with some effort. "The real question, the one that matters is, What do you want of me? No one finds their way here except in need."

"I had no need of you! Now look what you've done to me. How will I ever Dance again? I can scarcely walk. How will I make my way home?"

"The water has force. You need some help centering yourself." She reached out to put a hand on my arm.

"Don't touch me!" I shouted as I flinched away.

"You're a fool," she said waspishly. "You think you can handle that power all by yourself? Just look at you!"

Again, I felt that rush of fear. "Alright," I said through clenched teeth. "I suppose you can't do much worse than you've already done." Tensing against the terrible spasms that shook my body, I forced myself to endure the other's touch. This time the Old Woman didn't use her powerful grip but merely laid a light hand on my arm. Soon the tremors began to slow. "Still yourself as you would for the Dance," she said softly. "Go inward to the core of self." She repeated this or other words like them over and over. Her voice had a hypnotic drone. I closed my eyes and found myself spiraling inward until I reached a central place of calm where there was no sound, no pain and no tremors. I stayed suspended in stillness until, from somewhere outside, from some far other place, a voice said loudly, "Done!"

When I opened my eyes again the Old Woman was examining me with the look a potter might use to see if the pot was actually finished and ready for baking. "Well," she asked sharply. "How is it? Isn't that better? Didn't I tell you?"

I stretched out my arms and shifted my feet. "The shaking has passed," I said with amazement.

"Why are you so surprised? I told you I'd fix it. Now hold out your hands in front of you."

I did as I was told, raising my hands to eye level. They were dappled with leaf patterns of light and shade. They glistened with iridescent drops of moisture. They were still. Still! The shaking was gone! My hands, held out in front of me, were still and steady, under my control again. The tremors that had plagued me more and more these past few months were gone. My hands were my own again. I stared at them, open-mouthed.

"Well, young fool, that's the treasure I promised you, the treasure you kept refusing. That's your payment for that one last Dance. Did you really think I had a box of coins and baubles buried back here? What good would that do an Old Woman who lives by herself back in the woods?"

I kept looking at my hands in wonder, a smile growing on my face. Finally, I turned to the Old Woman. "It's really true, isn't it? They're mine again. How can I ever thank you? What is your name? I never thought to ask."

"My name is none of your business," she answered tartly. "All you need to know is that I'm the Keeper of the Spring. As for thanking me, you can't. There's no possible way of thanking someone for such a gift, such a treasure. All I ask now is that you go away, just go away quickly. You have already eaten much too much of my precious solitude." Her voice was rising in intensity, like a storm wind coming up to sweep everything before it. "Just go, go, be gone from here as fast as you can and hope that we never have a need to meet again." She began making quick gestures with her hands, as if she were shooing troublesome chickens out of the yard.

I began backing away from the force of her words and looking about me in bewilderment. "That way, that way, the path is over there." The Old Woman was shouting now as she pointed. I turned, almost in a panic, and found myself running frantically back down the path without a backward glance, trying not to stumble over roots and fallen branches as I went. I could still hear the voice of the Old Woman behind me, driving me on like a whip. "Go! Go! Out of my sight! Away from here!"

Faster than I could possibly have imagined, I stumbled out onto the road, panting and gasping for breath. I couldn't resist a quick, nervous glance up at the rock, though of course it was unoccupied. It took me a few anxious moments to find my pack under the concealment of the black cloak but just as the Old Woman had said nothing had been troubled or disturbed. Hastily

I gathered my things, stuffed them into my pack and hoisted the pack to my shoulders. Even in the silence of the woods I could still hear the Old Woman's driving voice in my head and had no wish to stay there a moment longer than necessary.

Even so, when I was done and had stepped out into the middle of the road, I couldn't refrain from stretching out my arms and holding up my hands before me one more time. They were still and steady and strong. The afternoon sun seemed to glow through my fingers. I could feel the gentle weight of the pendants between my breasts, warm now from my own warmth and remembered Margea's anxious eyes on my shaking hands.

Pressing my hands to the pendant she had given me, I said softly, "Thank you Mother, thank you for whatever happened here." With another little shiver of fear, I set off down the road, wanting to put distance between myself and those woods before nightfall. That night I slept in an open field under the stars.

Over and over I held out my hands in the morning light. Each time I was amazed to see that they were still steady, under my control again. The tremors were really gone—at least for the moment. So the Old Woman had been telling the truth after all. Only now could I admit to myself how grateful I was and how deeply frightened I'd been. Still it was time to go home, whatever home meant. I had fulfilled my five-year pledge and that part of my life was over. It was time to find out what the future held, now that I would no longer be a Dancer on the road.

CHAPTER 19

The Road Home

Filled with a mix of eagerness and regret, longing, anxiety and guilt, all tangled up with a strange sort of anguish, I set off down the road just as the sun was beginning to clear the hills. Part of me wanted to be there already, back in the city of Urshameel, back in the shelter of the Temple without the arduous effort of so many long days of walking. Another part of me wanted to delay as long as possible, delay the inevitability of meeting with all the problems I had left behind five years before, especially my mother's disapproval. Would Thea have softened at all with time and my long absence? Or would she be even more hostile and insistent? Was my father still alive? He had seemed surprisingly frail when I saw him last. Now I regretted not having gone home even once, but there had never seemed to be a right time.

Kendrin's Dance time on the road must be over. Was she already back at the Temple? I had never met with her in my five years away. Now I longed to see her again. Did she miss me too? When I allowed myself to think of Thesali much of the old pain seemed to be lying there, waiting to engulf me again. And when I thought of Thea my footsteps would slow to a crawl, but then my thoughts would turn to Melanthia and I would feel an urgency to rush on, almost at a run. I could hardly wait to hear the music of her stern voice again. Was she still teaching at the Temple? Would she be glad to see me? Or had she gone back to her natal village as she so often threatened to do when her students seemed hopelessly clumsy and inattentive? What if something had happened to her? My mind kept churning in a chaos of questions and fears.

Melanthia was the person I most needed to talk with, the only one who could help me understand that last Dance. Had I really Danced with the Goddess or had it only been imagination, or worse—madness? Was I going to become like Old Selvi? No one but Margea had claimed to see the Other Dancer. Was it the truth or was it only for my sake she had told me that? All the villagers believed so devoutly in the Goddess when She was safely encased in wood or stone and they could lay offerings at Her feet, but no one believed She could appear among them as a living being, a breathing, Dancing reality. And what of the Old Woman? Clearly she was more than she appeared to be. With all this on my mind, I went forward at a halting and uneven pace.

After a few hours of walking I almost wished I hadn't been so hasty in refusing their offer of a horse, but the thought of going back to Margail filled me with even more weariness. Besides, I'd never really learned to ride, trusting my sturdy Dancer legs to carry me wherever I wanted to go. Dancers were not encouraged to ride. It curved their legs. "Too late for a horse now," I said aloud.

When I passed some farm folk on the road they wanted me to Dance for their village and I found myself refusing, claiming to have Dance-fever. In spite of that, they blessed me and gave me food and wished me safely on my way. After that I took the Dancer's Knot out of my hair and put away my Dancewand. If I wasn't going to Dance, I shouldn't appear as a Dancer. If I ran out of food I would ask for some and really become the beggar my mother had so often accused me of being.

Even with the long walk ahead of me, I'd be back in the city of Urshameel in a week or two. My life on the road would be only a memory, an interesting series of stories to tell in the evening when our work was done. In spite of all my doubts and hesitation I began to move at a better pace after a while. Gradually the charm of the road won out. I even took my little travel drum out of my pack and found myself drumming and chanting to keep pace with my feet. The land lay peaceful and beautiful all around me. Birds sang, flowers bobbed in the wind, gardens were brimming with growing food. Sometimes I walked through fields of wheat, ripening on either side in golden waves. The days were blessedly uneventful. The violence I had witnessed and all that talk of death and destruction seemed to have happened far away, in another world. Perhaps it had run its course.

Late in the afternoon of the sixth or seventh day out of Margail, as I was trudging up a long hill with my pack growing heavier at each step, I saw a figure on horseback come over the rise leading another horse. For a moment I thought no more than to envy the rider her mount, though the horse's head hung low and it seemed dejected and weary. Then my heart leapt at the familiarity of that figure. Suddenly I heard my name being shouted. With a cry I dropped my pack by a tree and rushed up the hill, all my fatigue forgotten as horses and the rider came toward me at a shambling gait. As we neared each other I was shocked by Thesali's appearance. Her face was swollen and discolored with bruises, her hair in disarray and her clothes ragged, filthy and torn. When she reached me she slid off her horse and into my arms with a groan of pain. "Zaia! I found you! I found you! I can hardly believe it! Thank the Goddess I found you! I've been looking for you for days. I had to find you! I had to warn you!"

"Thesali, what's happened to you? What have you done to yourself? You knew I was coming home soon. Why didn't you just wait? You've worn yourself out with this ride. You're all ragged and you look ill. If you'd waited I would have been back in the city soon."

She was shaking her head wildly. "No! Not home! That's just what I was afraid of! That why I came to warn you. You can't go home, Zaia. There's no place to go to. Urshameel is gone! All gone! Nothing but ruins now, everyone is dead!"

In shock and surprise I grabbed her shoulders and shook her roughly. "What are you saying? That's not possible. Are you mad?"

With a cry of pain she pulled away. "Mad from what I've seen maybe, but I'm sane enough at this moment. And I know all too well what I'm saying." Then, with another groan, she started to topple sideways as if she were going to fall. I caught her around the waist. "The horses," she gasped. "Keep hold of the horses. They may mean our lives."

With one arm around her, half supporting and half carrying her, and the reins in my other hand, I led Thesali back to where I'd thrown down my pack. There I gently lowered her down to sit leaning against a tree. As fast as I could, I tied the horses to the next tree and then came to squat beside her. Her eyes were glazed over. She seemed to be lost in a sort of daze. I stared at her for a moment in silence with my mind reeling. Then I took her hand. Instantly she came back to herself. There was a wild, frightened look on her face. "Oh Zaia... So terrible... All gone... Blood everywhere..."

"How? What happened? Tell me! Was it a storm? An earthquake?"

Thesali was shaking her head again. Her words came out in broken bursts. "No...Nothing like that...Invaders...Men from the north...In broad daylight... Hundreds of them, shouting and howling...Riding into the city with their swords drawn and already bloody." She stopped abruptly and her head fell forward. I thought she'd fainted. I was so shocked by what she'd just said, by the horror of her words, that I was close to fainting myself. Then, seeing how pale and gray she looked, I started to rise, wanting to fetch a blanket for her.

She grabbed my arm with surprising strength and pulled me back down. "Wait...Not yet...Not finished."

"Later, Thesali, you can talk later. You're too weak right now. You should stop talking and get some rest. I was just going to get you a blanket. You looked so cold."

Her fingers bit into my arm like claws as she said with the fierceness of desperation, "No! Not yet! Have to talk...Need to tell it all...No one to talk to since it happened...Kept riding and riding, trying to find you..."

With that I sank back down to sit on the ground beside her. "I'm here now," I said softly. "You can talk and I'll listen." I nodded as I laid a gentling hand on her shaking arm.

She gave a deep sigh and seemed to be gathering what little strength she had left. Then she began speaking in a flat dead voice, as though telling some-one else's story. "We had no warning and no defense. Many of our people were in the streets. It was a market day; the markets were already open. Some were able to flee, but most died where they stood. Many of those who escaped were hunted down on horseback. I fled back to the Temple and ended up under a pile of bodies. I only got away because they thought I was dead." Her voice stopped again. She was staring straight ahead as if that terrible scene was playing itself out before her eyes.

Watching her, waiting in painful suspense for the next words, I finally broke the silence, asking in a hoarse frightened whisper, "My Father? Mother? Sister?" I was hardly able to believe I was asking such questions.

She nodded, her lips set in a grim line. At last she said, "Yes... All dead... Everyone. They broke into High Council and killed everyone there. Some people fled to the Temple and took refuge among us. We closed the great stone doors that hadn't been closed for a hundred years and put up the iron bars. It was terrible. We could hear shouts and screams, dreadful sounds coming from the city. Many of us watched from the upper walls, pouring down whatever we could on the invaders to drive them away. For a while we kept them off, but they kept coming back to try again. On the second day they broke down the east door. Those of us who could fled to the inner sanctuary. There was a huge crowd of us there, town folk and Temple folk all crammed together. We still had a final door with a great iron bar. It seemed to be holding, at least for a while."

Thesali stopped talking abruptly and shut her eyes. Moaning in pain and bending forward, she wrapped her arms around herself as if for comfort. Then she sat very still, seeming to have gone far inward.

I waited in silence for a few minutes, watching her with my heart aching. Finally I put a light hand on her shoulder and said gently in her ear. "Thesali, maybe it's time to stop talking now. Maybe you should lie down for a while and get some sleep."

Instantly her eyes snapped open again. The anger in them was like a blow. She shook off my hand, though the motion made her moan again. Then she straightened herself with effort. It was painful to watch, but I didn't try touching her again. When she turned to look at me, her eyes had a strange-ness in them that made me shiver. "No! I need to talk! I need to tell you everything! Someone has to hear it. Someone else has to bear witness. I can't live with this all locked up in my head. I have to speak for them, for the dead.

I didn't come all this way, suffer that terrible ride, keep myself alive when I might rather have died, just to sleep at the end of it. I need you to hear me, Zaia! I need your ear, not your hand on my arm! Do you understand?" I nodded silently, biting my lip to keep from speaking. I wanted so badly to hold her and comfort her. My whole body ached with it—but I didn't move.

When she continued, her voice took on a tone that sent chills up and down my back. "You need to hear this part, Zaia. Something happened that I can scarcely believe—even now. There was a woman among us named Hathi, a Dancer who came to us from the road. We took her in because she said she knew you, that she was your friend. I tried to like her because of you, but she always seemed angry and dissatisfied, seldom had a kind word for anyone.

"The men outside were shouting for us to open the door and we were piling things against it to hold them back. In spite of that, it seemed to be caving under their onslaught. Suddenly Hathi shouted, 'Yes! Yes!' and ran forward. Before we could stop her, before any of us knew what she was planning to do, she had climbed over our barrier, pushed things aside and drawn the bolt. She shouted "Yes!" again and was standing right in their path when they pushed open the door. They killed her first, before anyone else. I think she died laughing. It was the most terrible sound I've ever heard. They might have broken through anyhow, given a little more time, but she, a woman and a Dancer, she actually opened the way for those men."

Oh Goddess, how is this possible? Yes, I remembered Hathi, the Dancer from Chandairi, the one who was so full of hate and bitterness. "Hathi," I said with a sort of horrified wonder. "She said she would do it and she did." Hathi, you went there in my name and you opened the doors to death.

Thesali went on as if I hadn't even spoken. Her voice was getting stronger, but there was a harsh, grating edge to it, like metal on metal, as if it took everything she had to speak at all. "After that, they went about killing all the men left in the Temple and rounding up all the women. They forced us into the ritual chamber saying they would keep us for their use and amusement. For a whole day those men took turns with us and I wished myself dead. Then toward evening someone rushed in and shouted that the women were to be killed after all and that the Temple was to be torn down. With no hesitation those men drew their swords and began killing women all around me, the same women they had thrust themselves into with such lust just moments before. I think I must have fainted and it saved me." She had her hands pressed to her belly and her whole body was rocking back and forth, but I didn't dare intervene. I knew I had to let her keep talking. And I knew I couldn't voice my own rage at what I was hearing, though I was clenching my fists so hard my nails bit into my palms.

"When I came back to myself I was under a pile of bodies and soaked with blood, none of it mine. It was almost dark. Only a little light from the torches made its way down between the corpses. The smell of blood and smoke was everywhere. From somewhere else I could hear the cries of the wounded and dying, but in that chamber there was only silence."

I shook my head, not sure how much more I could hear. It was as if someone kept unrolling a tapestry of horrors before my eyes, the relentless turning of the wheel. I was stunned by what she was telling me. I could scarcely believe all this had happened. And yet I knew, with dreadful certainty, that the violence I'd seen on the road had all been leading up to this. Some part of me wanted to beg Thesali to stop, even to put my hand over her mouth, but I knew I had to hear her through to the end.

When I tried to put a reassuring arm around her shoulders, she shrugged me away again and said sharply, "Better not to touch me now." Then she went on, "Now that I was conscious again, I was in terror for my life. Before I had been numb, expecting to die at any moment. Now I wanted to live. I wanted to escape. I wanted to come and warn you. I began moving ever so slightly. When there was no outcry I kept moving, expecting at any moment to hear a shout and feel a sword thrust. When I got my head clear of the dead, I could see that it was night. There were only a few torches burning in the chamber and no other living person there. They had left the dead to take care of themselves.

"From far off, maybe the great chamber, I could hear the sound of blows, hammers against rock, loud crashes, many shouts, screams, cries. In that dim light I made my way through the bodies, trying not to fall or to cry out. As you know, from that ritual chamber there's a little door that leads to a small, almost secret passage out into the back alley behind the Temple. The door was unlocked. I doubt if those men even knew it was there. When I reached it I took a dark Dance cloak off a hook for concealment, wrapped it around myself, shut the door behind me and groped my way down the tunnel in utter darkness. When I reached the alley and peered out there was no one about. The invaders had business elsewhere. I slipped out into the night and crept from doorway to doorway, trying to reach the edge of the city. The darkness would be suddenly illuminated by huge bursts of flames from the burning city, but I did my best to keep to the shadows.

"A few times I thought I saw other dark shrouded figures, survivors of that massacre, but we each went our way in silence. Twice those men passed me with lines of people chained together while I hid in gutters or doorways, so close I could have reached out and touched them. I was terrified that dawn would come before I could make my way out of the city. Most of the invaders seemed to be drunk or guarding prisoners, or they were intent on tearing down our great buildings. That made them easier to evade but no less frightening and dangerous. When I finally reached the gates of the city they were open and unguarded. The invaders were too busy drinking and looting to worry about guarding the gates. Besides, they probably thought everyone was dead or captured. No need to guard the dead.

"When I finally got free of the city there were several loose horses wandering about, coming close enough to be tempting but not close enough to get caught. Badly frightened, they stayed just out of range of my reaching hands. At last, just as it was getting light, I found a horse tied up by a barn on a little farm. I called out but no one answered. I listened for a while and only heard the distant sounds from the city. At last I went into the house, trembling, fearful of a trap. Everyone there was dead, murdered, even the babies. There was no one to hurt me and no one I could help. I changed out of my bloody clothes, took food and a pack, found a second horse and two saddles in the barn and have been riding for seven or eight or nine days, hoping to intersect your path home. And now..." Thesali had finally come to the end of her story. She gave a great shuddering sigh, bent forward and sat staring in front of her as if I wasn't even there. Her face was so blank and still she looked hardly human.

I waited a while. At last I asked hesitantly, almost in a whisper, "My aunt Veraine, my cousin?

She was silent for so long I wasn't sure she would answer. I wasn't even sure she heard me and I didn't dare ask again. Then, without changing her expression or looking at me, she said in an almost normal voice, "Away on a trading trip for your mother. Goddess only knows, they may be safe or they may have met their fate sooner than the rest of us. We can only hope..."

The word hope sounded very strange to me in the midst of that litany of desolation. "And Anyashu, the boys, are they also..."

"How did you know about Anyashu?" This time she turned to look at me.

"I met Ushain on the road. She was carving pillars for a Dance Court in Shomar. Is Kendrin...?" I sucked in my breath and waited.

"I don't know. She may be safe. She was out of the city at the time."

I nodded and let out the breath I'd been holding. "Anyashu?" I asked again.

"Anyashu left me three years ago. She took the boys and went to her parents' village, said the boys were really more hers than mine. I went back to the city because I missed the Temple and the Dance. I was very angry at her then. Now I'm glad. At least they're all alive—I hope. Oh Zaia, how is it possible? All gone, everything gone, everything we knew..."

"Melanthia...?"

She nodded, but it took a few moments for her to say the words I was afraid to hear. "Dead. They killed her...I saw them..."

"Everything then." I pressed my hands against my heart and squeezed my eyes closed as if to shut out the sight. Melanthia...All so hard to believe... Urshameel had stood for hundreds of years and the Temple of Kernoss for even longer. I kept shaking my head. I still hadn't wept a tear. It wasn't real for me yet. "Hard to imagine it could all be gone in a day. I almost need to see it for myself to believe such a thing could happen."

"No, Zaia! No! You can't go near the city. They would kill you too."

"I have no doubt," I said with a harsh laugh. "You know I was dreading going back for fear my mother would still be angry with me. Also, I thought it might be hard to see you and Anyashu together. How little any of that matters now. Now I would give anything to hear my mother's sharp tongue again, to hear even one angry word from her. I think I could have learned to love her no matter what she said. Now I will never have the chance, not in this world. Is there anything left? The gardens? The Temple courtyard?" It was a foolish question and I knew it the moment those words were out of my mouth.

Thesali was shaking her head. "Nothing," she said flatly, "Nothing. Everything has been trampled and destroyed."

Suddenly I was remembering coming to the Temple as a child, seeing those glorious gardens for the first time and then discovering that my father had made them. For just a moment I could feel his hand holding mine. Then the dam broke and I began to cry. I hadn't been able to cry for all the people I loved. That terrible recitation had left me too numb. I couldn't believe they could all be dead, but I found myself weeping for my father's garden, could see all those bright, fragile flowers crushed under brutal feet. How could I even begin to comprehend it all? My whole world gone in an instant. But of course, it hadn't been an instant. I had seen it coming for a long while, ever since I first encountered that man in the woods. And to think that my mother had saved my life by driving me away.

Once I started crying, I couldn't stop. It took possession of me, went on and on. I was caught in a river of grief. Each time it began to slow down another beloved face would rise in my mind, with a new wrench of loss—or even a familiar building or street would appear in front of me to cause fresh grief. All gone! Everything! Then the weeping would start all over again.

Finally I felt Thesali's hand on my arm, shaking me hard. "Stop, Zaia!" I think she'd been saying it for a while. "Stop that now! You have to stay strong. You'll only make yourself sick with all that crying. Nothing you do will bring them back. Not all your tears can change a thing."

With a few final sobs, I turned to look at her. She'd been watching me cry all that time with her eyes dry, her face cool and remote. She hadn't even tried to comfort me. When I finally stopped, she said in that same dead, flat voice, "I've cried all my tears. There's nothing left and there's no comfort I can give you. You'll have to find that on your own. What's done is done."

Her coldness and her hardness frightened me. At that moment she seemed almost like a stranger. Shaking my head in disbelief, I cried out with a kind of bewildered desperation, "But where is the Goddess in all this? Has she turned her back on us?"

"The Goddess!?" Thesali gave a short harsh bark of bitter laughter. "What does the Goddess matter? What can She do for us now? All my life I've served the Goddess. Now She means nothing to me—less than nothing. She's left us at the mercy of men with swords. I put more trust in this poor dumb horse. At least he won't suddenly abandon me half way up the hill. Who knows if She even exists, if She ever existed. I have to tell you, Zaia, my faith in the Goddess died in the Temple that day, died along with everyone I loved. You can be sure it wasn't the Goddess I prayed to as I lay under a pile of bloody bodies. It was my own will I called on to get me out. And it was my own will that got me here—and my love for you." With that she leaned toward me, gripped my arm and said with fierce intensity, "Listen, Zaia, we don't need prayers and Dances now. If we want to stay alive, we need to learn how to use swords as well or better than those men. That's how we have to put our Dancer's skills to use, not in praising the Goddess, but in winning the next encounter."

I felt chilled all over by her words. This wasn't the Thesali I knew speaking, the kind and gentle girl who had been my lover. This was death speaking through her mouth, and I feared it was the truth. I certainly had nothing to counter her words and she'd seen the worst of it firsthand. I thought death was going to be gathering an abundant harvest this year and maybe for a long time to come. With that thought I suddenly became aware of how dangerous it was to be sitting right next to the road that way, how very vulnerable we were, one of us blinded by grief, the other too weak to move.

"It isn't safe here," I said abruptly. "We need to move back from the road, somewhere where we can't be seen so easily."

Thesali groaned and tried to rise. I was on my feet in an instant, slung my pack on my back and gently helped her to her feet. "How do I get you on your horse?"

She shook her head. "There's no way I can get back on a horse right now. Just help me walk. I can't go very far. I need water, food and sleep if I'm to be able to go on. I also need clean clothes. I reek of road filth."

While she held on to the tree for support I untied the horses. Then, at a slow halting pace, we moved away from the road and into the woods. In this way we came to a little clearing between the trees. From beyond it I could hear the sound of running water, a stream perhaps. I had hoped to reach the water, but Thesali suddenly said, "Far enough," and I could feel her weight sagging against me. I told her to lean against her horse while I pulled the blanket out of my pack and spread it on the ground. Then I helped her to sit down, again with her back against a tree. She clutched my hand. "Water, please. I've not been able to find much to drink and all that talking has dried me out."

I got out my water jug for her and held her shaky hands around it while she brought it to her mouth. Half of it ran down and soaked her shirt but at least she'd swallowed some of it. Then I took food from my pack, some trail bread thick with currants and nuts. I crumbled up a piece in a bowl for her, poured water to soften it and set the bowl in her hands. For a long while she sat staring at it without moving, seeming almost in a trance. At last I took her other hand and moved it toward the food. "Eat," I said gently. "If you want to live, you have to eat. Otherwise they've killed you after all." Very slowly she moved her hand, took a little morsel and began to eat, chewing mechanically with a vacant look on her face. After that I felt freed to eat myself, but the food tasted sour to me. When I looked down at my hands I almost expected to see blood dripping from between my fingers.

"My clothes," Thesali said, when she finally handed me back the empty bowl. "Help me get out of these awful clothes." They were so stiff from filth I had to cut them from her, and the smell was almost overpowering. I went back and forth to the stream several times with my little pot and a soft cloth before I could get her poor body clean. She was so bruised and thin! I felt the tears starting to rise again and bit my lip to stop them. She moaned a few times but never complained. When I finally had her in clean clothes she gave a huge sigh of contentment as she leaned back again. She even smiled. "Well, I may live after all. While I was on the road I wasn't so sure."

I tried to smile back at her, though it was probably more of a grimace. "You're very brave, Thesali. How did you learn to ride? I thought you were afraid of horses."

"I didn't learn. I was never on a horse before this except as a little girl on the farm with my father leading me. I got on a horse because I had no choice. I did it to save my life—and to warn you."

"So you didn't forget me altogether in these five years."

"I never forgot you. You were the one who left. I didn't want you to go, I always missed you. Not even Anyashu could take your place, though we both tried hard to make things work out between us. When I thought of you walking into that death-trap, I had to warn you."

"And you weren't afraid? You used to be so afraid of everything, especially horses."

She shook her head. "Afraid? No, I wasn't afraid." Her face, as she spoke, was stiff and harsh as a death mask. "What's left to be afraid of? Think on it, Zaia, I'm the walking dead. I've been violated and I've been killed. I'm a ghost left here among the living by accident. The dead aren't afraid. What can be worse than what I've already seen?"

I shook my head, thinking of all that had happened. Finally I said, "Thesali, there's something I have to do. I have to go back and warn the people of Margail, the last place were I Danced. I can't let the same thing happen to them."

"Oh Zaia, I tried to warn people along the way. They didn't believe me. They trust in the Goddess. They were kind and gave me food or I couldn't have gotten here, but I know they thought me mad. They couldn't imagine such things happening in their world—not to them. Most of them will die undefended just as the people of Urshameel died and there is nothing we can do to save them. They think their Goddess will protect them"

"If I'm with you, the people of Margail will believe us." Then I remembered how the Headwoman had looked at me and wondered if I would be believed after all. If nothing else, I would talk to Margea.

"Later maybe, if you really think it matters. Certainly not now. Right now I can't go another step. I can't move. Even if those men should ride down on us at this very moment I have no strength left to run. And my poor horse is lame and near to starving."

I nodded. "Tonight we rest here and let the horses graze. Tomorrow we can decide where to go and what to do."

The evening was turning cool and Thesali began to shiver. Soon her whole body was shaking. "I'm chilled through," she told me in a hoarse whisper. "It's as if I'll never be warm again." I tried holding her but it didn't seem to help. Instead she stiffened in my embrace as if she wasn't comfortable being held. "So cold," she kept saying. Finally I made her a little fire and the two of us sat there, staring into the flames in silence. What was there to be said when there was so much to say and none of it could fix anything? Eventually she dozed off sitting up. I eased her down, rolling some clothes under her head for a pillow. Then, very gently, I covered her with my sleep sack and threw some more sticks on the fire to keep it going.

After a while I made my way down to the stream at the edge of the clearing. I sat there for a long time just staring into the water, feeling as if I would crack in half with the pain of it all. I was trying to comprehend what had happened to my life and my world, to let the reality of it into my brain. Thesali's words about the Goddess kept running through my mind. At last, with my heart in anguish, I stood up and called aloud to the night, "Oh Mother, why have You abandoned us this way?"

There was a long moment of silence. I thought there would be no answer and that Thesali was right. Then the wind started up in the trees and I heard Her words on the wind. *Child, I wish it could be different, but this is how it is now. This the end of things and the beginning of things. My time here is over, at least for now. The golden times are at an end. For the next few thousand years, angry men will rule here on earth. Women will have to learn to survive and endure. There is nothing more I can give you.* The grief in her voice was beyond any human grief I could imagine.

"Will you come back?" I asked in despair.

Not for a long time. Not in your lifetime or in your daughter's lifetime, or in her daughter's lifetime, not for four thousand years or more. And then only if I'm summoned, only if enough of you remember me and call me back. Then that will begin a new time, another time of changes, a return to gentler ways. You must keep me always in your hearts, no matter what happens to you. You must remember and pass the knowledge on, for I am the hope and the light in the coming darkness, and knowledge of me can keep your hearts alive.

"Mother, is it the time for swords yet?"

Yes, Zaia, the time for swords has come. Again that terrible grief that made me want to weep.

"Should I break my Dancewand?"

"No!"

The word had been shouted in my head so loudly I threw up my hands to ward off the pain of it.

In a gentler voice, in the wind again, I heard: *No matter what else happens, no matter what you have to do, remember the Dance and pass it on, and hold on to your Dancewand. It's a little part of me. I'm leaving now and you'll never hear my voice again, but remember me...remember...remember...remember...*

The voice was fading and then it was gone, the voice that had accompanied every Dance for all those years. The silence was so huge, so sudden and thunderous that it seemed to have swallowed the entire world. I felt the pain of loss like a physical blow. I knew that nothing would ever be the same and that if I lived to be a hundred or Danced a hundred more times, I would never hear Her voice again, never feel Her presence in me or beside me again.

She had been speaking in the wind, but I had been answering aloud. Thesali heard me, even over the sound of the stream. She called out sharply, "Who are you talking to, Zaia? Are you alright?"

"Yes, fine, just saying a chant for protection."

How could I say I was fine? My whole world had just come to an end. But how could I tell Thesali I was speaking to the Goddess? It was not something she would want to hear at that moment—or perhaps ever.

That night we lay next to each other, though Thesali would not allow me to hold her. She said she couldn't let herself be touched right now, not after what had happened. I lay awake listening for sounds in the darkness. Finally, in her sleep, she moved closer to me. Feeling that familiar body pressed against mine, I could almost think we were still students at the Temple. Then the horror of it would come on me and I would remember all over again that there was no Temple. I wasn't going home after all. There was no home, no city, no Temple to go to. There was nothing left.

Against the darkness of my closed eyelids I could see piles of bloody bodies and flames rushing up into the sky. Then someone I knew would turn horror-stricken eyes toward me and reach out pleading hands before a sword cut them down. Each time it was as if I myself were dying. And it kept happening over and over. How much worse it must have been for Thesali who had seen it all with her own eyes. Though she said she was done with crying, I could feel her hot tears on my arm. Several times in the night she moaned and cried out, thrashing violently against me in her sleep. Then I would whisper to her and stroke her back to sleep again. I stayed up through the night, watching over us, worrying for the future and wondering if we would ever be safe again.

CHAPTER 20
Time of Changes

I was up at dawn, pacing up and down our little clearing, filled with turmoil and confusion. Each time I approached Thesali I was determined to wake her, but she looked so pitifully exhausted, so bruised and weary, that each time I backed away again, not having the heart to do it. Yet we had to leave this place—and soon. It wasn't safe to stay. It wasn't safe to be anywhere for long. But where were we to go? If such terrible things could happen to the great city of Urshameel, was there safety anywhere in the world?

I covered the ashes of last night's fire with dirt and leaves to hide this sign of our presence, then resumed pacing. Finally I stopped in front her. "Thesali," I whispered urgently. "Thesali, you have to get up. We need to go." Thesali stirred but didn't waken. I reached out a hand to shake her, then hesitated and stood gazing down at her.

Suddenly the hair went up on the back of my neck. We were being watched. I could feel it. "Thesali, danger!" I hissed. As if that had been the signal, a man charged out of the woods, running straight at me. I whirled to face him. At the same time I could hear the sound of other feet behind me.

The intruder stopped a few feet away and said in a coaxing tone, "Don't be afraid. We don't want to hurt you. We just want to talk." His speech was harsh, strangely accented and difficult for me to understand.

"Don't believe him," Thesali shouted as she struggled to her feet, fully awake now and with a knife in her hand. "They're invaders."

I glanced at her. In that instant, seeing me momentarily distracted, the other man tried to rush my back. I saw the motion out of the corner of my eye, spun and caught him in the stomach with such a hard kick that he doubled up with a cry. All pretense gone, the first man ran at me with his knife raised. I whirled away from the blade and caught him across the neck, a sharp blow with the edge of my hand. Then I kept whirling to where I could land a kick in his side that, from the sound of it, must have cracked ribs. With a shout of surprise he went down too, but now four more armed men dashed into the clearing. They stopped at the sight of their two companions on the ground, writhing and groaning in pain. I turned to face them, taking the Dancer pose of readiness, as if for the Stick Dance.

261

One of the four, better dressed than the others and looking more confident, seemed to be the leader. He took a step forward and gave me a predatory grin that moved his mouth but didn't touch his eyes. "Ah, a Dancer. Now there's a prize. You landed a couple of lucky kicks, but don't be fool enough to think you can hold off four armed men that way. We don't want to kill you. We just want you for our pleasure. Maybe we can even get you to Dance for us." His accent was closer to our own, and he spoke with more polish than the first man.

"Maybe you can," I told him with a grim smile. "But I promise it won't be a Dance you'll enjoy, though it might be one you'll remember." I tried to sound fearless; inside I was shaking. I knew well enough what such men were capable of doing and I had no idea if Thesali could help me in any way, or if I was facing all of them alone.

The leader gave me a nod and said curtly, "We'll see then, won't we?" With that he shouted to the others in some language I couldn't understand. They tried to surround me though none of them seemed eager to get within range of my feet or hands. This was like that man in the woods all over again, only this time there were four to deal with and their intentions were clear from the start.

I needed to draw one of them into range and at the same time keep clear of the others. They were armed with knives rather than swords, which gave me some advantage. With a roar I made a dash at the closest of them. He leapt back, startled. Instantly I jumped into the space he had vacated and so, for that moment, was no longer surrounded. The man to my side thought he saw his opportunity. He gave a shout and rushed at me, just the chance I was hoping for. I dodged out of his way. As he passed I aimed a fierce kick at the middle of his back that sent him sprawling to the ground. His knife flew from his hand. With that his comrade ran forward to help him, and Thesali, who had been dragging herself into the fray, caught that one in the back with a strong downward slash of her knife. When he turned with a startled sound she swung her arm so that a broad gash of red opened across his chest. He cried out, staggered and toppled over on his back with a look of pained surprise on his face.

I heard Thesali yell, "Not this time, Dog Turd! This time I live and you die!" I had caught the action out of the corner of my eye. I couldn't watch because I had to keep track of the two remaining men, the leader and a big burly angry-looking man with huge hands like slabs of rock. They were glancing back and forth between us, no longer sure of an easy conquest. After conferring quickly with each other the leader began running around me close enough to be a threat but just far enough away to be out of range of my feet. He no longer had a smile on his face. This little raid wasn't going as planned.

I had to keep turning so as not to lose sight of the man, knowing that all the while his companion was somewhere in back of me, just waiting for his chance. Then one of the first attackers tried to rise and Thesali rushed to deal with him. I turned in that direction and in that instant of inattention the man behind me saw his chance. He leapt on my back, intending to bring me down. I was staggering under his weight, expecting at any moment to feel the thrust of his knife between my ribs. Then there was a loud shout and I felt even more weight on my back. I stumbled forward under this sudden impact and fell to the ground. The man screamed and at the same moment I felt the weight on my back ease off. I rolled over and quickly sprang to my feet, amazed to see Margea standing in front of me with a bloody knife in her hand. My attacker was lying face down in the grass with blood spurting from his back, his big hands useless now. Above the cries and groans of the men, I could hear Thesali calling my name over and over. As I turned, I saw her standing over the last of them, the leader. He was spread out on his back with a knife in his chest. I couldn't imagine how she had managed this.

Not five minutes had passed and all our attackers were down, either dead or wounded. Miraculously we were still alive, but before I could even catch my breath or heave a sigh of relief, a hooded figure dressed in dark clothes stepped out from behind the trees. "Another one!" Margea shouted, holding her bloody knife out in front of her as a warning to the stranger to keep back.

I swung about too and took the Dancer pose of readiness again, only this time with a knife in my hand that I had snatched up from the ground. "Stop right where you are," I said fiercely, "or the same thing will happen to you."

The figure threw up its hands as if in surrender. "Peace! I'm a woman. I'm not one of them. I've been tracking these men for days, ever since they split off from the main part of their army. I think they've been sent to capture women for the use of their fighters. That's probably why they snuck up on you without their horses or swords and tried to take you alive. I would have been here sooner, but this time they left only one sentry. After doing away with him I took that chance to free the five women they had captured. Then I came on as fast as I could to see what other trouble they intended. I was just in time to see you take them down. If you'd needed my help I would have leapt into the fray, but you seemed to be doing well enough without me getting in your way. I never thought of the Dance as a weapon. Very educational. My name is Altra and I bow to your prowess, Lady Dancer. I wouldn't think to challenge the speed and power of your feet and hands."

As the woman stepped forward into the light, she looked like a living shadow. She had on a short black cloak with the hood drawn so snug it blended with her dark skin and almost concealed her face, a dark tunic and tight fitting black leather pants. On each hip she wore a long knife in a belt sheath. From the way she moved she seemed young and agile, but what could be seen of her face looked weathered, furrowed and very weary. Her voice was rough, almost hoarse.

While I stared open-mouthed at this new apparition, one of the men attempted to rise. Altra stepped forward quickly and casually knocked him back to the ground with one fast sweep of her arm. "Stay down, Scum!" she growled, adding two sharp kicks to emphasize her words. Then she turned to me. "We need to tie them up before they think to give the world any more grief, at least those of them that can still move." With those words she swung her pack from her back, pulled out what seemed like an endless length of rope and began cutting pieces from it with her knife.

The man she had struck hissed at me, "We were too nice. We should have killed you while we had the chance, instead of trying to capture you alive."

"Yes, true enough, because now you'll never get the chance." Altra spoke with a wolfish grin while giving him another kick. Then she beckoned to me. "Come help me tie this one up. You two watch the others. Man, roll over and make it easy for me," she ordered, "so I don't need to use my knife on you. And keep your silence, so I'm not tempted." Without a word the man complied, but not before turning on Altra a look of such pure hatred it made my stomach clench. I moved quickly to help her with the ropes. When we were done, she rolled him onto his back again. After that we walked around the clearing to check on the others. Two were dead, the one Margea had stabbed after he jumped on my back and the last one that Thesali had miraculously done in with her knife when he went for Margea. The other four were hurt, but still alive, moaning in pain. They silenced instantly when Altra approached them, looking like the shadowy figure of death itself.

When the men were all securely tied, Altra sank down against a tree with a groan of utter weariness. The three of us were staring down at her and I was suddenly full of questions. "Who are you? Where did you come from? Why were you following those men?"

Altra held up her hands. "Peace. If you have a little food you can share with me then I'll gladly answer all your questions and even ask some of my own, but I've run out of supplies and I'm weak from hunger. I've been traveling too fast in concealment to replenish my food."

Quickly I set about fishing in my pack for something to give her. When I saw to it that she had food in both hands and was chewing on a mouthful, I turned to Margea. "How is it that you appeared here at just the right moment?"

"I've been following you from a distance ever since you left the Old Woman. I had decided to go to Urshameel now instead of waiting for permission from my father in some far-off future time that might never come.

I wasn't sure you'd let me go with you so I stayed hidden, thinking to follow you back, or at least follow you far enough so you couldn't send me home again. Somehow I missed you on the road, retraced my steps and came upon these dangerous-looking men sneaking through the woods. I shadowed them at a distance. I had no idea you were their quarry until I got here and saw what was happening, just in time as it turned out."

"You saved my life. Thank the Goddess for your quick hand. If you hadn't come at just that moment I'd be lying there dead on the ground instead of that man." I tried to give Margea a hug of gratitude. Thesali came to hug her from the other side, but she quickly pulled away from us both. "I'm only too glad to do anything for you, Lady Dancer, even save your life, but you can't send me back. I won't go."

"But what about...?"

Altra paused from stuffing food in her mouth long enough to say, "Sit down, all of you. We need this moment to talk together and answer each other's questions. We have very little time. When these men don't return, others will come looking for them. Then not all your skilled Dancing will save us." This was more of an order than an invitation. Only too glad to comply, I sank down on the grass with a sigh. The other two followed my lead. "Now, for your questions," the stranger went on. "I am Altra from the city Jabul, many miles north of here. Jabul was once a beautiful city, a center of culture and trade. We had a fine Dance Temple there, one of the finest in the north. All gone now. Everything. Nothing but rubble left of what once was ours.

"These invaders are moving down from the desert places in the far north, destroying everything before them like a horde of locusts. My city fought back. We held out for almost two months. When they finally overran us they killed everyone, took everything that was useful to them, burned everything that would burn and tore down the rest. In the midst of the fighting I was able to kill one of them in an alley, slip into his clothes and make my way out of the city. A few other women escaped. Some of us found each other afterwards. We've gathered with fugitives from the surrounding villages, towns and cities and made a camp up in the hills, or actually several camps. From there we raid for supplies and horses. And you, who are you? And where are you from? And why are you here?"

I spoke first, saying my name, then quickly telling of my last Dance and my attempt to return home. After that I passed the story to Thesali, who told a much shorter version of the attack on Urshameel and her own horrifying escape. When it came Margea's turn she only said her name, where she was from and that she had been following me. "And why are you here so far from your encampment," she asked Altra boldly.

"We take turns trying to warn people of the coming invasions and gathering up the women who escape. Some of us went to warn the people of Urshameel. It grieves me that they didn't reach them in time."

"Perhaps they did," Thesali said, nodding her head sadly. "There was some talk, but who could believe such a thing? Just the babbling of mad-women. The people I warned did not take heed either and will probably die the same way."

"Why are you traveling alone?" Margea interrupted. "Isn't it foolish in the midst of such danger?"

"Probably. I left with a companion. She's dead now. She insisted on going back to her grandmother's village to try to save her. It was already too late. I warned her not to go but she wouldn't listen, so now I'm alone." From the way Altra spoke it seemed this woman had been more to her than a companion, and the finality of her tone made it clear that she wanted no more questions in that direction.

Margea was shaking her head, looking very distraught. "I have to go warn my village. They'll listen to me."

Shoving a last mouthful of food in her mouth, Altra got to her feet, wiping her greasy hands on her pants. "That's in the future. Right now we have to deal with this garbage." She made a contemptuous gesture at the bound men. "And then we need to be gone from here. Dancer, bring a knife and help me finish what you started. You'll need more than feet and hands for this kind of work."

"What do you mean? What do you want me to do?" I asked, looking fearfully at the knife in my hands.

"What do you think? Cut their throats, of course. What else would you do with a knife? Pick your teeth? Butter your bread? Surely not cut them loose?"

"Are you telling me to kill unarmed men? Men who are bound and helpless?"

"Yes, I should hope so. Or would you rather let them loose so they can have another chance at you or perhaps the opportunity to kill your friends? Think on it, Woman, the only reason they hesitated to kill you was because they wanted the use of your bodies first. Remember that. It was always their intent."

Two of the men were cursing angrily. The other two, seeing me hesitate, were begging for mercy or promising loyalty. One of them was calling out, "We never meant to hurt you, Lady." I was shaking my head, full of confusion. Altra grabbed my arm and shook me, saying fiercely, "Zaia, you have made your choice to live when you could easily have let them kill you. If you want to continue living you'll have to learn to kill. That's the unspoken bargain they've forced on us. Any of them that you leave alive will just be looking for the chance to kill you in the future, or to kill someone that you love. One look at a city they've taken would be enough to convince you. Do this now so I know I can trust you. I must ride with companions who'll defend my back. Otherwise, I leave you here."

Margea stepped forward suddenly. Her face was hard and stony, but her eyes flashed with fury as she raised her knife. The man she stood over was the first one who had run into the clearing. He tried to twist away, his eyes wide with terror.

"Wait!" I shouted, throwing up my hands, but it was too late. Already Margea was swinging the knife with a Dancer's grace and power. There was a strangled cry and then a hideous bloom of red across the man's throat. Margea's hands and face were spattered with blood. "You're next," she said to me with a bow. "I'm going with this woman no matter what and I don't want her to leave you behind."

I was shaking my head. "Leave me then. I don't know if I can live this way. This goes against everything I've ever been taught."

Thesali stepped forward and held up her knife. "So it does, but I can do it. If you'd seen what I have, you wouldn't hesitate. They killed everyone, even children, even little babies. They killed Melanthia, but first they used her body, one after the other." Then she dispatched the man who had been begging for mercy, did it as calmly as if she'd been slaughtering a goose for a feast day at the Temple. "Liar," she told his dead body as she wiped her hands on her pants. "I know how you would have used us. I've already had the pleasure."

Altra turned to me again. "Your turn, Dancer. Let's not stand here wasting time because we have precious little of it. We have bodies to dispose of and women to gather and a village to warn. After that I ride north with whoever wants to come with me. We'll circle around the enemy and join the others in the hills. If you're willing to learn to fight and ride and take care of you, you can come with me. There are many women like me in the hills. If you want to join us, cut his throat. Otherwise I have to leave you to your fate. I can't guard unarmed women. There's no safe place I can take you to. These men will soon overrun the whole region."

I stood staring down at the man, frozen in indecision. I could feel my stomach clenching and bile rising in my throat. My whole past spoke against this act, everything I'd ever been taught at the Temple. How could I actually take a human life that way with my own hands? For those of us who followed the Goddess this was the most forbidden act, the ultimate betrayal. She had created life. What right did I have to take it? Such things shouldn't happen. But my whole past also told me that what had happened in Urshameel was impossible. How could the Goddess allow such things? And yet, if that had truly been Her voice I'd heard in the wind, She herself had told me that the world was changing. And She had told me it was time for swords.

It felt as if I had stood there for a year in an agony of confusion, but it couldn't have been more than a minute or two. Then I heard Altra's voice cutting through my stupor, saying impatiently, "Come now, we need to get on with this. It must be done quickly and the bodies hidden in a gully. Then we must be well gone before nightfall. Thirty or more of them could come on us here at any time and believe me, they wouldn't stand around wondering whether or not to kill you."

I was still shaking my head in confusion when Thesali laid her bloody hand on my shoulder. I flinched away. "Think on it, Zaia," she hissed in my ear. "Picture Melanthia with a whole troupe of them pumping themselves into her. I think she was half dead before they finally strangled her."

Something in me turned. Thesali's words about Melanthia finally broke through my resistance and got me moving. Then fury took over and I had no more thoughts. With a sudden shout I raised the knife and wielded it on the nearest man. Rage for everything that had happened poured through my arm and powered my thrust. "This is for Melanthia," I shouted, stabbing him in the chest. "And this is for my father," another stab, "and for my mother," another stab, "for my sister, for my teachers, for the Dancers who were my friends, for my city." He shrieked and thrashed about, trying to avoid my blade. No use. The fury in me had turned to madness. I went on stabbing even after he was dead, even after I was covered with blood, screaming now with no words. I went on and on though Altra kept shouting at me to stop. Finally she grabbed my arms from behind and forcibly restrained me.

Panting for breath, I stood staring down at the object of my hatred through a red haze of madness. Altra said coolly, "Well, Zaia, now that you've proved you can do it, let me finish the last one. This sort of thing needs to be done swiftly and efficiently, not with all that messy passion. Go clean off the blood. Then come back and help us here. I have their horses hidden back in the woods. We'll need them for dragging the bodies away. There's a ravine in that direction we can use for dumping them. Then we'll have to cover them over with rocks and leaves and branches so the death-birds don't give away their location."

Without even waiting to see her kill the last man I staggered off into the trees and retched until there was nothing left in my stomach. Now that the haze of madness had lifted I felt totally empty, changed in ways I could hardly begin to comprehend. I had become one of "them."

Sick at the core, I went to the stream to wash off the blood. I needed that moment alone to think on what I'd just done. I knew I'd crossed a line from which there was no going back. The blood on my hands and face and clothes told me that. I walked into the water up to my neck and it ran red around me. "Mother, forgive me, I have become a killer," I said softly as I felt the cool water washing away my rage and their blood. After a minute or two the water returned to its natural blue-green, but when the others joined me in silence to wash in their turn it ran red again.

As we walked back up to the clearing, my heart was aching with hurt. I turned to Altra and said fiercely, "I need to break my Dancewand. You've proved to me that I can be a killer and I suppose, if I want to live, that's what I'll become, but no way can I be a killer and a Dancer at the same time. It's like living a terrible lie." Even as I said those words I remembered what the Goddess had said about the Dancewand, but at that moment I was too angry to care.

Altra shook her head, put a hand on my arm and moved to block my path. "No, Zaia, we will need the Dance if we are to survive this time of troubles in any human way. I can't stop you, but I ask you please to think on it first." Then she released my arm and went on ahead at a fast pace.

I stumbled after her. "But how can I ever Dance again after this?" I didn't say what I knew in my heart, that this time of troubles would not end in a short while, that it would last four thousand years or more, far beyond any life she and I would see or could even imagine.

Yet, even as I spoke, even with my heart filled with despair, I was seeing in my head a Dance unfolding, a Dance I could do for the women who had escaped the swords of the invaders, a Dance of anger and a Dance of strength and a Dance of hope. No, I wouldn't break my Dancewand after all, at least not yet. I would keep it a little while longer. "How can you bear it?" I asked when I caught up with her.

She turned and I saw in her eyes the sort of sadness I had seen in Jekartha's. "What choice do I have? What sort of a choice do they give us? If we fight back we become like them, cruel and merciless. If we don't, they kill us or worse still, take us as slaves and so doom our children and our children's children to a life of slavery. Believe me, Zaia, I used to be a kind person much like you, with love and compassion in my heart. I think I've seen too much. Watching my lover die ended any idea of mercy for me. Now I live to kill and kill to live. It is the thought of gathering up women like you that keeps me going through the hard times."

"I always thought we lived under the protection of the Goddess," I said bitterly.

"Ah yes, the Goddess." She shook her head. "I have no trust in the Goddess anymore, though She was once the very center of my world. Now I only trust my knife and my horse and the women who ride with me."

When we got back to the clearing we made our plans. Mounted on Thesali's two horses, Altra and Margea would go to meet with the freed captives and fetch the men's horses as well as Altra's horse that she had tied in the woods. They planned on bringing the horses back to the clearing so we could use them to dispose of the bodies, then we would take them with us into the hills. Meanwhile Thesali and I were to stay with the dead, pack our belongings and make ready to leave as soon as the others returned. As she was mounting, Altra gave me a stern-voiced order as if she were already my leader, "Strip the bodies of anything that may be useful to us and gather it all in a pile. And make sure to stay alert in case any more of them come."

Margea gave me a strange look. "You're not afraid to be left here with the dead?"

I shook my head. "No. They can't hurt me anymore and perhaps I need to make my peace with them." Seeing her so eager to ride off that way with Altra, I thought perhaps she had found someone new to follow—and I was glad of it.

Altra turned back for one last look around the clearing. "Not bad for a morning's work. Six of them dead, seven if you count the guard, three new women for us, eight in all if the freed ones choose to join us, food, weapons, clothes and maybe as many as ten or eleven horses. Women at camp will be well pleased." In her tally she made no mention of the companion who had lost her life on the way. It was almost as if she had never existed.

Margea turned to look at her. "What do they call themselves, these women who are learning to hide and ride and fight?"

"They are called different things in other places. The ones just north of here, the ones we go to join, they call themselves Amazons."

With that word I felt a chill run up my back. That's what I would be from now on, not a Dancer but an Amazon. I would learn things and see things and do things that a month ago I could not even have imagined.

After the others left Thesali sank down on the ground with a groan of weariness and leaned her back against a tree. "I'm sorry, Zaia, I can't help you with this task. I can't even stay upright on my feet. Too much has..." Her words stopped in mid-sentence, her eyes closed and her head fell forward.

Alone I walked about among the dead, closing their eyes and singing the death chant for them. My red anger was all gone. All I felt was a deep sadness, but also a sort of weary acceptance. In another world I might have known these men. They might even have been my friends but not in this world. Everything was changing and I was changing with it. Staring down at those dead faces I wondered at their intentions. Had they left their horses tied up thinking to sneak up on us unawares and capture us with little or no resistance? If so, we must have been almost as much of a surprise to them as they were to us. And how had they even known we were there? Perhaps the little fire I had made for Thesali the night before...

I really didn't want Thesali's help in doing this grisly task. She had already dealt with enough horror. Later she would have to ride and ride hard. Better that she rest for a little and maybe gain some strength. Still there were moments when I wished I had a second pair of hands to help me roll the bodies over. What was especially hard was trying to pry the boots off their dead feet, but I thought boots might be much more useful for this new rough life than the sort of sandals I was used to wearing on the road.

After a while I knelt on the bloody ground, bowed my head and whispered, "Goddess, why have you revealed yourself to me that way in my life, if this is the end of everything and not a beginning, if the world is about to all go dark?" The answer came back as clear as spoken words, *In a world of chaos someone must remember the promise and Dance it and teach it, even in the worst of times. That is yours to do.* I thought the Goddess had gone silent, so perhaps this was my own heart speaking back to me. I nodded, stood up slowly and picked up a knife. From now on I would wear one in my sash along with my Dancewand. I was going to go live among the Amazons.

Acknowledgments

I want to thank my artist friend Cedar Kindy, who did the cover art for the book, for introducing me to women's spirituality many years ago. I also want to thank Liz Lester for her help in getting my book ready for publication. And to thank Susanna Brinnon who carefully edited this book. I want to express my gratitude to Cindy Heulsmann for bringing Goddess ritual and sacred singing into my life.

About the Author

Diana Rivers, author of the seven-novel Hadra Series, is an artist as well as a writer. She has lived in intentional community much of her adult life. For more than thirty years she has been living on women's land in the hills of Northwest Arkansas. Her house was built entirely by women's hands, including her own. She has been a lifelong activist in the Peace and Justice movement and describes herself as an eco-feminist. Through her passion for empowering women, she has originated and helped organize several venues for women in the arts. She is an amateur naturalist who finds the natural world to be constantly full of wonders and surprises. She is a Lambda Literary Awards finalist and a winner of the Golden Crown Literary Award for Speculative Fiction.

Other Books
by Diana Rivers

Books in The Hadra Series

Daughters of the Great Star

The Hadra

Clouds of War

The Red Line of Yarmald

Her Sister's Keeper

The Smuggler, The Spy, and The Spider

Journey to Zelindar

City of Strangers

Snake Memories and Other Stories

Dancer for the Goddess

See more about Diana Rivers at www.thehadra.com